W9-BSU-146

THE SHOWSTONE

A selection of recent titles by Glenn Cooper

The Cal Donovan series

SIGN OF THE CROSS *
THREE MARYS *
THE DEBT *
THE SHOWSTONE *

The Will Piper library series

LIBRARY OF THE DEAD
BOOK OF SOULS
THE KEEPERS OF THE LIBRARY

The John Camp Down series

PINHOLE
PORTAL
FLOODGATE

* *available from Severn House*

to him. A display at the British Museum some years ago. However, that object was not quite as fine and lustrous.

Again? Was that the sound of a distant voice again?

Najib's broom-work done, he stood with a dustpan to be emptied. The reflected light from the black mirrored surface briefly caught his attention but this wasn't any business of his. He told his boss he needed to use the latrine.

Donovan dismissed him and re-wrapped the stone in the washcloth. He placed it inside a padded envelope, between two archeology monographs for added protection. Then he wrote a note on a card, referencing his British Museum recollection, placed it inside, then slipped the envelope into his desk drawer. When Najib returned, humming as was his want, Donovan let him know that he would need a car in the morning. He passed along a few coins as baksheesh to make sure he made the arrangements promptly. He would drive to the post office in Mosul and fill out a customs declaration that listed used books and send the package to his Cambridge, Massachusetts home address.

In Arabic the servant asked, 'You need a driver?'

'No, I'll drive myself. I need my satellite phone. Where is it?'

The old man pointed to the corner of his desk where it was hiding in plain sight. Donovan took it and went outside in the chill air to place a call.

The phone was balky, and he reached his wife on the third attempt.

'Bess, it's me.'

She was restrained in her response. She always was. It was 11 a.m. back in Cambridge. He pictured her, slim, in a demure slip choosing an outfit for a luncheon with friends. 'Hiram. This is unexpected. Are you all right?'

'I'm fine. I just wanted to let you know that I'm sending an envelope addressed to you. I'd appreciate it if you would simply tuck it away somewhere, unopened, for my return.'

There was some distortion on the line.

'I'm sorry, did you say to open it?'

'No, the opposite. Please don't open it.'

'What is it?'

'A curiosity, that's all.'

'It's nothing illegal, is it?'

'Why would you ask me something like that?'

'I don't know. Maybe it's because you sound awfully mysterious.'

'There's no mystery. Please give me a call when it arrives.'

'Yes, yes. I thought you were ringing for another reason.'

'What reason?'

Despite the connection he made out a sharp breath. 'I thought that maybe you'd heard about Cal.'

'Cal? Has something happened?'

'Why don't I let you speak to him?'

'He's in Cambridge?'

'He is.'

'Why isn't he at the base?'

He heard his wife calling for their son. Truth be told, Hiram wasn't entirely keen to talk to the young man, who was just shy of his twentieth birthday. Their last conversation had ended in a shouting match, two stiff-necked men butting horns like a couple of rams. He had been apoplectic at Cal's decision to forgo college and enlist in the army at age eighteen. Neither parent had seen it coming. The boy had grown up alongside high-achieving children of Harvard faculty members and he had been a star student-athlete at the Buckingham Browne & Nichols prep school in Cambridge, a reliable feeder to Harvard and other Ivy League universities. Yes, he had been a rebellious teenager who liked the girls and the parties and yes, he had developed an ominously early taste for vodka, especially expensive brands, but his parents had assumed that he would pass through his rebellious phase and get with the program. He didn't. Instead, according to his father's view of things, he pissed on his future by enlisting in the army instead of going to college, walking away from his early-decision admission to Harvard. One day after high school graduation, the obstinate only-child decamped for basic training in the Deep South leaving behind a confused girlfriend, a crying mother, and a furious, inconsolable father. Cal had returned on leave to Cambridge shortly before Hiram left for the current season in Iraq, but he had stayed at a friend's house. He ran into his father the day he showed up at the house to pick up a few things and the two of them had gone at it. Bess broke up the argument before it turned physical and Cal stormed out, banging doors.

A sullen, deep voice came on the line. 'Hello, Dad.'

'Cal, why are you home?'

He sounded halfway drunk and it wasn't even noon. 'You'll be happy to hear that I got kicked out.'

'I'm sorry, did you say kicked out?'

'You heard me.'

'How does one get kicked out of the army?'

'There's lots of ways. Mine was punching my sergeant.'

The moon was a sliver and the only light was from the gauzy glow of lamps inside tents. Hiram was tramping around the camp in the dark, paying more attention to his sat-phone than the terrain. He caught himself at the edge of the cutting where he had found the obsidian.

'Why the hell did you do that?'

'It's a long story. He was a sadistic dick.'

'Toward you?'

'I can defend myself. He was tormenting a guy in my squad.'

'And punching him was a solution?'

'Not really, but it fucking well felt great.'

'So, what's going to happen to you?'

'Dishonorable discharge probably.'

'You can't have that on your record, Cal.'

'Screw it. It is what it is.'

'You may say that but that's never something I'll say. There's always a way to make things right. I'll call Senator Kennedy and have him take care of this.'

'The great Hiram Donovan to the rescue. No thanks.'

'I'm afraid you can't stop me. I'm calling Kennedy's chief of staff as soon as we hang up. Then I'm calling Dean Fletcher at the admission's office. You're going to do what you should have done all along. You're going to enter the Harvard class of '93 in September.'

'Did I ever tell you that you're an overbearing son-of-a-bitch?'

'On more than one occasion.'

'Good. I'm saying it again. You do whatever you've got to do. I've got a date with someone who gets me.'

'And who is that?'

'A Russian named Stolichnaya.'

Over the following week, Hiram Donovan ran up an astronomical satellite-phone bill in aid of rehabilitating his disgraced son. Fortunately, he was a wealthy man and to him, it was merely a trifle. The Donovans were main-line Boston Catholics who had made a fortune trading textiles at the turn of the previous century, later acquiring substantial real-estate holdings and becoming tenement landlords to waves of immigrants arriving in Boston from Europe. Hiram's father had known Senator Kennedy's father, Joe, and had done some deals with him. He had been a guest at the presidential inauguration of John Kennedy. A call from Hiram Donovan carried weight and Ted Kennedy personally placed a call over to the Pentagon, and the Secretary of the Army set an honorable discharge in motion. It went without saying that despite the lateness of the calendar, Harvard College readily agreed to accept Cal into the freshman class. So, Donovan was reveling in the smugness of a successful fixer the evening that two men came to visit him at his field tent.

He was working at his desk and Najib was whisking when a voice called out in a heavily accented English.

'Excuse me, is this the tent of Professor Donovan?'

Donovan unzipped the flap and saw a squat Iraqi gentleman, perhaps forty, dressed formally in a black Western suit. He was with a much larger and much younger companion who wore a traditional flowing dishdasha.

'Yes, I'm Donovan.'

The older man said, 'Apologies for arriving unannounced, at nightfall no less. My name is Hamid. Mustafa Hamid, although my Western friends call me George. This man is my assistant. I wonder if I might have a word with you regarding a matter of great interest.'

Donovan didn't like being disturbed while he was working, and this had the look of some kind of a shakedown by a local official.

'I'm sorry, who are you with?'

'With? I am with no one, Professor. It is simply me, George Hamid.'

'You're not with the government?'

'No, no, no, nothing like that. I try to stay away from politics, if I am being completely honest. May we enter?'

Donovan mumbled something about the infernal sand and had them remove their shoes.

'My man can make you some tea.'

'No, we are fine,' Hamid said. 'Please do not trouble yourself.'

Hamid accepted a chair but the younger man declined one and stood by the entrance, clasping his hands at his waist, his face something of a cipher.

Before his guest could speak Donovan began. 'So, you're not with the government. What is it you do?'

'I am a businessman,' Hamid answered.

'From Mosul?'

'Not Mosul. Kirkuk.'

Donovan saw the man eyeing Najib's sweeping and told the servant to hold off. The fellow happily sat on his haunches in the corner.

'Your Arabic is good,' Hamid said.

'Thank you. Tell me how I can help you.'

'What you do here interests me, Professor. I have a great appreciation for the wonders of antiquity. So many of my friends and colleagues care only about the wonders of modern life – the latest electronics, automobiles, and the like. I care passionately about the wonders of the past.'

'Well, I'm glad to hear that. Do you have any background in archeology?'

'Unfortunately, not. I studied economics in college. It was very practical but very dry. I happened to be in the area this evening – I rarely get up this way – and thought that perhaps I might steal a few minutes of your valuable time.'

Donovan was getting impatient. 'Toward what end?'

'I was hoping to see some of the treasures you have been able to pull from the ground.'

'Well, look, Mr Hamid, I would love to give you a tour of

the site and show you some of the artifacts we've discovered but it's very late and that's just not possible. Let's set a date for your return, all right?'

Hamid's thick black mustache twitched with displeasure.

'You see, Professor Donovan, I have been fortunate in life. I am a rather wealthy man who dearly loves his country and its historical legacy. If you would honor my impudent request I would see fit to make a donation, a sizable donation, to support your illustrious work here.'

'Well, that's very generous, sir, but we have adequate funding. I'm sure the museum in Mosul would love to have your support. Now, if you want to pick a convenient date I promise you an excellent tour when you return.'

Hamid shook his head and gave Donovan a sad smile. His swarthy, stubbled face became flushed and he loosened his tie as if the maneuver might help drain the color.

'Actually, there is only one particular treasure I wish to see. Surely you can spare a small amount of time to honor my request.'

Donovan ran his hand over his bushy beard. 'And what treasure is that?'

'It is a piece of round obsidian. I believe you discovered it only a week ago. Please, may I see it?'

Donovan could feel his blood pressure rising. 'I have no idea what you're talking about.'

Hamid literally made a clucking sound. 'Please do not sully your reputation with a lie. I made certain inquiries about you, Professor, and you are an esteemed gentleman. You are also a Catholic, are you not?'

'I am. What does that have to do with anything?'

'I only mention it to invite a sense of camaraderie. I too am Catholic. Syriac Catholic. That is why I have always been keenly interested in what might be discovered at the Rabban Hurmizd Monastery. Perhaps you intended to eventually declare your discovery to your Iraqi colleagues. Surely you are not a thief, a looter of our sovereign treasures. Imagine the scandal if you were to be found to be a looter.'

'I thought you said you weren't with the government,' Donovan said. 'Are you a policeman?'

'Nothing of the sort. As I mentioned, I am only a businessman. Show me the black stone and I will say nothing. I only wish to see it.'

'I said I don't know what you're talking about. Now please, leave.'

Neither visitor moved from their spots.

'Your student, the girl, Mina. She makes reports to me. She saw the stone.'

'Mina? You hired her to watch over me? Why?'

'There were legends, Professor, but who knows about legends? Mina is my eyes and ears in case the legends were true. The stone, please.'

Donovan stood up. 'I don't know what she thinks she saw but I don't have what you're looking for.'

The large man seemed attuned to Hamid's intentions. At the slightest nod of his boss's head, he produced a pistol and pointed it at Donovan.

'I ask again,' Hamid said.

Najib looked alarmed but stayed glued to the floor when Hamid waved a menacing finger at him.

Donovan sat back down. 'I don't know what to tell you. I don't have any obsidian.'

'Please remain seated,' Hamid said before politely apologizing as he began searching the tent.

'These are my things!' Donovan exclaimed.

'Don't worry. I will be respectful.'

He seemed to be just that. The man's methods were careful and neat. Everything he searched – the desk drawer, the filing cabinet, the foot locker, the suitcase, the shaving kit, the mattress and bedclothes – he returned to their natural state. When he had finished examining every last centimeter of the tent and its contents he sighed through his nostrils and sat on the chair to rest.

'I know you did not deposit the stone with the other excavated artifacts. Mina told us this. And it is not in the tent.'

Hamid stood over Najib and asked him in Arabic about the stone, describing it in such perfect detail that Donovan became confused. He said it resembled a black mirror. He made a circle with his hands to show its circumference. How did he know what it looked like? The servant replied that he had seen nothing like this black stone.

'You are sure?' Hamid asked.

Yes, he was sure.

'Don't worry, I believe you,' Hamid told him. Turning back to Donovan he said, 'But you sir, you I don't believe. So, for the last time, where is it?'

Donovan remained defiant. By his calculus, his best tactic was to continue to stonewall. This man, whoever he was, would not find the disk. If he admitted his crime he'd be charged with a crime, removed from the excavation, and his positions at Harvard and within the international archeology community would be jeopardized. He wished he could take back a very bad decision, but that was water well under the bridge.

'For my last time, I don't know what you're talking about. What is it about this piece of obsidian that's so interesting anyway?'

'Ah, a salient question. I was wondering when you would ask. I am sure you have no idea what it is you found. Even the greatest expert may stumble around in the dark sometimes. The short answer is this: it is not for you to know. It is something that I have been searching for my entire adult life. It is an object that has been sought by others for centuries. It has great importance and for this reason your obstinacy pains me. The stone is closer than I ever imagined but alas, still far away.'

Hamid gave another small nod and the large man pocketed his gun into his robe. At this, Donovan looked relieved until the man strode toward him and roughly clamped his meaty hands over his ears.

'Hey!' he shouted, trying to wriggle free.

His cry was short-lived and when police would arrive the next day to interview the diggers in the tent village, it seemed that no one had heard anything unusual. The brute pulled Donovan's head all the way forward until his chin thudded against his own breastbone, then snapped it back with astonishing speed and force. As his occiput rammed into the hollow between his shoulder blades, Donovan's thick neck gave way in a sickening crunch. He fell onto the floor where his body convulsed for a time until it went still.

Najib said nothing but a pool of urine spread from under his rump.

Hamid said to him, 'You are afraid, Najib Toubi. Yes, I know your name. I know your village. I know the names of your wife and daughters. You are a countryman and more importantly, you are a fellow Christian. You do not need to die. Your family does not need to die. Will you be silent?'

The servant nodded.

'Will you tell anyone we were here?'

Najib shook his head.

'Will you clean up your puddle and go back to your village for the night?'

'*Balaa.*'

'Good. Do it and get out. Say nothing and live long. Talk and this man will kill you and all those you hold dear. I hear everything.'

Hamid addressed the large man by his name, Tariq, and told him what to do. He hoisted Donovan's body onto his shoulder as easily as if it were a sack of flour and stood by the desk, waiting. When Najib finished mopping up his mess and scurried away, Hamid left the tent, looking around to see if anyone was about. When he was satisfied the coast was clear, he whistled for Tariq to follow. The deep cutting where Donovan had found the black stone was only a short walk from the camp.

It was there that his body was dumped, and it was there that he was discovered by a digger the next morning, the apparent victim of a tragic, late-night fall that had broken the neck of the famous archeologist. He had been perfectly fine, working at his desk when the servant had left him the night before, Najib told the police. Then the servant broke down in tears and one of the policemen patted him on the shoulder and told him he was a good man.

'What happened was God's will,' the policeman assured the servant, but Najib was inconsolable.

TWO

Baghdad, Iraq, the present

The surgeon, a middle-aged man in sweat-stained scrubs, had been on his feet for nearly thirty-six hours. He looked marginally worse than his patient, who had at least slept through the night. The patient's chart was hanging at the foot of his bed in a crowded, noisy surgical ward that smelled of strong disinfectant. The doctor picked it up and scanned the newest entries.

'Was the sump emptied during the night?' he asked the nurse.

She checked the tube emerging from the surgical wound and the plastic bottle it drained into. 'It should have been emptied on the night shift. Doesn't it say?'

'No, there's nothing. Look.'

She glanced at the chart and shrugged. 'There was a new girl on last night. Maybe she forgot.'

'Forgot to empty or forgot to write it down?'

'Either is possible.'

'This is unacceptable! How can I do my job?' the surgeon said, his voice rising above the ward chatter.

The patient, an elderly skeleton of a man, awoke at the outburst, and looked at the surgeon through watery gray eyes.

'How are you feeling this morning?' the surgeon asked.

The septuagenarian shrugged. He pointed at his nasogastric tube.

'That must stay another day, maybe two,' the doctor said. 'We only did your operation two days ago, you know. It's too soon to take it out.'

Another passive shrug.

'How's your pain?'

'My belly hurts,' the man rasped.

'The nurse will give you morphine soon.'

The doctor noticed the small amount of almost orange fluid in his catheter bag.

'He's not making much urine,' he told the nurse. 'What's his IV rate?'

She told him and he grunted that she should draw blood to check his kidney function. Then he asked her if the patient knew his diagnosis.

'I don't think he was told,' she said. 'It would have come from you.'

'To be honest, I can't remember if I told him. Yesterday is a blur.' Leaning over the bed, the surgeon said, 'We found why you were vomiting blood. You have a tumor in your stomach. I stopped the bleeding, but the tumor was very large, and I had to leave most of it. Do you understand what I am saying?'

The old man nodded and whispered something the doctor couldn't quite hear. He put his ear closer. The man repeated himself.

'Please ask a Catholic priest to come.'

The priest was summoned to the Baghdad Medical City from the Chaldean Catholic Archdiocese on the other side of the Tigris River. These days there were only about a hundred fifty thousand Catholics in Baghdad but there were never very many more. The priest's hair looked particularly white atop his black garments and when he entered the surgical ward, the Muslim patients and their families regarded him with some curiosity. He looked around for a staff member to help him but seeing none, he called out for Najib Toubi.

The wife of a patient whose bed was next to his raised her hand and called for the priest.

'That's the fellow, there.'

The priest stood over the sleeping man and cleared his throat to try to rouse him and when that didn't work, he touched his shoulder. Najib blinked awake in gratitude and extended a shaking arm.

'I am Father Warda,' the priest said. 'How are you, my son?'

'I am dying, Father.'

'I am most sorry to hear that. Do you wish to confess your sins? Is that why I was summoned?'

'Yes, Father. I want to confess one particular sin. A great one.'

The priest pulled the curtains around the bed to give the man a modicum of privacy.

'Unburden yourself, Najib Toubi, and I will give you absolution.'

The old man's voice was thin and weak. The priest had to strain to hear.

'Nearly thirty years ago I witnessed the murder of a man and I did nothing,'

'Tell me more.'

'Do you know the Rabban Hurmizd Monastery?'

'Of course. I am from Kirkuk.'

'I worked as a manservant to an American. His name was Donovan. He was a famous archeologist who was exploring the ancient ruins. He was a good man, a Catholic man. One night, two Iraqis came to his tent. They wanted an object he found.'

'What object?'

'It was a polished black stone that was like a mirror. When the light struck it, it made the light come alive.'

The priest leaned closer. 'This American. Donovan. He found this stone under the ground at Rabban Hurmizd?'

'I believe so, yes.'

'And you saw it yourself?'

'Only for a few moments.'

'The Iraqi men. What did they say?'

'Only one spoke. The older of the two. He wanted to see the stone but Donovan lied to him. He told them he did not know of it. They searched the tent, but they were never going to find it.'

'Why is that?'

'The day after Donovan discovered the stone he went to Mosul with a large envelope.'

'You think he mailed it?'

'The package had the name of his wife. I saw it before he left that morning.'

'And what did the men do when they could not find what they were looking for?'

'They asked me if I knew. I told them I knew nothing. Then the other man who was young and very strong broke Donovan's neck. They threw him into the deep hole where Donovan had been digging so that it would appear as an accident. They told me if I said anything they would kill me and kill my family. They knew my name and where I lived.'

'Why do you think you were spared?'

'The older man said it was because I was a Christian.'

'This man was Christian?'

'Yes, a Catholic man.'

'Did he reveal his name?'

'Hamid. Mustafa Hamid.'

The priest all but gasped.

'You know him, Father?'

'Everyone from Kirkuk knows him.'

The old man said earnestly, 'I feared this man for the rest of my life. Now my life is over. My family are dead in the war. I am all alone. I don't fear him any longer, but I fear God.'

The priest nodded and said, 'Then let us pray. God, the Father of mercies, through the death and resurrection of his Son has reconciled the world to himself and sent the Holy Spirit among us for the forgiveness of sins; through the ministry of the Church may God give you pardon and peace, and I absolve you from your sins in the name of the Father, and of the Son, and of the Holy Spirit.'

The old man reached under his hospital gown and clutched the silver crucifix that Hiram Donovan had given him. He began to sob.

Father Warda returned to the rectory at the Cathedral of Mother Mary of Sorrows and immediately sought out one of his younger brothers.

'Father Zora, you are quite clever on the computer, are you not?'

The younger priest replied modestly that he was not without certain skills.

'Then please help me with a task. I need to find the telephone number of an Iraqi who left the country for America shortly after the first Gulf War. He was from an important Catholic family in Kirkuk.'

'Where in America, do you know?'

'It was New York City.'

'Do you know if he is still there?'

'I am not certain.'

'All right, what is his name?'

'Mustafa Hamid, but he also went by a Western name. He called himself George Hamid.'

THREE

Cambridge, Massachusetts, the present

Cal Donovan felt like an idiot, but this was his punishment for doing something terrible.

Only he couldn't quite remember his transgression. Whatever he had done or said had happened months earlier during the dead of winter when his girlfriend's chosen punishment and his agreed upon amends were impractical, to say the least. It probably had to do with standing her up for a date or saying something unspeakable in the heat of an alcohol-fueled argument. Although Cal spent some of his time doing archeology, nothing would be gained by digging up his sin. Better just to take his punishment like a man and get it over with.

He winced at his reflection in his bedroom mirror. The polo shirt was pink. Pastel pink. It was the only pastel article that had ever made its way into his closet. She had bought it for the occasion and had insisted he wear it. She'd also bought him a pair of golf shoes that, mercifully, were brown, not her alternative choice of buckskin white. At least he got to wear his own khaki trousers, not the micro-fiber Tiger Woods brand that she'd purchased in the wrong size. Why that particular brand, he had asked, walking into the punch? Because you're both pigs.

Jessica Nelson emerged from the bathroom in her own little golf outfit, a short white skirt that flattered her long, tanned legs and, unfortunately for him, a matching pink polo shirt.

'Great, just great,' Cal said.

'Twins!' she exclaimed.

He looked out the window onto his leafy Cambridge street, a manageable walk to his Harvard office. It was a gloriously sunny June morning.

'Looks like rain. We should cancel.'

'I'll drive,' she said, grabbing the keys to her Mercedes.

She was a member at the Dedham Country and Polo Club, located about twenty miles south of Boston, and she was an excellent golfer, one of the best women at the club. Cal had never played a round. As the CEO of an important Cambridge biotech company, Jessica used the club for business a fair deal. She'd taken Cal there for dinner once and though he drank a fair number of vodka martinis (hold the vermouth) that night, he'd done nothing to besmirch her member-in-good-standing reputation. Defying the predictions of Jessica's friends, their relationship seemed to have some staying power and it was probably because of parity. They were about the same age, both in their late forties. They both had big jobs. She was one of the better-known and best-regarded young healthcare CEOs in the country. He was a full professor of the history of religion at the Harvard Divinity School with a joint appointment at the Harvard University Department of Anthropology, where he also taught biblical archeology. In the world in which he inhabited, the name Cal Donovan was a conversation-stopper. He was a rock-star academic, an expert in the history of the Catholic Church, a personal friend of the Pope. She had been the youngest female biotech CEO in the country when she landed her current job. He had been one of the youngest full professors in the history of Harvard. They were both wealthy. She'd made her money from stock options, he'd inherited his from a trust fund. They both enjoyed their wealth without pretension, and both dabbled in philanthropy. They were equally strong-willed and could dish it out to each other and absorb the blows without being steam-rollered. And, not for the least of it, they were both handsome physical specimens who were sexually compatible to beat the band.

On arrival at the club, Cal unloaded his clubs from the trunk. An eager young man rushed over to collect them.

'I've got a 10:15 tee time,' Jessica told him, 'a twosome.'

'Of course, Miss Nelson.'

'I didn't ask where you got the clubs,' she said to Cal.

'A kid on the Harvard golf team.'

'Well, they're an excellent set. Try not to snap them in frustration.'

He met her outside the locker rooms and the two of them headed to the first tee where a foursome of men in their fifties were getting ready to hit off. Jessica knew them in passing and exchanged some pleasantries about the weather and how the wet and chilly New England spring was becoming a distant memory. To be sure, the fairway that stretched before them was an emerald incantation for the coming of summer.

Compared to Cal, the men looked remarkably unfit. They had spindly legs, overhanging guts, and puny arms. He was flat-bellied with heavily muscled arms that stretched the sleeves of his silly pink shirt. Golf was not and would never be his sport. He had played football in high school and boxed in the army. When he washed out of the service and landed at Harvard College, football seemed too tame. Rugby was more primal, more like combat, and he had been a bruiser as an undergraduate. He continued to play in local leagues when he was a junior faculty member, but the sport took its toll on his joints and he eventually retired his rugby cleats. But he still boxed at the club level at Harvard to keep fit.

One of the guys asked if he'd missed the memo. Jessica smiled sweetly and asked what he meant. 'I didn't know it was matching shirt day.' Cal wondered if it would be too impolite to punch the guy's lights out.

The men teed off. Their shots weren't all that long but they were straight. They waved goodbye and marched down the fairway.

'That guy who said the shirt thing,' Jessica said, 'is a state Supreme Court judge.'

'Wouldn't have been good to send him to the hospital, I guess,' Cal said.

'Not good, no. They're all lawyers.' She kissed his cheek. 'I'm going to hit from the ladies' tees,' she said. 'You should do the same.'

'Not a chance.'

'Okay, macho man. You'll be sorry. Let me see you take a practice swing.'

'Which club should I use?'

'It's a long hole. Use the big dog.'

'I assume that means the driver.'

'Clever boy. Put your little glove on.'

He took the driver out of its cover and took a swing so hard that he almost lost his footing.

'You're too damned strong,' she said and advised him to take a little off it. 'And try not to lift your head on the follow-through.'

'Head down, got it.'

She kept feeding him tips until the foursome ahead of them shrunk to tiny figures.

'I think it's safe for you to go,' she said.

'Oh yeah? How far do you think they are?'

'Two-eighty.'

'What if I hit them?'

'Well, number one, that would be bad, but number two, you've never played before. You're not going to hit the ball two hundred eighty yards straight. You'll be lucky not to top it and have it squittle onto the ladies' tee-box.'

'I don't know, Jess.'

'Would you hit already? Let's go! The next group is coming.'

He flashed her a smile. 'Okay, whatever you say.'

He put a ball on a tee, stood over it, then took a deep breath and swung away, every bit as hard as his first practice shot. But his balance was good this time and his head stayed down. The ball sailed off, rising straight and long into the bright sky, splitting the fairway.

She muttered something unintelligible at first, then shouted, 'Fore!' when it became all too clear that the foursome was in harm's way.

The lawyers scattered as the ball bounced in their midst before rolling another twenty yards past them. The wind carried some of the horrible things the men were shouting.

'Sorry!' she screamed, waving her club.

'Yeah, sorry,' Cal said under his breath.

'You hit a three-hundred-yard drive,' she said in a menacing tone, hands on hips.

'Lucky shot?'

'Don't give me that crap. Did you take lessons?'

He grinned. 'I didn't want to make a fool out of myself. The captain of the golf team gave me a few pointers.'

'How many lessons did you take?'

'Is a dozen a lot?'

'You bastard. I'm going to get kicked out of the club or sued by those guys or both.'

'I'll buy their drinks after the round. We'll be best buddies. And Jess?'

'What?'

'Still want me to hit from the ladies' tees?'

Cal mainly taught Church history at the Divinity School but this semester he had been teaching a popular undergraduate course on the archeology of the Holy Lands, something of a sweeping view of the field. He maintained an office on the third floor of the Peabody Museum, just large enough to keep a few books and papers and entertain one student at a time for office hours. It was a pale comparison to the spacious digs he had across the street at the Divinity School, but what he liked about the space was that it was next door to his father's old office, now occupied by the chairman of the anthropology department. Outside the door, a small brass plaque honored the memory of Professor Hiram Donovan and Cal, when the spirit moved him, would sometimes run a finger over it.

He was alone with a stack of blue books on his desk, marking final exams, when there was a knock.

'Yeah, come in,' he said.

Father Joseph Murphy, Cal's former graduate student, now a junior faculty member in the history department, was carrying two paper cups.

'I come bearing coffee.'

Cal took one and thanked the Irishman. 'How'd you find me?'

'I stopped by across the way. Trish knew you were over here.'

Cal patted his stack of paper. 'Exam books. No joy until they're done. You finished?'

Murphy gave a thumbs-up. 'I am officially a free man.'

'What's the plan for the summer?'

'I'm off to Galway to see my mom for a week, then I'll try to get stuck into my book on Irish saints. You?'

'Same old same old,' Cal said, peeling the lid off his cup. 'I'm editing a book of papers from last year's Danish congress then back to Rome in August for the usual couple of weeks of prowling around the archives. Pope Celestine's invited me to spend a few days with him on holiday at Castel Gandolfo, so I'll do that too.'

'How's he doing?'

'You know, hanging in there. Tough job but someone's got to do it.'

Through a series of shared crises, Cal and Celestine had become close friends, and Cal continued to enjoy the rare privilege of being the only outsider to have unfettered browsing rights at the Vatican Apostolic Library and the Vatican Secret Archives.

'Sounds like you won't have much time for golf, then.'

'Allow me to raise my middle finger to both of you.'

Murphy and Jessica had a standing monthly dinner date but often saw each other more frequently. They'd met through Cal but had become something along the lines of best friends forever, pledging that – as she put it – when, not if, she and Cal broke up that she and Murphy would remain pals. She loved having a funny and wise guy as a friend who didn't harbor aspirations and moon all over her. He's not gay, Jessica told her girlfriends, but he's the next best thing, a priest.

'She's still somewhat traumatized by your prodigious drive.'

'Fortunately for her, I couldn't chip or putt for shit. She beat me senseless.'

'She did mention that too. You're off to Foxwoods tonight, I hear.'

Cal nodded. 'My life's an open book.' He glanced at the wall clock. It was almost five. 'Screw it. The coffee's fine but let's toast the end of the semester with something stronger. I've got my overnight bag. Jess can pick me up from the bar.'

Jessica had never been to a boxing match and the thought of the violence she was about to watch seemed to unleash animal spirits. Seated at the ringside seats at the Foxwoods Resort that Cal had wrangled, she watched the first two fighters on the under-card go through their introductions and last-minute preparations.

She leaned over to Cal, her breath hot and boozy from her last cocktail at the casino. 'They're magnificent,' she said to Cal.

'They're good athletes but wait till you see the title match. Those guys are incredible.'

'Why have I never done this before?' she asked.

'Because you weren't with me before.'

She squeezed the top of his leg when the bell rang.

By the time the middleweight championship bout started, it was after midnight. It was a classic slugfest and Cal and Jessica were so close to the action they were sprayed with sweat. The challenger was taking the worst of it in the early rounds, but Cal told Jessica that he thought the guy was holding off, trying to tire out the older champ. Sure enough, in round nine, the challenger awoke alike a hibernating beast and started to show his true self. Jessica had started out as a passive spectator but by the time the bell rang for the last round, she was on her feet, screaming and waving her program.

At the decision – the challenger eked out a two-judge to one victory on points – she whooped for joy and threw her arms around Cal, whispering hoarsely into his ear, 'That was so amazing. I want to go upstairs and go fifteen rounds with you. Now.'

He whispered back, 'Not going to say no to that.'

It was nearly 3 a.m. when their bodies finally gave out. Cal rolled over, drenched in sweat despite the air conditioning. He lifted the bottle of Grey Goose from the hotel ice bucket, surprised that there was still some left.

'Want another shot?' he said.

'God no,' Jessica croaked, pulling a sheet over her ass. 'Get me some water and Tylenol. Hangover, I'm talking to you. Do not invade my person.'

He was about to pour himself a last cold one when his cell phone rang, showing a 212 number.

'Who the hell's calling me from New York?' he mumbled.

'Make that noise stop,' she said, draping a pillow over her head.

'Hello? Donovan here.'

'Mr Donovan, this is Detective Atwal from the NYPD. Are you the son of Bess Donovan?'

'Yeah, I'm her son. What's going on?'

'I'm over here at your mother's apartment on Park Avenue. I'm afraid there's been a situation.'

Cal winced hard. When he clamped his eyes shut he was half-drunk. When he opened them he was all but sober.

'What do you mean, situation?'

Jessica took the pillow off her head and turned her head toward Cal.

Considering what he had to say, the detective's voice was jarringly neutral. 'I'm very sorry to inform you that your mother has been murdered.'

FOUR

It was a full moon and a super moon at that, low in the sky, cartoonishly large and glowing above the cooling Arizona desert. Eve Riley was getting things set for the arrival of that rare and precious individual, a paying client. She had a patio at the back of her house where four rather uncomfortable chairs stood on flagstones around an empty space. Eve buzzed around, carefully positioning an assortment of candles on a tall wrought-iron candelabra. She caught a look at herself in the reflection of a sliding door and ran back inside to do something about her hair. Her bangs were a mess. She'd have to make an appointment to get them trimmed but for now, some clips would have to do the trick.

From the bathroom, she heard a car in the driveway. Peeking out the bedroom window, she swore. It wasn't her client, it was Henry's truck.

He bounded in without knocking, which wasn't all that unusual, but tonight she took offense.

'There's a doorbell, you know,' she called from the bedroom.

He headed for the fridge, got a beer, and tossed his cowboy hat onto a leather footstool. It kept going and wound up on the floor.

'Yeah, so?'

'So, you can use it sometimes,' she said. 'Your phone too.'

'Why?'

'In case I was busy.'

'When are you busy?'

'Tonight.'

'Busy how?'

'I got a client.'

'Hell you do.'

'It's the truth.'

She came in, scowled at his hat, and hung it on a peg.

He slurped down a quarter of a can. 'Well, I don't see no client.'

'He's coming. I don't want you here tonight, if you've got to know the truth. You should've called.'

'Doorbells, phones,' he muttered. 'You'd think we were strangers or some such shit. Well I'm here. I'm not driving all the way back to Tucson.'

Jason was, as her female friends put it, a healthy specimen. More brawn than brains, but not all together lacking in cerebral function, he sold and installed solar panels. They'd met at City Hall. He needed a permit to do an installation. She worked as a clerk in the planning and development department. He flirted. She was thirty-eight and available, he was age-appropriate and not a bad looker despite the early makings of a beer belly. She took the bait. The first time he made the trek to her place he asked her how come she lived all the way the hell out in Amado, and she had slid open the patio doors of her little bungalow and pointed toward the vast expanse of nothing but desert with low brown mountains at the shimmering horizon, and replied, 'That's why.'

'Well, at least park yourself in the bedroom,' she told him. 'It's not professional for him to see you in here drinking beer.'

'Professional?' he scoffed. 'You think you're a doctor or something?'

She let the comment pass, transferred her dinner dishes from the sink to the dishwasher, then gave the counter a wipe.

'It's a him, you say?' Jason asked.

'Yes, he's a him.'

'How old?'

'I don't know how old he is,' she said in exasperation. 'Would you move your carcass to the other room?'

'There's no TV in there.'

'Read a book.'

'Very funny.'

He grunted himself out of his boots and she immediately tossed them into the bedroom.

'How'd you find the guy?' he asked.

'He found me. Someone gave him my number.'

'You talked to him?'

'Yeah, he was nice.'

'How do you know he's not a psycho killer?'

'He didn't sound like one.'

Jason finished the beer and padded in his socks to the fridge for another one.

'Did you ask Pothnir about him?' he said sarcastically.

'Don't make fun of what I do,' she said. 'Maybe you should leave.'

He chugged the second beer and crushed the can. 'Can't now. Over the limit. Besides, I'm sorry, okay?'

'He's a retired professor,' she said, softening in the wake of the unexpected apology. 'If he were a solar-panel guy I'd be worried about the psycho-killer thing.'

Car headlights shone into the living room.

'All right, you need to make yourself scarce,' she said.

'How much is this guy paying you anyway?'

'Two hundred dollars.'

'I'll give you two-fifty to send him packing.'

'Jason, I'm not fucking playing around here,' she shouted.

'All right, all right,' he said taking the rest of the six-pack with him to the bedroom. 'But I don't like playing second fiddle.'

She answered the door to find a gentleman in his seventies with a goatee, an earnest smile, and a book in his hand.

'You must be Sam,' she said.

'Sam Benjamin, yes,' he said pumping her hand. 'And you must be Eve Riley.' He held up the book, back cover first, with an author photo of her.

'Come on in,' she said. 'Found me okay?'

'Satnav led me right to your door. Getting around is so much easier than the folded-map days.'

'Would you like a cup of tea?' she asked.

'If you're having some.'

She put the kettle on.

'So, Sam, I'm still not completely sure how you found me.'

He sank into her sectional. He was slightly tubby with that western-gentleman look that a bolo tie conferred.

'I teach at Arizona State. In the engineering department.'

'You drove all the way from Tempe?' she asked.

'No, I have a friend in Tucson. Anyway, I was at a conference – you know, one of those academic conferences where the most interesting stuff happens in bars – and late one night, I struck up a conversation with a colleague of mine from Michigan. It wasn't about engineering. It was about religion, which can be a fraught subject although this time it wasn't. The two of us were awfully simpatico despite the fact that he's a Methodist and I'm a Lutheran. There's plenty of doctrinal differences between the camps as you may well know, but we're on the same page in that we find Catholics to be on the wrong page.' He frowned, seemingly at himself. 'Now, Sam, here you go again. Eve, for all I know you're Catholic and I've offended you.'

'I'm not a Catholic and I'm not. Offended, that is.'

'Well, good. So, this buddy of mine and I are united in the sense that we Protestants are awfully comfortable having direct communion with God without needing all the intercessions and trappings of the Church of Rome to get through to the big guy in the sky. Only I wasn't having any luck accomplishing that.'

The kettle whistled and she got up to make the tea. 'Go on, I'm listening.'

'Are you married, Eve?'

'No, why?'

'Oh dear, I hope you didn't take that the wrong way. An old, not-wealthy fellow like me isn't going to be making advances on a young, beautiful woman. I asked because I was married for thirty-five years. No children, mind you, so my wife, Pat and I, well, our relationship was undiluted. Just the two of us. We shared interests. When I traveled, she went too. From the day we got married to the day she died we never spent a single night apart.'

'Milk?' she asked.

'Lemon if you have it.'

She squirted some lemon juice in both cups and asked how long it had been since his wife's death.

'Two years this October. I don't have to tell you how lonely it's been for a man like me who had this sort of seminal relationship in my life come to an end. But I'm not the sort who's at all comfortable with the notion of hanging out at drinking holes or doing online dating to meet women – swiping right, swiping left, whatever the lingo. Hell, I don't want a new woman. I want my old one! What I'm saying is I really want to talk to her again. To see how she's doing. Can you understand that?'

They took their first sips simultaneously, which made her smile. 'Yes, I understand. Of course.'

'So, at every chance I get – when I'm in bed, when I'm shaving, when I'm driving – I pray to God and ask Him to let me speak with her. But nothing. Not like I was really expecting God to connect a person-to-person call to Heaven. But maybe I'd at least see her in a dream? Not even that. So, I'm telling this Methodist buddy of mine about this and he says to me, why are you so arrogant to think that God, with all that's on His plate, is going to have the time to deal with a solitary old fart of a mechanical engineer in Arizona?

He says I'm aiming too high, that I need to go down lower on the Heavenly organizational chart. That's when he tells me about your book.'

'I see,' she said. 'But look, Sam, full disclosure. What I do—'

There was a thud from the bedroom and an 'Ow!'

'Oh, is there someone here?' the man asked.

'It's just my boyfriend. Don't mind him.'

'Is he all right?'

'I'm sure he's fine. What I was saying is that what I do takes years of study and practice. It's not something you can just pick up and do yourself right off the bat.'

'I realize that. I do. I'm willing to start the process. In fact, I've already started.'

He cleared his throat and awkwardly said, '*Ol sonf vors g, goho Iad Balt, lonsh calz vonpho.*'

Eve smiled and politely nodded.

'Well, how was that?' he asked. 'It's the beginning of the First Call.'

'Yes, so it is. The pronunciation is going to need a lot of work, Sam, but it's a great start.'

The engineer slurped his tea then leaned toward her as far as he might without pitching off his chair. 'Now Eve, I realize I've got a long road ahead before I can do what you can do and I'm committed to learning. As a teacher myself, I know the importance of having a good teacher and that's why I'm here.' He reached into his coat pocket, took out an envelope, and placed it beside the tea cup on the end table. 'That's why I'm more than happy to pay for your time. But what I'd like – and I'll pay you more for the opportunity – is to be able, through you, to speak to my wife as soon as possible. Actually, I was hoping we could make contact tonight.'

Eve was only a little surprised. The people who sought her out often had the same goal – to communicate with the dearly departed – but on the phone he had represented himself as someone who intended to invest the time to become a practitioner. When she had asked why, he had told her it was to expand his consciousness, part of his quest to become a better Christian and a better man. She had liked his answer and his ready acceptance of her fee structure. First session in person, future ones via Skype.

'Sam, I can feel how desperately you want to be able to contact Pat. I think that in time, you might be successful, but this will have to be something that you do yourself when you've amassed the skills to make it happen. It's something that's best done personally. It's not what I do. Through my teachings I enable people to act on their own behalf to achieve their personal goals.'

'But could you if you were so inclined? I have money in the bank I have no intention of spending in my lifetime. Eventually, it's going to go to a nephew I'm not even all that close to. What would it take, money-wise, to get you interested in helping me?'

She got up to put her cup in the sink and buy herself a slice of time to think how to respond. When she turned to face him again she said, 'It's not a matter of money although I admit my own bank account is a bit of a barren landscape. It would be an enormous commitment on my part without any guarantee for you of the result. You can't dial this stuff in, Sam, it's highly individualized. But if you do the work on your own, put in your own time and energy, at the end of the day, you're more likely to have success than me. I'll teach you the tools, but I can't be an intermediary. I hope you understand.'

He got a handkerchief and wiped the disappointment from his eyes. 'Yes, I understand. Of course I do. When can we start?'

'As soon as you finish your tea,' she said lightly. 'We'll work outside on the patio. I'll just get my gear from the closet. It's a beautiful night. The moon can't get any bigger.'

His tea was cool enough to chug and he declared his readiness at the very moment Jason threw open the bedroom door. He had a small pink trash bin in his arms and weaved across the living room purposely rattling the empty beer cans he'd tossed into it.

'Excuse me,' Eve said. 'I'm in a meeting, Jason.'

Jason was drunk, that much was obvious. 'Well, I finished my meeting with my six-pack and I'm fixing to have a new meeting with another six-pack, if you don't mind.'

He noisily emptied the bin under the kitchen sink and threw open the refrigerator looking for more beer.

The engineer stood up and said, 'I'm sorry, Eve. Maybe I came at a bad time.'

'Damned straight you did,' Jason fumed. 'A guy – a guy who works his butt off – comes over to see his girlfriend and she tells him to go fuck off into another room while she has a quote-unquote meeting. With another man? Even if he's an ancient geezer like you. I mean that's fucked up, right?'

'Jason, get the hell out of here right now,' Eve said. 'You sat in there like a juvenile, shotgunning your beers, and now you're a full-blown asshole. Congratulations.'

Sam looked like he wanted the carpet to swallow him whole. 'I'm not comfortable being in the middle of this, Eve. Maybe some other time, okay?'

Jason interrupted her response. 'Yeah, it's okay, old-timer. See you around.'

'Sam, I'm so sorry,' she said. 'I wasn't expecting him tonight, honestly.'

'It was lovely meeting you,' the engineer said making his way to the door while awkwardly avoiding eye contact with either of them.

'Your envelope,' she said.

'You keep it,' Sam said. 'For your time.'

She stood there crying until she heard the engine start and the car pull away. Then her lit fuse reached the explosives.

'Get the fuck out of my house!' she raged. 'Get out! Now! I never want to see you again. Don't text me. Don't call me. Don't come to my house. Don't come to my office.'

'How'm I supposed to get permits if I don't come to the permitting department?'

'Hell if I care. Now get out before I call the sheriff.'

'I'm not fit to drive back to Tucson, can't you see that?'

'Well you're fit to drive fifty yards down the road, park, and sleep it off in your truck. You've got ten seconds to pick up your boots and your stupid hat and get out of my life forever.'

*   *   *

She couldn't sleep. Her insomnia bubbled up from a witches' brew of agitation and anger. Fear, however, didn't enter into the mix. She wasn't the least afraid that Jason would try to get back into the house. She didn't think he was capable of it, especially when he sobered up, and besides, could take care of herself. Her snub-nosed Colt by her bedside was a handy piece of insurance.

Finally, she got dressed in jeans and a sweatshirt and went outside into the cool stillness of the desert night. She spent a while gazing at the gigantic orange moon before deciding that she had enough energy to proceed. She went to her closet and made two trips to the patio to get set up. There was a howl so far away she couldn't be sure it was a coyote's. What else could it be? Jason, still drunk, wandering the wilderness? There were no further cries from the dark and she lit her candles. Gazing into the shiny orb, she began to chant.

Ol sonf vors g, goho Iad Balt, lonsh calz vonpho; sobra zol ror i ta nazps od graa ta malprg.

The starting words were the same as Sam's effort but in pitch and cadence and pronunciation, they sounded completely different. But this first sentence was only the beginning. By the time she reached the Call of the Thirty Aethyrs several minutes had passed but to her, it felt as if no time had elapsed. It wasn't that she was in a trance. The altered reality came from the focus brought on by the rhythmical chanting. It divorced her from everything, even a sense of existence. The universe was reduced to only two elements – the sound of the chant and the sight of the shiny crystal.

Madriaax ds praf paz, chis micaolz saanir caosgo, od fifis balzizras iaida! Nonca gohulim: micma adoian mad, iaod bliorb, soba ooaona chis luciftias piripsol; ds abraasa noncf netaaib caosgi, od tilb adphaht damploz.

She went on, chanting in the strange tongue, until she stopped, nearly out of breath, air streaming through her nostrils.

She never knew where the voice came from. The surface of the crystal? The air? The inside of her own brain? It didn't matter. What mattered was that she could hear it and that she could understand the language she had been chanting.

I was expecting you.

'You were?' she replied in the same tongue.
I have a message.
'I'm ready to hear it.'
A man will reach out to you soon.
'What man?'
You will have common purpose.
'What purpose?'
The world as you know it is a world graced by the light of God. But it sits on a knife edge teetering over an infinite abyss. Know this: a great evil is coming. It threatens to tip all you know into a pit of darkness. Is the fate of your world darkness or light? I cannot say. Do you know the reason you became a scryer?
'No.'
This is why.

FIVE

'Where is she?' was the first thing Cal asked.
The detective was a turbaned Sikh who looked like he was about to extend his hand. That was before Cal tried to blow past him at the entrance to his mother's apartment. The policeman blocked his way with his stout body. 'The medical examiner took her. She's on her way downtown. I'm Detective Atwal. This is still an active crime scene.'

'I can't go into my own mother's apartment?' Cal said, thrusting his jaw.

'Oh yes, I would like you to come in, but you'll need to put on shoe covers and gloves. Fibers and fingerprints, you know. Here, please.'

As Cal slipped on the protective gear Atwal extended his condolences. It was the standard thing that policemen said to victims' families, but it came off sounding awfully heartfelt and authentic.

'I appreciate it,' Cal said.

'You drove from Connecticut?'

'My girlfriend did. I wasn't in a state to drive.'

'Your shock, I'm sure,' Atwal said.

'I was drunk. I'm sober now.'

'I see. All right, let's go inside, why don't we?'

The marble entrance hall gave no hints of the mayhem beyond. Everything was perfectly in place. The outgoing mail was on an ornate table, stamped and addressed, ready to be taken to the lobby in the morning. A vase held fresh flowers.

'She let the intruder in,' the detective said. 'See, the door is perfectly fine.'

'It was one man who did this?'

'It seems so from what I've seen from the cameras in the lobby and the Park Avenue entrance. He came in at about nine-thirty wearing a baseball cap and sunglasses. Sunglasses at night. And what looks like a pair of leather gloves. Large man, broad shoulders, race difficult to say. He pulls a gun on the doorman and forces him to disable the internal security cameras then binds the fellow with zip ties in the mail room. He makes his way to the ninth floor and knocks on your mother's door. The woman in 9F had just come home and was in her entrance hall so she hears the knocking, which she says was unusual because according to her, Mrs Donovan rarely has visitors at night. Your mother must have looked through her peephole and asked who he was. The woman in 9F describes herself as nosy. This woman opens her door a crack and hears him call through the door that he is a friend of her son, Calvin Donovan.'

'Jesus,' Cal whispered. 'You mean she was targeted?'

'It seems likely, yes. We've talked to every resident and this man approached no one else.'

Cal followed the detective into the living room, which bore scars of the intrusion. The large park-facing room was in shambles. Every book had been tossed from the shelves, every desk drawer and side board were open, their contents strewn on the floor. A bottle of India Ink had leaked onto a yellow and blue rug, staining it black. The blotch reminded Cal of a Rorschach test. It looked like a camel with two humps.

'He was looking for something,' Atwal said.

'She has a lot of jewelry.'

'In her bedroom. I saw it.'

'You mean it's still there?'

'I can't say that nothing is missing but there are a lot of expensive necklaces, earrings, and the like. This is what I need from you, Mr Donovan. I need to know what you believe might be missing.'

That was going to be a tall order. His mother had moved back to Manhattan from Cambridge after Hiram Donovan died. She was from the city and, truth be told, had never much liked life in the provinces, as she called Massachusetts. She and Hiram had been high-level hoarders, cherishing and preserving the relics of their lives. This eight-room apartment might have seemed like an awfully large space for a solitary woman in her nineties, but it was bursting at the seams with accumulations.

'Tell me what happened,' Cal said.

The detective fingered his thick, salted beard. 'We don't know precisely how long the assailant was up here. It was at least an hour. A resident who came in late went to the mail room to retrieve an Amazon package and found the doorman close to midnight. When uniformed officers arrived they did a unit-by-unit search and the woman in 9F told them about the man at your mother's door. They made entry and found Mrs Donovan in the bedroom.'

'How was she—?'

'I shouldn't say. The coroner, you know—'

'Just tell me what you saw, okay?'

'I believe it was manual strangulation.' The detective looked away. 'There were no signs of other abuse.'

'Thank you.' Cal swallowed the secretions that had built up in his throat. 'Anything else I should know?'

'She had been bound hand and foot by plastic ties, presumably while he searched for whatever it was he sought.'

Cal heard something in the kitchen and went to take a look. A man and a woman clothed in Tyvek suits were dusting surfaces for fingerprints. The contents of drawers and cupboards were all over the floor and countertops.

'Forensics,' Atwal said at his back.

Cal said out loud what he was thinking. 'What was he looking for?'

'That is what we would like to know, of course. Also, whether or not he found it. Did your mother have anything of great value beyond her jewelry and the paintings and other objects of art that we can see here?'

'I really don't know. Some of the art is quite valuable, I suppose. My father collected antiquities, some of which have value. I'll be able to see if anything like that's missing. She didn't keep much cash at home or gold bars or anything like that as far as I know. I don't think she even has a safe. She has bank accounts and brokerage accounts, of course. That's where she keeps most of her assets.'

The detective nodded. 'We haven't seen a safe. Is there anyone besides you who knows about her financial affairs? Do you have brothers and sisters?'

'I'm an only child. Most of her relatives are dead. She outlived them.'

'And your father?'

'He passed away almost thirty years ago.'

'I see. Well, Mr Donovan, it's very late and I'm sure you're very tired. I don't think it's reasonable to have you do an exhaustive search tonight. Perhaps we can do a brief walk-through and see if anything pops out. You have a hotel or some place to stay?'

'My girlfriend checked into the Pierre.'

'Fine. After we're done tonight, you can get some sleep. I can meet you back here in the afternoon to conduct a more thorough search.'

Cal spent about a half hour at a preliminary inspection. He kept his emotions in check everywhere but the master bedroom where a yellow stain on the white carpet marked the spot of her killing. The detective backed away and respectfully let him sob until he was able to resume his survey. Every room – even the bathrooms – and every closet told the same story of a frenzied, unfocused search for something the intruder knew or suspected the old woman had hidden somewhere. Cal was a frequent visitor to the place and had last come by around Christmas time. He had a fairly acute mental map of the contents of the apartment and over the years had seen his mother wear all her significant pieces of jewelry. Beyond that, he was the executor of her estate and he had reviewed the last iteration of her trust documents only two years earlier. As far as he could tell, nothing of significance was missing. When he delivered his verdict to the detective, Atwal flattened his thick, moist lips and nodded.

'Somehow, I'm not surprised,' he said.

'Why?'

'This is not the behavior of a typical robber to leave behind so many things like diamond necklaces and emerald rings he could easily carry. There is something about this crime we do not understand. Here, take my card. Get some rest and meet me here at two o'clock and we can spend as much time as needed searching for – well, an explanation. And again, Mr Donovan, I am most sorry for your loss.'

Jessica awoke briefly when Cal returned to the hotel, but he didn't want to talk. He crawled into bed beside her and both of them slept till noon when housekeeping tried to make up the room. He let Jessica know he needed to get back to the apartment and told her she ought to return to Boston.

'I'm staying with you.'

'You don't need to.'

She touched his back. 'I want to.'

Detective Atwal was wearing the same suit and tie as the night before. Cal wondered if he'd gone home. He peeled away the crime-scene tape from the front door and led Cal inside. The forensic team had finished its work. Every room, every nook and cranny had been dusted and photographed. This session lasted three hours. Cal went through everything, stretching his memory to its limits, and nothing seemed to be missing. This assertion was bolstered by a home-insurance rider he found in one of his mother's file drawers, a schedule of high-value possessions and their assessed valuations. Each item on the list was present and accounted for.

'So, nothing has been taken,' Atwal said wearily.

'Certainly nothing significant,' Cal said.

'This is difficult to understand,' the detective said.

'Where do we go from here?'

'I'll be trying to get better images of the perpetrator from

CCTV cameras in the area. I've got people reviewing them now. Hopefully we can get a look at his face and push it out to the public for help in identifying him. Otherwise, he left no physical evidence behind. I can release the crime scene back to you now. If we need to come again, I'll call. I'll keep you informed of any developments.' He extended a hand. 'Once again, I'm very sorry that this misfortune fell upon you.'

On his way out, Atwal removed the yellow NYPD tape from the door and Cal was alone. He planted himself in a living-room armchair and kicked off his shoes. The sun was still high enough in the sky to pour through the east-facing windows. A honking taxi nine stories below broke the silence. Cal had never felt at home here. It had always been very much his mother's place, not a family home. When Hiram Donovan died, she sold the Cambridge house where Cal had been raised and traded his father's old-world aesthetic for a décor that he would have despised – neutral-shaded, Park Avenue modern, something straight out of a 1990s issue of *Architectural Digest*. She sold all of Hiram's Edwardian library and study furniture prior to the move. What remained of him was his books, shelved (at least up until the intruder scattered them) in white built-in bookcases on one wall of the living room, some antiquities he'd collected over the years from Europe and the Middle East, and his papers and photographs, boxed into one of the guest-bedroom closets. These boxes too had been emptied onto the bedroom floor in an apparent frenzy of searching. Cal had long ago claimed some of his father's possessions and books that presently graced his own house but now he was faced with a monumental task of sorting and decision-making – what to sell, what to keep. He always knew this day was coming but now it was here by dint of violence, it seemed, in a way, more overwhelming.

Jessica picked up on the first ring.

'I'm alone,' Cal said. 'The detective left.'

'And?'

'And nothing. Nothing's missing.'

'So weird,' she said. 'You okay?'

'Tired. Can you come over?'

'Want me to?'

'Yeah. I could use some help.'

'I'm on my way. Need me to bring anything besides myself?'

'There's no vodka here.'

While he waited for her, he called the funeral home to start making the arrangements and found the contact details of his mother's rabbi in her address book. There were several numbers including a mobile and that was the one Rabbi Judith Bornstein answered. After Cal identified himself, the rabbi poured out her condolences and grief; she'd read about the murder in the papers. Cal mumbled something about needing to arrange a funeral as soon as the body was released by the medical examiner, and the rabbi insisted on making a house call.

Jessica's CEO instincts went into over-drive and when she arrived, Cal was happy to let her take charge for the time being. Beyond Cal's care and feeding and watering (plenty of vodka, plenty of ice), she threw herself into logistics. After Cal pointed her to the woman who was Bess's best friend – one of her circle of ladies-who-lunched – Jessica was able to assemble a contact list of funeral invitees, talk to prospective caterers for the shiva reception, and scope out the pricing for a death notice in the *Times*.

Rabbi Bornstein was a young woman, still in her thirties, but she had the measured calmness of an old hand at this kind of thing.

Grasping Cal's hand with both of hers she said, 'I am heartbroken. The entire congregation is in shock. How could something like this happen to such a sweet woman like your mother?'

'I know, it's horrible,' Cal said. 'It's not the way her life should have ended.'

The rabbi looked around the turned-upside-down living room. 'It was an unspeakable act, Cal. May I call you Cal? I know we haven't met but I feel like I know you. Your mother talked about you all the time.'

'I'm sure she did.'

'She was very proud.'

He ignored the second-hand praise. 'Would you like something to drink?' he asked.

'Maybe a soda water or plain water. Whatever you have.'

Jessica was listening from the kitchen and called out that she'd take care of it. She emerged with water and a fresh vodka for Cal.

'I'm the friend,' Jessica said.

'I'm the rabbi.'

'I'll leave you to it,' Jessica said. 'I'll just go back to putting the kitchen back together. One room at a time.'

'It was nice meeting you,' the rabbi said.

Cal and Bornstein sat on the sofa. Cal had picked up one of the photo albums thrown onto the floor and had it on the coffee table. The rabbi asked if she could look at it and thumbed through Bess Donovan's life.

'I only knew your mother for six years, Cal, but she made a big impression on me and I know how important she was to our congregation. I think I know a fair bit about her life but perhaps I should know more to be able to paint the fullest picture during my remarks at her service.'

He pulled at his drink. 'Whatever you want to know.'

'From what I can tell, there was a strong seam of faith running through your family life. Your father was a committed Catholic, your mother a committed Jew. And now you are a professor of religion. What was the religious dynamic in your family growing up?'

He snorted at the question and put his glass down next to the photo album. 'It was complicated. Both my parents were dogmatic and unyielding. They argued a great deal about many things, religion being one of them. They came to a rare detente with my name. My last name was always going to be Donovan, of course. She got the rights to my middle name – Abraham was her father's name. And Calvin was their solution for a first name.'

The rabbi chuckled. 'So, a famous Protestant's name was the great compromise.'

'There you have it. I'm not really sure why they stayed together.' He looked at the ceiling and answered his own question. 'I suppose they hung in there for me. Years after he died, she hinted that they probably would have split up once I was in college. We'll never know.'

'Parents often bury their hatchets for the sake of children.'

'In the case of Hiram and Bess, they were more likely to bury their hatchets in each other's skulls.'

'Oh my. That's strong. I might not use that.'

'Yeah. Probably better to talk about her philanthropy, her indomitable spirit, those sorts of things.'

'I will, for sure. But tell me, how did their religious arguments play out with respect to your upbringing? The subject interests me.'

'It was a fault line. He wanted me raised Catholic. She insisted that Jewish law made me a Jew. I kind of wished they would have thought about the issue before they decided to get married but apparently they both assumed the other would relent.'

'And who won, if I may ask?'

'For many years, neither. I was aggressively non-religious as a kid and young adult. I refused to go to church with him or synagogue with her.'

'No Bar Mitzvah?'

'Nope. Refused. It was only during my Ph.D. studies when I got very interested in European history, and the role the Catholic Church played in shaping that history, that I began to embrace Catholicism. Of course, my father was long dead at that point.'

'But your mother wasn't.'

'No, Bess wasn't best pleased. I was a serious Catholic for many years but for the last decade not so much.'

'A crisis of faith?'

'No, I still believe in God, or at least a strong notion of God, but the mechanics of faith have worn thin. Put it this way, I've given confession only once in the last ten years or so.'

'And how did that go?'

'Well, Pope Celestine took it, so it was interesting.'

She furrowed her brow and stared at him for a while until she concluded, 'You're being serious.'

'I spend a lot of time at the Vatican doing research. He and I have become rather friendly.'

She shook her head in amazement and told him that she

would love to spend time in the future discussing religion with him. Then again, she supposed they should continue talking about the life and times of Bess Donovan.

'She was big into funerals,' Cal said. 'She was old enough that she buried most of her friends. When I talked to her she gave each funeral a review, like it was a movie or a play. She wanted her own funeral to be as epic as possible so yeah, let's make sure you've got all the material you need.'

'And you'll do the eulogy?' she asked.

He nodded and smiled at her. 'Is the Pope Catholic?'

The next day, Cal and Jessica were back at the apartment continuing to put the place back together so when he got around to hiring a real-estate broker it would be ready for showings. The medical examiner was going to release the body to the funeral home the following day and the funeral would be held the next. They were in the dining room, bagging broken china, when the doorbell rang.

Cal didn't know the man at the door, a middle-aged fellow in a sharp suit.

'I'm terribly sorry to bother you,' he said. 'I'm a neighbor of Mrs Donovan's in 10G, right above you. Are you a relative?'

'I'm her son, Cal Donovan.'

'Look, it's a horrible, horrible affair, this. The whole building is rattled, the board especially. I'm on the board, the vice-chairman, actually. Here's my card.'

Cal looked at it. The guy was a lawyer at a big firm.

'Have the police made any progress?' the lawyer asked.

'Nothing yet.'

'Terrible, terrible. I didn't know your mother, but everyone says she was a heck of a gal.'

'That she was.'

'The reason I'm intruding on you is this: have you given any thought of what you want to do with the apartment? I hope it's not too inappropriate to ask so soon after everything.'

Cal had taken an immediate dislike to him. He was too damned slick and smarmy and yes, it was fucking inappropriate.

But he was too weary to tell him that and he resisted the impulse to slam the door.

'I'm going to sell it.'

'Well, here's the deal,' the lawyer said. 'My wife and I would very much like to buy it with the aim of making it into a duplex, you know, combining the two units with an internal staircase. I'd like to make you an offer you can't refuse. I've got all the previous sales in the building for the past couple of years for you to review. You're going to see that my cash offer is ridiculously good. And we'd be looking for a very fast closing.'

After a night's ponder, Cal made a decision. It was going to be a hassle to liquidate his mother's apartment and her possessions in any scenario, so it might as well be done quickly. Armed with Jessica's unconditional help – she called her office and took a week's vacation – he threw himself into the whirlwind. He accepted the lawyer's offer and began simultaneously juggling the funeral and the estate liquidation.

Of course, the funeral took precedence. His mother was seen off in a heavily attended service at her Upper East Side synagogue followed by an interment in a Jewish cemetery on Long Island. Bess Donovan's religious strife with her husband continued into the afterlife. Hiram was buried in a Catholic cemetery in Boston. She had harbored no interest whatsoever in eternal rest among Irish Catholics. Cal held the reception for her venerable circle of socialite friends and members of her congregation at the apartment, which he and Jessica had put back together in the nick of time.

The liquidation followed in short order. After undoing the chaotic work of the intruder, Cal and Jessica began reversing all their efforts, once again emptying drawers, shelves, and cabinets and placing the contents on the floor in rather more organized piles. Some piles were for charity, others for Cal to box up and ship to Cambridge, more for an estate sale. Jessica lined up an estate company to purchase most of the furniture and higher-value bric-a-brac. A representative from an auction house came by to do an assessment of the notable paintings and objets d'art that Cal had no interest in keeping. The largest pile were books, particularly books that had belonged to his father, which Cal was going to merge with his own considerable Cambridge library.

One night, after several long days chipping at the rock face, Cal and Jessica collapsed on the living-room floor with their drinks, the room now largely depleted. Cal absently leafed through a photo album of one of his father's excavations in Israel. His mother had brought Cal to visit Hiram that summer. The boy had been six. Cal lingered over a shot of the three of them, mugging for the camera from a bone-dry trench, each of them holding a spade.

Jessica turned her head and said, 'Finally.'

'Finally what?' he replied.

'You're crying.'

He wiped his cheeks with the heels of his hands. 'It's dusty in here.'

'Oh please. I know you're one blocked dude, but it's been weird watching you act like a zombie.'

'I didn't cry at his funeral either.'

'You were an angry, macho twenty-year-old who'd just been booted out of the army, right?'

'As I recall.'

'How did he die?' she asked.

'In a fall at a dig in Iraq.'

'Booze on board?' she asked.

'Who knows? He was no teetotaler but Muslim country and all – I kind of doubt it. It's a pity . . .' His voice petered out.

'What is?'

'I've wanted to have a conversation with him. You know, Cal, the forty-something Harvard professor, with Hiram, the sixty-something Harvard professor. I've got an office next door to his old one at the museum, did I ever tell you that?'

'No, you did not. What would you say to him?'

Cal shook his head and reached for the bottle of cold Grey Goose. 'Not going to go there, kiddo, in fact, I'm going to change the conversation.'

'Said you were blocked.'

'I want to tell you how much I appreciate your hanging in there and doing this week with me. It means a lot.'

She pulled her red hair to the side so she could peck his cheek.

'I think we make pretty good funeral buddies,' she said. 'I wish I didn't have to abandon ship tomorrow. You going to be all right for the end game?'

'I'll be fine. The place should be cleared out by Friday.'

'You won't drink yourself silly, will you?'

'No promises.'

Jessica used his shoulder to push herself to her feet and told him she had one more job she wanted to finish. She had declared herself highly qualified to go through Bess Donovan's clothes and jewelry to sort them for donation or consignment sale. The old woman had been a clothes horse who had attended numerous charity galas annually, year after year. She had a lot of dresses, some of them from top designers. More than once, Jessica had told Cal she wished she were a size zero so she could use this skirt or that jacket. Now, all that was left was to plow through were her shoes, current ones in racks, older ones in dozens of shoeboxes stacked at the back of her many closets.

An hour later Jessica came into the living room holding a shoebox. Cal looked up from a box of books he was taping up.

'Almost done?' he asked. 'I'm fried.'

'Yeah. Last couple. You should look at this.'

'Jimmy Choos?'

'Wow, I'm impressed. A man who knows his way around boxing matches and designer shoes. But no, not Jimmy Choos. This was inside.'

He took the padded envelope that had been folded to fit inside the shoebox. It had been addressed to his mother in his father's own distinctive calligraphic handwriting with a return address in Mosul, Iraq.

'It's postmarked July 1989,' he said, 'the month he died. It doesn't look like it's ever been opened.'

'Well, open it,' Jessica said impatiently.

The adhesive was still strong. Inside were a couple of his father's monographs, titles from the 1980s that Cal knew well, and sandwiched between them was a dusty old washcloth and an index card with a notation, also in his father's calligraphy.

John Dee?
British Museum/Scrying stone?

The washcloth concealed something with heft. He unwrapped it. The obsidian disk slipped into his hand. The polished surface caught the light from the crystal chandelier and played it back into his face, shrinking his pupils.

He suddenly looked over his shoulder.

'You okay?' Jessica asked.

'I thought I heard something.' It had sounded like someone far away had whispered something he couldn't understand. 'It's nothing. I'm just tired.'

She pointed at the disk. 'What is it?'

'I know who John Dee is,' Cal said, 'but I don't have a clue what it is. It was in a shoe closet?'

'Right at the back.'

He wrapped it in the cloth and put it inside the envelope again.

'Why the hell would he have mailed her something she didn't open?' he asked.

She shrugged a little and yawned a lot. 'Want me to put it in one of your boxes of books?' she asked.

He handed it to her then thought the better of it and took it back.

'No, I'll take it with me. I like a good mystery.'

SIX

Cassie Ferguson was nervous as hell. Peering into the ladies'-room mirror, she reapplied her lipstick, restoring the layer she had lost kissing the cheeks of analyst friends. For an investor-relations person, the first presentation on the first day of a roadshow for an initial public

offering was always going to be anxiety-producing but she
had the willies in spades. Her chairman and CEO was more
than a loose cannon. He was a dozen pieces of heavy artillery
rolling around the deck in a Force 12 hurricane.

She had been hired on the recommendation of one of the
board members, who rated George Hamid as the number-one
asset of the company and its number-one liability. During her
interview with the clean-shaven, kinetic Iraqi-American,
Hamid had leapt from his chair and pointed aggressively
through the windows toward lower Manhattan and the Harbor.

'You see this view?'

'I see it,' she said.

'It's a good view, isn't it?'

'It's a very good view.'

'You see this office? It's a fabulous office, isn't it? One of
the finest you've ever seen, isn't it?'

'Where are you going with this, Mr Hamid?'

'Here is where I am going. I arrived in this country with
nothing in my pocket. I lost everything during the first Gulf
War. I slept on sofas of Iraqi ex-pats willing to help me, I
scratched for every dime. I started this company with two
thousand dollars and a line of credit guaranteed by a friend.
And now I am the ninth largest residential landlord in America.
I've become a billionaire. Check my ranking on Forbes – you'll
see. How do you think I did that?'

'I know your history, Mr Hamid. I've done my
homework.'

He clearly didn't like her answer. He thrust out his lower
lip showing a purple mucosa full of veins. With his palms he
smoothed hair that didn't need smoothing. It was as gray and
dense as a wire bristle brush and hardly moved under his
touch. His demeanor was part anger and part pout.

'I built this company on the back of my salesmanship, some
might even say showmanship. I am my own best spokesman.
I'm a seasoned businessman. I'm seventy-three years old, for
God's sake. Why would I need someone like you, a very young
woman, to come and tell me what to do?'

She put on a sweet face and said, 'Well, thank you for
calling me that. I'm not as young as you might think but I'll

pass on the compliment to Anton, the gentleman who colors my hair. I've been in the investor-relations game for seventeen years. I'm the senior vice-president of IR at Bates and Modine, the largest publicly traded commercial real-estate company in the country. I know all the buy-side and sell-side real-estate analysts on the Street – more than superficially. I know their spouses' and kids' names, their birthdays, their likes and dislikes, the way they construct their financial models, the corporate-speak that drives them crazy-bad and crazy-good. I even know dirt on some of them. I've never had to use any of it but it's there as a nuclear option. It's your story, Mr Hamid. You will always be the principal story-teller, but I know how to craft the story so you're able to sell the company's vision for growth without running afoul of regulatory boundaries and getting yourself in serious hot water. Besides, I used to rent one of your apartments in Brooklyn.'

His frown disappeared. 'You did? When? Where?'

'When I first moved to New York, when I was getting started. It was all I could afford. To be honest, it wasn't great, but the heat worked and I could afford it.'

He wanted to know which building it was, how long she stayed, how much the rent was. She told him the details.

'Did you pay the rent on time?' he asked.

'Never late,' she said.

He turned his back to her, drank in his world-class view, and said, 'Okay, Miss Ferguson, you are hired on one condition.'

'Oh yes? What's that?'

'My accounting department will go back into our records to verify that you paid your rent on time.'

She assumed that he was kidding but he wasn't. Her rental records were located and scrutinized. Fortunately, she hadn't been lying.

When she started at Hamid Property Holdings, the board's plan had been to go public within a year, but George Hamid's impatience condensed the timeline. Now, eight months into her job, the IPO roadshow was happening but her plan for reining in her boss was on ever-thinning ice. He had refused to participate in the dry-runs of his roadshow presentation the bankers had penciled in, saying that any notion he needed to practice was ludicrous. The first time he publicly ran through the full PowerPoint deck was the night before the first investor meeting. At a presentation to the stockbrokers from the investment bank who'd be selling the deal to their institutional clients, Hamid had strayed off script, sometimes wildly, and a twenty-minute talk stretched to a rambling thirty-five. And during the question-and-answer session that followed, he had gone off the reservation and descended into hyperbole, boasts, and downright falsehoods. The lawyers had pressed the head of investment banking at the firm to try to reason with the bombastic CEO and later he reported back to his troops his belief that Hamid understood the stakes and everyone's concerns, and that he would behave.

One of the senior investment bankers on the deal button-holed Ferguson as soon as she stepped out of the restroom.

'Big crowd,' he said. 'Did you see inside the room?'

'I saw.'

'Must be a hundred analysts.'

'There's a lot of interest,' she replied.

'So, how's our guy going to do? You feel okay about this?'

'If feeling okay is feeling like I want to puke then I'm good.'

'Christ, Cassie, I feel like heaving too. He can't go spouting off bullshit like last night. He's got to stick to the verifiable facts. You've got to be prepared to jump in if he starts to say something bat-shit crazy, okay?'

'It'll be like throwing myself in front of a moving train but, sure, why not?'

She sidled over to Hamid before he took the stage and said to him in her sweetest and most cajoling voice, 'So George, you're going to stick to the facts and figures? No embellishments? No speculations?'

Hamid winked and pinched her arm with his sausage-like fingers. 'Come on, Cassie, you worry too much. I know what I'm doing.'

He walked to the podium sporting a huge smile that showed his gleaming teeth, whiter and shinier than anything found in the natural world. One of the first things he had done upon emigrating to the United States was get his teeth capped by a top cosmetic dentist. He believed that a good smile would be important to making it big in America and he never missed a chance to dazzle. The first slide of his presentation was a pro forma summary of the terms of the stock offering. The script had him reading it to the audience, word for word. He looked at it, looked at the audience, and immediately veered into unchartered territory.

'You know, ladies and gentlemen, it is such a pleasure and an honor for me to address you today. I am an immigrant. I am from Iraq. I was a very successful businessman there but nothing like I am now. I was a big enemy of Saddam Hussein and a big help to your government during the first Gulf War, Bush Senior's war. This country took me in and I have devoted myself to becoming a great American.'

The banker was standing next to Ferguson at the back of the room.

'Oh, Jesus,' he whispered. 'Just read the slide, George. And anyway, I thought we found out he was one of Saddam's cronies before he flipped sides,' he whispered.

Her eyes were closed. 'Whatever,' she whispered back.

Hamid continued to massacre slide number one.

'I hope you're going to buy a lot of shares in my company,' he said, 'because you look like nice young people and I would like you to make a lot of money from your investment. You know, some people say I can see into the future, you know, like a fortune-teller.' He laughed; no one else joined in. 'Maybe it's true, maybe not. But I can see the future of Hamid Property Holdings very clearly indeed and it's really quite amazing. At the offering price of eighteen dollars a share, how could you not buy this stock? What are you going to say if you missed the boat and it goes to a hundred?'

The banker exchanged panicky glances with the lawyers. 'Shoot me now,' he whispered.

When Hamid finished his talk, followed by a dangerously freewheeling question-and-answer session with the Wall Street analysts, his bankers and lawyers huddled to figure out how many financial regulatory landmines he had stepped on and whether they could salvage the rest of the multi-city roadshow. Ferguson wasn't invited into the gaggle, but she stood a short distance away to eavesdrop when she saw one of her least-favorite people poke his bald head through a side door of the ball room, then fill its frame with his slab of a body. Tariq Barzani was the director of security at the company and more than that, he was George Hamid's shadow, a bulldog body-guard, surrogate son, and fixer rolled into one. He had emigrated alongside his older companion in the early nineties and had supposedly fulfilled a similar role in Hamid's construc-tion company in Kirkuk. She had heard that Barzani had been an Olympic-level powerlifter in his younger days, but she never bothered to look it up. His neck was as big as her thigh, so the story was plausible. She knew he spoke English but rarely heard him converse in anything but Arabic around the office because the only person he interacted with was his boss. She had stopped trying to pretend to be nice to him because all he did was scowl at her and follow her with cold eyes as if he was a hungry dog and she was meat.

Hamid excused himself from a conversation with a couple of lingering analysts and waved Barzani over.

'What is happening?' he asked the younger man in Arabic.

'I have the building under surveillance with some of my men,' he said. 'I do not think anyone saw me that night, but I do not want to trigger a memory in case I am wrong. Her son is still there. A truck came from a company that buys furniture. There was also a moving company. I had a man speak to the driver of the van. The delivery is going to Massachusetts.'

'He must have been going through her belongings, deciding what to keep and what to sell. What you could not find, perhaps he can.'

'I am sorry I failed you.'

'Please, you did not fail me, Tariq. It was a large apartment and you had limited time. And we cannot be certain that Donovan's wife even kept the mirror. But thanks to the old man, Najib Toubi, we have a chance to find it. I am happy we did not kill him all those years ago.'

'I should have loosened his tongue back then.'

'We must look forward, not back. Are the police continuing to come to the apartment building?'

'No longer. The detective in charge of the investigation was interviewed in the newspaper yesterday. He said they had no leads.'

'Good, good.'

'What would you have me do?'

'We must rely on ourselves. On this matter, the angels are not speaking.'

'Do you want me to search the son's house when the moving company delivers the goods?'

'Not now. I'm worried that could allow the police to make a link. Watch him very carefully. Do this personally. I want to know everything he does.'

'But you will be traveling this week. I should not leave your side.'

'I'll be perfectly fine. Look at them back there.' Hamid caught a furtive glance from the lead investment banker at the back of the room and waved at him cheerily. The fellow returned an awkward smile and resumed his huddled conversation. 'See how they love me, Tariq? I am their cash cow. Pull my udder and dollars flow out. These men will take good care of me. Find the mirror, Tariq, and God willing, George Hamid will be able to wipe out that which is rotten in the world.'

SEVEN

Although it was only June, it might as well have been a high summer day. The spring had been warm and wet. Lilac blossoms were waning, but daffodils and tulips were in bloom, and honey bees flitted from flower to flower. Cal had thought to fill the hummingbird feeder on his porch and the tiny creatures began to plunge their beaks into the sugary water. It was hot, but it was a dry, comfortable heat. A slight breeze passed into his living room through screened windows. Then one of his neighbors, an architect who was fastidious to the extreme about his weekend yard work, fired up his leaf blower, forcing Cal off the sofa to slam his windows shut.

He didn't stay on his feet for long. The funeral and the great dismantling had taken an emotional toll, and the mysteries of the mind–body connection made him feel like a physical wreck. Heavy drinking hadn't helped. His head and body felt wooden and the spectacle of his living room and hall stacked with packing crates was stupefying. Whenever he allowed himself to look at the cardboard stalagmites on the floor, he audibly groaned.

The doorbell forced him up again.

Through the frosted glass he saw a black shirt with white collar. 'Priest alert,' he mumbled.

Joe Murphy gave his condolences at the door and continued to offer sympathies into the kitchen where Cal poured him a coffee from a half-filled pot.

'I'm sorry I wasn't around for the funeral.'

'Seen one, seen 'em all.'

'Catholic affairs, I'd have to agree. I've not been to all that many Jewish ones.'

'There's a lot less drinking.'

'So I've observed but I expect you wore some of your Irish.'

'I tried to do the Donovans proud. Even switched to Jameson's that night.'

'Jessica filled me in.'

'She was an extraordinarily good egg,' Cal said. 'I don't like depending on people—'

'One of your few flaws,' the priest interrupted.

Cal guffawed. 'But I don't know what I would have done without her.'

'I'd urge you to hold that thought for the next time you're about to do something unfortunate concerning our dear friend.'

'Christ, Joe, you know me too damn well.'

'Jessica tells me the police haven't found the killer.'

'No killer, no motive. It's maddening.'

'I'm sure it is. So, tell your parish priest, how're you really doing?'

'I'm hanging in there.'

'Well, you look sad, which is understandable, but you also look pale and listless, which is not.'

'Like I said, hanging in there.' He seemed keen to change the subject. 'How's your mother?'

'Fast with a cup of tea, slow with most everything else. Tell me, Cal, what in God's name are you going to do with all your mom's stuff? Look at all of it!'

'Three of every four boxes are books. Mostly my father's but she had a pretty good collection too. I'm going to have to convert a spare bedroom and build a second library.'

'Can't have too many books, right?'

'Truer words . . .'

Murphy casually volunteered to help lug the boxes of books up to the sacrificial guest bedroom. He didn't have to offer twice; Cal immediately pressed him into service. The young priest rolled up his sleeves and the two of them labored for the better part of an hour, then sat in the much-improved living room sharing a couple of cold beers. The room was now uncluttered enough for Murphy to notice something on an end table that had been obscured by a tower of book boxes.

'Now what is that?'

He got up to have a better look.

'Go ahead,' Cal said, 'you can pick it up.'

Murphy carefully plucked the black obsidian disk from the old padded envelope on which it had been resting. Cal noticed a flicker of an odd look cross his face.

'All right. I'm stumped,' Murphy said.

'I can't tell you what it is, but I'll tell you what I know,' Cal said. 'It was in the back of my mother's closet in a shoebox. Jessica found it doing triage on her shoes.'

'Now there's a woman who knows her footwear,' Murphy said. 'The two most prevalent items in Jessica's apartment, as you well know, are bottles of wine and pairs of shoes.'

'You've been in her closet?'

'She gave me the tour, yes. It's approximately the size of my flat. She's quite proud of it, not in a boastful way, mind you, more in a sweet way. So, this little beauty was in a shoebox.'

'In that envelope, sandwiched between a couple of my

father's monographs. The writing is his. He mailed it from Iraq. It's a little bit chilling. It's postmarked the day before he died. For all I know it's one of the last things he wrote.'

'Lovely bit of calligraphy.'

'That was his everyday handwriting. He was old-school.'

'He was on a dig when he died, I recall you telling me.'

'He was north of Mosul at the Rabban Hurmizd Monastery founded by the Chaldean Catholics in the seventh century. As far as I know he was excavating an eleventh-century scriptorium when he died in 1989.'

'You think this came from there?'

'I'd have a hard time believing that. He wouldn't have stolen an artifact from a dig. It wasn't like him. It wouldn't be something that any professional archeologist would do. It's more likely that he found it for sale in some bazaar.'

'Is it old?'

'All I can say is that I don't think it's modern. Oh, there was a card with it inside the envelope.'

Murphy found it, lettered in the same calligraphy. 'John Dee?' he said. '*The* John Dee, you think?'

'I mean, probably, but I can't be certain.'

'He was Queen Elizabeth's alchemist, right?'

'And her astrologer.'

'What, pray tell, is scrying?'

'I only did a quick look-up. It's gazing into reflective surfaces like polished stones or pools of water to see spiritual visions.'

'So, your father thought it might be intended for magic and the like.'

Cal shrugged. 'Maybe. It's a mystery.'

'Well, how curious are you?'

'Scale of one to ten? Maybe a five or six.'

'Well, that's good enough.'

'For what?'

'To get you off your *duff* into some wholesome sunshine. I happen to know a fellow who might know something about this stone of yours. Right up his alley. Come on, let's take a walk.'

The bookstore was at the edge of Harvard Square on Brattle Street, in the basement of an apartment building. Cal must have passed the Orb and the Serpent a thousand times over the years but to the best of his recollection he had only been inside once and that was when he was an undergraduate. Standing in front of the Celtic-style signage and a mandala decal on the door, he flashed back to the early 1990s and a small, dark room that reeked of incense where some type of breathy pan-pipes music was looping on a tape. He would have been in an altered state, he imagined, in a haze of booze, weed, or both.

'You know the owner?' Cal asked Murphy outside the premises.

'Jeremy Mulligan's his name. I wandered in a couple of years ago for no other reason than here's a bookseller in the Square I hadn't visited. Mind you the occult isn't really my thing, but it turns out that Jeremy's also from County Galway and we bonded. We see each other from time to time. If he's not the man with answers he'll likely have some ideas on where you might go for more information.'

Mulligan came from the back room alerted to their presence by the tinkling of a brass bell the opening door swatted. As soon as Cal caught sight of him he was sure he was the same guy he'd seen at the store all those years ago. Here was the same thin face made long by an unforgettable fleshy chin that hung like a nut sack, the same hippie hair tied back into a pony-tail that was, in his mind's eye, jet black and was now cotton-wool white. And for all Cal knew he was wearing the same tie-dyed shirt.

Mulligan grinned at Murphy and pointed at Cal and said in an accent flattened by decades away from the old country, 'Are you a rabbi?'

'Am I a rabbi?' Cal repeated, befuddled. Burning sandal-wood oil tickled his nostrils.

'That's right. Are you?'

'As it happens, no.'

'Pity,' Mulligan said. 'I always wanted to say, a priest and a rabbi walked into a bookshop.'

'And what would the punchline have been?' Cal asked.

'Haven't gotten that far, friend. Something will come to mind if the situation presents itself.'

The two Irishmen exchanged greetings while Cal had a look around the store. There were cases of paperbacks covering the full gamut of occult magic and mythological topics, small tables crammed with Hindu and Vedic figurines, incense sticks and burners, candles, Tarot cards, and by the counter, a couple of racks of posters of colorful occult symbology.

Murphy steered the conversation to the purpose of the visit. 'Jeremy, my friend here, Professor Donovan, has something we'd like you to take a look at to see if you can shed some light.'

'Donovan, eh?' Mulligan said. 'Your people from Limerick, Cork, or Kilkenny?'

'Limerick.'

'Ah, the way-back Donovans.'

'You know your genealogy.'

'I possess a plethora of non-marketable skills. Show me your mystery object, Donovan of Limerick.'

Cal had the washcloth-wrapped obsidian in a messenger bag. He placed it on the counter next to the cash register and did a reveal.

Mulligan's eyes widened. 'She's a beauty. May I?' On Cal's nod, he took it into his outstretched palm. 'Hello, darling, where've you come from?'

'Iraq,' Cal said.

'She can speak for herself, you know,' Mulligan said.

Murphy looked bemused. 'How do you know it's a she?'

'Well now, Father, to me, all lovely things are a she.'

'Why do you say it – she – can talk for herself?' Cal asked.

'Because that's what she's made for. Now I'll need some quiet.' Mulligan turned the volume knob on his sound system to zero and stared into the reflective surface. After a full minute of contemplation he shook his head and said, 'For a fellow who traffics in the magical arts, I've really got no special abilities, none at all. It's always made me rather sad. Did either of you notice anything when you held this black beauty in your mitt?'

Every time Cal picked it up there was always the faintest of murmuring, impossible to place. But he kept quiet and shook his head.

'Well, some folks have it, most don't. I'm not saying you can't get anything from her if you're lacking in these abilities, but she's intended for those that do.'

Cal was getting restless. 'I'm sorry, but you haven't said what it is.'

'She's a showstone. At least that's what I reckon.'

'Is that the same as a scrying stone?' Cal asked.

'One and the same. If you knew what it was, Donovan of Limerick, why'd you come in saying you didn't?'

Murphy knew Cal well enough to see from his reddening ears that he was about to get short with the aging hippie. He intervened by telling Mulligan that the obsidian arrived with some morsels of information, but they needed an expert's help to flesh them out.

'Right,' Mulligan said, placing the obsidian back onto the counter. 'These beasties are known by a number of names – showstones, shew-stones – the Elizabethan spelling (with an E-W), Aztec mirrors for the obsidian kind, scrying mirrors. They're all for the same thing. Conversing with spirits. Ever hear of a chappie named John Dee?'

'We have indeed,' Murphy said.

'Then you might know that Dee was the father of a school of magic that's come to be called Enochian. It's not a well-known form of magic, and it never had much of a following, owing to the fact that it requires considerable study and scholarship to become proficient. Dee was something of a genius. He worked out all the particulars of scrying and communication with the great beyond. Mind you, he wasn't a scryer himself. He didn't have the gift, you see. He relied on a number of gentlemen to do the scrying on his behalf. A curious fellow named Edward Kelley was his main man.'

'They were mediums?' Cal asked.

'Something like that. They used shiny objects in their work like crystals, vessels of water, polished stones like the black beauty here. Dee somehow got his hands on an obsidian mirror. He called it his Aztec mirror, but who's to say where it came from? You can find obsidian rock all over the world. By all accounts, it was his favorite instrument. It's sitting in the British Museum, actually, with some other of his mystical gear.'

Cal smiled. His father had gotten it right.

'There's pictures of it you can find online,' Mulligan added. 'And now it's time for me to monetize your visit, gentleman. I've got a couple of books on Enochian magic I will sell you for the price marked on their covers, not a penny more, not a penny less. I'll fetch them for you.'

Cal bought both, *Enochian Vision Magic – A Beginner's Guide*, by Malcolm Ebersole, whose author photo showed an elderly, unsmiling British fellow in a tweed jacket, and the earlier, *Enochian Magic – A Journey into the World of John Dee*, by an Eve Riley, an attractive young woman with raven hair photographed seated on a stone wall before a desert backdrop.

'Now that we've met, Donovan of Limerick,' Mulligan said, handing Cal a paper bag, 'don't be a stranger. And as for you, Father Joe, try not to get too hot under that collar of yours.'

The bell at the bookshop door rang again and Mulligan came out, swallowing the last bite of his ham sandwich.

'Like Pavlov's dog, here I come,' he said to the bald, swarthy man whose size made the shop seem even smaller.

Tariq Barzani didn't seem to understand the comment. 'You work here on your own?' he asked, expressionless, in a sonorous Middle-Eastern accent.

'Just the three of us – me, myself, and I. How can I help you?'

'This is magic store, right?'

'Magic, occult, astrology, mysticism, you name it.'

'There was a man just here. What did he want?'

'This is a book and curio shop, friend, not a spy on my customers shop. You look like you could maybe use something on Zen philosophy. Third shelf on your left.'

'His name is Donovan. He had a leather bag. What was in it? Did he show you something?'

Mulligan gave him a few tuts in reply and said, 'Unless you're a member of the constabulary, I'll not be answering inappropriate questions. Now buy something or skedaddle.'

Barzani bolted the door and flipped its sign to *Closed*. Over Mulligan's protestations, he shuffled forward. He still had the massive legs of a powerlifter and his inner thighs scraped against one another.

'Did he have a black mirror?' he asked. 'Did he have a showstone?'

'All right, enough is enough. Leave or I'm calling the cops.'

Barzani kept coming, slowly like a tank, but fast enough to yank the phone from Mulligan's hand and force him into the back room.

On Sunday morning, Cal was lounging on his sofa, sections of the *New York Times* tossed untidily onto the floor. His cellphone went off across the room. He groaned at it pleadingly, but it would not come to him, so he lifted himself up and saw it was Joe Murphy.

'Hey, Joe, what's up?'

From the priest's first breath, Cal could tell there was a problem.

'Jesus, did you hear the news?'

The doorbell rang. Cal saw through his front windows that a police cruiser was at the curb.

'What news? What's going on? The police are here.'

'You go talk to them and call me back,' Murphy said. 'Jeremy Mulligan's been killed.'

The man at the door was a few years younger than Cal with thinning blond hair and a wispy mustache. He asked if this was Calvin Donovan's house.

'That's me.'

The man reached into his tan sport coat and pulled out a badge wallet. 'I'm Detective Gilroy, Cambridge Police. Could I come inside, Mr Donovan?'

'Is this about Jeremy Mulligan?'

'How did you know that?'

'I just got a call from a friend. What happened?'

'Can I come in?'

'Of course. Sorry, the place is a bit of a mess. I inherited my mother's things. She just passed away.'

'My condolences.'

Cal cleared off a chair for the detective and squared off with him on the sofa.

'Mr Mulligan was found this morning at his store on Brattle Street. He was the victim of an apparent violent crime. He never made it to an engagement with a friend in Somerville last night and this friend went looking for him this morning at his apartment in Medford and then at the bookstore. He had a spare key, made entry, and found Mulligan in his stock room.'

Cal was shaking his head at the story. 'How was he killed?'

'We're not divulging that at this time. The reason I'm here is that it appears that you were the last customer he had yesterday.'

'I was there at midday with a friend, Joseph Murphy.'

'I'll need his particulars.'

'Of course. You identified me from a security camera?'

'The store didn't have cameras. I found your credit card receipt.'

'I see.'

'The time stamp on your credit card transaction was 12:46. Sometime around two in the afternoon, a building resident noticed the shop was closed, which was unusual for a Saturday, but she figured he just knocked off early. What time did you and Mr Murphy leave?'

'It was within a minute or two of making the purchase.'

'A couple of books, I saw.'

'That's right.' He pointed to the paper bag on the coffee table. 'There they are.'

'Go there frequently? Did you know the deceased?'

'It was my first time in a very long while. It was really my first time meeting him. Joe Murphy knew him fairly well. They were both from the same place in Ireland and had that in common.'

'How did Mr Mulligan seem to you? Any signs of stress?'

'Not at all. He was relaxed and joking around.'

'Was anyone else in the store?'

'Not in the front room at least.'

'Could anyone have been in the storeroom at the rear?'

'I didn't hear anything, but I couldn't say for sure.'

'And why specifically did you decide to go there yesterday?'

'I inherited an artifact from my mother. Joe Murphy thought that Jeremy might know what it was?'

'Did he?'

'Actually, he did.'

'Could I see it?'

Cal told him he didn't see why not and got the stone from the messenger bag. The detective looked at it, unimpressed.

'And what did he say it was?'

'It's for talking to the spirit world.'

The detective deadpanned, 'Maybe I could borrow it sometime as an investigative tool. So, nothing was out of the ordinary?'

'I didn't notice anything unusual.'

'And what is it you do, Mr Donovan?'

'I'm a professor here at Harvard.'

Out of the blue, Cal felt himself tearing up.

'Professor's row. Might have figured.' The detective looked up from his notebook. 'You okay?'

'It's upsetting, I guess. My mother was murdered two weeks ago. Now this.'

'Where did the murder occur?'

'Manhattan.'

'We live in a violent society. In my line of work you get used to it. What is it you teach?'

'Religion.'

The detective closed his pad. 'I'm not big into religion myself but it seems to work for some folks.'

Cal swiped his stinging eyes with his fist. 'It comes in handy from time to time.'

Barzani was lying on a bed in his boxer shorts watching a German Bundesliga soccer match on cable TV when his phone buzzed.

'Hey boss.'

'Are you still in Cambridge?'

'Across the river in Boston. The only hotels I could get there were too expensive.'

'You're on an expense account, Tariq. Why are you so cheap?'

'It is your money, not mine. I do not like to be wasteful.'

George Hamid said he wished his other employees were as frugal. 'I've been thinking about our situation.'

'Yes?'

'I'm willing to risk it. We know now that the son has the mirror. It's within our grasp. Listen, are you sure Donovan didn't ask the shopkeeper about the 49th Call?'

'He was motivated to give me the information. He told me about the mirror after the first punch. He didn't know what I was talking about when I asked about the call.'

'All right, I've decided. Go there tonight and persuade the son to give you the stone. Press him about the call too. When you have the stone, kill him and come back home.'

EIGHT

Mortlake, England, 1582

It was a rambling old house proudly sitting on the High Street, sandwiched between a sharp bend in the River Thames and St Mary's Church behind it. To the tradesmen and craftsmen who rumbled by on their horse carts it appeared to be the house of a wealthy gentleman, but the truth was otherwise. Its owner was an impecunious scholar who obsessed day and night about making ends meet and securing the kind of royal patronage to provide a steady income to support his many and varied research activities. Yes, he had a wife and a growing number of children to feed and clothe, but every shilling and crown that made it into his purse – beyond what was needed for basic necessities, of course – was put toward the acquisition of books and manuscripts. Years earlier, when he was a young man, at a time when the Queen's half-sister, Mary Tudor, sat upon the throne for her brief, five-year reign, he had lobbied Her Majesty to establish a grand royal library, but the scheme had never materialized. Therefore, he had taken it unto himself to amass an important personal library at

Mortlake. He started with a handful of books but in time, his library outgrew the single room he had designated for the collection and his children outgrew their single bedroom. Not wanting to move house, he added to it by degree, purchasing small tenements on either side of the property, constructing rooms for books and studies, laboratory spaces for his experiments, and bedrooms for the children and servants. Not to be left out, his wife occupied a set of small rooms on her own account. Owing to the higgledy-piggledy way the house came together, the layout was something of a maze, and in the main, the only way to get from one place to another was by walking through the rooms of others. His own studies and laboratories, however, were sacrosanct. A child or servant – or even his wife for that matter – who wandered into the inner *sancti* could be expected to be severely reprimanded and very possibly lashed. At its peak, his library was the largest in England, with some four thousand books and a thousand manuscripts he had acquired in the course of his domestic and Continental travels. There were books on the celestial sciences, mathematics, cryptography, alchemy, cabalistic magic, philosophy, religion, and a large collection of anatomy texts and other medical subjects. These works fed the furnace of a burning, polymathic intellect and Dee was generally considered the most learned man in all of England, a skilled mathematician, philosopher, geographer, astrologer, alchemist, and practitioner of magical arts. In addition, his more than passing interest in medicine earned him the honorific title of Doctor Dee that he carried throughout his life.

A library like his attracted scholars and dilettantes like flies to honey and the location of Mortlake proved expedient to the flow of intellectual commerce as the town was an ideal rest stop for learned nobles traveling between their great estates in the southwest and the royal palaces of Greenwich and Whitehall. Indeed, the library was so illustrious that Queen Elizabeth herself and her entire Privy Council had deigned to visit Mortlake in 1575.

Dee was holed up in the book-filled room with the best early light the morning a highly anticipated visitor rapped on the door with the brass head of his walking stick. At fifty-five, Dee was old but spry. He wore his long gray beard in the pointy style favored by academics and certain men of the cloth, and because his face was extremely narrow with hollowed-out cheeks, the beard gave him the look of some sort of giant sea bird with a great spear of a beak.

When the rapping persisted, Dee called out, 'Jane, will you ask why Robert is not seeing to the door?'

His wife called back, 'I believe he is in the garden in the privy.'

Dee yelled that he would come down himself. It would not have been proper for Jane to receive the visitor. He marked his page with a bookmark and closed the leather-bound text he had been annotating with marginalia. His threadbare black scholar's cloak, the same one he had first worn as a junior fellow at Trinity College in Cambridge during the reign of King Henry VIII, billowed as he flew down his staircase and when he got to the front door, he paused to catch his breath, not wanting to appear anything less than serene.

The visitor was a young man, younger than Dee had been led to believe, only a year past his twenty-fifth birthday, he would soon ascertain.

'Ah, Mr Talbot, I presume,' Dee said.

The accent was by and large, cultured, although perhaps too practiced, as if honed well after childhood. 'At your service, sir. I hope I was expected.'

'Yes, of course, please come in. Mr Clerkson told me the time you would arrive and you are punctual.'

'I strive to be so.'

Talbot was not tall, not short, but he ran to fat, with black hair that overflowed his collar. When he removed his overcoat, moist from a cold March drizzle, Dee saw that he wore a gown resembling an artist's with hanging sleeves that had slits to free one's hands for work. Framed by a beard that was almost as black as his hair, his clear, bloodless complexion made his crudely carved face seem all the more white. He used a stick to walk, favoring his right leg – whether he had been injured or palsied from disease, Dee could not tell. As he hung his coat on a peg, Dee asked him if he had trouble finding the place.

'As Clerkson advised, I inquired as to the position of the

church then looked for the largest house about. And here I am.'

'Very good, very good. Others simply have asked for the location of Doctor Dee's famous library.'

'I would not be so impertinent as to bandy about your name.'

Dee's manservant appeared, wiping his hands on his breeches.

'There you are, Robert. Is your horse tethered at the front, Mr Talbot?'

'It is. The tawny mare.'

'Robert, take it to the stables, dry it, and give it some hay. Please follow me to my study, Mr Talbot, so that we might converse. I have a small but pleasant fire going.'

At the top of the stairs Dee unlatched a door and led the young man through a book-lined room but he had to pause when Talbot stopped dead to peruse the spine of one of the volumes.

'Dear Lord, is that really a copy of Agrippa's *De Occulta Philosophia*?'

'It is, indeed, and much read and studied, I might add. You know it?'

'I have only read accounts of the central theses,' Talbot said. 'Wherever did you obtain it?'

'In Louvain, actually, where the great Agrippa wrote the text. I resided at the university for a time when I took my leave from Cambridge. I could ill afford the book, but I could equally ill afford not purchasing it after deciding I might never have another opportunity. It was during my travels in those bygone years that I acquired a good many important books that were to become central to my library and thus my life's work.'

'During this sojourn you studied with Frisius and Mercator, did you not?'

Dee's mouth cracked open in a self-deprecating smile. 'You are well versed in my background, Mr Talbot.'

'Might I ask a burning question?'

'Very well.'

'Is it true that Queen Elizabeth commissioned you to consult the stars to determine the most propitious time for her coronation?'

Dee looked down in modesty. 'I did play a part in the affair. Come along now.'

Dee's study had a large writing table spanning two windows that fronted onto the High Street. As it was a gray day, Dee had positioned two table-top candelabras to throw off much-needed light, but the floor-to-ceiling bookcases, crammed with bound books and manuscripts, were shrouded in shadows. A small fire took the chill off the air, but did little to make the room brighter. Against the opposite wall, with only enough room to squeeze past to retrieve a book, sat another long table, this one filled with alchemical glasswork and vials of colorful solids and liquids.

Talbot made a show of inspecting the vessels and asked playfully if any of them contained the philosopher's stone.

Clearly, Dee did not detect the lighthearted nature of the comment for he replied, 'I can assure you, sir, that should I have made that discovery, you and the rest of the world would have heard about it. Might I trouble you to add a log to the fire?'

Talbot stooped to accomplish the task and when he did, his hair fell forward, revealing an anatomical peculiarity. The tops of his ears were missing.

Dee had the young man take a chair by the improved fire and he turned his writing chair to face him.

'I am remiss,' Dee said. 'Do you desire a libation?'

'Perhaps some water.'

Dee bellowed for Robert but when there was no reply he mumbled that he was probably in the stables. He next called out for his wife, who shortly afterwards knocked gently on the study door. She was a small, pretty woman, almost three decades her husband's junior. Her hair was severely pulled-back and her high-necked dress was as drab as a bucket of oats. The only color about her came from naturally pink cheeks and luxuriously blue eyes.

'Mr Talbot, may I introduce my wife, Jane? Jane, this is the young man I spoke of.'

Talbot sprang to his feet and grabbed a small hand, hesitantly offered, bringing it to moist lips. While he planted his greeting, she seemed fixated on the same abnormality of his ears her husband had noted.

'I am most pleased and enchanted to make your acquaintance, madam,' Talbot said.

'And I yours,' she said, reclaiming her hand.

'Might you have one of the girls bring up a pitcher of water?' Dee asked her.

'Of course. Nothing else?'

'That will suffice,' her husband said.

'May I compliment you on the beauty of your wife, sir,' Talbot gushed when she had left.

'I had very little to do with her natural attributes,' Dee said. 'That was entirely the work of our Lord.'

'Yes, of course,' the young man said quickly.

Dee was anxious to attend to business. 'My colleague, Mr Clerkson, recommended you to me.'

'I am grateful to him for his kind attentions. The opportunity to make the acquaintance of an illustrious man such as yourself does not often arise.'

'Might you enlighten me as to your background?'

Talbot leaned forward and eagerly recounted his personal story. His people were of the Uí Maine clan of Connacht in Ireland, but he was born in England, in Worcester. An able student, he gained entry to Oxford University, where he studied Greek and Latin and divinity.

'Of course, I was not destined to be a scholar such as yourself and other distinguished gentlemen,' he said. 'My aptitude, alas, was not sufficient for a career in scholarly pursuits.'

'And how have you occupied yourself since your Oxford days?'

'I have tried my hand in business, sir. Importing goods from the Low Countries, for the most part, and selling them on to the trades.'

'Have your ventures been profitable?'

'Enough to live on but if I may be frank, not enough to elevate myself sufficiently.'

'Sufficiently toward what end?'

'To afford a comfortable house, to marry a woman

approaching the gentility and beauty of Mrs Dee, if I might be so bold.'

'I see. But I haven't asked you here for your business acumen, have I? You are here regarding an entirely different skill.'

'So I was given to understand.'

Dee's servant girl knocked and was allowed to enter. She nervously placed a tray with a jug of water and two glasses onto a table, gave a little curtsey, and withdrew.

Dee poured for his visitor and said, 'Please tell me about your gift. When did it first become manifest?'

'When I was quite young, perhaps ten years of age. I was by myself on the bank of the River Severn in Worcester. It was late in the afternoon and the river was free of boatmen. When I had tired of skipping stones I sat and gazed upon the water. There must have been no wind and the current must have been imperceptible for the surface was as smooth and clear as pond water. Suddenly, I heard a low murmur, a most gentle and soothing voice, seemingly far, far away and then, in the water, I saw him.'

Dee unclasped his hands and leaned forward. 'What did you see, tell me?'

Talbot also leaned in so that the two men were intimately close. 'He wore a white robe and a crown of flames. It was as if he was standing within the river, looking at me from below the surface.'

'Did the murmur become a language that you could decipher?'

'It did. When it became clearer, it was apparent he spoke in Latin. Alas, I was only just beginning to engage in my Latin studies in school, so the meaning was mostly obscure. However, I did understand him to speak his name.'

'And what was it?'

'Hamaliel.'

'Most consequential!' Dee exclaimed. 'Hamaliel is the angel of the month of August and the governor of the zodiacal sign of Virgo.'

'The month I was born and my star house.'

'This was a powerful and auspicious connection, Mr Talbot. Tell me, is there a proclivity to scrying within your line?'

'My father has told me that my dear departed mother had the gift.'

'Have you had repeated contact with this angel – with your scrying?'

'Indeed I have. From that youthful day I learned that I might summon Hamaliel and other entities by gazing upon all manner of reflective surfaces.'

'To what effect?'

'I am ashamed to say that my aspirations have not been, on the main, lofty. Oftentimes I have asked for guidance in matters of commerce and love.'

'And what say you of the guidance received?'

'I would say, dear Doctor, that what success I have achieved, I lay at the feet of Hamaliel. However, Clerkson has told me that your aspirations are on a very much higher plane. Might I inquire further?'

'You may indeed. Plainly, my interests are spiritual, Mr Talbot. Ever since my Cambridge days, I have immersed myself in the study of Kabbalistic and linguistic principles. I am convinced that by the study of ancient languages, including the very form of their letters and hieroglyphs, that one might get closer to the original language of God Almighty. And I have hoped that these contemplations might lead me to discover the divinely inspired hidden meanings that might inform our knowledge and understanding of our universe.'

'Another question, Doctor Dee. How does this pursuit relate to the practice of scrying?'

'The central question, Mr Talbot! Let me take you back to the origins of my interests in scrying, to a time some twenty-five years ago. I had returned to Cambridge following my period in Louvain and Paris.'

'This was when Queen Mary was on the throne, was it not?'

'Precisely.'

'I do not wish to divert your discourse but was this the time you ran afoul of the monarchy by assisting Princess Elizabeth.'

Dee's shoulders drooped. 'A difficult time it was. Mary had recently married Philip of Spain. If Mary died without issue, Philip would have no claim to the throne and Elizabeth would ascend. The Princess asked me to divine the future that awaited her and what I saw from her horoscopes did indeed come to pass. Mary's pregnancy was false and when she did die of a tumor, the throne belonged to Elizabeth. But before that occurred, a member or members of Mary's Privy Council had me arrested and taken to the Tower. I thought I would be released quickly but a child of one of my accusers went blind and I was wickedly accused of malicious conjuring.'

'Is it true you were tortured?'

'I do not wish to revisit that unhappy time.'

'I do apologize, sir. My curiosity knows no bounds and it leads to impertinent questions and interruptions.'

'I admire and encourage curious minds, Mr Talbot. But allow me to return to your central question. In the year of our Lord 1555, I began to concentrate on the study of optics and light. Since the body of Christ can assuredly move through solid objects, it stands to reason that angelic spirits of Christ's realm can become manifest in this world. I thus began my experiments with techniques for summoning spirits into crystals. Yes, scrying is an ancient art, and I was not the first practitioner, but I believe I did make strides in applying mathematical rules of perspective to the endeavor. Vision occurs when beams of light emitted by the soul through the eyes encounter physical objects. When reflected from highly polished surfaces such as crystals or pools of water, as in your youthful experience, those beams may set the soul, particularly in men such as yourself who have a particular gift, into a reflexive sort of spiritual awareness and rapture, allowing visions of angelic messengers to make their appearance.'

Talbot was nodding like an eager student. 'Rapture is indeed a word I might use to describe my inner joy when I practice my scrying, Doctor Dee.'

'My personal efforts at scrying have been disappointing, I'm afraid,' Dee said. 'I do not seem to possess a gift. Early on I made brief contact with a spirit, Prince Befafes, but my interactions, while interesting, did not bear the desired fruit. That is why, in recent years, I have employed able scryers who have greatly facilitated my spiritual dialogues with angelic beings. My desire has been to entice the spirits to impart their language unto me.'

'Towards what end?'

'I am convinced that the angelic tongue is God's own. Knowing it will place me at the gateway of understanding God's universal plan.'

Talbot had some more water and offered to refill Dee's glass. 'Have the angels revealed their language to you?'

'Although I have had untold spiritual actions over the years and have communicated most freely in Latin with several spirits, especially the angel Anael, they have not deemed me worthy to receive the prize.'

'Perhaps it is not you who are unworthy, sir. Perhaps it is your scryers. May I ask which gentlemen you have employed?'

'Bartholomew Hickman for many years but of late, Barnabus Saul. Do you know them by acquaintance, or know of them?'

Talbot scratched at his beard. 'The names are familiar.'

'Have you an opinion as to their skills?'

'I have no direct knowledge and I am not one to engage in hearsay.'

'Very well. I do have direct knowledge, as you put it, and therefore will share my observations. Mr Hickman had some skill but Mr Saul, in particular, was very able and I was making good progress with him, when to my surprise, only a fortnight ago, he announced that he had utterly lost his spiritual insight. We parted ways as a result.'

The fire was faltering and without being asked, Talbot tended to it, much to Dee's satisfaction.

Retaking his seat, the young man said, 'And thus you have summoned me.'

'Via Mr Clerkson, who has vouched for you, yes.'

'You seek to perfect your dialogue with spirits and coax them to reveal the secrets of God's realm.'

'Precisely.'

'These gentlemen, your scryers, did they possess their own showstones?'

'An interesting question, Mr Talbot. No, they did not. They utilized mine. Would you like to see it?'

Dee had a beautifully carved wooden box upon his desk. Inside was a perfectly round and clear crystal ball, the diameter of half the length of a thumb. It rested on a squat tripod of brass.

'May I?' Talbot asked, and Dee let him take it up for inspection. The young man held it up to the light from the fireplace and stared into it intently.

'What say you?' Dee asked.

'It is a fine stone,' he said, 'with nary an imperfection. I do believe it is serviceable.'

'Serviceable? Is that all? I have put it to much good use and the archemaster from whom I obtained it in Paris did likewise find it to be a laudable instrument.'

'I believe I might offer up one that is even finer, my good Doctor.'

With that, Talbot reached into the largest pocket of his gown and produced a thin pouch made of supple leather. He uncinched it and pulled out a round black mirror. It was fashioned of shiny stone, about the size of a smaller supper plate. The thickness was no more than thirty pages of one of Doctor Dee's books. It had a short handle chiseled of the same black stone in which a hole had been drilled so that one might dangle the object by a leather thong or silk string. The surface of the stone had been meticulously polished into a brilliant gloss. Dee feasted his eyes on it and eagerly held out his hands to receive it. He moved it around to catch the reflection of the fire, the window, his own face.

'Its refractive properties are most excellent,' he murmured. 'What is its origin? I have heard of these mirror stones but have never seen one. Is it from the conquistador expeditions to New Spain?'

'I worked for a time in Cheshire as a tutor to a nobleman's son. He had the stone kept in a curio cabinet. I believe it had been in his family for some time, so I imagine it came to England well before the Spanish conquests in New Spain. I believe that similar stones come from the Holy Lands. In any event, when first I examined the mirror, I immediately did incur a spiritual action – and a powerful one, at that – and cognizant that it would make a potent showstone, I asked my good lord whether he might give me the mirror in lieu of a portion of my wages. He readily agreed.'

Dee reluctantly parted with the mirror. 'If you were to come into my employ, Mr Talbot, would you propose using your showstone?'

'Indeed I would.'

Dee gazed out the window. The rain had stopped and the sky was lightening considerably. 'And if I were to employ you, what would you require as a stipend?'

The answer was crisp and emphatic. 'Fifty pounds sterling per annum.'

'A great deal of money, Mr Talbot.'

'I would prefer you think of it as a great deal of value, sir. I assure you, you will not be disappointed with my abilities.'

At supper that night John Dee led his young family in prayer before tucking into a meal of roasted venison and a spread of root and leafy vegetables. Two of the children were old enough to sit at the table. The baby was up in the nursery with the wet-nurse. Jane, newly pregnant, was expecting their fourth child in as many years. She was Dee's third wife and was as fecund as his first two had been barren. Arthur, the three-year-old, was fidgeting in his chair and fussing noisily, prompting his father to point his spearing knife at him and warn him to remain silent at the table.

'What did you think of Mr Talbot?' Dee asked his wife.

'An honest opinion, husband?'

'Of course.'

'I did not like his manner.'

'Oh yes?'

'I detected an insincerity.'

'Did you?'

'And a forwardness.'

'I believe he found you beautiful, as do I.'

'It is not his place to express such opinions.'

'Perhaps not. Anything else?'

She put down her knife and said softly, 'Did you notice his ears?'

'I did, actually.'

'They were cropped, John. Do you know whose ears are cropped?'

'Forgers, counterfeiters to name a few,' Dee said.

'Did you seek an explanation?'

'I did not. I was more interested in his skills as a scryer, my dear. I have asked him to return in two days' time to assist me in a spiritual action. With the departure of Mr Saul, I am bereft of a spirit guide. My work has suffered in the interim. If he proves able, I will take him into my employ.'

Her face flushed with anger. 'You would have a forger or counterfeiter in our house?'

'Some men are falsely accused of crimes, my dear wife,' he said tartly. 'I, for one, spent a lamentable time within the Tower of London at Queen Mary's pleasure, falsely charged with conjuring. I beg you not to forget this.'

NINE

They didn't stick to a set schedule, but Cal and Jessica tried to manage sleepover dates as frequently as their calendars allowed. Busy as they were – she the CEO of a high-profile company, he a star professor sought after for conferences and speaking engagements – their dates were somewhat irregular. Nevertheless, they tried to alternate between her condo in Boston and his house in Cambridge and this night they were at his place, after a dinner in Harvard Square at a favorite spot. Though they played at domesticity they weren't much good at the game. Neither had been married and their past relationships, though multitudinous, tended to be measured in months rather than years. And neither was the type to graciously bend to the whims of another, a function perhaps of two pampered, only-children who never had to learn to make nice with siblings who grew up to become willful adults.

After a brief, animated argument over which film to watch, they abandoned the idea and parked themselves under the two best reading lamps in the living room. Ordinarily, Jessica would have happily escalated a trivial spat into World War Three, but she had been sensitive to all he had been through recently and let it go. She quietly tucked into the half-read spy thriller she'd brought with her, while Cal picked up one of the books he'd purchased from the doomed Irish bookseller.

As he flipped through the Ebersole book, *Enochian Vision Magic – A Beginner's Guide*, Cal gritted his teeth at its breezy, almost juvenile style and went back to the introduction to see what kind of credentials this Ebersole had. The answer seemed to be, not many, and certainly nothing remotely academic or scholarly. He was a self-proclaimed expert best known in Enochian magic circles as the presenter of a series of YouTube videos on the subject. Cal briefly went online to check out amateurish productions where Ebersole offered pompous narrations over hokey PowerPoint slides and graphics. Cal was about to toss the book aside when he read the following in the acknowledgements section:

> *Though half my age, Eve Riley has been my mentor in my quest to understand the complexities and promise of angel magic. No modern practitioner can match Eve's skills as an expert scryer or her insights into the Elizabethan world of Dr Dee and Edward Kelley that she gained during her Master's studies in history at the University of Arizona. I am forever grateful to her and will long and fondly remember my time spent with her in the Arizona desert.*

'Screw this guy,' Cal said out loud, dropping the book onto the coffee table and picking up his glass of vodka.

Jessica looked up and said, 'What?'

'I'm not going to read a book written by a jackass when I've got another one by a bona fide expert. I'd return it to the bookstore if the guy wasn't dead.'

'Did the police find out who did it?' she asked over the top of her book.

'Not that I've heard. I'm fried. Want to read in bed?'

'Sure.'

While she was taking off her makeup, Cal flopped onto the bed with the Riley book. He took to it right away. She wasn't as good a writer as he was (in his own not-so-humble opinion) but she wasn't bad and the first couple of chapters on the role of magic and its interplay with traditional religion in sixteenth-century England and the life of John Dee were credible and well-referenced. But any notion of making a dent in the book was sidelined when Jessica came in, wearing something short, new, and lacy.

'Damn,' he said.

'What's wrong?'

'I guess we're not going to read.'

'Oh no?' she said innocently. 'Why ever not?'

Cal's house was on a side street. It only saw traffic during commuting hours and it was far enough away from Harvard Square to be free of nocturnal drunkenness and antics. In the wee hours it was about as silent as an urban street could be. The intruder broke the silence. Despite taking care to put masking tape on the window pane before breaking it, a piece of glass dislodged and hit the tiled kitchen floor. Jessica was a heavy sleeper who needed a jackhammer to wake her, but Cal slept lightly and his eyes blinked open. The sound didn't register as a glass break, only something vaguely high-pitched. He'd had plenty to drink but now, in the middle of the night, he was mostly sober but awfully groggy. He listened hard for a few moments, reluctant to get out from under the soft duvet, then drifted back to sleep, only to be awakened again by a few indistinct but out-of-place sounds downstairs.

He swore softly enough as not to bother Jessica, got up, and fumbled for his boxer shorts on the floor where Jessica had tossed them after pulling them off. Unlike most of his neighbors he'd never installed a security system. His insurance broker told him he was nuts to forego the discount on his homeowner's policy, but it was something he'd never felt the need for. As far as he knew, for as long as he lived there, his street had never been hit by a burglary. Making his way cautiously down the stairs he wondered whether that might have been a poor decision.

At the bottom of the stairs, he hit a light switch and tossed out a 'Hey, anyone there?'

He stopped to listen but didn't hear anything.

His hands felt uncomfortably empty. He thought about making a stop in the kitchen for a chef's knife, but he felt silly and went into the dark living room instead.

'Don't move.'

The voice came from the darkest part of the room near a corner bookcase. A hulking shape, black as the shadows, materialized as the intruder took a step forward. There was no face to latch onto, only a huge body and it took a few moments for Cal to understand that he was looking at a black balaclava. The fireplace, with its iron poker and shovel, was a few paces to Cal's right.

Barzani seemed to anticipate Cal's instinct, took another step forward and said, 'Don't.'

It was then that he saw the pistol in his hand. It was either a very large hand or a very small gun and when the man took another step toward the hall light, Cal had a better idea about the weapon. He wasn't an expert, but he was knowledgeable about firearms. He didn't own a gun – Massachusetts, putting it mildly, wasn't the most accommodating state in the country for gun owners – but he'd been a good shot in the army and from time to time over the years he'd gone target-shooting with buddies. The pistol aimed at him was a compact 1911-style semi-automatic, capable of leaving a whopping exit wound at close range.

'Whatever you say. How about I get you my wallet and you can leave the way you came? I'll even wait a while to call the cops once you're gone.'

'I don't want your wallet.'

The man's accent was distinctive. Low, thick, and Middle Eastern.

'What do you want?'

Barzani answered the question with one of his own. 'Who else is here?'

'No one.'

'Two cars in the driveway.'

'I've got two cars. You want one of them? I'll get you the keys.'

'You have one car. Someone's here.'

Cal tried to process that. Had he been watching the house? Was this more than a garden-variety burglary?

'I'm telling you, I'm alone. Just tell me what you're after and we can work something out, okay?'

'Let's go upstairs.'

Cal dug in. 'No, listen.'

'I'll kill you. I don't care. Upstairs.'

Cal took a step toward the fireplace, but the intruder cut off the angle with his big body and his gun. Once more he demanded that Cal head up the stairs. Reluctantly, Cal began walking, slowly enough to try to think through his options. Once Jessica was in the mix, things might get really ugly. He could turn and engage the man in the hall. If he didn't get shot right away, he could fight it out. He was still a good boxer and could probably get in some licks until he was overwhelmed by the brute's physical size. He could wait until they were both on the stairs and launch himself backward. In the tumble, maybe he'd get lucky and the gunman would be hurt worse. He landed on a third.

'Jess! Get up! Climb out the window and get the hell out! Now!'

A sleepy voice came back, 'What?'

Cal felt the steel barrel poking him hard in the ribs.

'Go,' Barzani said.

Jessica was in bed looking dazed when Cal appeared at the doorway. He switched on the light.

'What's the matter?' she asked. 'What were you shouting?'

'We've got a problem,' Cal said before a hand shoved him into the room.

When Jessica saw the man with the balaclava she said a quiet, 'Oh my God,' but didn't freak out. She had the presence of mind to reach for her night dress at the foot of the bed and throw it over her head.

'Stay there,' Barzani said, waving his pistol. 'You, Donovan, take these.'

Cal turned toward him. There were a couple of long plastic zip ties in his free, gloved hand.

'You know my name,' Cal said.

He ignored Cal's statement and said, 'Tie her to the bed.'

Jessica looked hard at Cal and seemed to read his mind. He didn't want to go along with the intruder. He wanted to chance it and lunge at him.

'Do what he says, Cal,' she said calmly.

'Jess.'

She repeated herself.

The man tossed the plastic ties onto the bed and Cal zipped one of her hands to the bed board, then the second, leaving enough slack for her to wriggle free.

'Tighter,' the man said.

'I don't want to cut off her blood,' Cal protested.

'Tighter or I'll shoot her.' He picked a throw pillow off the floor and buried the barrel of his gun in it.

'It's okay, Cal,' Jessica said.

He pulled the slack out of the ties and moved to position himself between the gunman and Jessica.

'Now tell me what you want,' Cal said.

'The black mirror. Where is it?'

It hit Cal at the speed of light – not the why but the who. He didn't know why the obsidian stone was so important but the huge man in his bedroom was surely the who – the instrument of death of the bookseller and quite possibly his mother too.

'I don't know what you're talking about.'

'You do. You showed it to the man in the shop.'

'You're mistaking me for someone else.'

'Look, Donovan, this is waste of time. It's stupid to make me mad. Really stupid for a smart guy. Where is the mirror?'

'I don't have what you're looking for.'

Cal saw the black balaclava shaking back and forth. 'Here's what's going to happen,' the man said. 'You're going to give it to me right now or I'm going to kill both of you and spend the rest of the night tearing your place apart. Maybe I'll fuck her first. She looks good.'

Jessica clamped her lips in anger and looked to Cal.

'Okay,' Cal said. 'It's downstairs. Come with me.'

'Bring it to me here.'

'If you want it, come with me. I'm not leaving you with her.'

The big shoulders shrugged.

As soon as Cal left with the intruder, Jessica began to strain at the plastic ties. It didn't take her long to figure out that they were too thick and tight and that the oak bed board was too sturdy. She stopped struggling when her wrists throbbed terribly and she strained to hear what was going on downstairs.

Cal went straight for the shoulder bag and was about to open it when Barzani told him to stop what he was doing and toss it to him.

'Why?' Cal asked.

'Maybe you've got a gun in there.'

'You think we're in Texas?'

'Give it to me.'

Cal tossed him the bag. The big man kept his gun trained on Cal while opening it. He immediately felt the stone through its cloth and smiled when he exposed its blackness by partially unwrapping it with his thumb. He put the bag down on a chair to give Cal his full attention again but before he could speak Cal preempted him with a question.

'Did you kill my mother?'

Barzani's expression was a cipher of impassivity. 'We don't need to discuss this.'

'I think we do,' Cal said.

'This gun says we don't, okay? This is what we need to discuss. Do you have the 49th Call?'

Cal looked confused and asked him to repeat the question. He said it again. The 49th Call.

'I don't have the slightest idea what you're talking about.'

Maybe it was because he was telling the truth but Barzani seemed to believe him. He shifted to a different question.

'What about an old paper with writing? Was this with the mirror?'

Cal still didn't know what he was talking about, but a faint survival plan hatched. Despite the anonymity that a balaclava and gloves provided, Cal knew he wasn't going to just walk away after this. 'What kind of writing?'

'Old writing. Arabaic? What's the word?'

'Aramaic,' Cal said.

'Yeah, that.'

'Why didn't you say so.'

'You have it? The paper?'

'It's papyrus. Aramaic was written mainly on papyrus. People wrote Aramaic way before there was paper. You didn't make yourself clear.'

'You have it?'

'Yeah.'

'Give it to me.' Barzani's voice showed excitement. Urgency. 'Hurry.'

'It's here in my desk. I'll get it for you.'

Cal took a step toward his desk but was told to stop. The intruder probably figured that a desk would be an even better place for a gun.

Barzani came around and had a look at all the little drawers in Cal's father's old roll-top desk.

'Which one?'

'Bottom left, second down.'

His eyes didn't leave Cal until the split second he reached for the drawer handle.

That's when Cal made his desperation move. He closed the distance between the two of them in one flying leap and used his clenched fist to chop down as hard as he could on the man's gun hand.

The element of surprise and the force of his blow were enough for the pistol to drop to the rug but Barzani was quick enough to loop his other arm around Cal's neck from behind. Cal felt it clamping down. He could tell the man was strong enough to squeeze the life out of him, the way he'd likely done to his mother. So, he fought like hell.

He rammed a heel into his knee.

He slammed an elbow into his gut.

He hammered his right fist four times in rapid succession over his head into the man's nose.

The last of the hammer-blows might have cracked cartilage. Barzani yelped and loosened his vise grip enough for Cal to squirm free and turn to face him squarely. They both eyed the pistol, but Cal got to it first with his bare foot, kicking it across the room where it came to rest partly under a colonial tall-boy chest that held a collection of his father's artifacts.

Barzani swore at him in Arabic then switched to English. 'Now I'm going to kill you fast and kill your woman slow.'

It was time to see if the guy could box.

From upstairs, Jessica heard the sounds of fists landing on flesh and bone, shouts, and grunts. She started working the zip ties harder.

Cal ignored the pain from his knuckles pounding the concrete block that was Barzani's skull and he quickly had his answer. The man was no boxer. He was slow and wild with his punches. His instincts were more of a wrestler trying to get into a clinch to throw his opponent down. A strange calm settled over Cal as he faced his foe. Boxing was one of his comfort zones, a place where he could unhitch intellect and rely on pure physical skills. A lot of years had passed since he won prizes in the army, but he was still pretty good at it. When slamming into a rock-hard chin didn't make inroads, he tried tagging the guy's nose but the intruder's long wingspan made it hard to reliably reach it. Cal sampled his midsection which was, unfortunately, hard as wood. The few times Cal got hit squarely weren't pleasant. The man's gloved fists were like iron mallets and the blows put him back on his heels. The one thing he couldn't let happen was getting close enough to be ensnared in a wrestling move.

After a minute or so of giving more than taking but not getting an upper hand, Cal decided that the Marquis of Queensberry's rules were bullshit in a street fight. When the first opportunity presented itself, he planted a back foot and kicked him ferociously in the groin.

Barzani didn't go down but he gave out a low grunt and bowed his head. That gave Cal the chance to really lay a right uppercut into his bloody nose. That was the punch that staggered him and sent him down on one knee.

Cal had the advantage now, but he hadn't won. He'd been on the receiving end of fights that seemed over but had turned around in an ugly way. Before the guy could get himself straight, Cal made the decision to go for the gun. He took off across the room, but the big man pulled himself together enough to follow a couple of strides behind. Two trains barreled toward the same junction and Cal got his hand around the pistol grip first.

He wheeled around without having a moment to check whether a round was chambered or if the safety was off but with only an arm's length separating the men, Barzani stopped short and backed off. That's when Cal glanced at the pistol. The safety showed a red dot – red is dead – and it was cocked.

'Get down on the floor,' Cal shouted between panting breaths, 'or I will shoot you.'

Barzani kept backing up but when he got to the chair with the shoulder bag and the stone, he paused to look at it.

'Don't even think about it,' Cal warned, but Barzani ignored him and moved his arm to reach for it.

It would have been the easiest thing in the world to aim center mass and put rounds into his vitals. The bastard killed his mother. He killed the bookseller. But as primitive as the fight had made him feel, he wasn't an executioner, so the bullet he let fly blasted through the floor and wound up in his basement.

The man froze; Jessica screamed from the bedroom.

'The next one's in your chest,' Cal said. 'Your choice. Get down on the floor or I'll shoot you.'

He heard Jessica call his name and he shouted back that he was okay and was calling the police.

Barzani backed off a few paces without the bag.

'You're not going to shoot me,' Barzani said, breathing hard. A short, deep snort came from the mouth hole of the balaclava. 'You're too fucking civilized.'

Then Barzani did something that Cal, under the circumstances, failed to notice. He slid a finger under the band of his wrist watch and pulled out a round piece of metal, the size of a nickel, that he flicked onto the floor. It came to rest under one of the sofas.

Cal was looking down the iron sights, lining up the perfect shot and thought: the son-of-a-bitch had gotten it right. Too fucking civilized.

TEN

The doorbell rang and one of the Cambridge policemen answered it. A group of officers and a couple of crime-scene investigators had been on the scene for an hour when Detective Gilroy made his entrance. The blonde detective put on booties and gloves and asked where Donovan was.

Cal and Jessica were in the kitchen drinking one coffee after another.

When Cal saw Gilroy he said, 'We've got to stop meeting like this.'

'You think?'

Gilroy and Jessica introduced themselves and the detective pulled up a chair.

'From what I've been told by the ranking officer this was a traumatic event for the both of you, but while it's still fresh I need you to take me through what happened,' he said. 'Don't leave out any details.'

'You want a coffee first?' Cal asked.

The detective nodded. 'Nothing's open yet. I thought you'd never ask.'

Cal started to spit out the events in sequence and when he got to what happened in the bedroom, Gilroy asked, 'Okay, I know you say he was wearing a balaclava, but you both heard his voice. Did he have an accent?'

'Definitely,' Jessica said. 'Middle Eastern maybe.'

'Yeah, I'd agree,' Cal said.

'Can you pin it down more than that?'

'I can't,' Jessica said.

'Me neither,' Cal said. 'I'm not an expert in accents.'

'By the way, any cameras in the house?'

Cal shook his head.

'Outside cameras?'

There were none.

'Do your neighbors have outdoor cameras?'

'I wouldn't know.'

Cal kept going with his story. Hearing that the intruder referenced Mulligan, the bookseller, Gilroy interrupted him.

'He said, "You showed it to the man in the shop?" Exactly that?'

'I think that's verbatim.'

'Did he say he killed Mr Mulligan?'

'No and he didn't make any other mention of him.'

'You sure?'

Cal thought for a few seconds and said he was absolutely certain.

Then Cal got to the black mirror.

'So, he was specifically after it,' Gilroy said.

'Except for something I'll get to, he wasn't interested in anything else in the house.'

'And he'd been doing some kind of surveillance prior to the break-in. He knew you had only one car. He knew you had a visitor by the second car.'

Cal said, 'That's my conclusion, yes.'

'When was the last time you were here, Dr Nelson?'

'You mean for a sleepover?' she asked with a smile.

'Anytime.'

She had to check the calendar on her phone. It had been three weeks.

'So not recently,' Gilroy said. 'Professor, this black mirror – this was the same one you showed me before? The one for talking to spirits.'

'The same one.'

'It didn't look like much to me. Is it valuable? I mean, how much do you think it's worth?'

'I've got no idea,' Cal said. 'From the little I know about it, it doesn't have the type of provenance that would command big money at auction.'

Gilroy looked up from his note pad. 'I'm sorry but I didn't go to Harvard myself. I don't know what provenance is.'

Cal was too tired and stressed out to apologize for using big words. 'It means ownership and where it came from. If someone famous owned it and that was well-documented, then it might be worth a lot. As it is, I don't know. A few hundred bucks, maybe more. As a curiosity.'

'But he's willing to go through all of this, maybe including a murder, to get his hands on it.'

'Two murders.'

'How do you mean?'

'Mulligan and my mother.'

'I don't know anything about her situation.'

Cal remedied that.

When he was done the detective said, 'Based on the little you've told me, I'd say it's a leap to think your guy was the perpetrator in New York. You're the one who found the black mirror anyway, right?'

'I think that's what he was looking for.'

'Look, color me skeptical. Let's not get sidetracked, okay. Keep going with what happened here tonight in my city.'

Cal didn't fight it. He carried on and talked about the intruder asking for the 49th Call.

'And what is that?' Gilroy asked.

'I'm afraid I don't know.'

Gilroy seemed exasperated, prompting Jessica to say, 'Well don't look at me. It's not a scientific or medical term, that's for damned sure.'

'So, he asks for something you've never heard of and then what happens?'

'I pretended I had a papyrus written in Aramaic in a drawer. He said it was written in Aramaic. I assumed he meant papyrus, not paper. He wanted to get it himself because he was worried I might have a weapon. That's when I jumped him.'

'You jumped a guy almost twice your size with a gun.'

Cal shrugged wearily. 'I didn't love my odds, but I hated them if I didn't do anything.'

'Explain.'

'He wasn't going to leave us alive.'

'How do you know that? His face was covered. He was wearing gloves. You couldn't identify the guy, not definitively anyway. What does he gain by killing you?'

'He killed before.'

'Chances are he didn't walk into the book store wearing a balaclava. Mulligan could have ID'd him.'

'I don't know,' Cal said. 'I just think he was going to shoot us. Call it a strong impression.'

'I think Cal's right,' Jessica said. 'I think we'd be leaving here in body bags. That's my strong impression too.'

'All right, noted. Go on.'

Gilroy stopped taking notes during Cal's rendition of the fight. Jessica had heard an abbreviated version that Cal had given to the uniformed cops but its detail made her shudder. Cal stopped to make sure she was okay.

'The two of us went to a boxing match at Foxwoods a couple of weeks ago,' she said to the detective. Her voice trailed off a bit. 'And now this.'

'It's a good thing you're handy with your fists, Professor. Otherwise, well. You think this guy was a wrestler?'

Cal played back the way he moved in his mind. 'I can't say for sure but his foot work, the way he held his arms – that's what he seemed like. He was looking for an angle to do a takedown.'

'Then you get to the gun first.'

'Yeah.'

'And you fire one off into the floor.'

'Well, I wasn't going to go for the ceiling. The bedroom's above the living room.'

Gilroy shouted for someone to bring him the gun. It was in a see-through evidence bag.

'The serial number's been filed off clean,' Gilroy said. 'Very professional of him. Still, we'll see if the ballistics match any other spent casings in NIBIN.' Jessica made him explain the acronym. 'Sorry, it's the national ballistics database system. Okay, so you get the guy to leave the bag with the black mirror behind and he leaves.'

'That's what happened.'

'You let him leave.'

'I ordered him to lie on the floor while I called 911 but he wouldn't. What was I supposed to do? If I shot him, you'd have me in handcuffs now, wouldn't you?'

'Maybe yes, maybe no.'

'That's what I thought.'

Gilroy put his empty coffee cup into the sink and told them that he was done for now, but that he might come back later with more questions.

'What about my mother?' Cal asked.

'I'm sorry, I don't understand the question.'

'How are you going to investigate the link between what happened here to my mother's murder?'

Gilroy stuffed his notepad into his jacket. 'First of all, I think it's a stretch to link the cases. Second, New York City isn't my jurisdiction. I've got enough on my plate, thank you. You do want me to catch the guy who did this to you, am I right?'

Cal felt his blood rising. 'Seems to me that this is something the FBI would be interested in.'

Gilroy gave him a snarky look and said, 'Knock yourself out, Professor. Their number's in the phone book.'

When the house emptied out, they crawled up to bed, dead tired. A marked police car with a couple of officers was parked out front for the night in case the attacker returned.

'You can't stay here, you know,' Jessica said. 'At least not without an alarm system installed and maybe a giant dog.'

'I like dogs but I'd need a bunch of cute dog sitters and walkers, preferably in short-shorts and tank tops.'

'I'm serious.'

'Yeah, I know.'

'Stay with me.'

'No way. I'm not exposing you to more of this.'

'My building's got security.'

'So did my mother's. No, I'll check into a hotel and order up a burglar alarm for the house.'

'Are you really going to call the FBI?'

'Hell yes. I'm not going to rely on some dumb-ass local detective.'

She pulled the covers up to her neck. 'Did you really not know what he was talking about? The 49th Call?'

'That was the truth. I didn't.' He reached for Eve Riley's book on the night table. Before Jessica had come in and interrupted his reading with her lacy gear, he'd scanned the table of contents and its chapter titled 'Learning the 48 Calls'. 'But I'm betting that this gal knows the answer.'

Five days passed and Cal was in his Divinity School office tying up the loose ends of the semester and shooting the breeze with Joe Murphy, who'd stopped by for a chat and a coffee.

'Any news then about your mystery man?'

'The Cambridge police won't tell me more than "we're working on a variety of leads."'

'Did the FBI ring you back?'

'They did, actually. A nice enough fellow from the Boston office called and asked me a bunch of questions.'

'And?'

'And nothing. Haven't heard jack shit.'

'Jessica tells me you haven't been back home since.'

'When'd you speak to her?'

'Last night.'

'How'd she sound?'

'You know, it was a traumatic thing for her. She thought the worst was going to happen. To the both of you.'

'I feel terrible and yeah, I've been staying at the Charles Hotel.'

It was as swanky as Cambridge got and Murphy knew it. 'Slumming it. You should get in touch. She says you've been ducking her calls.'

'I should. I will. I feel guilty for what happened to her.'

'Wasn't exactly your fault.'

'You know how the mind works.'

'Unfortunately, I do. Still, call her.'

'Yes, Father. And I'll say ten Hail Marys.'

'Twenty. So, where's the magic mirror?'

Cal had the shoulder bag under his desk. He brought it out to show Murphy then slid it back, saying he wasn't letting it out of his sight.

'You're taking it with you to Arizona, I expect,' Murphy said.

'More important than a toothbrush and change of underwear.'

'What'd you think of Eve Riley?'

'Actually, it was kind of strange. I got the impression she'd been expecting my call.'

'She said that?'

'Not in so many words.'

The department secretary knocked on the open door, some mild concern creasing her face.

'Sorry to bother you, Cal, but you've got some visitors to see you.' She dialed herself back to a loud whisper. 'The FBI.'

Murphy sprang up. 'That would be my cue to take my leave. Stay safe and keep in touch, will you?'

The two special agents were wearing suits. His gray one was a half-size too large, her pants suit, a bland ecru, a half-size too small. Richard Nesserian produced a business card from the Boston office. Julia D'Auria's was from New York City.

'I'm surprised you're here,' Cal said.

Nesserian asked, 'Why is that?'

'Because I didn't get any response after my call.'

'This is the response,' D'Auria said. 'Maybe things work faster at a university.'

'I very much doubt that,' Cal said.

'The matter was referred to me,' Nesserian said. 'I did a little digging around here then got Special Agent D'Auria involved down in Manhattan.'

D'Auria said, 'We'd like to ask you a few questions.'

She was a small woman with brown hair feathered to a short length and a nose a tad too delicate for the rest of her squared-off features. Cal guessed she was somewhere in her thirties.

'Yes, of course. I can have some coffee brought in.'

She answered no, her partner yes. Nesserian was a good two decades older than D'Auria. His face was as baggy and rumpled as his suit. Its centerpiece was a mustache that looked like a couple of dirty toothbrushes had been pasted onto his upper lip.

Nesserian reacted to a shirty look from her and said, 'You know what, forget the coffee, I'm good.'

'You gave a description of your attacker to the Cambridge police,' she said. 'Tell us again what he looked like.'

'Big guy, very big actually. I'd say six-four, maybe six-five or six, the better part of three hundred pounds. But solid pounds, not a lot of flab.'

'How could you be sure of that?' Nesserian asked.

'Because I slammed my fists into his gut a few times. I'm a boxer. Club-level. I've hit my fair share of guts. This guy works out.'

'But you got the better of him,' D'Auria said.

'I kicked him in the nuts. Works wonders.'

Her shoulder bag was generous enough to hold a folder. She drew out some photos, and showed him one.

'Think this is your attacker?'

It was a screen grab from a security camera of a large man with an untucked, loose-fitting dark shirt and a baseball cap. Because of the high camera-angle, his face was obscured by the bill of the cap.

'Where was this taken?' Cal asked.

Nesserian told him it was on Brattle Street, the day the bookseller was killed.

'It could be him,' Cal said. 'I mean it's hard to gauge his size without some kind of reference, but his shoulders are massive like the guy.'

She threw down another photo. 'What about this?'

The first image was in bright sunlight. The second was in the dark, a sidewalk lit by street lights and maybe the head-lights of passing cars. It showed the same man, similar loose shirt, similar baseball hat. Again, his face wasn't visible.

'It could be the same guy,' Cal said. 'I wish I could tell his size.'

'We had some work done on the photos, looking at some of the image references – size of the sidewalk squares, that type of thing,' D'Auria said. 'This man is six-five, approximately three hundred pounds, just like you indicated. In these and every frame we have on him he's savvy enough to know the cameras are above him and he doesn't look up. He's a pro.'

'Where was this one taken?'

'On your mother's block on the night she was killed.'

Cal looked out the window. Pale-green early summer foliage moved in the breeze.

'Looks like you were right,' Nesserian said. 'He was probably looking for your – what-do-you-call-it – your artifact thing.'

'Now we need to figure out why,' D'Auria said.

'So, is the FBI going to take the case?'

'We already asserted jurisdiction based on crimes committed in New York and Massachusetts,' she said.

'I'm relieved to hear it. Look, there's a lot I don't understand about motives, but for the life of me, I can't figure out how he knew my mother even had the stone. I didn't know she had it. I'm not even sure she knew she had it. It's been sitting in the back of her closet for thirty years.'

'It's going to be one of the things we investigate,' D'Auria said. 'We're going to need to have a look at it.'

Cal told then they could see it now and pulled it from his bag. She handled it first and unimpressed, passed it to her partner, who laid it on Cal's desk and snapped a series of photos with his phone.

'I can't believe people got killed over this,' he muttered.

'You made some statements to Detective Gilroy about the piece,' D'Auria said, referring to her notes. 'You said you understood that it was something called a showstone that was allegedly used to communicate with spirits.'

'That's right.'

'And you told him that you didn't think it had a particularly great monetary value.'

'Look, I could be wrong about that but it's hard to believe it would fetch more than a few hundred to a few thousand at auction.'

She said she understood and asked about this thing the intruder was also looking for – this 49th Call. 'You told the detective you didn't know what that was. On further thought, any ideas?'

'I think it may have something to do with how one supposedly makes contact with spirits. I'm going to be visiting with an expert in the field, a woman in Arizona.'

'You'll let us know, right?' Nesserian said.

'I will. Which one of you should I contact?'

Nesserian pointed to D'Auria. 'I'm the pretty one but she's the smart one.'

'You realize he could come back,' D'Auria said. 'He seems pretty determined to get his hands on the stone.'

'I haven't gone home since the night it happened and I'm having a security system installed.'

'That may not be enough to keep you safe,' she said.

'What do you suggest?'

'Do you own a gun?'

'Nope.'

'You should get one,' D'Auria said.

'Getting a permit in Cambridge, Massachusetts is a bitch,' Nesserian said.

D'Auria said that getting one in Manhattan was probably even harder but that they'd try to pull strings at the local police department and the state firearms bureau.

'That would be good, I guess,' Cal said.

D'Auria smiled for the first time. 'Can you shoot? I mean other than nailing your floor?'

Cal smiled back. 'I hit the exact spot on the floor I was aiming at.'

ELEVEN

Mortlake, England, 1582

Edward Talbot returned to Mortlake at his appointed time. It was evening and the river traffic on the Thames had thinned to a few barges and skiffs making their way to night dockages. Talbot stopped for a moment outside John Dee's door to compose himself and steady his breathing. He had ridden his horse hard from London so as not to be late, but he did not wish to present himself as a man lacking in steadiness and composure.

He had come from Whitehall Palace, where he had taken his first meeting with Francis Walsingham. Walsingham was a fearsome presence. He was not given to ranting or indeed raising his voice beyond a mild, conversational tone. If

anything, it was his calm demeanor and quietness that proved
so disconcerting to Talbot and all others who found themselves
summoned for an audience. Walsingham, with his own hand,
had never killed or even harmed a man. Yet, as the Queen's
spymaster, he could destroy lives simply by affixing his signa-
ture to a writ of arrest or torture. After a long presence at
court, Walsingham had been elevated to Secretary of State.
Elizabeth did not like him, for how could one take to a man
with the personality of a viper, even one's own reptilian
servant? But she valued him for what he did, which was to
dedicate his life to keeping her safe from plotters, foreign and
domestic.

Talbot, when finally ushered into Walsingham's chambers,
felt his knee joints go soft. He leaned heavily on his walking
stick. The Secretary of State clearly knew he was standing
there in front of his mighty desk, but he kept his eyes glued
to a letter and kept his visitor in an uncomfortable state of
suspended animation. Walsingham's hair and beard were
unusually dark for a man of fifty but it was his eyes that
defined him. They were set wide, deeply buried in their sockets,
with hooded lids that seemed so weighty, it was a miracle they
were not tightly shut. And when he finally put his parchment
down and looked up at Talbot, those eyes revealed themselves
to be as dark and blue as the finest lapis stones.

'Tell me what I should call you?' Walsingham asked.

'Talbot, my lord. Edward Talbot.'

'But that is not your real name.'

'It is the name I am currently assuming, my lord.'

'Why the subterfuge?'

'Doctor Dee has many colleagues and acquaintances. I wish
to remain beyond reproach should he make inquiries.'

'But you are not beyond reproach, are you?'

'I have led a colorful life.'

Talbot then noticed that a middle-aged man as small as a
boy was in the chamber, stoking the hearth and making the
flames leap. Had he been there the entire time or had he snuck
in like a furtive creature? The flames conjured a vision of Hell
fires.

Walsingham was talking again. 'In fact, you are a scoundrel, sir. You have borrowed irresponsibly and failed to repay debts. You have fraudulently altered bills of lading. You are a liar and a cheat.'

'I have paid a price for my crimes, my lord.'

'Some say you should have lost more than the tops of your ears and the use of two good legs.'

'I assure you, I am a changed man.'

'If so, it affirms the righteousness of a good cropping and a vigorous beating that has left you crippled. In any event, Mr Clerkson vouches for your piety and that is why you are recruited to my service. I am told you are a scryer.'

'I am.'

'Further, I am told you have considerable talents in this regard.'

'I cannot deny that.'

Walsingham lifted his eyelids to the utmost and fixed his visitor with a luminous, blue stare. 'How am I to know if your scrying is real or the product of a devious heart?'

Talbot's walking stick shook from the pressure he was applying. He looked toward a chair but permission to sit was not forthcoming.

'You will simply have to believe me, my lord. I have had the gift since my youth.'

Talbot could not have known that Walsingham's interrogation methods included sudden shifts of subject.

'What will you say to Doctor Dee when he discovers your true name, as he surely will?'

'Hopefully I will have engendered enough trust, if and when this should happen, that I will be able to weather the storm.'

Another shift. 'What do you know of Doctor Dee's past?'

'That he is a very learned man, expert in the natural sciences, languages, and philosophy and that he has a profound interest in Kabbalistic and spiritual realms. He is said to be a foremost magus. This from Clerkson and others I have met in scrying circles.'

'My interest in John Dee arises not from these pursuits. I want to know if he is a traitor.'

'A traitor, my lord?'

'Her Majesty has many enemies. Some Catholics are as

easy to spot as a pope bedecked in red robes and bearing a scepter. Others are cleverly hidden from view and must be ferreted out. Doctor Dee may be such a man.'

'I am ignorant of this side to him, my lord.'

Walsingham finally seemed to notice Talbot's difficulty standing.

'You look like a tree about to topple. Sit yourself down before you fall.'

He found the cushion just in time and thanked Walsingham for the kindness.

'Were you aware that thirty years ago, Dee was ordained as a Catholic priest?'

'I was unaware.'

'It was done under the direction of the then Earl of Pembroke at a time, following the death of young King Edward, when Mary Tudor, during her unfortunate reign, was purging the Church of Protestant clergymen. Dee took his holy orders from none other than the notorious priest and traitor, Edmund Bonner.'

Talbot could have continued to listen passively, but he had a lively mind and had been an active debater at university. 'I had thought that many young men made such a decision if for no other reason than to stay in the good graces of the Crown for purposes of advancement.'

Walsingham did not seem annoyed by the challenge. 'True enough and not in and of itself grounds for branding Dee a menace to Her Majesty. I offer it as one brick in a wall.'

Talbot, encouraged by the benign response, weighed in further. 'And I have heard that when Queen Elizabeth was a young princess, she consulted with Doctor Dee and asked him to cast her horoscope to divine the future that awaited her. Was she not aware that he was a priest?'

'Indeed she was. I do not believe she was troubled. The times were different, the threats of a different nature.'

'Surely Doctor Dee has abandoned his vow of celibacy. He is thrice married with children. Is this not a mark in his favor?'

'Certain men will go to great lengths to hide their true religion.'

'You mentioned a wall,' Talbot said. 'There are other bricks?'

'Indeed there are. My predecessor, Lord Burghley, long harbored suspicions that Doctor Dee did engage in conjurations and incantations of evil spirits, contravening the Witchcraft Act that Parliament did enact. This goes back many a year, but when he was arrested and confined to the Tower on charges of treason during the reign of Queen Mary, the child of one of his accusers went blind and the suspicion turned to Dee as a conjuror.'

'But he was acquitted by the Star Chamber, as I understand.'

'He was set free, yes, but this was Catholic justice which, as we know, was an imperfect instrument. It was the priest, Bonner, who argued for his innocence, the same Bonner who later ordained him. That alone was enough to bring Dee to my attention and over the years, I have encouraged my network of informers to keep a watch on his activities both in England and during his various and sundry sojourns abroad. From time to time I have received reports regarding his spiritual actions. Some recent reports suggest that he may have strayed into the realm of the dark arts.'

The small man by the hearth poked at the fire again and made it roar. Talbot might have wondered whether this had been done to effect.

'Toward what end, my lord?' he asked.

Color came to the minister's pale face. 'Conjuration of evil spirits, man! To subvert and weaken Her Majesty the Queen! This is my vexation. This is my fear. A papist plot against her person.'

'You have evidence for this?'

'Hearsay evidence, I would say. We have a man inside Dee's household who has heard certain cries and incantations.'

'Not his scryer, Barnabus Saul.'

'Not Saul, no. He is loyal to Dee and not to be turned. There is another, his servant, Robert Hilton, who is in my employ, although his access to Dee's spiritual actions is limited. Barnabus Saul could not be cajoled into becoming our ears and eyes but we were able to persuade him to cease his scrying and leave Dee's service.'

The way he said persuade made Talbot shudder.

'I understand.'

'You met with Doctor Dee last week. How was that meeting?'

'I believe it went well. Clearly, he was interested in seeing me again. When I leave you today I will proceed apace to Mortlake for supper, to be followed by a scrying action.'

'I will want to hear your report from this and all other spiritual actions. Be keenly aware of Doctor Dee's attitudes and adverse motives with respect to Her Majesty.'

'Of course, my lord.'

'And make sure and certain that you poison the well of Master Barnabus Saul. We do not wish Doctor Dee to feel that he can return to that bosom. In future, you are the only scryer that gentleman shall use. Do I make myself clear?'

Dee's servant, Robert Hilton, answered the door. If Talbot had given Hilton a knowing, conspiratorial glance, it went unanswered. Perhaps Walsingham's other man did not know that he too was a spy. Perhaps the servant had also been instructed to spy on Talbot. Such were Walsingham's methods.

Talbot was received in the sitting room, where Dee was lounging with his second eldest son, Rowland, a gangly youth. For sport, Dee was drilling the lad in Greek grammar, and Talbot's entry allowed Rowland to escape his father's academic clutches and seek out one of his sisters for a game of Nine Men's Morris.

'Ah, Talbot, here you are. Would you care for a glass of sack?'

Hilton brought a bottle and two pretty glasses and left when Dee dismissed him.

'We will eat shortly,' Dee said. 'And then we will retire to my chambers for our business. You have the showstone, I trust.'

'I would sooner forget to bring my head, good sir.'

The remark delighted Dee who laughed heartily and offered a toast.

Supper was served in the dining room. The cook served a nice joint accompanied by a savory pudding. Hilton stood by, pouring the wine and, Talbot imagined, listening and remembering. John

Dee controlled the conversation, steering it mainly toward his subjects of interest, Kabbalistic linguistics and optics, while Talbot played the role of keen student, asking leading or clarifying questions. Jane Dee was a model of matrimonial decorum, eating in silence, motioning for Hilton to fill glasses, and ringing a small bell to summon the cook.

'Do you know why I have devoted so much of my work to understanding the optical properties of light?' Dee asked, picking a stray bit of leek from the sleeve of his robe.

'Pray, tell me why, Doctor?'

'It is known that celestial light is emitted by the Creator and imagined through the eyes. I and others have developed mathematical rules to demonstrate that when such light is reflected by polished surfaces, as in crystals or your Aztec stone as I will call it, the rays when entering the eyes may send the soul, particularly the virgin soul, into a state of intense awareness. Angelic spirits may travel on these rays and when the archemaster has properly prepared himself through prayer and meditation he may thereby perceive these angelic spirits. A scryer such as yourself may receive such rays of light in concert with their winged travelers. If you like I will share my mathematical equations with you.'

'I would like to see them, although I confess, I may not fully understand. I was not a particularly excellent student of mathematics.'

While Dee was speaking, Talbot was furtively noticing Jane Dee. Her brown dress was exceedingly modest with a high neckline and cloth to the wrists and ankles, but Talbot could follow the contour of her thin neck to the point where it disappeared under her collar and imagine more of her feminine anatomy. When there was an opening he attempted to draw her into the conversation, perhaps to enjoy the melodious sound of her voice.

'I wonder, madam, whether you share your husband's interest in the realm of the spirits?'

Dee stopped chewing, seemingly taken aback by Talbot's sudden questioning of his wife. For her part, she took the cloth napkin draped over her shoulder and serenely dabbed at the corner of her mouth.

'My role is to serve my good husband and raise his children. In matters of his spiritual research, I can best be his helper by keeping the young ones from wandering into his rooms during his actions and interrupting his important work.'

Talbot nodded but before he could ask more of her, Jane rang her bell and asked the cook to remove the plates.

Dee removed his napkin, placed it over the arm of his chair and, pointing toward the window, declared that the evening was well enough along that he and Talbot might begin their night work.

Jane had not betrayed any emotion during the meal but when the men rose, she frowned, evidently anxious to ask a burning question.

'I wonder, Master Talbot, whether you have made the acquaintance of my husband's last scryer, Barnabus Saul?'

'I do not know him, madam, but I do know some gentlemen who have had the pleasure.'

'And what have you heard of him from these gentlemen?'

Talbot ran his hands through his hair to make sure his locks fell sufficiently over his ears to conceal his deformities.

He answered her question with one of his own. 'May I ask your opinion of Master Saul, madam?'

'I found him most agreeable.'

'I see. I would not wish to taint your considered opinion of him so I will keep my tongue.'

John Dee was having none of it. He ordered his guest to say what he knew.

Clearing his throat and showing some discomfort Talbot said, 'Well, sir, I was told that Barnabus Saul has been speaking behind your back of the discomfort he had at continuing in your employ.'

'And why is that?' Dee demanded.

'He said he was poorly paid for his services and implied that he was coerced to make contact with darker sorts of spiritual presences.'

Dee slammed a hand down on the table, upsetting a goblet. 'That is an outrageous lie. Hear you this, Jane? It is well that he is gone from our household. Come upstairs, Talbot, I will show you how I do, in truth, operate.'

The little chamber where Dee and Talbot retired was through his book-lined study, the last in a series of linked rooms. It was the quietest in the house, at the rear, and the one least likely for the smaller children to wander into. The room, because of its lack of proximity to the central chimney stack, had no fireplace. At night, the light came only from candles, so Dee went about lighting them from the one he carried up the stairs. The candle holders were iron tripods that stood on the floor, and Dee mumbled that they were of his own design. Once the room was alight, he pulled the curtain over the sole window. It overlooked the churchyard and he did not want to tempt the curiosity of the prying minister out for an evening constitutional.

Talbot looked around at the sparse furnishings. In the center of the room on a bare floor was a low square table, only a few inches off the ground. A red cushion lay before it. A small writing desk and chair stood facing the table. There was a chest of drawers against one wall topped by a cabinet with glass doors. Inside it, wooden shelves held two rows of leather-bound books.

'Well then,' Dee said, 'where is your black beauty?'

Talbot reached into his capacious robe and removed his leather pouch and a folded brass stand that he said was purpose-made for the stone.

'This table?' Talbot asked.

'Yes, right there, if you will.'

The obsidian mirror fit snugly onto the stand. He placed it at the center of the table and Dee bade him to kneel on the cushion. Then he began moving candles and stands around, checking on how they were reflecting onto the surface of the stone, and seeking Talbot's opinion on their placement. When they were both satisfied, Dee procured the materials he needed from the cabinet: a bound book of parchment for his notations, a pot of ink, a pair of spectacles he had obtained during one of his journeys to the Low Countries, and a fresh quill that he proceeded to sharpen with a knife. Then he pulled up the chair to the small desk so that he was facing Talbot.

'Shall we begin?' Dee asked.

'I will follow your lead, sir,' Talbot said from his kneeling position.

'Then let us seek the Blessed Angels of God and let us pray.'

In unison they said, '*Gloria patri et filio et Spiritui Sancto. Sicut erat in principio, et nunc et semper: et in saecula saeculorum. Amen.*'

Dee pinched the spectacles to his narrow nose, dipped his quill, and wrote at the top of a blank page: *Anno 1582, Martii Die 10, Hora 11 ¼ Ante Meridiem*. Then he began to stare at the young man who was staring into the showstone. They spoke no words between themselves for five minutes, ten, then fifteen when Dee saw Talbot suddenly stiffening, his eyes widening.

'What see you?' Dee whispered.

Talbot said, 'A man clothed with a long robe of purple all spangled with gold. On his head, a garland of gold.'

'Has he—'

Talbot put a finger across his lips, then said, 'His name, he says, is Uriel.'

Dee became excited and attempted to write the name on his parchment, but the ink had dried. As he re-dipped his quill he muttered that Uriel was the fire of God, the archangel of salvation. 'Has Uriel appeared to you before?'

Talbot replied that he had not and that this was an auspicious start to their action.

'Ask him if he is answerable to this stone.'

Talbot repeated the question then relayed the answer. 'He says, "I am."'

Dee knew that were he to come around the table and gaze into the showstone he would see nothing, nor did he expect to hear Uriel's speech. The angelic spirits made themselves manifest only to the scryer.

'Are there more beside you?' Dee asked via Talbot.

Uriel replied, 'Michael and Rafael but Michael is foremost in our works.'

Dee marveled at hearing the names of the two great archangels, then scribbled the answer and asked Talbot what language Uriel was employing.

'Latin, dear Doctor,' he said excitedly. 'Clear and excellent Latin.'

'I have so many questions for him,' Dee murmured. 'I hardly know where to start.'

He asked if one of the earlier books he had written, *The Book of Soyga*, had merit. It was a manuscript including Kabbalistic tables and magical squares of letters passed down over the centuries from magus to magus. To Dee's amazement, Uriel replied that the book had been revealed to Adam in Paradise by the good angels of God.

Dee had, for a great while, been frustrated at his inability to decipher the magical tables. He said, 'Oh, my great and long desire has been to be able to read those Tables of Soyga.'

Uriel replied, 'These things mostly involve Michael. Michael is the angel who illuminates your path. And these things are revealed in virtue and in faith, not by force.'

Dee nodded at the wisdom and after he wrote down the answer he was emboldened to ask how long he might live.

'A hundred and odd years,' Uriel said.

A smile cracked Dee's dour countenance. Talbot couldn't help but to smile as well.

Dee continued, 'Is there a special time or hour to be observed to deal for the enjoining of Michael?'

Suddenly Talbot went quiet and after a time, Dee asked him why.

'A strange image has appeared in the stone,' Talbot whispered. 'I know not what it is.'

'Can you draw it onto my parchment?' Dee asked.

Talbot labored for several minutes with pen and ink and passed the leather book back to Dee. He saw written upon it a broad-based triangle, filled with odd pictograms he could not fathom.

'Good Lord!' Dee whispered. 'This must be angel writing. Ask Uriel what is the intent of this.'

The answer came quickly. 'It is from Michael. Engrave this seal in gold for protecting the body in all places, time, and occasions. It is to be worn on the chest.'

And with that, Uriel was gone.

Talbot pushed himself up from the cushion and rubbed hard

at his aching leg. Dee was fast to hand him his walking stick that had been left against a wall.

'Robert!' Dee bellowed. 'Robert, come here.'

Robert Hilton immediately appeared from the adjoining study. While Dee did not seem to be put off by his servant's close presence, Talbot looked on suspiciously, worried perhaps that indeed Walsingham's man was spying not on his master this night, but on him.

'Robert, bring us some wine,' Dee said. 'We will have it in my study.'

Hilton bowed slightly then left them.

'An invigorating and illuminating start to our action,' Dee declared.

'It was indeed,' Talbot said. 'I see you are pleased.'

'I am utmost pleased, good sir. Your showstone is powerful and your scrying is most excellent.'

'Perhaps I can return in a few days.'

'Nonsense!' the magus exclaimed. 'You will rest here tonight as my guest. Robert will prepare a bed. Tomorrow night we will have our second spiritual action. I cannot wait for several days to pass. To think, man! Michael made his presence known through Uriel. Michael! The greatest of the angels all but spoke to me.'

Dee crawled into his bed wearing only his night shirt. Jane stirred beside him. He could tell by her ordinary breathing that she was awake.

'Wife? Why are you not asleep?'

'I could not.'

'Are you troubled?'

'Less so now that Master Talbot has departed.'

'But he has not. He is staying the night so that we may resume our work tomorrow evening.'

She said nothing.

Dee filled the void with his enthusiasm, recounting what had occurred. When still she said nothing, he asked what troubled her.

'I do not like Edward Talbot,' she said. 'I do not trust his intentions. If I had a say in this I would not have him sleeping under a roof that shelters our children.'

'Nonsense, woman. He is a fine enough fellow. Clerkson assures me of his character.'

'And his cropped ears?'

'Surely a misunderstanding lay at the root of whatever the misfortune that befell him. Now we must sleep. I will surely dream of angels and I pray they will visit you as well.'

Late the following night, Dee and Talbot once again took their positions on either side of Talbot's showstone and after offering up prayers, the scryer began to stare into the reflected candle-light. Giddy with anticipation, Dee waited for Talbot to speak. Before very long he whispered that Uriel had returned.

'Tell him that I desire to learn the mysteries of his realm. Tell him I wish to invoke the help of Michael and other great angels.'

Uriel replied enigmatically, 'There is a seat of perfection from which things shall be shown unto thee which thou hast long desired.'

Dee wrote furiously then told Talbot to ask what was meant by a seat of perfection. The series of answers startled him. As he transcribed what were in essence a series of instructions, the small room filled with the sound of Talbot's voice and the scratchings of quill upon parchment. There was more to it than Uriel's words. Talbot also had to pause to write down the symbols and pictograms that appeared to him on the smooth surface of the polished obsidian.

Uriel commanded that a new scrying table be built for the showstone. By the angel's orders, the table was to be made of sweet wood, two cubits high and two cubits square. Four rows of names and symbols were to be carved on each side of the table and stained with yellow oil. The showstone was to be set atop a Sigillum Dei, or seal of God, as he put it, 'already perfected in a book of thyne.' Dee had earlier published his modification of the ancient seal, a magical diagram consisting of two circles, a pentagram, and three heptagons, labeled with the name of God and his angels. It was an amulet intended to give the initiated and blessed magician power over all creatures save the mighty archangels. According to Uriel, the Sigillum had to be made of perfect, clean wax, without color, and needed to be nine inches in diameter and an inch and a half thick. On the back surface, a peculiar cross pictogram was to be engraved. Under each of the table legs, a miniature copy of the Sigillum was to be placed. Finally, a square of fine red silk was to be placed on the table, over the large Sigillum, hanging down with four tassels at the corners.

A good hour had passed, and Dee was exhausted by the demands flung at him by the angel and his need to carefully write down every detail.

'Is there more?' he asked Talbot, who was wincing from the pain shooting down from his withered leg.

Talbot looked again into the showstone. Uriel was gone. He heard something at the study door and he imagined that Robert Hilton was there with his ear pressed into it.

'Uriel says one more thing,' Talbot said.

'Tell me.'

Talbot lowered his voice to a conspiratorial whisper. 'He says there is an evil spirit in the house named Lundrumguffa who seeks your destruction. He has entered into the bodies of one of your manservants. He seeks the destruction of your daughter and your wife too.'

His daughter was only nine months old. 'My daughter, Katherine?'

'Yes, her. If you do not discharge this servant from your house on the morrow, he will harm Katherine and your Jane.'

'Which servant?' Dee asked in utter alarm. 'George, who toils in the stables, or Robert Hilton?'

'He says the man possessed by evil is Robert Hilton.'

'Then he will be gone, I say!'

Talbot set his jaw in satisfaction. Two spies in one household was one too many. He announced that Uriel had taken his leave, although the angel had, in truth, departed before Talbot began his slander of Robert Hilton.

The two men got to their feet and Talbot leaned heavily on his stick.

'What say you, Doctor Dee? Are you satisfied with this action?'

'More than satisfied, Talbot. This has been an extraordinary evening. There is much work to do. I must commission a carpenter to build me a table and molds for wax Sigilli. I must procure perfect wax and red silk. The sooner I have fashioned these spirit furnishings the sooner we may get to our work of mastering the angel mysteries and indeed all the mysteries of the world.'

'So, you will want me as your scryer?'

'Of course, my good man, of course! How could you think otherwise?'

'And my salary of fifty pounds per annum?'

Dee stroked at his beard. 'A great deal, sir. Could you be content for less?'

Talbot stared at the magus. All the mysteries of the world to be revealed and he was haggling?

'I would not be content for less, Doctor Dee.'

TWELVE

Eve took a sick day and spent it cleaning every inch of her bungalow. By the early evening, when Cal pulled into her driveway, the place was pristine. The only thing that would have made it nicer was a fresh coat of paint. It had only been three days since his call. He had apologized, told her he'd gotten her number online from a White Pages site. It wasn't major sleuthing. There was only one Eve Riley in Arizona her approximate age, assuming her author photo was of recent vintage. By now, she knew about him too. Cal Donovan was all over the Internet. Dozens of photos from web sites, conference agendas, press conferences, his own author head-shots. She sorted through them, found a favorite, a manly sort of shot, taken at an archeological dig in Turkey, and printed it out. When his car door slammed shut, she realized it was still on the cork board in her kitchen, and she hurriedly pulled it down and put it in the cutlery drawer.

Cal was wearing his usual travel clothes – khakis, white oxford shirt, blue blazer, his messenger bag slung over a shoulder. The sun, while moving toward the horizon, was still bright. He forgot he was wearing sunglasses and peeled them off when she appeared at the door.

'I'm Cal.'

She seemed shy. 'Eve.'

There was a mutual awkwardness that came from a situation that felt more like a first date than a business meeting. He checked her out in one of those head-to-toe scans that took a second but seemed to him to last longer. He was sufficiently self-aware to know he was an inveterate womanizer, but he prided himself on being a subtle and respectful one. Women always had been attracted to him and he had always enthusiastically reciprocated. If he wasn't keen on a woman who showed an interest in him, he usually found the sweetest possible way to let her know the score. He wasn't going to be flashing the brake lights with Eve Riley. She was more beautiful and exotic than her book-cover picture made her out. For her book, maybe she had been going for a librarian look to draw in religious types. In her author photo she had severely pulled-back hair, a blousy shirt buttoned high, and a ground-brushing denim skirt, but tonight her black hair was loose and long, her cowboy shirt was open to cleavage, and her jeans were hip-hugging. She was deeply tanned without much makeup. If her name weren't Riley, he'd have pegged her for Native American, but maybe Riley wasn't her maiden name. He'd figure it out.

'This is a beautiful spot,' he said.

'It's heaven. At least for me. Please come in.'

She offered something to drink. It was the time of day when a glass of vodka usually called his name, but he took a lemonade from a frosty pitcher. It was homemade and awfully wholesome. The bungalow – from what he could see of it – exuded a singular personality. There were black-and-white photographs on the walls – hers, she said – of desert flowers, lizards, and sunsets. There was a lot of tribal pottery and a horse-hair blanket thrown over an old saddle horse. The furniture pieces were small and feminine. He might be wrong, but it didn't look like a man was in the frame.

When he'd finished admiring her photography he broke the ice on his visit.

'You know, I thought your book was really excellent.'

She beamed like a child. 'Really?'

'Yeah. Look, I understand the audience you're trying to reach – the want-something-practical, spiritual-seeking crowd – but your writing is a cut above the usual how-to book and there's a scholarship that comes through.'

Her skin was too dark to show a blush, but she acted like she was blushing and repeated an eyelid-fluttering, 'Really? You really think so?'

'I do.'

'That means a lot coming from you. I mean you're famous. I looked you up.'

He shrugged modestly. 'And I looked you up too. I see you got your master's from University of Arizona. I know a few people at the history department. Carson Miller's the chairman.'

'He wasn't chairman when I was there but his courses in Tudor and Elizabethan England were terrific. But I have to correct you, I didn't quite get my degree. I had to drop out several credits and a thesis short when I got pregnant.'

'That's too bad. You never went back?'

'It was kind of a messed-up time for me. I wasn't ever seriously with the father and I was really young. I didn't want to be a mother, so I put the kid up for adoption. I wasn't going to have an abortion. Anyway, giving the baby away sent me into a downward spiral. My head wasn't right for going back to school and I really couldn't see racking up more student debt in the state I was in.' The corner of her mouth twitched. 'I started working shit jobs and that was that. I'm still in a shit job. For the city of Tucson. I issue permits for the building department. Fortunately, living out here in the middle of nowhere is cheap.'

Cal pulled her book out of his bag. 'But you're an author too.'

She laughed. 'I sat down once and calculated the hourly wage I earned off of that book. I think it was ten cents or thereabouts.'

'Well, like I said, it was very well done. I learned a lot from it.'

She asked if he wanted to have a look at her 'back yard' and led him onto the patio. The desert began on the other side of her low stone wall and spread out brown and flat for a hundred miles to the Baboquivari Mountains, purple in the evening light.

'You like it?' she asked.

'It's spectacular. Is this where the magic happens?'

Caught off balance, she laughed heartily. 'How did you know? Yeah, this is where I practice my magic.'

'It seems like an excellent place for it.'

'The energy. Can you feel it?'

He wasn't into New Age sentiments, but he had to admit that the atmosphere was special.

She moved one of the opposing patio chairs, so they were both facing the lowering sun, and they sat there, talking toward the desert and noticing the occasional lizard flying over the flagstones in a hurry to get somewhere.

'So, you inherited a showstone,' she said. He had said as much when he telephoned.

'It wasn't a formal bequest,' he said lightly. 'I found it in the back of a closet after my mother died.'

'It was hers?'

'No, my father's. He was an archeologist. He found it on a dig in Iraq nearly thirty years ago.'

'How did you know what it was?'

'He labeled it. I don't know how he knew.'

She asked to see it. She wanted to unwrap it for herself. One of its surfaces caught the setting sun and was reflected into his face. She whispered an apology but otherwise she was totally focused on the obsidian disk, holding it cupped in her hands, running a finger over it, lost in thought. He didn't interrupt her.

Finally, she pushed a rush of air through her nostrils and shook her head several times, her face flickering in gratitude or awe, he couldn't tell which.

'It's remarkable,' she said.

'Tell me about it.'

'Your father was right. It is a showstone. Definitely.'

'How can you tell?'

She looked like she was carefully choosing her words. 'Well, it looks very similar to one of the most famous showstones in history, the one belonging to John Dee. If you read my book you know who he is.'

'I do know him. And I read your book too.'

She rolled her eyes at herself. 'You're a Harvard professor, of course you know who he is. Anyway, beyond that – I just *know* what it is.'

'Can you explain that to me?'

She hadn't taken her eyes off it. 'It's speaking to me.'

'Literally?'

She looked up at him sheepishly. 'It's special, really special.'

He didn't press her further – not right now at least – but let her see the card his father had included with the obsidian, the one marked with Dee's name and the British Museum.

'So, Doctor Dee came to his mind too,' she said. 'Did you talk to him about it?'

'My father died in Iraq shortly after he mailed it home to the States. He fell. An accident. I don't think that he had a particular expertise in Elizabethan England, but the British Museum was a home away from home. Maybe he saw the piece there. Have you seen it?'

She lifted her head toward the mountain range. 'The only place I've ever been to outside America is Mexico and you can practically walk there from here. I'd love to go to England. I'd love to go anywhere. When you stamp building permits all day your horizons get kind of limited.'

'I would have thought that scrying can expand one's horizons considerably.'

She lit up to the comment and told him she was happy to hear him say it. 'Magic takes me places, that's for sure.' She wrapped the stone in its cloth but kept it on her lap. 'Tell me, Cal, why are you here? I mean, you could have emailed me a picture of your stone. You didn't have to get on a plane and fly to Arizona. There's something more going on, isn't there?'

He hadn't planned on it but there was something about the way she asked the question. He opened up and let the story tumble out. His mother's murder. The killing of the bookstore owner. His home invasion. She listened with a studious stillness.

She didn't ask a single question, but he had the feeling she was processing every detail. He searched her face for reactions, but she didn't show any, even when he told her that the intruder was looking for the 49th Call.

'In your book you wrote about forty-eight calls,' he said, 'nothing about a 49th. Maybe you know what he was talking about. I don't.'

She didn't answer right away but he noticed she was holding the showstone tighter.

'I guess I'm here for answers,' he said. 'I can spend days or weeks approaching this academically and reading a bunch of primary and secondary sources on John Dee's magic, or I can cut to the chase and pick the brain of a real expert. I want to know why this man killed two people and almost killed two more – me and my girlfriend.'

'Did you consider that he might have killed three people?'

'What do you mean?'

'Your father.'

The comment hit him hard and straightened his spine. He couldn't stay seated. He got up and walked to the edge of the patio. The sun was giving up the ghost, turning the sky orange and the mountains black.

'It never occurred to me,' he said. 'His accent. He could have been Iraqi.'

'Was he old enough? In 1989?'

'He was wearing a balaclava. I don't know.'

Perhaps she picked up on his agitation and wanted to hit the pause button, because she also got up and said, 'I'm hungry. You?'

'I'll take you out to dinner,' he said.

'There's nothing around here for miles and besides, I make a pretty good chopped salad. Later, we can do some magic if you like.'

'I was hoping you'd say that.' He paused then said something that had been lingering on his mind. 'When I rang you, you weren't the least surprised. I got the feeling you were expecting my call.'

She handed the showstone back. 'I would have been surprised if you hadn't called.'

*   *   *

Over dinner Cal brought up his father again. He couldn't shake her suggestion that the man in the balaclava was the one who had killed both his parents. He told her it was wildly out of character that Hiram Donovan would have taken an artifact from a dig and mailed it home.

'Maybe it spoke to him,' she said. 'Maybe he couldn't let it go.'

'Spoke to him how?' he asked hesitantly.

'The way it spoke to me when I held it. Scryers have a connection to their showstones. The stronger the stone, the stronger the scryer, the stronger the connection.'

'What did it say?'

She smiled a little. 'It's a beckoning, a call to action, a call to have a conversation with angels. If you didn't know angel language you wouldn't understand it.'

He started to say something but only a syllable came out before he stopped himself.

'Maybe your father had some gift as a scryer and didn't even know it. Maybe that's why he kept it.'

'Maybe,' he mumbled.

'You know, the gift runs in families. Maybe you've got a connection to the stone too?'

That ever-so-faint murmuring every time the disk rested in his hand.

'Maybe,' he said again.

A weather system was pushing a bank of low clouds that blotted out the moon making the night sky blotchy dark. Eve was in her closet getting the things she needed for their spiritual action. She used the term John Dee used.

'Need a hand?' Cal asked.

'Sure. Take the table.'

On the patio she had him prop the small folded table against the stone wall while she put her other materials to the side.

'Let's wait till the top of the hour to start,' she said. 'It's not a requirement or anything. It's just one of my little quirks.'

'So, I'm about to see some Enochian magic,' he said.

She took one of the chairs and he took another. Without the mountains as a line of reference, the desert might as well have been infinite. The air was cool and dry, alive with chirping crickets.

'Doctor Dee is the father of Enochian magic, but he never used the term. Later magicians slapped that label on it. He called it angel magic. The prophet Enoch was very important to him. He was Methuselah's father and according to the Book of Genesis, after living for three hundred sixty-five years, Enoch, who walked with God, was no more, for God took him.'

'Which Christians have interpreted to mean that he entered Heaven alive,' Cal said. 'He and the prophet Elijah were the only people said to have ever done so.'

'God, I love talking to an educated man,' she laughed. 'You have no idea what it's like out here. My last boyfriend was an expert in football and beer. So, yeah, Enoch was able to talk with angels. We don't know how he did that but maybe that made him the first scryer. They taught him their angel alphabet and their angel language and once he understood it, he was able to read the Book of Nature.'

'And that gave him full knowledge of the universe,' Cal said.

'Exactly. And that's what Doctor Dee wanted too. He wanted to read the Book of Nature himself and help usher in humanity's return to a life of perfection in perfect harmony with nature.'

Cal was in a rhythm with her. 'The Hermetic tradition of spiritual rebirth through the enlightenment of the mind.'

'He also had a practical goal, I think,' she said. 'He was born a Catholic during Henry VIII's reign and had to basically become a Protestant to survive under Queen Elizabeth. Europe was torn apart by the split in the Church and the angels told Dee that there was another way for Christians to live, that they could reveal to him a new religion, kind of a merger of Protestantism and Catholicism—'

Cal couldn't help himself. 'But even beyond that, a universal faith that would include Jews and Muslims as well as Protestants and Catholics.'

She clucked at him and accused him of sandbagging her, but he assured her that he only knew about Dee's theology, not the nuts and bolts of his angel communications.

'Okay, five minutes to blast off,' she said after checking her watch. 'When Doctor Dee started his angel conversations his scryers weren't all that good and he didn't make a great deal of progress. There are shitty scryers, decent ones, and great ones, just the same as with anything. I imagine you're a great professor, for example.'

'And I imagine you're a great scryer.'

She answered without a trace of modesty. 'Actually I am. I was born with it. I didn't know my father, but my mother had the gift, though she was generally too fucked up to put it to practical use. From the earliest age I saw visions in pools of water and shiny things. In high school I found a book on Enochian magic and that set me on my journey. It's why I wanted to study history and write scholarly books about Doctor Dee but, hey, it wasn't to be. Anyway, where I was going with this is that Dee didn't really crack the code until he hooked up with a great scryer, a man named Edward Kelley. The two of them entered into a collaboration over several years where the angels revealed to them the crown jewels – their language and how to penetrate the different levels of the angelic universe by using calls to open the gates of nature. It's all there in Doctor Dee's detailed diaries and notes that were discovered after he died. Even their discovery is kind of interesting. When he died his furniture from his house in Mortlake near London was sold to a dealer. A family bought a chest of his and years later, they were moving it around when they heard something shifting inside. It turns out there was a hidden compartment where Dee kept his angel diaries. That's how we know about angel language and Enochian magic.'

'From Enoch to Dee is a pretty long swath of history,' Cal said. 'Are we to believe that no one else between them ever learned the language of the calls?'

'I've wondered about that,' she said. 'There's no record of anyone else but it can't be possible, can it? There've always been people with the gift of scrying. Somewhere along the line, I feel there must have been others who received the knowledge.'

'Okay, tell me about the calls.'

'Sometimes you'll see them referred to as keys or claves.

To understand them, you've got to understand the Enochian map of the universe. Picture a bunch of concentric circles extending out into the universe. There are thirty circles representing a realm, each one presided over by a spiritual being known as an angelic governor. A call is a prayer or a chant in angel language that allows you to get in contact with these realms. There are forty-eight calls that were revealed to Doctor Dee. The first eighteen have a variety of special purposes I don't need to get into. It's the next thirty calls that are going to interest you most, I think. They're called the Call of the Thirty Aethyrs. They connect you to one of the governors who rule the thirty Aethyrs or Aires as they're called. The thirtieth is the lowest Aethyr. The first Aethyr is the highest. It's the last concentric circle. It represents the pure and undifferentiated mind of God. Most experienced magicians go straight to their guardian angelic governor in one of the Aethyrs. Mine is called Pothnir. He resides in the fourth Aethyr. I reach him with the forty-fourth call.'

'Can I ask what you talk to him about?'

She looked into the darkness. 'I'm not an important person or a big thinker like Doctor Dee was. I don't fuss with cosmic issues. Mostly I ask his advice about small things – well, big for me but super-small for mankind if you know what I'm saying. Just talking to him helps me sometimes. Makes me feel closer to God.'

'So, let me understand this,' he said. 'In the Enochian scheme of things, the fourth Aethyr is close to the first Aethyr and therefore God. Is your ability to get high up on the totem pole a marker for your abilities as a scryer?'

Again, she showed little modesty. 'I've never met a scryer who had a higher level of access.'

'Okay, now the big question. Was this guy talking nonsense when he asked me if I had the 49th Call?'

'Nonsense? Hardly,' she said. 'When you mentioned it on the phone I got chills.'

'Go on.'

'The angels told Doctor Dee that there were really forty-nine calls but that they would hold back one of them because it was too powerful and couldn't be revealed.'

'You're saying no one has ever seen it?'

'As far as I know, it's never been revealed.'

'But we have this guy thinking I might have it.'

'I don't know what to say, Cal.'

'And what would this forty-ninth call be used for?'

'I haven't a clue. The mind boggles. Maybe it's a direct connection to God or maybe—?'

'Maybe what?'

'Maybe it's a direct connection to something we weren't intended to reach.'

'You believe that?'

She said that she didn't know what she thought; he had no way of knowing that she was playing back the conversation she'd had with Pothnir about the world teetering over an infinite abyss.

'It's time,' she said. 'Let's get started.'

As she set up the table at the center of the patio, she explained that she had it made to match the design for a scrying table the angels had given Doctor Dee. Like Dee's, her table, made of laurel, had folding legs for travel. Dee had taken his on his journeys throughout Europe and she too took her tools on the road for seminars and private actions with students. She told him wistfully that these days she didn't travel much and that paying students were few and far between. By the light of the sconces on either side of her patio doors, Cal saw that the borders of the table were segmented into twenty-one cells on each side, each cell containing a runic kind of script that Eve said were angel letters. A large hexagram was inscribed onto the table and at its center was a 3 x 4 cell of more angel letters.

She opened a wooden box that contained several objects. First, she took out a thick disk, the size of a fruitcake. It was made of cream-colored wax engraved with a complex concoction of circles, interlacing geometric forms, and runic letters and words.

'This is the Sigillum Dei Aemeth,' she said. 'The seal of God, also given to Dee from the angels.'

She gently placed it at the center of the table then got a folded square of red silk from the box and placed it over the wax seal and the table, so its tassels hung down from the corners.

There were four more wooden boxes inside the larger box, the size of a couple of packs of playing cards. Each box, she, explained held a miniature wax version of the Sigillum Dei Aemeth, and with his help, she placed one box under each table leg.

Next, she lit candles on standing holders and placed them around one side of the table then turned off the sconces so that the patio was lit only by the flickering wicks.

The last small box within the larger box held her scrying stone, a flawless crystal ball, but she asked Cal if it was okay with him to use his obsidian mirror instead.

'I'd love to give it a test drive,' she said.

'I was kind of hoping you would.'

She used a small plate holder as a stand for the stone and adjusted the candles. She had him sit opposite her as she faced the showstone and began to chant the 1st Call.

'*Ol sonf vors g, goho Iad Balt, lonsh calz vonpho; sobra zol ror i ta nazps od graa ta malprg.*'

In time, she reached the Call of the Thirty Aethyrs.

'*Madriaax ds praf paz, chis micaolz saanir caosgo, od fifis balzizras iaida!*'

Cal watched her closely. The candles were behind her; her features were lost to the darkness. The angel language was guttural, but somehow, in her voice, it sounded sweet. Her chant lasted a couple of minutes. It seemed to take something out of her because he could see her shoulders begin to droop.

Then, apart from the crickets, there was silence.

Until.

He saw her leaning in, her face closer to the showstone.

'He's here,' she said. 'His image is so vivid. This mirror is incredible.'

Cal was about to ask who was there, but she began speaking in the guttural language. Then silence again.

She spoke in English now. 'Pothnir knows you're here. He says your showstone is very powerful. He says it allows him to tell me things he couldn't before. He says you are permitted to question him.'

Cal felt like he was watching an act and his skepticism was running wild. He was a practicing Catholic, which made him a card-carrying believer in miracles, but this? It seemed a bridge too far.

'Can I come over to your side and speak to him directly?'

'You won't see anything other than your own reflection and you won't hear anything either. Ask through me.'

'I want to ask him something that only I would know.'

She sounded hurt. 'You don't believe me, do you? You think this is bullshit. Go on, ask him anything you like.'

Undaunted, he thought for a moment and said, 'Ask him what memento of my father I keep on my desk.' It was something he was sure had never appeared in anything written about him.

She spoke in angel tongue and soon relayed an answer. 'He says, you have your father's tool that he used for digging artifacts from the soil. He says the handle is engraved with the letters HD.'

Cal felt lightheaded. The cricket chirps were drowned out by the sound of blood rushing through his ears.

Eve must have noticed him wobble. She asked if he was all right.

'Yeah, I'm okay.'

'He nailed it, didn't he?'

'Yeah, he got it right. No one knows about that trowel.'

'Shall we continue, then?'

Questions swam through his head but the first one was for Eve, not the angel.

'He told you I'd be calling you, didn't he?'

'Yes.'

'Ask him if the man who came into my house killed my mother.'

She spoke to Pothnir then told Cal, 'He killed her. He wanted the stone.'

'Does he know who he is, his name?'

Cal waited.

'He doesn't know his name but there is a powerful man, a magician, who controls him. That man's name is also unknown to him.'

'Can you ask him if the man who killed my mother also killed my father?'

He held his breath.

'He says that this man did kill your father. He says it happened in Al-Iraq. The magician was present.'

He tried to compose himself, but he was shaking. 'Why do they want this showstone?' he asked.

'It is very powerful,' Eve replied once she received the answer. 'A strong magician, one of the strongest ever known, made it from a very pure lump of black glass. With this stone, a powerful magician can use it to learn the 49th Call.'

'What is the 49th Call?' Cal asked.

The answer came. 'With it, a magician can summon the great evil.'

'What is the great evil?'

'The evil that arises from a fallen one.'

Cal wished he could see Eve's eyes better. 'A fallen one?' he asked. 'Do you mean a fallen angel?'

The answer was simple. 'Yes.'

Cal asked this: 'The killer asked about something written in Aramaic. Probably on papyrus. Do you know what he was talking about?'

Eve conveyed the answer. 'The great magician wrote it. Your father found it.'

'In Iraq?' He corrected himself and used the medieval Arabic name for the territory. 'Al-Iraq?'

'Yes.'

'Where is it now?'

'I do not know.'

'What should we do?' Cal asked.

Eve spoke into the showstone then listened to the words that only she could hear. Before she gave Cal Pothnir's answer she told him that she had never before heard the angel raise his voice. Her own voice was quavering. Later, he would see she'd been crying.

'He says that we must stop these men from possessing the showstone and the 49th Call. If we cannot, the world will be plunged into a pit of evil the likes of which has never been seen.'

THIRTEEN

Al-Iraq, 1095

I t was an oasis, not in the sense of a fertile spot in the desert where water nurtures the barren land, but in a religious sense. In the eleventh century, the Rabban Hurmizd Monastery, located in the mountains to the north of the ancient city of Mosul, was a religious oasis, a Christian enclave surrounded by the Seljuk Turks, who were recent and fervent converts to Islam. The bishop of the monastery, an elderly cleric named Cyril bar Aggai, ruled his enclave with a firm hand, but his inner streak of kindness was known to his acolytes and to Christians in this hostile land, and this attribute had, over the years, served as a recruiting tool for young men contemplating a life of prayerful service. One of these young men was Daniel Basidi, who entered into holy orders at a tender age. His parents had too many mouths to feed and they welcomed his decision, even though it meant losing the affable youth to a cloistered life.

The day that Daniel presented himself to the gate of the monastery was the second time he had met Cyril. The bishop remembered him instantly even though it had been a decade earlier, when Daniel was only a boy. His parents, devotees of the Church of the East, had sought the bishop out for his counsel. The small boy had been acting strangely and they were concerned that the devil had a hand in his affliction. For days he had been staring into bowls of water, cups of wine – anything with a reflective surface – and he had been heard to murmur furtively. When asked what he was doing and what he was saying, the boy was evasive. At first Cyril had been curt and dismissive but then, out of earshot of his parents, Daniel said something that caught his attention. He then questioned the lad more closely for several minutes before taking his father aside and telling him that in his opinion, the boy was not cursed but blessed, and that he should be encouraged to pray regularly and learn the scriptures.

On the day of their second meeting, the old bishop nodded at the strapping youth standing before him and said, 'So, Daniel, you wish to become a priest?'

'I do, father bishop.'

'And tell me, do you still converse with angels?'

'I do.'

'And what do they tell you?'

'That I should become a priest and devote myself to God.'

Cyril reached for his stick, pushed himself upright, and took a few steps on arthritic hips.

'Then all I can say is welcome, Daniel. You will be one novice I will be watching with particular interest.'

Now, Daniel was a priest, and according to his superiors he was the most attentive and intellectually adventurous member of the spiritual community. He already knew the scriptures by rote when he entered the monastery, but during his tutelage as a novice and as a young priest he excelled in doctrinal analysis and commentary. His discourses and disputations were held in high esteem. But he did have his detractors for his habit of closeting himself away for stolen moments to devote himself to scrying. Cyril, who now had become practically bed-bound by his arthritis, wearily summoned him each time one of the brothers complained. He had an obligation to do so, but he harbored little worry for he believed in his heart of hearts that Daniel was a good and pure soul, albeit a special one. Once, a few years past, a traveling mystic had stopped at the monastery for rest and sustenance and Cyril, on learning the man was himself a scryer, had introduced him to the young priest. When the bishop later questioned the mystic about Daniel's skills, the wizened fellow replied that he had never heard of or met a scryer with the powers that Daniel Basidi possessed. The mystic was so moved by the experience of watching Daniel scry that he could hardly speak.

'Enter, Daniel. I have had another report,' the bishop said.

'I will not ask from whom,' Daniel replied, his hands folded over his rough brown robe.

There was a wink from an old eye. 'That is good, because

I would not tell you. Now, Daniel, you know the question I am once again obligated to ask.'

'You wish to know if, in the course of my scrying, I have engaged in any conversations with dark spirits. You wish to know if I have been practicing black magic.'

'And what would your answer be?'

'My answer is no, father bishop. The angels with whom I converse are sons of the light. They are the minions of God Almighty.'

'The calls that you have learned from them – do they still number forty-five?'

'I have recently learned three more. They have allowed me to penetrate the second Aethyr, only one Aethyr from where God Himself does reside.'

'And what will happen when you reach the first Aethyr?'

'I do not know if mortal man can ever attain this realm but if I am the fortunate one to do so, I hope to learn ultimate truth and divine enlightenment.'

'If a brother asks, might I tell him that you continue to use your scrying for good, not evil purposes?'

'That is the truth.'

'One last question, Daniel. Have the angels informed you of my fate?'

'They have, father bishop.'

'And?'

'You should prepare yourself.'

The old bishop closed his eyes tightly and nodded. 'Thank you, Daniel. You may go.'

Daniel returned to his stifling, airless cell in a mud-brick dormitory, to get his walking staff. He had two hours before evening prayers, led these days by the assistant bishop given Cyril's infirmity. It was just enough time to take a brisk walk down the steep path from the monastery to a plateau blessed with a smattering of wild flowers. He would pick a bouquet and give colorful sprigs as treats to the other priests at the conclusion of the church service. And if he was lucky, he might catch a few gusts of warm wind on his face, the kind that made him feel as if he was being brushed by the hand of God.

He reached the plateau and his sandals slipped and shifted on sweaty soles as he collected his blossoms – fluffy purple squills, blue thistles, and yellow chamomiles – but when he had almost gotten to the limit of what he could hold in his fist he spotted a stone protruding from the ground that caught his interest. It was half-buried in the pebbly soil, rounded and knobby, and he knew from its thick matrix of powdery chalk what it was – a good-sized nodule of obsidian, the size of a big melon. He put his flowers aside and pulled the stone from the earth, then brushed it off and admired its heft. If it was pure and black, he reckoned that Brother Thaddeus, the most able knapper in the monastery, could produce hundreds of sharp scythe blades from it. Bronze was expensive in these parts and the local farmers still used obsidian blades set into antlers at harvest time, as their ancestors had done for tens of thousands of years. The monastery traded scythes for grain and kegs of beer. A good hunk of obsidian was God-sent.

The only way to tell whether the stone was of high quality was to split it and that's what Daniel sought to do. A short distance away, he found a round hammer stone the size of his fist, and dropped to his haunches. With one stiff blow to the chalky nodule, it cleaved down the middle and he saw that it was the blackest black and flawless. One half was slightly concave, the other convex. He chose the concave one for closer inspection and saw his own image on its surface, distorted only by the percussion ridges from the cleavage.

In an instant, his reflection gave way to something else that arose from the depths of the blackness. He lost himself in the image and soon was hearing words in his head in a language that only he knew. The words were as clear as if one of his brother priests was whispering directly into his ear, clearer by far than he had ever heard them.

Gulping, he replied, '*Zirdo aqlo noco. Gemeganza.*'
I am thy servant. Thy will be done.

They made a curious pair. If Daniel was a twig, Thaddeus was the trunk of the tree. Not so many years separated them but Thaddeus, with his enormous girth and great height, seemed like a much older brother. Daniel was cerebral and clumsy.

Thaddeus was not stupid but his mind was not his strongest asset. It was his hands that were special. He was a wizard with his big, thick hands and it was in these hands that he held half of Daniel's nodule.

'It is a nice piece of obsidian,' Thaddeus said, his heavy hindquarters indenting the thin rush mattress on his bed frame. 'One of the best I have ever seen. Do you know how many scythes I can make from it?'

'You can make your little blades from the other half,' Daniel said. 'I would like you to make me something from this half.'

'What?'

'A scrying mirror.'

'I thought you use a bowl of water for your magic.'

'I do. I did. This will be better.'

He looked up at Daniel with dull eyes and asked, 'Better how?'

'More powerful.'

The large young man thought for a moment then asked what Daniel had in mind.

'Chip away the chalk from the other side and make it thin and round.'

'How thin?'

'Maybe the thickness of my thumb. Any thinner and it might break. Grind the ridges off the faces and polish them so it they are as smooth as the bottom of a baby and as shiny as a still pool of clear water.'

'Anything else?'

'Yes. Carve a piece of wood to hold the mirror upright.'

'Anything else?'

'No, nothing else.'

'And what will I get for doing this for you?'

'What do you want?'

Without hesitation he replied, 'I want you to teach me how to speak to the angels.'

'Why do you want to speak with them?'

'Because I want them to show me my parents. I want to see them again.'

Daniel reacted kindly to the sadness in his friend's eyes. 'I am afraid it does not happen thusly. The angels do not show me souls who have ascended to Heaven. They only reveal their own visages.'

'Then I would ask them to pass messages to them. I want to know how they are faring and I want them to know how I am faring.'

'But do you not seek this in your own prayers?' Daniel asked.

'I do, but I receive no reply.'

Daniel weighed his response. He hesitated to take on a student. After all, other priests would be envious and would want to know why they were not given a similar opportunity. And his scrying time was precious, carved out from the brief intervals between monastery work, organized prayer, and sleep. But this obsidian stone had a power like none he had ever seen. Without so much as a call, he had seen not one of the minor angels he had conversed with in years past, he had seen *Michael*. The Archangel Michael! The angel who had led God's armies and defeated Satan! And it was Michael who had commanded him to make this mirror. Still, if Thaddeus did not possess a glimmer of scrying ability, then teaching him would be pointless.

'Tell me, Thaddeus,' he said, 'as you hold the stone in your hands, do you notice anything?'

The big priest scrunched his face in thought. 'I notice the stone is heavy.'

'Anything else?'

'I notice it was cool to the touch and now it is warm.'

'Anything else?'

'I notice someone whispering from somewhere in this chamber.'

'Why in Heaven's name did you not mention this in the first instance?' Daniel exclaimed.

'Because I could not understand what was being said and wondered if it was just the rumbling of my belly.'

Daniel ran a hand through his curls then said in exasperation, 'Begin your grinding and your polishing, Thaddeus, and when you are done, I will teach you what you wish to learn. I will teach you how to scry.'

*   *   *

Thaddeus had been in Daniel's cell before, but he had never seen what was hidden under the frame of his bed. Inside a large red pilgrim's bag that Daniel's mother had woven for him when he left home he kept the tools of his spiritual trade, objects the angels had painstakingly instructed him to manufacture. As Thaddeus stood over him, Daniel took out each object, one after another, and laid them carefully upon his mattress.

'What is that?' Thaddeus asked.

'That is the Sigillum Dei Aemeth,' Daniel said. 'The Seal of God. The angels told me what it should look like. I got wax from the beekeepers and had Brother Dinkha inscribe the magic symbols and letters for me. I am not good with my hands, as you know.'

'And that?'

Daniel laid a wooden square on the bed. It too was inscribed with all manner of letters and symbols.

'It is the magic table on which I lay the seal. And these small seals are placed under each corner. Like this.'

By the light of two candles he assembled his magical furniture on the floor. It was nighttime, after compline prayers, and the monastery was dark and still.

'This is the copper bowl that I fill with water,' Daniel said, 'but tonight we will use the black mirror.'

Thaddeus had done a fine job on the stone. Its surfaces were silky smooth now, black as a bottomless pit, and they caught every ray of light.

'Is the mirror better than your bowl?' Thaddeus asked.

Daniel replied, 'I could tell at first glance that it was a miraculous stone. God must have left in my path so that I would find it. I believe in all my heart that with this scrying mirror I will be able to plunge even further into the realm of angels which is the realm of God. Archangel Michael himself revealed himself to me without so much as a call.'

Thaddeus scratched at a sand-fly bite on his arm. 'What is a call?'

'These you will have to learn, Thaddeus if you are to speak to the angels. As you learned Latin, you will learn the angel tongue.'

'Latin was difficult.'

'Angel language is even more difficult. The letters are peculiar. The words do not flow off the tongue with ease. I will help you but you will have to apply yourself.'

'I will try.'

Daniel positioned the candles just so and he and the big priest sat cross-legged, shoulder to shoulder, facing the show-stone in its wooden stand.

'This is the 1st Call,' Daniel said. 'It opens the first gate. I will write it down for you to memorize. But before we begin, heed me. This magic – it must only be used for good. You must never cross into the black arts. Do you understand?'

The big head bobbed in a nod.

'Then we will begin. Are you ready?'

'I am fearful, Daniel, but I am ready.'

Daniel stared into the mirror and chanted. '*Ol sonf vors g, goho Iad Balt, lonsh calz vonpho; sobra zol ror i ta nazps od graa ta malprg; ds holq qaa nothoa zimz, od commah ta nobloh zien; soba thil gnonp prge aldi; ds urbs oboleh grsam; casarm ohorela taba pir; ds zonrensg cab erm iadnah. Pilah farzm znurza adna gono iadpil, ds hom od toh; soba i pam lu ipamis; ds loholo vep zomd poamal, od bogpa aai ta piap piamol od vooan. Zacare, ca, od zamran; odo cicle qaa; zorge, lap zirdo noco mad, hoath Iaida.*'

'What does it mean,' Thaddeus whispered.

Daniel patiently responded, 'This is what I said: I reign over you, sayeth the God of Justice, in power exalted above the firmaments of wrath; in whose hands the Sun is as a sword and the Moon as a through-thrusting fire; which measureth your garments in the midst of my vestures, and trussed you together as the palms of my hands; whose seats I garnished with the fire of gathering, and beautified your garments with admiration. To whom I made a law to govern the holy ones and delivered you a rod with the ark of knowledge. Moreover, you lifted up your voices and swore obedience and faith to him that liveth and triumpheth; whose beginning is not, nor end cannot be, which shineth as a flame in the midst of your palace, and reigneth amongst you as the balance of righteous-ness and truth. Move, therefore, and show yourselves; open the Mysteries of your Creation; be friendly unto me; for I am the servant of the same your God, the true worshipper of the Highest.'

'Oh,' was the fullness of Thaddeus's reply.

Daniel turned back to the stone. 'Now, the second call.'

Daniel slowly worked his way through forty-six of the calls without pausing to translate them for his companion. Even so, it took the better part of an hour for his recitations to be completed. At times he noticed the big priest nodding off and once he felt his block of a head coming onto his shoulder. Each time he nudged him to attention.

Finally, he reached the place he aspired to be – the second Aethyr – where he had his most productive and illuminating conversations. All at once, Daniel's own face disappeared from the surface of the obsidian disk, replaced by a figure of a man with a golden robe and a golden beard riding into view on a golden chariot.

Daniel heard a voice, but it was not coming from the man in the stone. It was Thaddeus asking who the man was.

'You can see him?' Daniel asked.

'Of course I see him. He is right there.'

'That is good, Thaddeus. You will be a scryer one day! This is Archangel Selaphiel, the patron saint of prayer in our Church of the East. He is my teacher. He is my guide.'

The angel spoke to Daniel in his guttural language and Daniel replied.

'What are you saying?' Thaddeus asked.

'He asks who you are. I told him.'

Daniel and the angel spoke more but Daniel would no longer let Thaddeus interrupt him. Only when he was ready did he tell his companion what had transpired. The angel Selaphiel knew that Archangel Michael had commanded him to prepare the powerful black showstone so that Daniel could learn further truths. With this mirror, a great scryer such as Daniel might hope to be granted ever-greater revelations about the universe.

Thaddeus looked into the showstone and told Daniel that Selaphiel was no longer there.

'He has gone,' Daniel said. 'Our time with him has ended.'

'But I wanted to ask him about my parents.'

'Not tonight. In time. Let me say a closing prayer.'

Afterwards, while stashing his spiritual tools in the red bag and sliding it under the bed, Daniel told Thaddeus that he was more than a little surprised that he had been able to see and hear Selaphiel.

'Why?' Thaddeus asked.

'Because few men have the gift of scrying. It is not something that can be taught to one who has no natural ability. Have you ever had visions?'

'Only when I drink too much wine.'

'This is a serious question, Thaddeus.'

The big priest got himself to his feet and rubbed his sore rump. 'Once I looked down into the well to see if the bucket had dropped all the way down and I saw a face in the dark water. Is that a vision?'

'It seems you really do have the gift.'

'What does that mean?'

'If you learn the angel language then you might be able to have your own angel guide and you may have a conversation with him about your parents without me. Tonight, I will write down the first call and tomorrow in your free time you can start to learn it. But do not tell any of the other brothers about what we have done or what we may do in the future. Some will be envious. Others will be fearful, suspecting black magic. It is better to keep it to ourselves.'

'When can we do this again?'

'Learn the 1st Call. Then we will enter the Aethyrs together.'

Weeks passed, then months. Tutoring Thaddeus required infinite patience, but Daniel felt in a curious way that it was a kind of penance to try to teach a new language to a lad who bumbled his Latin and even his native Aramaic. But painstakingly, he was able to get Thaddeus to memorize the calls and to initiate him into the realm of the angels. Daniel was constantly surprised that this rather simple young fellow had a facility for scrying, but it was not for him to judge whom the angels blessed with the knack. Nevertheless, on his own, even with the obsidian showstone, Thaddeus was not able to progress beyond the seventeenth Aethyr. His angel-guide in that realm was a spirit named Kokbiel, whom Daniel (ever the observer) came to know as having something of a dual nature. He was part virtuous and part mischievously bad, seemingly preying on Thaddeus's dark side. Whereas Daniel was a seeker of universal truths who engaged his guiding angel, Selaphiel, in esoteric theological discourse, Thaddeus was rooted in the temporal world. Early on, he had asked about the fate of his parents but Kokbiel told him that such knowledge was held in higher Aethyrs. So instead, he questioned Kokbiel incessantly on matters that Daniel considered furiously mundane. Which of the brother priests was helping himself to extra rations of beer? Would the new bishop – Cyril had died – ever grant him his wished-for assistant in his scythe-making workshop? Had a rich man ever buried gold in the fields surrounding the monastery?

He allowed Thaddeus to observe his own scrying sessions with the new showstone, sessions that were getting him ever closer to the ultimate knowledge contained within the first Aethyr. One night he had this conversation:

Daniel – What will I find when I get there?

Selaphiel – It is a place beyond human existence as you know it.

Daniel – Can you tell me more?

Selaphiel – No.

Daniel – Is it wonderful?

Selaphiel – Yes.

Daniel – Is God there?

Selaphiel – Of course.

Daniel – Has a mortal man ever gone there?

Selaphiel – No.

Daniel – If I get there will you be my guide?

Selaphiel – It will be Michael, the archangel.

Daniel – You have told me before that there is one missing call. Do I require it to gain entry?

Selaphiel – The 49th Call is not for that purpose.

Daniel – What purpose does it have?

Selaphiel – It is for summoning the fallen ones. It is for evil. That is why God does not wish mortal men to learn it. Evil exists in your world, this you know. Yet there is a greater evil.

Thaddeus sometimes let his attention drift away during
Daniel's spiritual actions; sometimes he even fell asleep.
Tonight, he was in rapt attention and after hearing Selaphiel's
pronouncement, he prodded Daniel to ask this question:
Notwithstanding God's concern, could the 49th Call be learned?

Selaphiel – It has never before been passed to mortal man
but yes, even a good angel such as myself could be compelled
to pass the 49th Call to a great magician with a powerful
showstone.

Daniel – Am I such a magician and is this such a stone?

Selaphiel – The stone is powerful and you are the greatest
magician the world has ever known.

Daniel ended his action abruptly, stood, and snuffed out the
candles. The room darkened.

'Why did you not ask him for the 49th Call?' Thaddeus
asked.

'I have no wish to converse with fallen angels. I have no
wish to converse with demons. I have no wish to summon evil.'

The usually phlegmatic Thaddeus became animated and
said, 'But, Daniel, you are the one who always talks about
wanting to know more about God and the universe. Did not
God cast down those angels who sinned against Him? Surely,
you would wish to speak to the fallen ones to greater understand their sins and transgressions and the consequences of
their evil works.'

Daniel was gathering up his spiritual objects. 'It is late,
Thaddeus, and I am tired. Please go now.'

But Thaddeus would not let the matter rest. Day after day,
he pestered Daniel to learn the 49th Call and peppered him
with reasons he should do so. It will increase your enlightenment. Just speaking with the fallen ones does not mean you
will bring down evil. You will become the greatest magician
of all time. Your name will be known through the ages.

Finally, Daniel was worn down by Thaddeus's persistence
and also, perhaps, by his own curiosity and vanity. On a moonless night, he retired to his stuffy cell with Thaddeus and
assembled his table and his seals and his showstone. He
summoned the angel, Selaphiel, who seemed to know what
his intensions were.

'Are you certain you wish to know the 49th Call?' the angel asked.

'I do.'

'Use it with great care, Daniel. The Lord will judge you harshly if you do not. It is for your ears only.'

Soon, a guttural chant that only Daniel could hear was emanating from the showstone. Thaddeus grunted in frustration at not being privy to the call but there was nothing he could do until a visibly shaken Daniel ended the action with his usual prayer.

'Well?' Thaddeus asked. 'Did you get it?'

Daniel's throat was dry and his voice was scratchy. 'It was given, yes.'

'And who was the entity named in the call?'

'I dare not use his name.'

Thaddeus gulped. 'Was the call a long one?'

'Not long, not short.'

'Will you remember it?'

'My mind is troubled. I do not know.'

'You must write it down then lest you forget it.'

'I do not want to remember it.'

'You must write it down. Think of all the questions you might ask. Your learnings will multiply. Your knowledge will be legendary. I will get papyrus and ink from the scriptorium and you must set down the words.'

When Thaddeus returned, Daniel was lying on his bed, curled up and rocking himself. The big priest had to prod and coax him to sit up and write down the call using his magic table as desk. The minute Daniel finished the task, writing the phonemes of angel language in his native Aramaic, he folded the papyrus in two and thrust it down the neck of his robe.

'Let me see it!' Thaddeus said.

'No!' Daniel said. 'It is meant for me and me alone.'

'But I must see it.'

Daniel shooed Thaddeus away with both hands. 'Leave me now. Please. My mind is troubled and I am for sleep.'

But Thaddeus had no intention of leaving. It was the easiest thing for the brute to rip Daniel's robe half off and seize the papyrus.

When Daniel tried to grab it back, Thaddeus delivered a back-handed swat to his face that left him with a bleeding mouth.

'What are you doing, Thaddeus? Why are you treating me to such hard punishment?'

'I am sorry, Daniel. You are a good man, better than me, but I must speak to the fallen ones. I want their help.'

'For what purpose?'

'For avenging my parents. I have never spoken of this. The Turks came to my village when I was a boy. They took all the Christians from their homes and made them stand around the well. They made them renounce Jesus Christ and embrace their faith. Those who did not – their throats were cut. I ran away. Christians found me and took me to this monastery, where I have remained. But I never forgot. I want revenge and I pray the fallen ones will help me if I summon them.'

Daniel was staunching the blood from his lip with his torn garment. 'I am sorry for what happened to you. I truly am. But I cannot allow you to use the call. I swore to Selaphiel.'

'You cannot stop me, Daniel.'

Daniel picked himself off the hard-packed dirt floor. 'We will not be scrying any more. I will not allow you to use my mirror or the other holy objects. Our work together has ended. Give me the papyrus.'

'No.'

'Then I will have no choice but to denounce you to the bishop as a practitioner of black magic.'

In the flickering light of one small candle, Daniel could see Thaddeus's face set and harden. He saw him slowly approach, his meaty hands extended. He felt strong thumbs pressing against his windpipe until not even the softest sound could escape his throat.

And when his lifeless body was dropped to the floor, Thaddeus put the seals, and the table, and the showstone into Daniel's red bag, and left the cell, and left the dormitory. He kept on walking out of the monastery gate and into the darkest night he could ever remember.

FOURTEEN

George Hamid didn't like going to other people's offices. He always wanted them to come to his. This had everything to do with power. The weak visited the strong. He'd learned that during his salad days in Kirkuk, a young man trying to make his way in business, buying this, selling that, observing the habits of men who were many rungs higher on the ladder. When he had become what he then thought was wealthy, he was determined to get into the military surplus business, selling off unused (often pilfered) merchandise such as uniforms, field rations, spare parts for trucks and the like. To do so he started bribing low-level officers then over time he worked his way up the ranks to brigadier generals. When eventually he became known as the surplus king, not only in his province but across the country, men started coming to him, looking for opportunities. At his zenith within his home country, the only time he went calling was to visit Iraqis who were richer and more powerful than he and his most memorable visit was in 1990, four months before the US invasion in the first Gulf War. The man he sought was the richest by far and the most powerful.

Standing in front of the vast pink confection that was Saddam's palace in Kirkuk, his emotions were decidedly mixed. On one hand, his chest swelled with pride at how far his ambitions had taken him. On the other hand, his heart boiled in anger.

Tariq Barzani looked at the building through his mirrored sunglasses and told him that it looked like a hotel, adding that it seemed a bit much for one man.

'It is not just for him,' Hamid said. 'He keeps some whores here for when he comes to Kirkuk. At least that is what the generals tell me.'

Barzani had been made to wait at the guard station when Hamid was shown inside and in an anteroom the size of a basketball court, he had been made to wait for three hours without so much as a soda water. It was another lesson learned. Powerful men knew how to make lesser men understand their weakness.

When he was finally granted admission to a monumental receiving hall decorated with a quarry of pink marble, Saddam was seated in a snow-white armchair decorated with his presidential seal woven in gold thread. A *fareeq*, a lieutenant general, stood by his side and a praetorian guard of soldiers with Belgian sub-machine guns lined the walls.

Even now, Hamid remembered the wave of nausea and disgust he felt at seeing Saddam's coarse face, being there in the belly of the beast.

The general reminded Saddam who Hamid was.

'What is it you want from me?' Saddam said.

Hamid bowed and scraped as required but he did not take the obsequious tone that others had recommended. He had an ace up his sleeve and it gave him confidence.

'Mr President, I would like to receive your permission to sell heavy military surplus equipment you no longer require.'

'What kind of equipment?' Saddam asked.

'Tanks, rocket launchers, aircraft engines – surplus materials the army purchased in years past from Yugoslavia and Ukraine through the Syrians.'

'For a small-time provincial man you seem well informed about where I make my purchases.'

'Mr President, you are correct that I am small-time and provincial and you are also correct that I am well informed.'

That elicited a laugh.

'I have men from Baghdad who are big businessmen, Ba'athists, Muslims who can sell heavy goods. I am aware you have made a lot of money, but it is money you made from buying and selling little things. You are like a little Kirkuk ant. And you are a Christian.'

Today, Hamid perfectly remembered the way Saddam had spat out the word, Christian. He had gone through life in Iraq as a second-class citizen, despised by the majority of his countrymen. He looked at the smug thug of a man and thought, Muslim bastard, I would kill you with my own hands this very minute if I could.

But he would not let his anger show.

'Correct again, Mr President,' he said with confidence.

His swagger must have piqued Saddam's interest. 'Who would you sell to?'

'Africans in half a dozen countries. I have excellent connections.'

'No, it's impossible, isn't it, General?'

The general agreed that it was indeed impossible.

Hamid smiled, again, further driving Saddam's interest. 'I am not an ordinary businessman, Mr President. I have some remarkable powers. If I demonstrate these powers would you consider my proposal?'

'I have ears,' Saddam said. 'Speak.'

'Last week you were staying at the Republican Palace in Baghdad. Late at night you went for a stroll around the swimming pool. Except for your guards you were alone. Two eagles came down from the sky and perched on a date palm. You took it as a good omen.'

Saddam's thick mustache twitched in anger. 'Who told you this?'

'I assure you, Mr President, I do not know a soul in your inner circles and I have never even been to your palace.'

'Then how did you know about the eagles?'

'An angel told me, Mr President.'

Saddam looked up at the general, who responded with a shrug. Then Saddam laughed again a little nervously. 'How much will you give me on the sale of this military equipment?' he asked.

'Fifty percent, Mr President.'

'I require seventy-five.'

'Then it will be seventy-five, Mr President,' Hamid said, extending a hand, surprised that the palm of the most powerful man in the country was moist.

And that was that, if not for this irony: while Hamid had foreseen the eagles, he had not thought to ask the angels about the Americans, who would soon invade, sending Iraq into paroxysms of paranoia and chaos. Power vacuums were to form, old checks and balances would evaporate. Ba'athist officials in Kirkuk would manage to seize Hamid's businesses and drive him into poverty. He would save himself and what remained of his family, by spying on Saddam's government for a CIA operative who infiltrated Kirkuk. Had he not done so, his US visa would not have materialized and he would have likely died in Iraq during the subsequent years of conflict.

He rode to the top floor of the midtown Manhattan office building with Barzani at his side, then presented himself to the woman who was waiting at the elevator doors.

'Mr Hamid, let me take you to see Mr Stern.' She asked for Barzani's name, but Hamid told her not to worry, that his associate would wait in the reception area.

Leonard Stern played in the same space as Hamid, mid-tier residential rental buildings that boasted hundred-percent occupancy. The two men had been not-so-friendly competitors for years. Time and time again they went after the same assets, whether they really wanted to own them or not, sometimes just to bid up a building and drop out when the other man trumped their offer, leaving the sucker holding the bag. But a year earlier, there had been a property in Brooklyn – a four-hundred-unit building – that Hamid really wanted to own, only to be outgunned by Stern.

Stern wasn't as flashy as Hamid. His office was relatively small with a rather ordinary view. Hamid forced a smile.

Stern said, 'George, come in, have a seat. Can I get you anything?'

'I'm good, Lennie.'

'I was surprised you called me,' Stern said, settling down in one of the armchairs. 'I think this is the first time you've been up here.'

'I think that's correct. You've been to mine, right?'

'Once, if I recall. Killer views.'

'They are,' Hamid agreed.

'Congratulations on going public. Sounds like a great deal.'

'It was. We raised a lot of money. The stock's up. I'm worth a few billion more.'

Through an artificial smile Stern said, 'Glad to hear you're doing well. So, to what do I owe the honor of your presence?'

Hamid went right for it. 'I want to buy Grayson Court.'

Stern looked over the top of his glasses. 'My Grayson? In Carroll Gardens?'

'The very one.'

'My Grayson that I outbid you on a year ago?'

'That's right, Lennie.'

'Why would I do that?'

'Because I'm going to give you a good price.'

Ever-practical, Stern said, 'Shoot.'

Stern almost slid off his chair at the number. 'Are you crazy, George? That was your last bid before I raised it by ten percent! On top of that I've done some improvements. On top of that the market's up in that neighborhood. So, with all due respect, jump in the river.'

Hamid nodded as if he understood the points but said, 'It's a very generous offer, actually. I could have come in lower given the circumstances.'

'What circumstances?'

Hamid was ready. This was going down perfectly. 'Seven months ago you had a bit of a family problem. You were successful in covering it up. Life went on. Smooth sailing on the good ship Stern.'

'I don't know what you're talking about but whatever it is has nothing to do with real estate.'

'It's got everything to do with it. You're a fortunate man, Lennie. You've got a son who's going to take over your business one day. A good kid, I understand. Me? My son got killed in Iraq in George Bush's war. Bush One. Remember it? Anyway, your boy was at a party seven months ago where a girl had an overdose of drugs. These drugs. Such a problem. Your son and two of his friends didn't do nothing for her. They didn't call 911. They didn't take the girl to the hospital. She died. But your son made one call. He called you and you came. You paid his two friends a lot of money to take the fall and say your son wasn't even there. They went to jail. Your son is back at college up in Boston. Lennie, Lennie, if you don't take my offer, I'll pay these boys much more to tell the truth and drag your son back into it. He'll go to jail too, I think. There. That's it. A very simple offer. You can see that I could have been a real bastard and offered you a lot less.

As I'm thinking about it, if you take too much offense, I will drop the price and I will keep dropping it until you say, thank you, George, we have a deal.'

Stern looked like he'd lost most of his muscle tone. He went pale and could hardly speak. 'How? Who the hell told you about this?'

'Some people talk to little birdies. I talk to angels.'

'That's not fucking funny. Where did you get your information?'

'Believe me or don't believe me. I don't care. All you need to do is tell me this, Lennie. Do we have a deal?'

Hamid lived in one of the premier buildings in Manhattan. When he was merely very rich he bought one of the penthouses and when he became a billionaire he bought a second one, combined the units, and did a gut renovation. His daughter was married now and his wife thought it was ridiculous for only two people to live in eighteen thousand square feet of space on two floors. Not Hamid. He had heard from the condo board chairman that another unit just below him was coming to the market and he wanted that one too. For the staff.

The apartment was so large that he didn't bother calling out for her. It was pointless and she never cared to learn how to use the room-to-room intercoms. She was usually in the kitchen and that's where he found her. She was as wide in the beam as he was, but it didn't bother him. He wasn't particularly interested in sex – nor was she – and he didn't look for it elsewhere. His doctor had asked him about his libido once and wanted to check his testosterone, but Hamid had told him no thanks, he was fine. He also didn't read books or watch much television other than Fox News, which was on mute stand-by in most rooms. What he did was work – sixteen hours a day – and pray frequently, not in a church, but in his own way.

'How was your day?' his wife asked in Arabic.

'Good. I bought a building.'

'That's nice,' she said in a way that showed she didn't give a damn. 'I'm going to the kids. They've got a dinner at Arthur's boss's apartment and I'm going to babysit.'

Their daughter was ten when they came to America. Her first husband was an American loser, in the opinion of her parents. They were happy there hadn't been any children from that marriage and happier still that he was out of their lives. Her second husband was Iraqi-American, a Christian, and an anesthesiologist. It was all good except that his new son-in-law had zero interest in the real-estate business so, God willing, he would have to keep himself in the saddle until his grandson was ready to take the reins. Hamid's only son was nineteen when he was conscripted into Saddam's army just before the Americans invaded. He died in a bombing raid in the defense of Baghdad. When he fled Iraq in 1994, he had been forced to leave his elderly parents behind but before he could send for them a mob looted their clothing store and shot them dead, leaving anti-Christian slogans on the walls in their own blood.

'I'll have Tariq drive you,' Hamid said.

'I can take a taxi.'

'Use Tariq. I don't need him tonight. I don't need Sara either.'

'She left lamb in the refrigerator.'

'I'll be fine. Kiss the little ones for me.'

After he finished his supper, it was still light. His huge office on the upper floor of his apartment was through-to-through east to west, with one balcony overlooking the Hudson, the other, the East River. He had a smartphone app that allowed him, with the push of a button, to lower the window shades and once the space was all but blacked out, he went to a locked closet and opened it.

He had fled Iraq with only three suitcases for his entire family and one of the cases was half-taken up by the objects now in the closet. He had wrapped them in his shirts, trousers, and underwear. His wife had complained about leaving behind other possessions, but he would not budge. These things were more precious than anything else. He was only glad he didn't have to choose between them and say, his daughter. He had sawn off the legs of the ceremonial table; new ones could be fashioned. The wax seals were the most fragile and required the most padding. His showstone, a small, pretty crystal ball, took up the least space. That went into his shaving bag cushioned by a Kirkuk Football Club T-shirt.

His routine was a well-worn one. After positioning the ceremonial table legs on the four small seals, placing the large seal on the table, and draping everything with a red silk cloth, he put his showstone at the center of the Sigillum Dei Aemeth and set his candles to cast their light on the crystal. His prayers to God were in Arabic. His calls were in angel language. He was aware that in the modern world of Enochian magic, no practitioner was said to have reached the second Aethyr. He had been a constant visitor to that exalted realm for forty years. He was discreet. Other than his wife and Tariq no one knew about his magic and he had no intention of ever widening the circle.

The angel was waiting for him standing on his golden chariot. Hamid greeted him in angel language like an old friend.

'I have returned,' he said.

The Archangel Selaphiel opened the conversation as he always did. 'What do you seek?'

'I seek truth. I seek enlightenment.'

Again, his standard reply. 'You have come to the right place.'

'What you told me about my rival, Leonard Stern, was true. I gained an advantage.'

'I will always speak the truth.'

'I know.'

'Has this truth brought you peace?'

Hamid thought before answering. 'It brought me more wealth. Wealth brings me satisfaction, not peace. Only one outcome will bring me that.'

The angel knew what that was. Hamid had spoken his mind before, many, many times.

'You are the most powerful magician alive but nevertheless you cannot have what you desire.'

'I almost had the black showstone but I am certain I will get it. I also seek the 49th Call.'

'There were only two in the history of mankind who had the power to obtain the forbidden call.'

'How did they obtain it?'

'I gave it to them.'

Hamid was incredulous. The angel had never told him this. 'Then why will you not give it to me?'

Selaphiel's golden robe glowed brighter. 'The evil that was set upon the Earth was too great. Such an evil must never be allowed to rain down again. I will not be the giver of the call. But hear me. You are not the only seeker.'

Hamid stiffened. 'Who else?'

'Calvin Donovan, the man who possesses the black showstone, and Eve Riley, a strong magician.'

Hamid leaned in until his face was only inches from his crystal ball. 'Tell me more.'

'They have scryed together. Her angel is Pothnir. He resides in the fourth Aethyr. There are powerful ripples moving through the Aethyrs. This man and this woman seek the forbidden call.'

'Toward what end?'

'They wish to stop you from possessing it.'

'Do they know my intentions?'

'They know only that you have a great evil in your heart.'

'It is true, Lord Selaphiel. I cannot rest until I have gotten my full measure of revenge.'

FIFTEEN

On a hot and hazy day, Cal drove to Fort Devens, about forty miles west of Boston. Ever since the closure of the army base, the FBI operated a firearms training center on the sprawling campus. Cal drove around lost until he found the place and presented himself to a guard. His name was on a list. Inside the range clubhouse Julia D'Auria was waiting in a pair of khakis and an FBI polo shirt.

'Sorry I'm late,' Cal said. 'This place is a labyrinth.'

She looked somewhere between pissed off and cheerful. 'No problem. Special Agent Nesserian got tied up. It's just me. You ready?'

'Absolutely. Thanks for doing this.'

He heard something that sounded like a grunt.

D'Auria was suffering the consequences for strong-arming the Cambridge police chief to not only approve but fast-track Cal's conceal/carry firearms permit. Cambridge had one of the lowest per capita license rates in the state and the chief wasn't thrilled about being pressured. His response to Nesserian's call was basically, fine, if you're such an advocate, personally certify that the applicant is competent in firearm safety and use. And that meant blowing a Saturday morning. When Nesserian got called into another case, the burden fell to D'Auria, who was in Massachusetts working the bookstore murder.

D'Auria took Cal over to an indoor range with eight lanes and asked him by way of the first lesson, 'What do you need before we enter?'

'Plugs and glasses.'

He got nothing more than a curt nod and figured she was either always like this or just in a bad mood.

She gave him soft earplugs and safety glasses. Seven of the lanes were taken with special agents doing mandatory recertifications. A haze of gunpowder was in the air. Even with earplugs, the pistol fire was loud. Their reserved lane was down on the far end.

'You ready?' she said loud enough for him to hear.

He gave a thumbs-up and she pulled her sidearm from the molded plastic safety holster clipped to her waistband. She pointed the weapon downrange, ejected the magazine, and cleared the round in the chamber with a smooth pull, finishing the action with the flourish of catching the ejected round before it hit the counter.

The pistol was a small-frame Glock, but he didn't recognize the model. He asked what it was.

'Glock 19M,' she said loud enough. 'It's the new FBI standard issue. It's lightweight, shoots a 9 by 19-millimeter round, uses a fifteen-round mag, has excellent rapid-fire characteristics, low recoil, and just about never jams.'

'I used the Beretta M9 in the army,' he said over the racket.

'I didn't know you were a vet,' she said.

'It was a long time ago.'

She handed him the gun and watched what he did with it. He passed the first test by pointing downrange as she had done, and rechecking, manually and visibly, that the chamber was indeed cleared.

'Let me see you empty the mag and reload it,' she said.

He popped the ammo out with his thumb then smoothly filled the double-stack and seated the magazine. Then a pro move: he racked the slide, ejected the magazine, added one more round, then re-seated it. He placed the gun on the counter, barrel pointed downrange, and looked at her.

'Fifteen plus one,' he said.

He didn't expect any praise, so he wasn't disappointed. Instead she handed him a silhouette target and told him to send it out fifteen feet.

'How many rounds?' he asked.

'Empty the weapon. Take your time.'

There were things you didn't forget and shooting a pistol was one of them. He'd been drilled like crazy in the army and had achieved an expert marksmanship badge, the highest award. The gun felt good in his hands and the night sights were bright. He extended both arms and acquired the target then began squeezing off rounds, one every second. When the slide locked open, he ejected the empty mag, put the weapon down, and pushed the target-return button. He glanced at it before taking it down and handing it to her.

She was poker-faced at the four-inch grouping around the bullseye.

'Okay, reload and let's see how you do at twenty feet.'

They grabbed a table near some vending machines.

'You want a coffee or something?' Cal asked.

'The coffee here is lethal. I'll have a Diet Pepsi.'

She folded his targets while he got the drinks.

When he sat down he asked if he passed.

'You shoot better than I do,' she said, 'and I'm not bad.'

'Like riding a bicycle. I like your gun. I might as well get the same model. If I change careers and apply to the FBI I can say on the application I already have the gear.'

She finally smiled. 'You're a bit old for a recruit.'

'That hurts. How long have you been in?'

'Eleven years.'

'Always worked in New York?'

'I started in Columbus then got moved to Charleston, West Virginia. I've only been in New York for two years.'

'Like it?'

'It's pretty dynamic. Lots of big cases.'

'And then there's my case.'

'Two dead, one armed-home invasion. It's big to me.'

'Thanks for saying that.'

Her jaw rippled before she spat it out. 'I want to apologize.'

'For what?'

'I've been kind of a dick today. I'm carrying some domestic problems to work and I shouldn't do that. You ever been married?'

'Never.'

'You said that emphatically.'

'You noticed.'

'I'm on my first. We're having a moment. It's my third weekend in a row working.'

'And he's pissed at you?'

'*She's* pissed at me. Funnily enough her name's also Jessica. By the way, I thought your Jessica was pretty cool when I interviewed her.'

'She's a force of nature.'

'Mine is too and right now that force is basically volcanic.'

'Sorry to hear it. I'm afraid I'm the last person in the world to offer relationship advice.'

She changed the subject to his trip to Arizona. 'How'd it go?'

'It was interesting.'

'Yeah? Interesting how?'

'The woman I told you about, Eve Riley – she's very knowledgeable about magic and angels.'

'Name a subject, there's an expert,' she said. 'How did she get to be an expert? Don't tell me they teach it at some bullshit college.'

'Well, it's not taught at the Divinity School.'

'Yet.'

'Maybe I'll work in a course next year,' he joked. 'As I understand it, these scryers, which she is, are born with the ability to see angels in reflective surfaces like showstones. I don't think there are more than a few dozen of them in the United States but by all accounts, she's at the top of the pyramid.'

'What did she say about your stone?'

'She said it was very powerful.'

'So, it was the real deal, according to Ms Riley.'

'It was. Her angel told her it was powerful too.'

D'Auria slurped down some Pepsi. 'Her angel.'

'Your skepticism abounds,' Cal said.

'Does it show? Did her angel have a name?'

'Pothnir.'

'After Gabriel, that was the name I would have guessed.'

Cal snorted at that.

'This Pothnir – male or female?'

'Male. He's high up in the angel organizational chart. Apparently, all the important ones are male,' he said.

'So what else is new? What did he have to say about the 49th Call your attacker was looking for?'

'Well, that was the interesting part. He said that it was something for summoning evil. The great evil was how he put it. Marry up the 49th Call with my showstone and a powerful magician and the world's going to be in deep shit.'

'Deep shit. That's the technical term?'

'My description.'

'And did this angel of hers tell you where you could find the call?'

'He didn't, but he said my father found it. Presumably it was when he worked in Iraq, but I don't really know that. I do know that I didn't inherit any Aramaic papyri and I didn't find any among my mother's things. I'm going to see if I can find any of his papers and excavation notes floating around the Peabody Museum at Harvard. Anyway, that's my plan.'

'You were there, I wasn't. What's your opinion? Do you think Ms Riley fed you a bullcrap sandwich?'

Cal, ever the teacher, thought this was a pretty good teachable moment.

'You know, Special Agent D'Auria, I make a living studying and lecturing on religion. With the exception of miracles, which are tangible manifestations of spirituality that ordinary people might visualize, religion relies on faith. You believe something hard enough and it becomes real to you. I might not hold a particular belief that's held by another person, but I can appreciate their position. But I've got to tell you something about Eve Riley and her angel. He knew something about my father that no one but me could have known.'

'Oh yeah? What was that?'

'He knew I had his trowel, the one he used for archeology, with his initials carved into the handle.'

'You ever been to Las Vegas?'

'Sure. Why?'

'They've got mentalists who go on stage and do that shit all the time.'

'I suppose in your line of work it's good to be a skeptic,' he said. 'According to this angel, the same man who killed my mother and tried to kill me also killed my father thirty years ago.'

'I'll keep that in mind,' she said, draining her soda and landing a long-distance can-toss into the trash can.

'Basketball player?' Cal asked.

'Point guard in college.'

'Well, you've got my report from angel-land. Anything new on your end?'

'Unfortunately, not much. We released CCTV photos of the suspect from Cambridge and New York to the media and we've been working through tips from the public but nothing's panning out yet. Hope springs eternal.'

They got up to leave.

'Yes, it does,' he said.

On Sunday afternoons, the non-public areas at the Peabody Museum were usually quiet, particularly on a Sunday after the end of the Spring term. As soon as June hit, most of the grad students and faculty members in the Anthropology

Department beat a hasty retreat, and if not for his quest, Cal would have been among the evacuees.

Cal touched his museum keycard to the card reader. The door unlocked and he went in. The rooms where non-exhibited artifacts and supporting documentation were stored were not healthy places if you had a respiratory condition. The archives were musty and dusty – the kind of wooden-floored spaces found in nineteenth-century red-brick college buildings. Excavation notes, journals, and photos from archeological digs were generally considered to be the property of the professor, but many retiring faculty members left their papers at the Peabody for research purposes. When Hiram Donovan passed away his department contacted Cal's mother who willingly signed over her husband's papers to the museum where they had remained, rarely, if ever, consulted these past decades.

It had been years since Cal looked through his father's Peabody papers and that had been a cursory review on the occasion of him securing his joint appointment in anthropology. It had been that department's first dual professorship with the Divinity School, and given his father's outsize role in Near Eastern archeology, it had been a matter of pride all around. Now, with the memory of Hiram Donovan within the department fading, Cal felt nothing but melancholy standing before the file drawers that held his father's legacy.

Donovan's excavations at the Rabban Hurmizd Monastery had spanned four seasons, culminating in the fateful 1989 dig. Cal's first order of business was finding out whether any of the paperwork from the dig was archived and if so, whether the notes from the 1989 season had been transferred to Cambridge upon his father's death. He knew for a fact that there had never been comprehensive publications arising from the excavation, only a few cursory reports from the first two seasons. The full excavation report was among the professor's many unfinished professional tasks. What was clear, however, was that none of the excavated artifacts should have been shipped back to Cambridge – per the joint Harvard/Baghdad University Excavation Agreement, all the finds were required to go to the Baghdad Museum. And that made his pilfering of the obsidian mirror shocking to Cal. What could he have been thinking when he mailed it back to Cambridge? Was Eve right? Had the showstone had literally spoken to him?

When he opened the first file drawer he released more mustiness into the air. Someone had done a good filing job because the folders were in chronological order with clear, typed labels. The very earliest folders were from 1956. They contained research notes and photos from his father's initial excavation as a Harvard graduate student at a biblical site in Israel. The work had formed the basis for his doctoral disser- tation. Cal spent a few minutes perusing the material, purely out of nostalgia. Hiram Donovan had always written with a calligraphy nib on his fountain pen and that gave his writing an Edwardian flair. From the 1950s, Cal motored, opening up one drawer after another until he got to the last cabinet. There he found what he was looking for: *Rabban Hurmizd – 1986: 1 of 6*. Flipping forward, he quickly counted the six thick file folders from the first season of the excavation. Deeper in the drawer were binders from the 1987 and 1988 seasons but there was nothing from 1989. Had the notes from the last season remained in Iraq?

There was one last file cabinet drawer with his father's name. Cal opened it and saw several folders marked, *H. Donovan – Miscellaneous*. One of the them contained a jumble of material that Cal instantly recognized as coming from Iraq and when he pulled it out and had a closer look, it was clear these were the unsorted papers from the 1989 dig.

He took that folder to a reading table and began organizing the papers while looking for anything illuminating. In a bound excavation journal he found a grid map of a trench called Cutting 9 and a notation that immediately grabbed his atten- tion. One square meter, designated Cutting 9/G 18, was marked with a small X at a depth of 3.6 meters. The accompanying note written in his father's distinctive calligraphy read: 'Polished obsidian disk.' The notation was dated a week before the date that Cal always carried with him – the day his father died. He went through every entry in the journal looking for any mention of papyrus scrolls but came up empty. The very last item in the folder, however, was upsetting. It was a photo, apparently taken by someone from the top of the deep trench, clearly marked Cutting 9, showing a police officer crouching over Hiram Donovan's twisted body.

Phlegm filled his throat. He swallowed hard. His father had died in the same cutting where he had found the showstone. The family had been told that he died of a broken neck. Now Cal wondered that if he had been murdered, whether he had been alive or dead when someone threw him in.

All field archeologists knew that related objects were not always found during the same excavation season. With that in mind he started going through previous seasons, starting with the first in 1986, looking for items that might be temporally related to the obsidian disk. A great many artifacts had been found and logged and it took over an hour to slog through the material, but when he was done he had nothing to show for the time. The same was true for the 1987 season. The afternoon was turning to evening and he had a date with Jessica he didn't want to cancel. He thought that the 1988 season might have to wait for another day, but decided at least to take a peek to scope out the effort. But in the first folder from 1988, an index card with a name and address caught his eye. It was for someone named Omar Rasouly at the Institute of Archeology in London. He didn't know him personally, but he recognized the name as someone who'd been working in Middle Eastern archeology for decades. It was Rasouly's area of specialization that was more than a little interesting – he was an expert in translating and studying Aramaic papyrus manuscripts.

He called Jessica, who answered testily.

'You're not canceling on me.'

'Hell no.'

She sounded like she was on a hair-trigger. 'What then? You canceled our tennis date this morning to go shooting with your new FBI buddy.'

'She's married.'

'So that's stopped a determined woman before?'

'She's also gay.'

'Now you're making me feel better.'

'I was just hoping we could move the dinner from Boston to Cambridge.'

'Why?'

'I've got a little more work to do and I didn't want to be late. We can stay the night in my place or we can go back to Boston after dinner.'

She hadn't done a sleepover at Cal's house since the break-in.

'Is your new security system working?'

'It is.'

'Is the fucking black mirror there?'

'Nope.' It was in the bag by his feet.

'Then it's a date.'

The journal entry that would make all the difference was dated July 21, 1988. According to Hiram Donovan's notes, an Iraqi student had been digging in a relatively new area, Cutting 9, opened toward the end of the 1987 season. The first three meters of more modern deposits had been dug through relatively quickly, but work had slowed when they had reached the era of greatest interest to the dig. At a depth of three meters, they began seeing pottery and other artifacts of an eleventh-century origin – and subsequent radiocarbon data from charred human bones found within the burned and collapsed scriptorium had confirmed the dating. On July 21st the student named Mina Almasi found a shallow pit at a depth of 3.2 meters with sixty-two postage-stamp-size fragments of papyrus. The grid reference for the find was Cutting 9/L 14. According to his father, the writing on the papyri was Aramaic. A later journal entry noted that all paleographic material was being sent to Professor Omar Rasouly for analysis.

Cal rapidly leafed through the rest of the journal looking for more information about the papyri and found a second entry of interest, this one from late in the season, toward the end of August. In grid 9/N 13 another twenty-four papyrus fragments were found. And then, a week later, a third and final find of inscribed papyri (nineteen fragments), this one in grid 9/M 14. These too were sent to Rasouly. But that was the extent of it. There was no correspondence between Omar Rasouly and his father concerning the papyri, and no journal entries from any season concerning Rasouly's work. When he picked up the journal to put it back in the file cabinet, a never-posted air-mail envelope dropped from inside the back cover. Inside was a reminder note Hiram Donovan had written to himself.

One fragment from 9/M 14 omitted from last Rasouly batch. Need to send on.

A small glassine envelope, the kind used in stamp collecting, was inside the larger envelope. Cal opened it and a piece of papyrus fell onto his palm.

He got very excited very quickly. The lettering was Aramaic. His Aramaic was serviceable – not as good as an internationally known expert like Omar Rasouly, but he could do a reasonable translation of most variants. There were five distinct words on the papyrus but on fast inspection, they made no sense. It was gobbledygook.

A text from Jessica sent him scrambling. She was at the restaurant – where the hell was he?

He put everything back into the file drawer except for the piece of papyrus, which he slid back into its envelopes and into his bag. He had promised Jessica that the 'fucking black mirror' wouldn't be at his home so he took the padded envelope and slipped it among his father's papers.

'Here you go, Dad,' he said.

He turned out the lights and took off after noticing that the archive door hadn't completely shut on its own. He pushed it closed and made a mental note to let the maintenance people know.

Sunrise came early this time of year. Cal awoke when the first light began to leak around the bedroom curtains. He took care not to disturb Jessica, brewed a coffee, and went to the living room to place a call to London, where it was just past ten. A woman answered. Cal asked to speak with Omar Rasouly. He didn't know his exact age, but he reckoned, based on his curriculum vitae and when he had received his graduate degree from the University of Paris, that Rasouly was in his mid- to late seventies. The departmental secretary at the Institute of Archeology told him that Professor Rasouly no longer came into work on a regular basis but when Cal identified himself as a professional colleague from Harvard, she was more helpful. Cal wrangled Rasouly's home phone number from her and rang it straight away.

A craggy voice answered in a French accent.

Cal started to introduce himself but Rasouly interrupted.

'I used to know a Professor Donovan.'

'My father. Hiram Donovan.'

'Where was he? Was it Harvard or Yale?'

'Harvard. I'm at Harvard too.'

'I remember when he died. It was very sad.'

'Professor Rasouly, you were doing the paleographic work for the dig at Rabban Hurmizd. I wanted to revisit my father's research and perhaps pull together the excavation report that was never written.'

'That would be nice.'

'So, with that in mind, I was trying to find out if you had ever done any analysis on the papyrus fragments from the third season of the dig. That would have been in 1988.'

'Let me think. It was a long time ago, wasn't it? You know, I don't believe I did any analysis. When Hiram died the funding for the project died with him.'

'Where are the fragments now? Do you know?'

'I don't know. Somewhere at the Institute, I expect. These days I don't go into the office much, but they haven't locked me out yet.'

'If I come to the Institute later this week, say Friday, could you let me see them? I can do the translations myself if you're busy.'

'You know Aramaic?'

'Biblical Aramaic, mainly.'

'What day did you say?'

'Friday.'

'I'm sorry, what was your name again?'

'Calvin Donovan. I'll ring you on Thursday when I get to London to confirm.'

'Hiram Donovan was a wonderful man, you know. I do remember him.'

Tariq Barzani was waiting when his boss arrived for work. Hamid knew from his eager expression that Barzani had something for him.

'What is it?'

'The microphone I left at Donovan's house picked this up earlier this morning.'

He opened his laptop and played the file.

As Hamid listened his face softened into something approaching pleasure.

'Fly to London tonight,' he said when the recording was over. 'Find the papyrus before Donovan gets it.'

'And the black mirror?'

'I doubt Donovan will travel with it. He's probably got it hidden away somewhere. Once we have the 49th Call we can turn our attention to the showstone again. I have a mind to kidnap the woman who was with him that night. He'll trade it for her, don't you think?'

Barzani grinned at the prospect. 'Tying her up again will be my pleasure.'

SIXTEEN

Mortlake, England, 1582

John Dee was furiously spitting venom like a cornered serpent.

'Your name is Kelley! Edward Kelley. Edward Talbot is a fiction. You have deceived me! I invited you into my house. You supped at my table!'

Kelley's head was bowed in a show of penitence. He stood before a seated Dee in his inner sanctum like a naughty pupil. Under the name of Edward Talbot, he had scryed for Dee for several months. The two of them had made slow but steady progress, learning the angel alphabet, symbol by symbol, and the language, word by word. They had been given a glimpse of the celestial knowledge they might receive in the future when Dee learned of the subterfuge and abruptly put an end to their association. A distraught Kelley had fled north to his family home in Worcester and it had taken half a year for

Francis Walsingham to persuade him to return to London and attempt a reconciliation. Now, on a cold November night, he presented himself at the house by the Thames, prepared to do whatever it took to reestablish himself into Dee's good graces.

'It was but a trifle, Doctor Dee, but I do accept that I engaged in a deception. My reputation was sullied by false accusations and I did not wish those falsehoods to interfere with my prospects.'

'Well, sir, I know the reason,' Dee fumed. 'I had occasion during the month of May to speak with Barnabus Saul, who informed me of these so-called falsehoods. You are a forger. You are a thief. That is why I banished you from my employ.'

'None of this is true. I beg you to see through the veil of lies to the truth. Surely you must see that Barnabus Saul is a man embittered because I displaced him.'

'Yet you freely admit to using a false name! If the allegations are untrue why did you not give me your family name?'

'May I sit?' Despite his staff he was wobbling on his bad leg and Dee took pity on him. 'Thank you. The reason is a simple one. I greatly wished to secure employment in your household and I did not want false allegations about past misdeeds to intercede.'

'Once again, you make statement about false claims. Why do you suppose persons made such allegations?'

Kelley lowered his voice. 'The times we live in, Doctor.'

Dee asked him what he meant by such an enigmatic assertion.

'Some gentlemen with whom I was doing business – I was engaged in the export of certain goods to the Low Countries – these gentlemen sought to seize advantage by having false charges brought against me. I was held in an unhealthful prison for weeks and when my time came to answer these charges they whispered to the judge that I was a papist. My judgment came swiftly without any due consideration for the facts of the matter, and a harsh physical punishment was meted out. You can see the results inflicted upon my poor body with your own eyes.'

Dee listened in rapt attention, his visage losing some of its sharp edge. 'Is it true? Are you a Catholic?'

The man winced. 'Am I to be judged harshly again for my beliefs?'

Dee rose to pour two cups of watered wine. He offered one to Kelley.

'My past is known to many but perhaps not to you,' Dee said, sitting back down. 'I am a loyal subject of Her Most Gracious Majesty the Queen. Her realm is Protestant and this is a Protestant household. However, I was not always a Protestant, a common fact for men and women of my age. I was born a Catholic under a Catholic king. Beyond that fact of birth, as a young man I elected to become a priest and took Holy Orders.'

Kelley pretended he did not know. 'You, sir, a priest?'

'It is an indelible part of my history. However, as we are painfully aware, the circumstances in England changed. King Henry was the architect of these changes. He made the country Protestant. Young King Edward perpetuated the faith. With his untimely death, Queen Mary did reverse course and we were once again a Catholic land. Then, a few short years later, Queen Elizabeth did restore her father's religion. And all the while, Protestants and Catholics caught on the wrong side of history did suffer and burn. As for me, I renounced Holy Orders and my vow of celibacy and here I am, a devotee of the Queen's religion, a husband, and a father. But despite my devotion to the Crown and all my good work and services thereunder, my Catholic past has been an impediment toward my attaining royal patronage and remuneration. So, I say this to you, Master – Kelley, it is easy for me to believe that you might have been persecuted by unscrupulous men on account of your religion.'

Kelley broke down in tears which seemed to make the unsentimental Dee uncomfortable. He bade him to drink down his wine.

'Your kind words do touch me, Doctor Dee.' When his eyes were dry he looked up from his cup and asked, 'May I ask you something? When born a Catholic can one truly leave the old religion behind? Does it not bubble up in one's soul like a spring of fresh water?'

Dee looked at him through hooded eyes and answered cautiously, 'Is your soul bathed by this spring?'

Kelley whispered his reply, as if they were in a crowded tavern. It had been a while since he had spoken the truth about his life and this was the truth. 'I wear a Protestant cloak, but my flesh is Catholic. May I ask of your belief?'

Dee considered his reply and then said, 'I endeavor not to look back. I am a natural philosopher, a seeker of knowledge, and therefore I am inclined to look forward. I am also a practical man. If today the Queen tells me to wear black, I will wear black. If tomorrow she tells me to wear yellow, then yellow will be my color.'

Outside the window the daylight was gone and if it were not for the candles Dee had lit earlier, the room would have been dark. He asked Kelley if he was of a mind to stay the night and undertake a spiritual action.

'That would please me more than anything, Doctor Dee,' the young man gushed.

'Then I will go outside to use the privy and then we will get to our work to be followed by a late supper.'

Once alone, Kelley went limp like a rag doll, breathing hard in relief. He rapidly composed himself, seizing the opportunity, his actions guided by Walsingham's unseen hand. There was a pile of correspondence on Dee's desk and he began to rifle through it. One particular letter set his already fluttering heart beating even faster.

Dee found his wife in the kitchen plucking a chicken. His young son, Arthur, was crawling on the floorboards, chasing a bug.

She looked up from her task and simply asked, 'Well?'

'I did speak with him about his deceit,' he answered.

'I did not see him leave,' she said.

'He is still here. We will conduct a spiritual action and then we will eat. He will stay the night.'

Jane pursed her lips and said nothing. Dee imagined she was wordlessly counting to prevent an eruption.

'Do not hesitate to speak, Jane,' he said.

'Then I would ask you to explain yourself, husband.'

'When I put to him what I learned from Barnabus, he freely admitted the transgression. He told me he did not wish to lose the opportunity for employment. He maintains his good name was sullied by disreputable business partners who did influence a judge to rule in their favor by invoking his Catholic beliefs.'

'And you believed this?'

'I found him persuasive. He is not the only one in this country who has been cruelly persecuted for his faith.'

Her plucking became fiercer. Feathers fell like snowflakes. The toddler turned his attention to the shower and began gathering them up in his tiny hands.

'Husband, I applaud you for your Christian charity, but I shudder with the knowledge that this man remains under our roof. I will have no more to say on the matter.'

The two men fell back into their routine as if their last scrying session had only just taken place. Dee set up his holy furniture and his companion's black showstone, invoked a prayer, and watched Edward Kelley's face for the flicker of recognition that would signal an angelic presence.

Would it be Raphael? It had been Raphael who, until their sessions came to a halt, had been painstakingly teaching Dee the angel language. The basis for the language was twenty-one regular characters and an additional aspirated one, pronounced not with a hard sound but with a strong burst of air. Each of the characters bore a name and, as in Hebrew, when strung together to form words, they were read from right to left. Likewise, when the words formed the pages in revealed texts, the books were read back to front. There the comparison ended because angel language bore no other relationship to Hebrew or any other known tongue. To Dee, learning angel-speak was not the academic exercise of mastering a dead form. He considered it to be very much a living language that humanity had lost and would now reclaim. As he saw it, the knowledge would set him on a course toward the ultimate wisdom, to the long-awaited rediscovery of the Book of Nature, establishing the lost links between Adam and the angels and God Himself.

But the task was arduous. Although Dee was a linguistic scholar, this divine language did not conform to any known rules of grammar, syntax, or pronunciation and the angels had warned him that even the smallest error would have profound significance in obscuring the results. Dee spent a great deal of energy trying to master the way it was spoken so he could form his speech just like the angels to elevate it from the mortal to the immortal. The process was made even more difficult and complex by the very nature of the instruction. Everything had to pass through the eyes and mouth of his scryer who was the only one who could see and hear the angels within the showstone. For these lessons, it was Raphael who appeared in Kelley's black mirror standing on a table covered in the angelic letters, pointing with the tip of a long rod, spelling out long passages of text, letter by letter. Not surprisingly, some of the angelic sessions lasted for seven hours or longer, leaving Dee and Kelley exhausted. In frustration, Dee had asked whether there was some way to make the process go faster, but Raphael had scolded him for his presumption and demanded that he learn the language on God's terms, not his. If he persisted, divine wisdom would be his. The angels had told him that the divine language played the pivotal role in the creation of the world. The word of God, spoken in the angel tongue, created the cosmos and the first human, Adam, and the language was, as the angels put it, the 'plasmating' force for the Book of Nature that gave coherence to the universe.

And furthermore, the angels presented Dee with a carrot on a stick. If he followed their path diligently and mastered the language then great hidden texts such as the *Holy Book of Loagaeth*, the *Speech from God*, would be revealed to him. And beyond that were secret angelic calls that would allow him to communicate with ever-higher heavenly realms, bringing him closer and closer to the bosom of God Himself.

On this night as Dee waited for divine contact to occur, he dipped his quill and dated his notebook, *1582, Novembris 15*, then wrote, *Post reconciliationem Kellianam* – after the reconciliation with Kelley. Before the ink was dry, Kelley leaned forward, his gaze fixed hard on the stone.

'It is the angel Uriel!' Kelley exclaimed. Then he allowed himself a smile and whispered across the holy table, 'It is good to be scrying with you again, dear Doctor.'

*   *   *

Kelley scryed with Dee for several days in Mortlake before excusing himself to attend to personal business. That business was to report to the stately residence of Francis Walsingham at Seething Lane in London, uncomfortably close to the Tower of London. Walsingham had a fever and bade his secretary to send Kelley to his drafty bedchamber. The day was fair, but one might not have known it. Heavy curtains blotted out the light. The paneling was dark, the floorboards were dark, the tapestries were dark, the candles were few and scattered about on dark furniture. Walsingham was propped on pillows and covered in dark-colored brocaded bedclothes and was visible only from the shoulders up. To his visitor, the tableau had the hallmarks of a nightmare. Even in a state of infirmity, the dour visage of the Secretary of State pierced Kelley's breast with fear.

'Throw more logs onto the fire,' Walsingham commanded, but when Kelley turned to look for the basket of wood, Walsingham shouted, 'Not you, man! Are you dimwitted? My servant!'

The manservant who had been lurking in the shadows hopped to it while Kelley apologized and drew closer, unsure, where to sit or where to stand.

Walsingham lashed out again in a feverish pique and shouted at the scryer to take the chair nearest the bed.

'Give me your report, man. Don't dawdle.'

There was no small talk to be had with this man and Kelley was grateful for that. The sooner done, the sooner away.

'I returned to Mortlake as you ordered, my lord. Doctor Dee received me harshly, but I was able to persuade him that my deception was an innocent affair to conceal an identity that had suffered wrongful slander. I told him that my accusers influenced my judge to my detriment by claiming that I was sympathetic to Catholic causes.'

'There is cleverness in that tack,' Walsingham said. 'Unless—'

'Unless what, my lord?'

'Unless it is true.'

'Heavens, no!' Kelley said, his lie almost levitating him off the chair. 'I am a good and faithful Protestant! My family are of solid Protestant stock. Of this, there is no doubt.'

'Very well,' Walsingham replied wearily. 'What next occurred?'

'The Doctor's position did soften.'

'Did he confess to similar Catholic sympathies?'

'He did not. He merely said that he too was persecuted for his Catholic past despite having abandoned his old oaths and becoming a loyal member of Her Majesty's Church.'

'Pity. Tell me more.'

'He invited me to return to his employ so that we might resume our spiritual actions.'

'And did you commence these?'

'We did, deep into the night. The angel Uriel did introduce us to various kings of heavenly realms, though they did seem minor personages. The tedious work of imparting unto us the language of the angels appears to be done. Our lessons progress in other ways.'

'Were there any signs of black arts or the conjuration of unwholesome spirits?'

'No, my lord.'

'Then I am disappointed.'

'You should not be, my lord.'

'And why is that?'

'When he was gone from his study, I had occasion to peruse his correspondence. There was an interesting letter.'

'From whom?'

'Bernardino de Mendoza.'

Walsingham clucked in delight. 'The Spanish ambassador. His master, King Philip, is the arch-enemy of our good lady. Did this letter speak of plottings, perchance?'

'To my untrained eye, the Spaniard wrote in admiration of Doctor Dee's prowess as a mapmaker and navigator. He inquired whether he might one day inspect his collection of maps, globes, and navigational instruments.'

'Your untrained eye,' Walsingham repeated.

'I am wholly ignorant of coded messages, my lord. Perhaps there were hidden meanings.'

'Did you bring me the letter?'

'I could not. He would surely have known I had taken it.'

Walsingham had a brief coughing fit. When he composed

himself, he told Kelley that this was a promising development. 'Do your utmost to look for future correspondence between Dee and the ambassador. Steal Mendoza's letters if you can. Try to make faithful copies if you cannot. Let us see if we might discover a nest of vipers poised to strike against our lady. Earn your keep, Master Kelley. Now run along and let me convalesce in peace.'

SEVENTEEN

Cal was waiting for his Uber when Jessica called.

'Are you at the airport yet?' she asked.

'Still at the house but leaving any minute.'

'Well, be careful.'

'I don't think I'm going to be followed to London, Jess.'

'Did you buy a gun yet?'

'I ordered it the day I got my license. I'll have it when I get back. Look, there's something I probably ought to tell you. Eve Riley's joining me in London.'

He didn't know for sure that Jessica was going to be annoyed, but it was better to tell her beforehand. Her tone shifted abruptly. He could picture her squeezing her phone.

'Oh yes? Her idea?'

'Mine, actually. I don't exactly know what I'm looking for. She's the expert in this shit.'

'I thought you said she seemed as poor as a church mouse.'

'I sent her a ticket. We're meeting at Heathrow.'

'Won't that be cozy? Separate hotel rooms?'

'Of course. Strictly business.'

'Yeah, business. You're forgetting that I saw her photo. And you're also forgetting that I know you.'

'What's that supposed to mean?' He knew what she meant.

'You know exactly what I mean.'

'Relax. She's not my type. You're my type.'

'She's got two X chromosomes. That makes her your type.'

'I'll be good. I promise.'

'You'd better be. You've got enough people who want to kill you already.'

Cal arrived at Terminal 5 at Heathrow and took the shuttle bus to Terminal 3 to meet Eve's flight. He sipped a Starbucks while waiting for her in the arrival hall feeling a bit guilty that he'd only bought her a coach ticket. He flew business. He'd make it up to her. Their hotel was a good one. The Bloomsbury was a place he liked to hang his hat when he had business at the British Library or the British Museum, and it was only a short walk to the Institute of Archeology. If he was feeling expansive, maybe he'd upgrade her room to match his.

When she emerged from the customs hall, she looked like a backpacking college student heading out on a European tour. She wore a denim jacket over a hippy-ish floral dress, sneakers, and her hair was in pigtails. Plus a backpack. Seeing her, he felt like a preppy with his blue blazer and khakis. It was the way he always dressed and he presumed this was her usual wardrobe. Worlds colliding, he thought, but maybe that was being melodramatic.

She seemed happy to see him, but they settled for an awkward handshake and headed to the taxi rank. On the way into London, she seemed awfully wide-eyed, dropping comments about driving on the left, the size of the cars, and her difficulty understanding the driver's accent.

The driver overheard and offered that even his missus couldn't understand him.

'So, first time,' Cal said.

'Yep. Like I told you, the only place I've ever been outside the country is Mexico. If it weren't for that I wouldn't even have a passport.'

'Not everyone's a traveler.'

'I'd travel like mad if I had any money. I've been asked to go to Europe for Enochian conferences before – don't faint, they're a real thing – but they don't pay your way, so I never went. I've been to a bunch of them in the States, especially the ones in driving distance from Arizona.'

'How are they?' he asked. 'Pretty sober meetings or do angel people get freaky after knocking back a few?'

She laughed at the concept of freaky angel types. 'It's not a wild and crazy crowd for the most part, plus I'm usually the youngest person there by a decade or three. You must travel a lot.'

'I do, actually. Conferences, research. I'm in the UK every year or so, Israel, Turkey a lot, Rome and the Vatican usually at least twice a year.'

'I suppose you know the Pope.'

'I do, actually. We've grown quite close.'

'I was kidding,' she said.

'I wasn't. He's an impressive guy. I can't wait to tell him about the angels.'

They checked into the hotel and while she showered and set her alarm for a two-hour nap, Cal phoned Omar Rasouly to confirm their appointment for the next day. Rasouly's machine picked up and Cal left a message. After a shower and a shave, he tried again but there was still no reply. Eve was easier to reach. She picked up right away and sounded eager to get out and start looking around.

Cal made a conscious effort to purge his preppy look and he appeared in the lobby in jeans and an untucked shirt. Eve had apparently made a similar decision to purge her hippie look. She was sporting a knee-length skirt and a demure blouse with flat shoes. They chuckled at each other without referencing their fashion shifts and hit the street on a perfectly glorious sunny day.

'Hungry?' he asked.

'I could eat.'

He knew a good bistro in the neighborhood and they settled in at a window table watching a parade of tourists and Londoners on their lunch hour.

'It's so beautiful here,' she said, 'and so green.'

'Where you live is beautiful too.'

'It is, and I love it, but green is such a pleasant change to brown. Did you reach the man we're supposed to meet?'

'Left a couple of messages. I'll try him again later. Anyway, we've got an afternoon to do sightseeing and I'm a pretty reasonable tour guide. Any idea what you'd like to see?'

She replied instantly. 'The British Museum. Is it far?'

'Right around the corner. One of my favorite places on planet Earth. It's a big place. We'll need a game plan.'

'Oh, there's only one thing I want to see.'

'What's that?'

'Don't you know?'

She ate like a bird. He drank like a fish. She left the restaurant full. He left with a buzz. The afternoon was warm and glowing when they headed off to the museum. He enjoyed watching her reactions to ordinary things that no longer amazed him. In truth, he wished he could recapture the way he had felt when he was a teenager seeing London for the first time, tagging along with his father who had something important to do, whatever it was, long lost to the mists of time.

The sun shone through the steel and glass ceiling of the great court of the museum. Eve took it in, smiling, and then began fast-walking ahead of Cal.

He caught up to her and said, 'I can ask where we can find them.'

'It's this way,' she said.

'How do you know that?'

'I just do.'

Alongside the mummies and the Rosetta Stone, the Enlightenment Room was one of the most popular exhibits. It was a huge gallery that explored the sweeping age of Enlightenment, a time when a conflagration of reason and learning spread across Europe. Cal let her lead the way. She weaved around the cases and then stopped and stared several paces from one particular display.

'There,' she said.

She approached it hesitantly, Cal at her heels, and when she could get no closer than the glass, he saw she was crying.

'Look,' she said. 'The Sigillum Dei Aemeth, Dee's seal of God.'

The wax seal was oatmeal-colored, faintly incised with geometric shapes and squiggly characters. To Cal, it looked like an old overbaked cake that someone had left in a tin for a very long time. Next to it were a pair of smaller seals meant to sit under the legs of Dee's table.

She was breathing hard. 'His showstones.'

There was a small crystal ball, the size of a billiard ball, sitting on a tripod, but what drew their attention was a large obsidian mirror with a stubby handle drilled through with a hole. It was flat like Cal's, slightly thicker and larger, but its surface was not as shiny and brilliant. Still, it was obvious why his father had referenced Dee's mirror on the notecard.

Cal didn't want to interrupt her reverie. He occupied himself reading the background information on Dee printed on the display placard. He waited until she sighed before he spoke up.

'Did he use both showstones?'

'There's no way to know,' she said. 'He included a drawing of the crystal ball in one of the early diary entries but there isn't one of the obsidian mirror. Still, I can't believe he wouldn't have used it, or rather that one of his scryers like Edward Kelley wouldn't have used it. It's the powerful one.'

'You can tell?'

'Oh yes, I can tell. It's what guided me here.'

She stared for a while longer. Standing behind her he caught her reflection in the mirror, looking awfully dark and mysterious.

When she stepped away he asked, 'You want to take a picture?'

'There's no need. It's going to stay with me.'

That morning Omar Rasouly was eating a bowl of cereal in the kitchen of his north London house when the doorbell rang. The elderly man put down his spoon, blotted the milk from his lips, and slowly made his way to the front door where the silhouette of a very large man filled the frosted glass panel.

Barzani smiled when the old man opened the door and asked whether this was Professor Rasouly.

'Yes, I'm Omar Rasouly. How can I help you?'

'I was wondering if we could talk about a papyrus from Iraq you worked on some years ago?'

Rasouly wrinkled his face in puzzlement. 'Are you Professor Donovan from Harvard?'

Barzani quickly replied that he was.

'I'm terribly forgetful these days. Weren't we meant to meet at the Institute?'

'Yes, but I was passing your house and thought we could go together.'

'I see. Well, come inside. As you can see I'll need to get my shoes.'

Barzani thanked him and asked if he should remove his shoes too.

'You're fine. You know, you don't look anything like Hiram.'

'Who?'

'Your father, Hiram Donovan.'

'I get that a lot. The papyrus is in your office, right?'

'Well, I think so. We'll have to have a look, won't we?'

A few minutes later the professor appeared with shoes and sports jacket.

'I do hope that this isn't one of Bettina's days to come.'

'Who is she?' Barzani asked.

Rasouly went to the kitchen where a printed sheet was fixed by magnets to a board. It was a calendar with the name Bettina printed on every Tuesday, Thursday, and Saturday square. The sheet had the logo of a company, Home Memory Care Support.

'She helps around the house, that sort of thing,' Rasouly said. 'Do you know what day this is? Is it Thursday?'

Barzani inspected the sheet and lied. 'It's Friday.'

'Oh good.'

Barzani had a car parked outside Rasouly's unruly front garden. Traffic slowed their journey into town. Rasouly was chatty at first but then got sleepy and announced he would take a short nap. Barzani told him that was fine and drove on. It took him a while to find a place to park. Once on foot, Barzani got lost but Rasouly's mind happily kicked into gear and he led them straight to Gordon Square Garden and the Institute of Archeology. They took the lift to the third floor, and walking down the corridor one of the curators, a woman in a hijab, beamed.

'Omar, it's so good to see you.'

Rasouly smiled back and seemed to struggle to remember her name.

'It's Nadia, Omar, and I hope we can have a cup of tea together before too long.'

'That would be marvelous, Nadia. Thank you. I'm just in to find something. I don't come in very often, you know. Oh, this is Hiram Donovan's son, Calvin. He's at Harvard too I believe. Did you know Hiram?'

'I don't think I did,' she said.

She greeted Barzani who mumbled a hello back then dropped his head to look at his phone. The woman told Rasouly that she looked forward to seeing him again and went on her way.

Rasouly's office was locked. A plastic tag on his loop of keys was marked *office* and he opened the door. Inside, the small, windowless room to which he had been transferred when he was granted emeritus status was neat and uncluttered. A few pieces of unimportant mail had been held for him and a stack of recent and unread journals.

Barzani closed the door and folded his arms across his broad chest.

'Why was it we're here?' Rasouly asked.

'The papyrus! The papyrus that Hiram Donovan found in Iraq at Rabban Hurmizd. Before 1989. He sent it to you.'

'Oh yes. Now where might that be?'

'Can you look for it, please?'

'Yes, of course. I'll do that.'

Rasouly began pulling open file drawers all the while talking to himself about old projects, old publications, old friends. Every ten minutes or so he asked what he was looking for and Barzani repeated it with mounting impatience. Finally, there was an 'aha!' and Rasouly pulled out a thick folder with a tab, *Rabban Hurmizd Monastery – Harvard/Baghdad Excavations.*

'Let's see what we shall see,' the professor said, removing the folder to his desk.

Barzani hovered and asked if the papyrus was there but Rasouly ignored him because he was thumbing through papers, reading a line here, a paragraph there. He seemed focused and happy.

'I don't have all day,' Barzani said.

'Research takes time,' Rasouly replied gently. Then he came across a letter in a pale blue airmail envelope with *Rabban Hurmizd – Epigraphy* scrawled in his own handwriting.

'Maybe something here?' Rasouly said to himself.

The old man began reading the letter. Midway through the second page he stopped and began nodding to himself.

'That's right. Now I recall. That's where they are! Have a look.'

Barzani read the paragraph, grimacing. He asked Rasouly if he could keep the letter and the professor readily agreed, saying that it was good for a son to have an interest in his father's legacy.

Then he added, 'I should have my lunch before long. Do you know if Bettina is coming today?'

He stood up and Barzani told him to turn toward the door. The old man asked why.

'Just do it, please.'

Rasouly did a half-turn and Tariq reached his arms around his chest and began to squeeze. The air that slowly expelled from his lungs made a low whooshing sound. He tried to speak but the only thing that came out were some guttural clicks. His face screwed into an alarmed confusion before it got dusky, then purple. The big man continued to squeeze, hard enough to prevent Rasouly from expanding his chest with air, but gently enough not to break ribs. When the old man finally went limp, Tariq kept squeezing for another couple of minutes. Then, satisfied with the result, he opened his arms and let him fall onto the floor.

He checked to make sure there was no pulse, closed the file drawer with his foot, and shut the office door with a handkerchief on his way out.

That afternoon, Cal kept ringing Rasouly's number with increasing frustration. He took Eve to Covent Garden for dinner and an evening walkabout, and before they returned to their hotel, he told her she really had to experience a bit of pub life. He chose one about as close to a neighborhood pub as you could get in the area and insisted she try some real ale. She was a sport, sipping at her pint while he downed a couple.

'What are we going to do if he doesn't answer?' she asked over the clamor of the public bar.

'Go to the Institute, I guess,' he said, worried that he might have dragged her halfway around the world for a non-meeting.

After his third pint he got a little tipsy and then he got a little pushy, exhorting her to finish her drink before they left. It was bad luck to leave beer in the glass, he told her, making it up. The result was that she got tipsy too and they both laughed their way back to the hotel. In the lobby he caught himself. A pretty woman. Booze. A hotel. Was his promise to Jessica just a load of nonsense? Could he really not control himself?

'I'm going to call Rasouly one more time,' he told her. 'Let's meet for breakfast and if I still haven't reached him, we'll head over to the Institute.'

'My head's spinning,' she said. 'What do they put in their beer here, anyway?'

'A shit-ton of alcohol, that's what.'

When the lift stopped on her floor he asked if she could manage and when she said she'd be fine, she touched his arm to thank him for dinner. He smiled and let the door close behind her.

The following morning was bright but in the restaurant, Cal's mood was stormy. Rasouly still wasn't picking up and there was nothing to do but head over to the campus and make inquiries there. Eve seemed to pick up on his tension and neither of them talked much on their brief walk to Gordon Square.

When they rounded the park onto Endsleigh Place they saw that the street in front of the Institute of Archeology was clogged with police cars and an ambulance. A knot of Institute workers was on the street chatting and smoking. A police officer stood on the entrance stairs checking for university badges.

Cal went up to him and asked what was going on.

'Nothing that ought to concern you, sir. Are you an employee?'

'No, a visitor.'

'Do you have an appointment?'

'Yes, we're going to meet one of the members of staff.'

'We're just holding off on admittance for a short while until our incident team is finished.'

'Could I just ring up to Dr Rasouly's office to see if he's there?'

At the mention of the name, the officer puckered his mouth and asked Cal to wait at the bottom of the stairs until he got someone to speak with him.

Cal sidled up to a group of three women huddled on the sidewalk and asked them if they knew what was going on.

'Someone's had a heart attack, apparently. It's very sad.'

'Who is it?' Cal asked.

'Omar Rasouly. He was such a lovely man.'

EIGHTEEN

The call came in over the Wi-Fi network of George Hamid's Falcon jet. There was some distortion on the line and Hamid had to talk loudly. His wife, Nella, grimaced from her cross-aisle seat and took her fashion magazine to the rear. There was no one else in the cabin to disturb.

'Yes, I hear you now, Tariq. I know, I know. I'm on a flight to LA. You'll need to speak up. Tell me what's going on.'

Barzani was in an inexpensive hotel in the Paddington area. He was concerned about the thin walls; a couple having sex had kept him awake that night. He tried to find a level to be heard without having to shout.

He told his boss about meeting Rasouly and tried in his own way to describe his malady.

'He was all fucked up. He thought I was Donovan. And he couldn't remember shit.'

'What, like dementia?' Hamid suggested.

'Yeah, I guess.'

He told him about going to his office and finding the letter in his files.

Hamid was mightily disappointed. He asked what happened next.

'He's dead. I made it look natural.'

'Did anyone see you?'

'Yeah, but it looks like it was natural. No blood. Nothing broken. He was old.'

'Okay. Well you know where you've got to go next.'

'I already made the arrangements. I'm leaving today.'

'Good. Keep in touch.'

Hamid got up to use the lavatory. The Grand Canyon was off the port side. He pointed it out to his wife, who couldn't be bothered to look.

'Who called?' she asked.

'Tariq.'

'Where did you say he was? He usually comes with us.'

'He's doing something for me.'

'He's always doing something for you.'

'That's what I pay him for.'

The reception was at the Beverly Wiltshire Hotel and although Hamid's suite was over the top in size and appointments, he was fuming. He couldn't believe that he hadn't been booked into the Penthouse Suite or at least one of the two Presidential Suites. He complained to the front desk manager and when that didn't secure an upgrade, he took to the phone to savage his assistant back in New York. The problem was that the event was dripping with ultra-wealthy types who had snapped up the three best rooms, and his belated decision to attend had not helped. At 2,200 square feet, the Governor Suite was only half the size of the penthouse, his usual lodging at the hotel, and he was aggrieved.

'Who is in the penthouse?' he had demanded of the general manager, who scampered up to the suite to do damage control.

The reply in a high-brow French accent was, 'We cannot divulge guest details, Mr Hamid. I am sure you can understand?'

'Would I recognize the name?'

'Of that you can be sure.'

'If I had known I couldn't get the suite I wanted I would have gone elsewhere or rented a house.'

'Perhaps if you give us a touch more lead time on your next visit we will be able to accommodate you more appropriately. In the meanwhile, is there anything I can do for you to make your stay more comfortable?'

Hamid considered asking the fellow if he didn't mind screwing himself, but for the sake of his wife, who was looking miserable and waiting to unpack, he let the man off with a dismissive wave.

'I'm going to fire Tammy,' he told his wife when they were alone.

She didn't answer. How many times had he threatened to fire his assistant?

'No, I mean it this time.'

There were two master bedrooms.

'Which one do you want, George?' she asked.

'I don't care. They're both rather small.'

The ballroom was already crowded when Hamid and his wife made their entry. He hadn't been to the annual meeting of the ACRF in several years, but he had decided, spur-of-the-moment, that this would be a good year to make a grand reappearance. After all, his company had just gone public in a high-profile offering and he was aching for a shot of adoration and envy from his peers and competitors. And he was keen to meet this year's keynote speaker. The gala dinner was always for the benefit of charity and Hamid had paid enough for tickets to ensure a place at the speaker's table.

He picked up a couple of flutes of champagne from a waiter and whispered to his wife that he wanted to check out their seating. He had bought a new tuxedo for the occasion and strutted with the confidence of a man in a well-tailored suit that flattered his rotundity. Nella Hamid had a new sequined gown but was feeling low. She had emerged from her room wanting to know how she looked and he had asked in his typical marital ignorance if it wasn't a bit tight around the middle.

Table One, closest to the stage, sat eight and when no one was looking, Hamid swapped his name plate with the president of the organization so he would be next to the speaker.

'It's a good thing I checked,' he told his wife.

'Who am I next to?' she asked

'Lonergan's wife, I think. Don't do your usual thing.'

'And what is that?'

'You know. Acting like a turtle. I need you to stick your head out and be talkative. These are important people.'

A few attendees, mostly New Yorkers, came up to Hamid to congratulate him on his IPO and he basked in the attention. The lights flickered and several hundred guests began making their way to their tables. Hamid motioned for his wife to come along and hurried to make sure he claimed the coveted seat before anyone figured out they had been moved.

The president of the organization, a big developer from St Louis, approached the table with the keynote speaker and their wives. He looked a little confused when he saw Hamid sitting in his seat, but he graciously took it in stride and found his new spot.

'I think you're over there, Gabe,' the president said. 'And Gretchen, you're next to Gabe.'

Gabriel Lonergan held his wife's chair then unbuttoned his tuxedo jacket to sit down. He had patrician looks, neither handsome or plain but decidedly distinguished, with light-brown blow-dried hair, and a long tennis-player's body. When the sixty-year-old passed through the room his strides were fluid, his posture erect, his handshake firm, his eye-contact declaring a personal interest.

Lonergan struck first, turning to Hamid and offering his hand. 'Gabe Lonergan. Pleased to meet you.'

'George Hamid.'

'George, this is my wife, Gretchen. Is that lovely lady across the table your wife?'

'Nella, yes.'

Lonergan waved at her and made a joke about table decorations always getting in the way.

'I know we haven't met, George, because I never forget a face, but I know who you are. I've been reading about your company and its IPO. Hearty congratulations are in order.'

Hamid lit up. 'Thank you, Gabe. We're not in your league – yet – but it's nice that the market appreciated what we do.'

'And your stock's up a bunch over issue price. Good job all around. I'm going to have to beat up my broker for not getting me in on it.'

'If I had known I would have gotten you a friends and family allocation.'

'Well, next time.'

With that, the ACRF president got Lonergan's attention and the two of them began talking over Hamid.

If there was one thing that Hamid respected it was wealth, and Lonergan was said to be worth twenty billion, give or take. In his home state of California, a few Silicon Valley types were wealthier, but he was top of the pile in his native Los Angeles. But as the dinner progressed, Hamid sensed a bit of a cold shoulder. Lonergan was polite to him but downright jovial to the president and the other man in the grouping, an Orange County shopping-mall developer.

But just before dinner plates were about to be collected and the speeches begun, Lonergan said to Hamid, 'Say, George, you're an immigrant, right?'

'I am, Gabe. I came to America from Iraq after the first Gulf War. Nella and I came with nothing. America was very good to us.'

'The reason I ask is that I'm going to be making a few references to immigration during my speech. I have a couple of things to say about the Muslim situation and I wanted to make sure I wasn't going to offend you.'

'But I'm not a Muslim, Gabe.'

'What are you?'

'I'm a Christian. That's one of the reasons I left Iraq. We were a persecuted minority, you know.'

Lonergan's face brightened a few shades. 'I had no idea, George. I think I've got a couple of minutes before I'm called up. Tell me more about your story.'

They stopped chatting when the president took to the stage. He lowered the microphone that Lonergan's people had adjusted to his height ahead of time and welcomed the group.

'The American Commercial Real Estate Forum is honored to have a keynote speaker tonight who is a second-generation LA developer. Gabriel Lonergan inherited the company his father, Ralph, built and took a great company and made it a whole heck of a lot greater. You can't drive – or sit in traffic – in southern California without looking at dozens of Lonergan towers, hotels, and office complexes. And now he's even branched out into mixed-use commercial-residential planned communities. If you know Gabe as I know him, you'll understand that he isn't one of these plain-vanilla, politically correct types. He generally speaks his mind and even the few endangered species in the ballroom tonight – and by that, I mean Democrats – even they have got to respect him for that. I give you our speaker tonight, my friend, Gabe Lonergan.'

Lonergan sprang up and took the stairs to the stage in two big youthful leaps. He discreetly removed his speech from his pocket and smoothed the fold on the podium, then raised the microphone back where it should have been.

'Ladies and gentlemen, it's my honor to address our wonderful ACRF tonight, an organization that gives back to our communities all over this great country of ours and, I am pleased to say, is ranked number two in the country for its philanthropy out of all the nation's commercial interest associations. But let me tell you, I hate being number two in anything. Let's all make it our mission to get to number one.'

He paused for the applause and went for the obligatory humor.

'You know, how you can tell how wealthy this group is? I was told so many private jets flew into LAX today that the runway congestion got the pilots confused. They thought they were on Interstate 405 between Venice and Wiltshire at rush hour.'

There followed a nakedly political speech which was little surprise to most in the room. It was a matter of when-not-if speculation that Lonergan was going to be running for something on the state or federal level. A lot of his remarks revolved around economic prosperity and how too many politicians stupidly thought that government action, not an unbridled private sector, was the way to achieve accelerating growth. But then he segued into immigration, a favorite red-meat issue.

'Now we here in California know the importance of agriculture to our economy. And I've had people come up to me from all over and say, "Mr Lonergan, how can you be such a hawk on immigration when you know the farmers in California and other states can't get Americans to work the fields?" And I tell them what I'm about to tell you – I am not against immigrants. I am for legal immigrants but dead set against illegals. I say expand our seasonal visas for agricultural workers but when the season is over, see to it we have enough Immigration and Customs Enforcement officers on the job to make sure we kick every last backside back across the border! My friends, I love legal immigrants. They are one of the reasons we have a great country. Let me tell you one success story.'

Lonergan looked away from his text and pointed at his table.

'Hey, George Hamid, would you get up and take a bow.'

Hamid glanced at his wife who looked confused then stood to wave and smile.

'Okay, George,' Lonergan said, 'you can sit down again. You're stealing my thunder. Folks, George Hamid, came to this country from Iraq right after the first Gulf War. Saddam Hussein and his Muslim cronies persecuted the hell out of George and his fellow Christians. They forced his boy into the army where he was tragically killed by one of our boys or girls in the US military. But this country, the greatest country in the world, took George and his wife and their daughter in with open arms and George Hamid, who arrived with a few crumpled dollars in his pocket, built a great company in New York City, and that company just went public in one of the largest IPOs in the history of our sector.'

The audience clapped warmly and Hamid took it upon himself to stand and wave again, prompting Lonergan to point and laugh.

'Good man, good man,' Lonergan said. 'The Muslims in Iraq and other places wanted to grind our Christian brothers and sisters into dust and let me tell you something – we must never let that happen.'

When he was finished with his talk, Lonergan basked in the applause and settled back to his table. His wife pecked him on the cheek and everyone else tossed around praise.

Hamid waited his turn and said, 'Gabe, that was an amazing

speech. And I am so proud you used my story. You have made this a very special night for me.'

'Well, George, it went over well. I've been getting a lot of requests for speeches around the country lately. With your permission, I'd like to include you as a shining example of what can happen when immigration is done the right way, vetted, legal, and proper.'

'Of course, of course,' Hamid said. 'I've been following the speculation in the media that you might run for political office.'

'Yeah, the media likes to speculate about all sorts of things,' Lonergan said with a sly grin.

'What are your favorite speculations?' Hamid asked slyly.

'Well, you hear all sorts of things.'

'There's only one position you should consider,' Hamid said.

'Oh yeah?'

'Absolutely. The only office a man like yourself should bother with is the presidency of the United States.'

'That's interesting, George. Very interesting indeed. You're a bit of a mind-reader, aren't you? But if that time ever comes, I'll appreciate your support. Say, let me give you a date to hold on your calendar. Maybe we can see each other again soon.'

Hamid took down the details and said, 'I will definitely be there for you, Gabe. I will support you in ways you simply cannot believe.'

NINETEEN

Krakow, 1584

The winter journey across the Channel and into eastern Europe had been arduous and it had taken its toll on John Dee's family. The children were feverish and coughing, Jane Dee had withdrawn into a painful silence, and John Dee was given to rants at his servants and hostelers at every stop along the way. His flashpoints invariably involved the cost of things and suspicions he was being exploited by the locals. However, other members of Dee's entourage seemed to be enjoying themselves. Edward Kelley and his bride, Jane, who was several years older than he, were generally mirthful, bumping along in the back of one of the coaches. She was plump and plain and possessed a child-like simplicity that seemed to suit her new husband. This was her first trip abroad and she seemed tickled by the shifting languages and foods as they journeyed east. And as the party drew closer and closer to his ancestral home, their guide, Albrecht Laski, became more adept at navigating the local customs and he grew ever more animated.

'Do you smell it?' he would exclaim. 'The air of ancient Silesia! It is sweet as honey, is it not?'

Laski had appeared in Mortlake during a particularly painful period for the magus and Dee had declared him angel-sent. Dee had become increasingly desperate for funds to maintain his household and his scientific experiments, unaware that the unseen hand of Francis Walsingham had been thwarting him at every turn. Dee had spent years lobbying the Queen for the steady income of a royal commission, but as much as she valued his astrological, navigational, and map-making expertise, his promised alchemical advances to convert base metals into precious ones had not materialized. Nor had he made progress toward finding the philosopher's stone, the long-sought agent for permutating metals, healing illness, and conferring immortality. Absent an offering of something of demonstrable value, Dee was nothing more than one man in a huddle of Crown supplicants, albeit the most erudite one in all of England. Still, Elizabeth long held a soft spot for Dee and had urged Grindal, her archbishop – against the wishes of Walsingham – to grant the magus from Mortlake the dispensation to hold for life the two rectories at Upton and Long Leadenham, ecclesiastical positions that guaranteed him a sustainable annual income. However, Dee, distracted by his experiments, had failed to follow through on the legal necessity of having the seal of the archbishop attached to the Crown documents, and Walsingham pounced on the discovered error.

Despite Edward Kelley's spying, Walsingham had failed to confirm his suspicion that Dee was a papist plotter. Nevertheless, he preferred that Dee should wither on the vine of financial ruin and he pushed Grindal to withdraw the rectory positions on account of their invalidity. By late 1583, deprived of income, Dee was desperate.

Albrecht Laski seemed to breathe new life into his tired soul.

The flamboyant Polish lord arrived in England that year in an attempt to revive his own fortunes. Driven from his ancestral seat by the king of Poland, Stephen Bathory, Laski was received at court by the Queen, who had been thoroughly seduced by his reputation as a warrior-humanist and by the elegant letter he had written her in Italian, describing the lady as the refuge of the disconsolate and afflicted. His appearance at Whitehall Palace had caused a stir, and perhaps stirred the royal heart as well. He was tall and handsome with a pale complexion. He wore red, only red, except for yellow boots with curled toes, evocative of the Middle Ages. It seemed he had never ever trimmed his gigantic white beard, so long it was that he wore it tucked into his belt. And when he talked it was with the bookishness of a scholar and the resolute temperament of a military man. A smitten Elizabeth set him up at Winchester House in Southwark, where he began a round of expensive entertaining with money borrowed from a variety of Court grandees. No one apparently was fully aware just how impoverished the Polish palatine was. In truth, Laski had traveled to England to meet one man, John Dee, who had the reputation on the Continent as one of the preeminent alchemists of his day. If he could just convince Dee to work with him on the discovery of the philosopher's stone, then riches would follow, and his inherited lands and positions would be restored.

Laski first met Dee at a reception at Greenwich Palace and later came to Mortlake to witness one of the Doctor's famed angelic actions for himself. The Pole seduced Dee as thoroughly as he had seduced the Queen, although Dee was enchanted before he had even arrived. The angel Uriel had spoken well of Laski, implying that the nobleman would deliver unto him riches and further his opportunities for the acquisition of celestial knowledge.

When he met Edward Kelley at Mortlake on a fine May evening, Laski treated him like a functionary, but as he began to understand Kelley's pivotal role as a scryer, he came to offer up rather more respect. At his first spiritual session in Dee's inner study, Laski asked Kelley to transmit questions concerning his future in Poland. Would Laski prevail in his disputes? Would he succeed Stephen Bathory as king? The angel who replied was Madimi, who appeared in the showstone as a pretty young girl with a red and green dress. She replied that the prince would have a kingdom within a year. Laski returned to London that night, his chest puffed up like a mating bird, while Dee, also satisfied, wrote in his diary that Laski would 'strive to suppress and confound the malice and envy of my countrymen against me, for my better credit.'

Over the ensuing weeks, Laski became a steady presence in Dee's Mortlake study, participating in numerous actions and prodding the angels to divulge details of what the future held for him and for Doctor Dee. They were told to look to the east, for that was where all manner of treasures awaited them. Dee and the angels would profit Laski and he in turn would profit them once he was restored to his rightful positions in Poland.

By midsummer Laski declared to Dee and Kelley, 'We must go to Krakow.'

For Dee the timing seemed auspicious if only to escape his mounting financial obligations. He owed money to friends. He owed money to his brother-in-law. His suit to the Crown for the 200-pound pension he believed he was owed was squashed by Walsingham, who wished to turn the screws. He was at the end of his tether and he saw that Kelley was, perhaps, taking advantage of his weakened position. He caught wind of discussions between Laski and his scryer to the effect that Kelley alone could provide Laski what he needed – access to the angels via his showstone. He even overheard Laski and Kelley talking about attempting to conjure evil spirits to do damage to Laski's enemies at home. As to Dee's attraction as a great alchemist who might one day succeed in the transmutation of base metal into gold, Kelley assured Laski that he was learning that art too. Why not cut out the magus and decamp to Poland as a smaller party?

Increasingly desperate to leave his troubles behind, Dee reckoned that if he could make one more push to borrow funds, he would cement his pivotal role with Laski. He turned once again to his wealthy brother-in-law, Nicholas Fromoundes, and borrowed 400 pounds, secured by his only assets – his house and his books. That sum would provide what the penniless Laski and Kelley could not: the rental of two ships to carry his Mortlake household, several hundred books and manuscripts, Laski with his servants and horses, and Kelley's rather more meager household. Funds in hand, Dee made his final arrangements, dismantling and packing his paraphernalia for angel magic, closing his alchemical research facility, making provision for his students and alchemical research staff, and dodging a host of creditors. His wife, Jane, had the unhappy task of dismantling the domestic trappings she had spent these years of marriage constructing. She held her tongue, for she was nothing if not her husband's obedient mistress.

Before Dee packed his table and wax seals he held one final spiritual action in early September with Kelley and Laski. Auspiciously, God's covenant with Laski appeared to be solidified. Kelley saw in his obsidian mirror the angel Uriel holding a crown over Laski's head and promising kingship over three wicked nations. A fortnight later, they were on the high seas, sailing toward Holland, unaware that Nicholas Fromoundes, unwilling to bear the financial risk, was already selling off Dee's furniture and many of his rare books.

The winter crossing through the Low Countries, across northern Germany, and into Poland was arduous. While most of the party had to endure icy roads, spending nights in poor inns or huddled in wagons, Laski, traveling with his demanding Italian wife, generally had a more salubrious experience, riding off to stay in the houses and lodges of well-heeled friends along their route and rejoining the Dees and Kelleys after pleasant interludes. Along the way, Dee and Kelley anxiously consulted with the angels and were told to press on. During one of these actions Dee was perplexed and Kelley delighted by the assertion that Kelley was to become a great seer and supreme alchemist.

They arrived in Krakow, the Polish capital, in a frigid February, road-weary and eager to take up new lives. Dee scraped together the money to pay the rent for year on a house on St Stephen's Street, barely large enough for his family and the Kelleys, and Laski and his wife retired to the opulent residences at their disposal in their native city. While their wives toiled at feathering a nest, Dee and Kelley visited the renowned Jagiellonian University, where Dee secured a teaching post and Kelley insinuated himself into their alchemy laboratories.

It was not until April had come and the snows began to melt that Dee unpacked his magic table and his seals in a small room at the back of the ancient house.

'So, Edward,' Dee said when the house finally quieted after supper, 'we begin our angel conversations anew.'

They were pleasantly surprised at the immediate appearance of Nalvage, an angel who had not shown himself in a long while. What he told Kelley so excited Dee that his diary entry for the session betrayed his tremulous hand. Dee had learned from earlier sessions that the realms of Heaven were controlled by powerful angelic Governors. Yet however painstakingly he had mastered the angel language, they had no way of communicating with these Governors. On this night, Nalvage revealed that they would be taught the first of the calls to summon each Governor, although one call, the 49th and last, would not be revealed. Asked why, Nalvage told them that a single call was held back by God Himself and it was not for them to know it.

Nalvage promised them this: 'In time you may use the calls to move every gate save one, to call out as many as you please, to open unto you the secrets of their cities through which knowledge you will easily be able to judge, and of all things contained within the compass of nature, and of all things which are subject to an end.'

And with that the lesson began. Nalvage appeared in the showstone holding a rod. Standing within a grid of angelic letters he pointed to one letter at a time, slowly spelling out the first words of the 1st Call.

Ol sonf vors g, goho Iad Balt, lonsh calz vonpho.

It was slow, hard work receiving each call, letter by letter, and it took three months of scrying to receive the first eighteen calls. On a warm, moonless night in July, the angel Ilemese appeared in the showstone and dazzled Dee and Kelley with this revelation. He was about to impart unto them the 19th Call, which was in actuality, thirty calls, bringing the total to 48. The 19th Call, they learned, was a master call to access the next thirty Aethyrs. The only thing that differentiated the thirty calls was the insertion of the name of each of the Aethyrs in the first line.

When an exhausted Dee finished recording this lengthy call and all its embellishments, he wanted to know if he was the first man to know them.

'You are not the first, but few men have received them,' Ilemese replied.

Dee was elated. If nothing else was revealed to them, the journey to Poland had been worth the expense and discomfort. Kelley, however, was not fully satisfied. He inquired about the missing 49th Call, of which the angel Nalvage had spoken.

Ilemese rose from his chair and said sternly, 'God does not wish man to know the call.'

'But pray, tell us why?' Kelley asked.

Dee berated him. 'We have been told this call is reserved by God Almighty. Do not defy the angels, Edward!' But then his curiosity got the better of him and he asked, 'What sayeth Ilemese to your question?'

Kelley heard Ilemese's answer. 'It unlocks the realm of the fallen.'

Kelley gulped but chose not to pass the pronouncement along. Dee would never permit further inquiry if he had been truthful. Instead, he said, 'He refused to supply an answer.'

'Then it is a question well left,' Dee said. 'Do not ask it again.'

Kelley looked into the showstone again and said, 'The angel has stood up and he is gone in a great flame of fire upwards.'

That night, Jane Kelley was woken in bed by Kelley's restlessness.

'What is the matter, husband?' she asked.

'Doctor Dee is perfectly happy to accept the judgement that the 49th Call is not to be known by us. I am not.'

'Why do you wish it?'

'I feel it might open the gate of opportunity for me. Perhaps it is the gate to the philosopher's stone. Perhaps it is the gate to other knowledge and riches. I am tired of being poor as a mouse and living in another man's house.'

'But what if it opens a gate of evil and horror? Perhaps that is why it is not on offer.'

He had not told his wife what the angel had said about the realm of the fallen, but he silently credited her intuition. 'Then I would harness that evil to become powerful. Powerful men are invariably wealthy men.'

She let her hand wander onto the thigh of his withered leg, but he was uninterested. He had already tired of the plodding sexual congress to be had with his Jane. His interests lay elsewhere. He rolled onto his side and declared that he would sleep.

Just as it was in England, in Poland there was never enough money. Dee's teaching stipend from the university was barely enough to keep his large household afloat. To make ends meet he sold a book here, a book there. And he turned to the show-stone, scrying on his own when his master was gone, hopefully exploring the Aethyrs and exhorting the angels to help him find buried treasure or the alchemical powders he might need to make the elusive philosopher's stone. And every new angel he encountered, he asked about the 49th Call. His powers as a scryer allowed him to penetrate all the way to the fourth Aethyr, where he saw an angel named Selaphiel who told him that although he possessed knowledge of the 49th Call it was too dangerous for man to receive. But Kelley pleaded with the angel for help, complaining about the indignities of poverty he had suffered since Dee had been forced to suspend his annual wage. He could not afford to buy a new pair of boots or a thicker cloak for his shivering wife. He was trapped in servitude in a foreign land. Selaphiel seemed to take pity on him and dictated, using the grids of angelic letters, the holy words that an alchemist might use to compel darker angels to transmute base metals into gold and silver. He began using these chants, but the results were disappointing. His lumps of lead remained lead.

Count Laski was also spurred on by his mounting debts and royal aspirations. Encouraged as he was by angelic prophesies, he joined in a conspiracy to overthrow King Stephen, but the conspirators were routed. His compatriots were beheaded in Krakow's marketplace and Laski only escaped punishment with the support of the citizenry who held him up to be an estimable character duped by devious men.

On one occasion, three dispirited fellows, Dee, Kelley, and Laski, came together around the showstone to have an angel advise them to turn to the Holy Roman Emperor, Rudolf II, for financial assistance. Laski, a known Habsburg supporter, would surely get a favorable audience with Rudolf, and as the emperor had a keen interest in alchemy, Dee and Kelley might secure patronage. A plan was hatched. If they could raise money for the journey to Prague, then they would depart before the summer turned to fall.

On a Tuesday morning the Dee household was as quiet as it ever was. Jane Kelley had taken the children into the garden to play tag. Doctor Dee was at the university lecturing a class of advanced students in mathematics. Jane Dee was in the kitchen, plucking chickens and chopping vegetables. And Edward Kelley was at home, tired of reading one of Dee's particularly obtuse alchemy texts. He limped into the kitchen without his walking stick and stood at the doorway for a while, watching Dee's wife at work, admiring the faint outlines of her pert rump through the fabric of her dress.

When she realized she was being spied upon she said, 'Have you never seen a woman dressing a chicken, Master Kelley?'

'None as charming as yourself, Jane.'

'I believe your good wife is outside with the children.'

'The fresh air will do her good.'

'Perhaps you might join her. Fresh air is wholesome for men as well.'

He came toward her, the shoe on his palsied leg scraping the floorboards. 'What I find wholesome is the sight of a comely woman.'

She looked at him sharply, but he came closer.

'My husband would put you out on the street if he knew of your impertinence.'

'He need not know, Jane. He is an old man. I am a young, vital man and you are a young, vital woman. Do you not think that destiny has brought us together under the same roof?'

'Destiny?' she said. 'Nay, Master Kelley, it was not destiny. It was my husband who, for reasons I am unable to judge, sees fit to employ you. If you provide him with good services, then I have little reason to object. However, if your work is in any way suspect, then surely you will be judged harshly, in this world or the next.'

'What do you mean by suspect?'

'How am I to know if you really do see angels in that stone of yours?'

A frown darkened his face. 'Madam, I can assure you that the angels do indeed answer to my call.'

'I pray you say the truth, sir. Your ears have already been cropped. What parts could next be on the block to answer for so great a lie?'

As the hoped-for departure date for Prague approached, Kelley returned to the St Stephen's Street house from his alchemy studio in the university district to see a fine carriage and horses outside the front gate. He was weary from another day of little progress. He had obtained a large bladder stone from a physician, and having pulverized the specimen, he had not succeeded by means of chemical manipulation and chanting in angel tongue to transmute it into anything more valuable.

Kelley saw his wife in the front hall and asked who had come calling.

'I am not certain, husband, but I took his name to be Spanish.'

'How long has he been here?'

'He has just arrived.'

The parlor was unoccupied, so he climbed the stairs and walked as quietly as he could up to the door to Doctor Dee's outer study. That door was open but the door to the inner study where they conducted their scrying sessions was closed. He entered the first chamber and gently shut the door behind him so that Jane Dee or the children could not see him if they passed. With his ear to the inner door he instantly heard the voices of Dee and a gentleman with the distinct accent of a Spaniard.

Juan Carlos de Guzmán was the ambassador to Poland from the court of King Philip II. A proud Castilian from a family with long service to the Spanish Crown, he had sent a man to the university to see Dee and to arrange for a discreet visit at Dee's residence. Kelley could tell that the ambassador was being more than deferential to his master. He was being obsequious.

'This is surely, without a scintilla of doubt, one of the greatest days of my life meeting a man such as yourself, Doctor Dee. You must know that you are regarded as one of the finest intellects in all of Europe.'

'Please convey my good tidings to your king,' Dee said, making no acknowledgement of the praise.

'And I bring you the good tidings of my colleague, Bernardino de Mendoza, the ambassador to your queen.'

'He is a fine gentleman. He expressed an interest in my collection of navigational instruments. Sadly, I left those behind in Mortlake.'

'Yes, he told me. It was he who recommended I visit you in Krakow.'

'How might I be of service?'

'Your expertise in the zodiacal arts is well known. I was hoping to commission a horoscope concerning a certain English gentleman and some tasks my king desires him to perform. He wishes to know future dates that may prove to be auspicious concerning a business venture he intends to pursue.'

'This gentleman,' Dee said. 'May I know his name?'

'It is Sir Francis Throckmorton.'

Dee said that he knew of the man, but they had never met. Throckmorton's cousin was a lady in waiting for Elizabeth with whom Dee was acquainted. 'This work,' Dee added. 'I trust it has nothing to do with any differences that might exist between Catholic Spain and Protestant England.'

'Certainly not,' the ambassador said, 'but as you raise the matter, you were a Catholic priest when you were a younger man, is that not so?'

Kelley felt his heart beating in his throat. Walsingham would need to hear of this conversation. What an opportune moment to ask for funds to further various and sundry clandestine activities!

'I renounced my Catholic orders and I am now content as a Protestant,' Dee answered him.

'I pray that one day we all should be blessed with contentment.'

'This horoscope you seek,' Dee said. 'I find myself to be a very busy man these days. How much could you pay me to put aside present obligations and take up this task?'

'I can pay you very well and fairly, Doctor Dee. Of this you can be sure.'

That night in his bedroom, Kelley wrote a letter while his wife loudly snored. He knew that Francis Walsingham had little interest in small words, so he went straight to the matter at hand and described what he had overheard in the vivid detail he knew the spymaster craved. And now that he had an excuse to write, he decided to play another card he had been withholding for the right moment. Several weeks earlier he had found himself in the chambers of a wealthy Polish count who was interested to hear about the latest alchemical research from the new English arrivals to Krakow. When the count was briefly called away by a servant, Kelley casually opened a box on the man's desk and saw at least twenty gold pieces. He helped himself to two of them and when his business was done, he left the premises smiling. One coin he kept for his own coffers, the other, he melted down in a crucible and poured the molten metal into a dimple he carved in a flat piece of walnut. Now he intended to include this piece of wood inside the folded letter.

'Finally, Sir Francis, I would beseech you to present this gift to Her Gracious Majesty. My alchemical experiments have been progressing exceedingly well. I have been able to convert stones from the bladder of an afflicted man into a fine grade of gold, as you can clearly surmise. If Her Majesty could bestow unto me a stipend of 100 pounds to purchase the materials I require to produce larger quantities of gold, I will be able to greatly augment Her royal treasury.'

Francis Walsingham received Kelley's letter when the first leaves of autumn began fluttering to the ground. He had a stack of correspondence that day, but he opened that letter first. It was the first communication from his spy since he embarked for Poland and the letter was strangely heavy. The heaviness revealed itself as soon as he cracked the seal. A piece of wood inlaid with a glob of gold. He devoured the letter seeking an explanation.

But Kelley's claims for a breakthrough in alchemy were of less interest to a pragmatist like Walsingham than the name Throckmorton. He had been monitoring the Catholic brothers Francis and Thomas Throckmorton, whom he suspected of plotting to murder Queen Elizabeth to pave the way for her cousin, the Catholic Mary, Queen of Scots to take the throne. His web of informants in England, France, and Spain had been feeding him fragments of information that led him to believe that the Throckmortons were acting as go-betweens between Mary, under house arrest in Carlisle Castle, and Bernardino de Mendoza, the Spanish ambassador. The outlines of the plot involved the restoration of a Catholic monarchy brought about by the invasion of England by Henry I, the Duke of Guise, supported by King Philip of Spain and the Vatican. And now it seemed that John Dee might be a supporting character in the tale.

Walsingham showed the letter to his private secretary, Francis Mylles, who asked him what he intended to do about John Dee.

'I intend to do nothing for the moment. Being an old fool is not a crime. Being a Catholic plotter is quite another thing. Let us see whether he crosses the line. In the meanwhile, Dee will not receive any monies from the Crown. He may starve and wither for all I care.'

'And what of Edward Kelley's alchemy? Will you inform the Queen?'

Walsingham used his belt dagger to dig out the gold nugget

from the wood. 'Once a liar and a fraud, always a liar and a fraud.'

He slipped the piece of gold into his pocket and called for the next letter.

TWENTY

The director of the Institute of Archeology was a woman Cal knew only slightly. He had heard Eleanor Cartwright lecture once on her specialty area, pre-Columbian Meso-American archeology, and had met her at a cocktail party in Berlin, as he recalled. She remembered him somewhat better and warmly greeted him and Eve, brushing ringlets of wild red hair away from her eyes.

'Imagine, coming all this way to see Omar and then this,' she said. 'How dreadful for all of us. Did you know him well?'

'I'm afraid not,' Cal said. 'He was a colleague of my father. He did the paleography on his Near Eastern papyri.'

'He was very eminent in his field,' she said. 'Of course, in recent years, he had to slow down on account of his memory issues. Isn't dementia particularly cruel when a person's mind is full of a lifetime of learning and expertise?'

Cal admitted that in his brief telephone conversation with Rasouly he hadn't picked up the extent of his difficulties.

'And you, Ms Riley, are you an archeologist as well?'

'I'm not, I'm afraid. I'm not an academic at all.'

Cal stepped in. 'She's being modest. Eve is an expert in Elizabethan magic.'

'Ah, a John Dee disciple,' Cartwright said.

Eve relaxed at that. 'That's right!'

'I really don't know what to say about your aborted meeting, Professor Donovan.'

'Please, Cal.'

'Yes, of course. Cal. Is there anything I or a member of staff can do to try and salvage your mission?'

'I was trying to track down the location of an Aramaic papyrus my father found in Iraq in the late 1980s. He sent it to Omar for curation and translation but it's not clear the work was ever done. My father died in an accident at the dig and the funding for the project died with him.'

'And you think that he might have been in his office looking for the material when he had his heart attack?'

'It's possible.'

Cartwright chewed her lip. 'I really don't think I can let you root around in his files. That wouldn't be appropriate.'

Cal said he understood.

But she added with a wink, 'But now that the police has taken him away, perhaps we could just pop in and have a quick look on his desk to see if he managed to pull the relevant papers before he succumbed.'

On entering his office, Eve was immediately drawn to the spot on the floor where Rasouly's body had been found. Cal noticed her melancholy reaction. The carpet wasn't marked by the police, there were no stains, but Cal had little doubt that her sense of where he died was accurate.

Soon, Cal was drawn to something else. In the center of the desk was a thick folder, its label boldly referring to the Rabban Hurmizd excavation.

'Perhaps you're in luck,' Cartwright said.

Cal leaned over the desk and began flipping through the materials. In many ways they mirrored his father's own files in Cambridge. When he got to the last page he announced he had found nothing helpful.

'Are you sure I couldn't go through his other files?' he asked.

The director said she really wasn't comfortable letting an outsider do so but then she added, 'When are you scheduled to leave London?'

'Day after tomorrow. Why?'

'I placed a call to Omar's son this morning after his father was found. Marc is also on the faculty here, you know. He was in Jordan working on a pottery collection in Amman. He's returning to London tonight. If he's happy to let you search his father's things I certainly would have no objection.'

On the way out, they passed by a knot of female staff members talking among themselves. One of them, a woman in a hijab, was tearful. She saw the director and came over, asking whether she knew anything more about what had happened.

'I'm afraid not, Nadia. They believe it was a heart attack. It would have happened sometime yesterday.'

'I may have been the last person to see him alive,' the woman lamented.

'I'm sorry,' Cartwright said, 'I should make an introduction. Dr Nadia Ansour, please meet Professor Calvin Donovan from Harvard. And this is his friend, Ms Riley.'

Ansour took on a look of utter confusion. 'I don't know how to say this politely but are you sure this is Professor Donovan, Eleanor?'

'I'm pretty sure I am who I think I am,' Cal said, bemused. 'Why do you think I'm someone else?'

'Because yesterday when I saw Omar he was with Calvin Donovan.'

Detective Inspector Proctor from the Metropolitan Police set up shop in a small conference room a few doors down from Omar Rasouly's office. He interviewed Dr Ansour first, followed by Cal and Eve. After he took Cal's statement he inspected his passport, taking note of the 7:30 a.m. entry stamp at the airport the previous day.

'Dr Ansour tells me she saw Dr Rasouly near his office at approximately 11:15 a.m. with a man Dr Rasouly claimed was Calvin Donovan. How do you explain that?'

Cal tried hard not to get worked up by Proctor's officious tone. 'I don't think I can. It wasn't me.'

'It was certainly possible for you to get to central London from Heathrow by 11:15, isn't that so?'

'We got to our hotel before ten, actually.'

'And you didn't then come to the Institute?'

'No, we had a rest, left the hotel midday for lunch then went to the British Museum.'

'Can you confirm that Professor Donovan was with you the entirety of the morning, Miss Riley?'

'I'm sorry,' she said meekly. 'We have separate rooms. We met up for lunch.'

'So, Professor, you could have come over here at 11:15.'

'I could have but I didn't. I'm sure you spoke to Dr Ansour, same as me. Her description of the imposter didn't match me at all.'

'Just being thorough, sir.'

'Look, officer—'

'Detective.'

'Sorry, Detective. There's more to this than meets the eye. Dr Ansour's description of the guy sounds a lot like a man who killed two people back home and tried to kill me. The FBI is investigating.'

'And why would this man have come to London to murder an elderly gentleman with dementia?'

'He was probably after the same thing we are – an ancient papyrus that Dr Rasouly worked on thirty years ago.'

'And what is the significance of this papyrus?' He stumbled over the word and asked for the spelling and definition for his notes.

Cal glanced at Eve and sharply raised his eyes in a non-verbal signal for her to follow his lead. This detective wasn't going to be fertile ground for planting angel magic seeds.

'I believe it is valuable.'

'Valuable how?' the detective asked.

'Scientifically and financially. It's the scientific part that's of interest to me. I want to translate it, analyze it, and publish the findings. And there's a personal aspect to it also. My father was also an archeologist. He was the one who found it. It's part of his legacy.'

'What would this papyrus be worth?'

Cal made up something up. 'At auction, I'd say hundreds of thousands to the right private collector or museum.'

'And you, Miss Riley, what's your interest in this?'

'The same as Cal's,' she said.

'Are you a scientist too?'

'Me? I'm more of an amateur.'

Cal tried to cut off further questioning by telling Proctor

that he noticed CCTV cameras in the corridor outside Rasouly's office.

'You're quite the Renaissance man, aren't you, sir. Harvard professor and a detective to boot.'

Cal smiled. 'I was just going to give you the contact info for Special Agent D'Auria who's in charge of the case for the FBI. If you get a screen grab of the man who was with Rasouly then maybe the FBI and the Met can work together.'

The detective looked like he'd sucked on a lemon. 'We endeavor to cooperate with law-enforcement agencies around the world. This case will be no different.'

After they finished at the Institute Cal and Eve felt adrift. They slowly walked back to their hotel and Cal found himself looking over his shoulder in case the large man with a Middle Eastern accent was following. Eve eventually broke their silence.

'So, you want to tell me about this man?'

He was feeling guilty. 'Look, Eve. The last thing I wanted to do was expose you to any danger. If I thought for a second that this guy would have followed me to London I wouldn't have gotten you involved. I feel awful. Honestly, I've got no idea how he could have found out about the papyrus. The only people I told were you and Jessica.'

She went quiet.

'Yeah. Look, I think you should get on the first flight home we can book. I'll take care of everything.'

'Maybe you should just tell me what's going on first.'

He opened up to her. By the time they hit the lobby she knew everything.

'I'll go up to my room and sort out flights for you,' he said.

'I'm not leaving. I'm going to see this through. Maybe Omar's son will know where his dad kept the papyrus.'

'Can I try to change your mind?'

'Nope. Besides, when am I going to have the chance to be in London again?'

She was a fully informed adult so what could he say? 'In that case I owe you the Calvin Donovan special one-day VIP tour of London. Put your sneakers on.'

About twelve hours later they hobbled back to the hotel on sore feet. The activity tracker on Cal's watch showed they had clocked almost ten miles of streets, cathedrals, and museum galleries.

Over a late, boozy dinner at Veeraswamy, his favorite Indian restaurant in the city, he asked her to name the day's favorite.

'Let's see,' she said dreamily. 'The kid in me loved the London Eye and the Tower of London, the grown-up me loved Westminster Abbey and St Paul's, and the person I aspire to be loved the Tate and the National Gallery.'

The lift stopped on her floor.

'I'll ring Rasouly's son first thing in the morning and let you know,' he said.

'Could you see me to my door?' she asked.

She admitted that she had drunk too much and now she was swaying like she was on the deck of a gently rolling ship.

'You okay?' he asked, ready to steady her.

'I'm good. Actually, I'm really good.'

He got that unmistakable feeling he always had when a woman was interested.

'So, I'm just down there,' she said pointing her keycard down the hall.

At the door her slightly goofy smile vanished. 'Can I say something?'

'Sure.'

'I like you.'

Here it was.

'I like you too,' he said. 'You're a fascinating person. Fascinating woman.'

'Could I ask about Jessica?'

'We've been seeing each other for a couple of years.'

'Are you engaged?'

'Engaged?' He laughed and said no. He told her he wasn't sure he'd make a reliable husband, not that Jessica was looking for one.

'Here's the thing,' she said, referring to the brand of Indian beer they'd been knocking back. 'It's probably the Kingfisher truth serum talking but I've never, ever, never once in my life made love to a man I respected.'

This would not be an act of charity. He'd been smelling her black, perfumed hair all evening and having sly thoughts about how she'd look with her clothes on the floor. He briefly, very briefly, thought about his promise to Jessica then settled on a too-clever retort.

'I'm sorry to hear that. How do you know you'd still respect me in the morning?'

'We'd have to wait and see.'

When the morning came, they woke up early then made love again. When they were done she laughed and assured him she still did respect him. While she showered he called Marc Rasouly at the number Eleanor Cartwright had given him. When Cal began to introduce himself, Rasouly pre-empted him and told him that Cartwright had told him to expect the call.

'I'm so very sorry for your loss,' Cal said. 'I didn't know him, but he was a colleague of my father.'

'I know. They were frequent collaborators. I saw Hiram Donovan's name on several of my dad's papers.'

'This has got to be an awful time for you and your family, but do you think we could get together for a quick coffee to discuss the reason I came to London to see him?'

'Yes, of course. Could you come by the Institute in a couple of hours?'

Marc Rasouly's office was on a different floor to his father's. Cal and Eve arrived to find a sprig of a man in his late forties with a neat black beard. He was calm and composed and in short order admitted that he had been dreading the day when his father's dementia progressed to the stage when he'd have to go into a care facility.

'But I take it you believe my father may not have died of natural causes.'

'I'm afraid so,' Cal said.

'I suggested a post-mortem,' Rasouly said. 'I'm not sure they would have sought one if not for your suspicions.'

'It's possible the man who was seen with your father near his office was the same man who killed my mother last month.'

The man's composure broke. He looked aghast. 'My God, what is this all about? Eleanor said it was an Iraqi papyrus you were looking for? Someone would kill for that? I'm a pottery guy. Etruscan pottery. No one would kill for one of my pots.'

Cal told him about the papyrus. 'We think it might be a record of an ancient chant, a magical spell, if you will, intended to open up some sort of hidden realm of the heavens.'

'So what?' Rasouly said. 'Ancients believed in all sorts of magic and superstition. Modern, rational men don't.' When he saw Eve's expression he added, 'Or do they?'

'There's a field of magic called Enochian magic,' she said. 'And some people absolutely believe in its power to understand the cosmos. I'm one of them. And yes, I can understand why some terrible people might kill to get their hands on it. I think they believe they can make powerful magic with it.'

Rasouly shrugged. 'Look, put me down in the dyed-in-wool skeptic column. Frankly, I don't want to engage in a debate on something about which I am wholly ignorant, but you think this papyrus was sent to my father from your father?'

'Actually, it's not a single papyrus scroll or sheet. According to my father's field notes it's over a hundred fragments discovered during a 1988 excavation at a mediaeval Christian monastery in Iraq. Let me show you the single fragment that somehow didn't make its way into the assemblage sent to your father.'

Cal had the small glassine envelope with him. Rasouly took a pair of specimen forceps from his desk and examined it under a strong light.

'This is Aramaic?' he asked.

'It is.'

'Was anyone able to translate it?'

'We both did,' Cal said. 'It didn't make sense to me because it corresponds phonetically to a language called Enochian that only a very few people know. Eve is one of them.'

'It says, "the great one who,"' she said.

'And who is the great one?' Rasouly asked.

'We don't know that,' she answered.

'We're going to need the other fragments to make sense of it.'

Rasouly returned the papyrus to its envelope. He tented his long, delicate fingers, the kind of fingers well suited to assembling small pottery shards into whole ceramics. Then he surprised them with a bombshell.

'Well, I'm afraid you're not going to find what you're looking for in London.'

Cal swallowed. 'Okay—'

'I don't have to look anywhere. I remember my father telling me about this years ago when I was a graduate student here in the mid-nineties. He told me he had been commissioned to do restoration and translation of some epigraphy from a monastery in Mosul.'

'The site was close to Mosul,' Cal said.

'Well, then. It fits. He told me that all the artifacts from this dig, by edict of the Iraqi authorities, had to be sent to the Baghdad Museum. He was going to be doing his analysis in Baghdad.'

'Not London,' Cal said.

'Not London.'

'So, when my father wrote in his diary that he was sending the papyri to your father he meant care of the Baghdad Museum?'

'Almost certainly, I would say. But then Kuwait happened, and the Americans invaded, and Dad stopped going to Iraq. My mother thought it was too dangerous.'

'Your father told me over the phone that when my father died in 1989 the funding for the work dried up.'

'Well, probably that was an issue too.'

'Are you saying the papyri are in Baghdad?' Cal asked.

'Actually, I can tell you with some certainty that they are not.'

Cal stifled a few choice words in case Rasouly was the type of guy to take offense. 'How do you know that?' he said.

'Do you recall when the Americans invaded Iraq again in 2003 and all of us in the antiquities community watched in horror as the Baghdad Museum was looted? I may or may not have discussed this with my father at the time but a year or two after I remember very clearly having a conversation with him about whether he knew if the epigraphy he had worked on over the years stored in Baghdad had survived the war. He told me that he had corresponded with the director of the paleography department at the museum, who told him that after the invasion all of his specimens had been sent to the Cairo Museum for safekeeping.'

'Even though the material wasn't Egyptian?' Cal asked.

'I suppose the Egyptians did it as a courtesy of one Muslim museum director to another,' Rasouly said.

'And you think they're still there?'

'I really don't know but I don't believe they were ever sent back to my father. I believe that's where your papyri probably are.'

Cal slowly shook his head and said to Eve, 'How'd you like to go to Egypt?'

She grinned back, 'I'd like that very much.'

'You can do something for me, Professor Donovan,' Rasouly said.

'Anything I can.'

'If my father was indeed murdered, please do your utmost to help the authorities find the killer and bring him to justice.'

TWENTY-ONE

Constantinople, 1095

During the month after he murdered Daniel Basidi, Thaddeus aimlessly wandered the arid land, surviving mostly on alms and the rabbits and rats he snared. There were days when he had nothing to put in his belly. But the woven bag containing Daniel's precious scrying stone, wax seals, and magic table was rarely off his shoulder. Lacking a plan, he walked in circles and figure-eights, sometimes returning to the very spot where he had begun. Every dark-skinned soul he encountered stirred up new hatred and he uttered under his breath: Saracen bastard – were you the one who killed my parents?

Saracens.

The Christian term for the followers of the Prophet
Mohammed. It didn't matter whether they were Arabs or Seljuk
Turks, they were all Saracens to him. It was a Semitic word
meaning thief, marauder, plunderer, and it perfectly encapsu-
lated his contempt. Every so often he encountered one of the
rare souls who wore a crucifix around his neck or marked his
house with the Chi Rho christogram, or the outline of a fish.
He would approach them, invoking kinship, hoping for the
reward of a proper meal.

In one of these Christian houses, as far west as he had ever
been, he was invited inside.

The patriarch, a man who called himself Jeremiah of Jaza,
delighted at the sight of a Christian pilgrim in these parts and
lavished attention on the young man.

Thaddeus gaped at the bowls of roasted goat and flatbread
and dates beautifully presented on reed mats. He asked why
there was such bounty and why the members of the family
were dressed in finery.

'Do you not know what today is?' Jeremiah asked.

'I know not.'

'It is Midsummer Day, the Feast of St John the Baptist.'

Thaddeus began to sob, imagining the festivities that were
happening at this very moment at his monastery.

'What is the matter, my son?' his host asked.

'I was reminded of the feast that I am missing.'

'Where?'

'At my monastery.'

'You are a monk?'

At his nod, Jeremiah clasped his hands together and
exclaimed to his wife, sons, and daughters that they were
blessed to have a priest in their midst on a holy day.

Thaddeus lowered his head and said, 'I do not know whether
I am still a priest. I left my community.'

'Why is that?'

He was not going to explain. He could think of nothing to
say and remained silent.

Jeremiah seemed to read into his silence. 'The life of a
monk is surely hard for a young man such as yourself. Losing

one's way, losing one's faith for a time is, I would think, natural. You will regain what you have lost. I can see the light in your eyes. It is God's light.'

Thaddeus did not wish to opine on the ebb and flow of faith. He was more interested in the bowls of food and the jugs of beer so close at hand.

'For now, the life of a pilgrim suits me.'

'But you are a pilgrim priest and you do honor our home. Will you lead us in prayer, Brother Thaddeus?'

Reluctantly, Thaddeus did so and was rewarded with the biggest joint of goat.

After the meal, he reclined on a cushion and satisfied his host's curiosity but only to a point. He told Jeremiah that when he was just ten years of age the Turks butchered his family simply because they were Christian. He alone survived. A community of monks took him in. He began as an apprentice to a stone mason then became a novice and finally received Holy Orders. He was the best flint-knapper in the monastery and made all the sickle blades his brothers used to harvest grains for their bread and their beer. One day the bishop surely would have put him in charge of all the stone work.

'Then why did you leave, Thaddeus?' his host asked.

Now, well-supped with beer sloshing around his gut, he had an answer to give.

'The faith of Christ is about love,' the young man said. 'But I could not love. I am consumed by hate for the Saracens. I watched them cut the throats of my mother and my father and my brothers. I wish they had caught me too and thrown me down the village well with the other children, so I would not have had to live with hatred all my days. I had to leave the monastery to act upon my hatred.'

'But what can you do?' Jeremiah asked. 'What will you do?'

'If I were a soldier I would fight. Alas I know nothing of soldiering. But I have another weapon.'

'And what is this weapon?'

Thaddeus lowered his voice so that Jeremiah's lounging family could not hear. 'I know magic. I can speak to the angels. I will have them do my bidding.'

Jeremiah seemed fearful. 'But angels are good, Brother Thaddeus.'

'Some are good. Some are not,' he said without elaboration. 'The instruments of my magic are here in my bag. Would you like to see the stone I use to converse with them?'

He let his host peek at the obsidian mirror and hurriedly returned it to the sack.

'However, I am crippled by my ignorance,' Thaddeus said. 'I do not know how to direct the angels to my purpose.'

'Why can you not ask them to smite the Saracens who did evil unto your kin or to smite all the Saracens who occupy our land?'

'I do not think the angels can smite mortal men by their own hand. They must work through men.'

'What will you do, then?'

'I need the counsel of a wise and powerful Christian.'

Jeremiah thought for a while then said, 'Then you must go west to Constantinople and seek an audience with the wisest and most powerful Christian in the kingdom. You must see Emperor Alexios.'

It was a two-month trek through vast empty spaces of Syria and Asia Minor. Sometimes Thaddeus went days without seeing another person. Whenever he happened upon a Christian he asked about the nearest church or monastery where he might receive some succor.

On some solitary nights, when the moon was full and bright enough to reflect into the showstone, he set up his magic implements and summoned the angel who had been his companion on the journey. Jachniel had appeared to him in the thirteenth Aethyr, identifying himself as one of the guardians of the gates of the South Wind.

'Will I reach Constantinople?' Thaddeus would ask.

'You will,' the angel would respond.

'What will I find there?'

The answer was always the same. 'Your destiny.'

Once, in the Anatolian town of Kaisariyah, the halfway point on his journey, Thaddeus was set upon by Saracen thieves while trying to find some clean straw for the night and had to fight them off with his walking stick. He had cut three grooves into the lower half of the sturdy staff and, using his knapping skills, he had embedded and glued rows of flint blades. The thieves received the cutting end and fled, leaving trails of crimson. It was the first time the young man had ever drawn blood from a Saracen and he reveled in it. He ran a finger over the shiny, red-streaked flint and tasted the coppery blood. It tasted like revenge; it tasted like victory. Invigorated, he continued westward at a swifter pace.

The Christian city of Constantinople was protected by the Theodosian walls. Emperor Theodosius II had erected the massive, double-rowed stone walls six centuries earlier and they remained virtually impregnable. They had saved the Byzantine Empire time and again from marauding Arabs, Bulgars, and Slavs and now a solitary underweight pilgrim presented himself at one of its many gates.

One of the soldiers manning the gates asked what he wanted.

'I wish to enter the city, friend,' Thaddeus said.

'For what purpose?'

'I intend to join a monastery.'

'Bit old for a novice,' the soldier scoffed.

Thaddeus pulled out the silver crucifix hanging from his neck. 'I am a priest.'

The soldier cleared his throat. 'Sorry, father. You are free to enter.'

'Where is the Emperor's palace?' Thaddeus asked.

'No monastery there, father.'

'Seeing the place where the Emperor resides is part of my pilgrimage.'

'Keep walking toward the setting sun. It is close to the sea. You will come to the hippodrome first. The palace is nearby.'

The great palace stood on a steeply sloping hillside beside the hippodrome. It had been built seven hundred years earlier by the first Christian emperor, Constantine, and had survived all manner of man and God-made calamities – fires, earthquakes, riots, and sieges. The palace complex spread seaward toward the magnificent Hagia Sophia church on a series of earthwork terraces that Constantine had personally designed. The complex was so vast that a bewildered Thaddeus had no

idea where to approach it to seek entry, but everyone he questioned pointed him toward the Augustaion Square at the south
side of the Hagia Sophia and from there, the Chalke Gate, so
named because of gilded bronze tiles used on its roof. But
when he arrived, no amount of pleading his case could get
him past the grim-faced soldiers who manned the gate. He
returned again and again, and the answer was always the same.

This was a Christian city, a place where a priest was treated
kindly. Thaddeus ate well, slept in a proper bed most nights,
and regained his strength. In his second week in Constantinople,
he met the owner of a lodging house while begging for bread
in the Augustaion Square. The man offered him a tiny room
at no charge and in conversation one night told him that the
Patriarch of Constantinople had returned from a journey to
Rome and would be celebrating Mass the very next day at the
Hagia Sophia. That night Thaddeus entered the thirteenth
Aethyr and spoke with the angel Jachniel.

'I have not been able to speak with the Emperor,' he told
the angel.

'He is most high and esteemed,' Jachniel replied.

'Tomorrow I will try to speak with the Patriarch of this
city.'

'Tell the Patriarch that Pope Urban II did whisper into his
ear as he was departing Rome, and this is what he said: "You
stand between two worlds, the noble world of our Lord, Jesus
Christ, and the dark world of the heathen Turk. Be as unyielding
as a great boulder for you are the sword of Christ."'

'And if I tell him what the Pope said unto him, will he help
me have audience with the Emperor?'

'He will.'

'And what should I tell the Emperor so that he will heed
my words?'

'You will tell him about his son.'

It seemed as if the entire city had turned out to celebrate
Mass with the returning Patriarch. Nicholas III Grammatikos
was rather tall and skeletal with a long white beard, but
his voice was uncommonly strong. The great Hagia Sophia
dome seemed to amplify it. It reached the back of the church
where an enthralled Thaddeus, crushed in the throng like one

olive too many in a stuffed jar, hung on every word of prayer.
When it was time for the Patriarch to perform the eucharist,
the faithful presented themselves one by one for communion.
Finally, it was Thaddeus's turn. He took the bread and the
wine, but he did not move along swiftly like the others.

The old Patriarch looked at him with a furrowed brow and
a younger priest was about to intervene when Thaddeus blurted
out, 'You stand between two worlds, the noble world of our
Lord, Jesus Christ, and the dark world of the heathen Turk.
Be as unyielding as a great boulder for you are the sword of
Christ.'

The Patriarch said, 'How knowest you these words?'

'I speak with angels, Holy Father. I have a message for the
Emperor.'

The palace was so vast that if Thaddeus's life depended on
his finding his way back to the Chalke Gate on his own, he
would have perished. A palace official led him through myriad
chambers, corridors, and courtyards until they reached a
surprisingly small, though well-appointed room where the
Emperor was lounging on a divan. Alexios Komnenos, who
was known as Alexios I, had been emperor for fourteen years.
He had the compact body of a soldier who had distinguished
himself on the battlefield against Seljuk Turks and other
invaders. His shaggy brown beard and fitful eyes gave him
more the appearance of a ruffian than the Byzantine Emperor
and he immediately challenged Thaddeus.

'What about my son?' he barked. 'Patriarch Nicholas tells
me you accosted him at Mass about my son. He tells me you
speak with angels. Out with it, man.'

'I do speak with angels, Your Majesty. The angel Jachniel
spoke about your son to me not three days ago.'

Alexios unleashed a torrent of flippancy. 'Never heard of
him. How many angels are there, anyway? I cannot keep them
straight.'

'There are myriad angels, Your Excellency. Jachniel is one
of the guardians of the South Wind. He resides in the thirteenth
Aethyr of Heaven.'

'I like a good south wind. We do not get south winds that

often. They come off the sea from the east mainly. Tell me, priest, which of my sons were you gossiping about?'

'John, Your Excellency.'

He was the eldest son, the heir apparent.

'Well, spit it out.'

'It concerns a snake,' Thaddeus said.

The Emperor swung his muscular legs to a sitting position and glowered at the young priest.

'Speak more,' he demanded.

'A fortnight ago, in a palace garden, he was bitten on the great toe by a green snake. Though it was a poisonous viper, the surgeon did suck out the poison. That action together with your vigorous prayer did save him from mortal harm.'

Alexios was on his feet now, closing the distance to where Thaddeus stood in three angry strides. The Emperor's guards lifted their spears to a two-handed ready position.

'Who told you this?' he bellowed.

Thaddeus flinched but held his ground. He could smell the spices from Alexios's last meal on his hot breath. 'The angel.'

'Who do you know in my palace? The surgeon? A servant? Tell me now.'

'I know no one, Your Excellency. I have just arrived in the city. I am a stranger to these parts. I hail from Al-Iraq, where I lived in a cloistered monastery.'

'Which monastery?'

'Rabban Hurmizd.'

'I know of it. Why did you leave it?'

'Because of my hatred of the Saracens. They butchered my family. I decided to use my powers as a scryer who communes with angels to bring vengeance upon them. Yet I need your help, Your Excellency. My guardian angel informed me about your son as a means to convince you of my powers.'

The Emperor backed off and returned to his divan and the palace guard relaxed their postures.

'No one despises the Saracen more than I,' Alexios said. 'The Normans attack me from the west, the Saracens from the east but at least the Normans share our one and true God. The Saracen is a heathen, an abomination upon my realm, and my dream is to be the agent of their destruction. What angels do you commune with who might help us? This Jachniel? Are not the angels of Heaven mainly gentle beings lacking in bellicosity?'

'That is indeed so, Your Excellency. But I am not speaking of the angels in Heaven.'

The Emperor became angry again. 'What are you, priest? Are you a conjurer? Do you practice dark magic? I could have you burned at the stake!'

'Surely, Your Excellency, you would agree that conjuring to rid the world of the Saracen would not be an act of evil. Would it not be to the benefit of all good and faithful Christians?'

Alexios went quiet and said that he would have to confer with his council of noblemen and with the Patriarch on the matter. In the meanwhile, Thaddeus would remain in the palace in the custody of his guards. The young priest thanked him and bowed obsequiously.

As he was being led away the Emperor suddenly told his guards to halt. 'Tell me, priest,' he said, 'how do you summon the angels?'

'With the use of the tools in this bag,' Thaddeus replied.

'Show me.'

Alexios took the red bag and looked inside it. 'These are unfamiliar objects.'

'I can show you how I perform my magic, Your Excellency. You can speak to the angels through me.'

'Is that so?' the Emperor said. 'I will take counsel, but I alone will decide what shall be done. Guards, take this priest away.'

'My bag, Your Excellency?' Thaddeus said.

'If you were a soldier I would confiscate your sword and your shield to diminish the threat to my person. As you are a conjurer, I will confiscate the tools of your magic.'

Thaddeus was treated well. Although he was locked inside a room, it was larger and far better appointed than his monk's cell at the monastery and the food he was given was fresh and appetizing. It came almost as a disappointment when a guard announced that he was to be freed from confinement.

As he was taken through dark corridors he asked, 'Where are we going?'

When he received no answer he began to panic, wondering if these were to be the last moments of his life.

He was brought into a large room festooned with candles. On a green and gold rug in the middle of the room sat his red bag.

Emperor Alexios entered and sat on a padded bench.

'My advisors were unanimous in their opinion. Speaking for the Council, would you care to know what Patriarch Nicholas advised?'

Thaddeus nodded hesitantly.

'He believes you should be burned alive, depriving whatever remains of your bones a Christian burial. What think you of that?'

'I am not overly fond of his advice, Your Majesty.'

He held his breath until Alexios said, 'I am not fond of it myself. In the end, I have made a contrary decision. Nothing is more vital than the defeat of the Saracen plague. You will do your magic, right here, right now, and I will observe. I presume it is a fallen angel whom you will summon.'

A visibly relieved Thaddeus told him that was so.

Alexios said, 'If I am satisfied your angel will smite the Saracens then you will live. If I am unsatisfied, then you will not see the sun again.'

The Emperor was brought a cup of wine and he watched Thaddeus assemble the magic table and place the black scrying stone atop the largest of the wax seals, the Sigillum Dei Aemeth. As the monk positioned candles so that the showstone would catch the light, he felt his sweat beading on his forehead and dripping from his armpits. He had only invoked the 49th Call a single time. He had bucked up the courage one night during one of the early days of his journey from Al-Iraq to Constantinople, for if the call had not worked, why make the dangerous trek at all? Better to open a vein as penance for his murder of Daniel and lie down to drain his blood upon the soil of his homeland. But the call had worked, though he had been too frightened to continue. He had tipped over the showstone and backed away until he could muster the courage to pack up his implements.

'I am ready to begin, Your Excellency,' he said.

'Shall I join you?' Alexios asked. 'Will I be able to look upon your stone and see what you see, hear what you hear?'

'Please sit opposite me, Your Excellency. Only the scryer sees and hears but you may ask questions through my voice.'

The time had come.

Thaddeus had used his time trekking through the wilderness to commit the 49th Call to memory, but now he was so nervous that he placed Daniel's papyrus on his lap lest he forgot any of the words.

He slowly intoned the call and when he was done all he could do was wait.

The wait was short.

The surface of the showstone came alive with the image he had seen that one time before.

His guardian angel, Jachniel, was a rather flamboyant figure with a red robe, gold-colored sandals, and an animated face. This angel who appeared in the stone sat still upon a plain throne, his head slightly bowed to the ground. He wore a simple gray robe. He was neither handsome nor ugly, his beard neither long or short. If one had encountered such a personage upon the road or at the market, he would have made a light impression. He spoke the angel language smoothly with almost a soothing cadence.

'I am Satanail. Why have you summoned me?'

That is when the angel cocked his head and stared through the showstone, locking his black eyes on the young priest, imbuing him with fear.

Thaddeus somehow found the courage to translate the question.

The Emperor sucked in air as if punched in the gut. Satanail was the name given to him in the Book of Enoch, but most knew him by his shortened name, Satan. He had been an archangel, the leader of the Watchers, the angels who chose to cohabitate with human women and thereby fell from God's grace. Now he was Prince of the fallen angels, the great architect of evil.

The Emperor was too shocked to speak. Thaddeus struggled to find his own words, the ones he had rehearsed in his head.

After he spoke them in angel tongue he whispered a quick translation for Alexios.

This is what he said: 'Lord Satanail, I need your help to bring destruction down upon the heads of the Saracens who have killed innocent Christians and who threaten our land.'

The angel's mouth thinned. Was it a smile or a frown? 'Why do you not seek help from the king who sits before you?'

Thaddeus asked Alexios how he should reply.

'Tell him that although I am indeed a king and emperor, I do not have the power to smite so powerful an enemy. Implore him to act as our sword and spear.'

Satanail leaned forward on his throne and said, 'I can but act on Earth through the body of a man. If this king is not powerful enough to raise an army to smite your enemy, which man is so?'

The Emperor did not have to think long. 'There is but one man who possesses this power. Yet on his own he lacks the resolve for action.'

On hearing the name, the angel's lips parted into a full-on smile, revealing rows of plump yellow teeth.

'I know of this man,' Satanail said. 'Ask the king if he understands the magnitude of death and misery that such an action will bring upon your Earthly realm?'

Alexios answered without hesitation, 'I know full well. Tell him it will be worth every drop of spilled blood.'

Thaddeus felt a chill run through his feverish body at the sight of Satanail laughing and slapping his thigh.

'Drops of blood?' the angel cried gleefully. 'I think not. Prepare ye for rivers of blood!'

TWENTY-TWO

Cal woke to a harsh sunlight pouring through the parted curtains. Eve was sleeping beside him. There had been no point getting two rooms. Both of them wanted to keep whatever it was they had going, at least for a while.

He showered, ordered room service for two, and made an outside call. When the breakfast arrived, he had it brought onto the balcony then woke Eve with a playful pat to her rear.

'Are we still in Cairo?' she asked, her eyes a couple of slits.

'Come outside and see for yourself.'

The view from a high floor of the Four Seasons at the Nile Plaza was worth the crazy price of the suite. The river, brownish-blue and swiftly flowing, snaked around both sides of Gezira Island. The low, sprawling cityscape was punctuated by the spires of mosques and a few skyscrapers. Eve clutched her robe to her chest and took it in.

Cal pointed toward the island and said, 'There's the Opera House and next to it, just there, is the Museum of Modern Egyptian Art. And over there on the mainland – the orange building – that's where we're headed this morning. The Egyptian Museum.'

'You know your way around.'

'A little. Egyptian archeology isn't my thing, but I've been here for conferences. And as a tourist.'

'It's so beautiful. You think we'll be able to see the pyramids?'

Tourism was far from his mind. 'We'll see. Work comes first.'

She nodded and gulped down a glass of freshly squeezed orange juice.

While she dressed, he tackled an email reply he'd been avoiding. Jessica had shot him a message, asking how things were going in Cairo, and wondering whether Eve Riley had returned to the States. The question had been put so benignly, without her usual barbs or sarcasm, that he almost felt she knew with certainty that he'd already fallen off the monogamy wagon. He tapped an artful reply that Eve had, in fact, come to Egypt because, assuming the papyri were found, he wouldn't be able to make sense of them without her. Then he added that he missed her.

He pocketed his phone and sank into a shallow gulley of guilt.

He was remarkably disciplined when it came to some parts of his life, the academic and scholarly parts, and so reckless in others. His drinking still veered out of control, but he'd

found that Jessica had largely tamed his roving eye. She
punched every one of his tickets. They were so well matched
in intellect and finances that there weren't any of the superiority/
inferiority games that had torpedoed so many of his past relationships. She was also funny, rather beautiful, and well read,
which was important to him. She had even made the effort to
tackle some of his more rarefied books on religion. She was
also a Catholic, which mattered to him only insofar as she intui-
tively understood the concept of Catholic guilt. It was always
handy, he reckoned, to be on the same guilt wavelength as a
girlfriend. So why was he cheating? If he ever was forced into
therapy, he'd have to ask his shrink. For now, he comforted
himself in the knowledge that at least it had been Eve who
had made the first move. That had to count for something.

The morning was already steamy when he and Eve strolled
through a bustling Tahrir Square on the brief walk to the
Egyptian Museum. Cal only knew the museum as a tourist.
Egyptian archeology was far afield from his areas of interest
and he had been forced to cold-call the museum director, who,
based on Cal's credentials, had kindly put him in touch with
the curator of the papyrus collections, a fellow named Osama
Nawal. It was Dr Nawal who came to meet them in an entry
hall teeming with a tour group from Japan and local school
children on field trips.

Nawal was a clean-shaven, bespectacled man in a loose
plaid sport shirt. He spoke excellent English. He was older
than Cal, but he came across deferentially, making a point of
telling him that he had reviewed Cal's bona fides online and
was most pleased to be of any possible assistance to such an
illustrious professor. He treated Eve somewhat as an after-
thought, directing his full attention to the Harvard academic
whom he led, talking non-stop, through the crowds, and past
a guard station into a staff area, and from there, to a staircase
to the basement.

'I have been the curator for the papyrus department for only
five years,' Nawal said. 'It was my predecessor who I have
been able to ascertain was responsible for receiving Professor
Rasouly's materials from the Baghdad Museum after the war.
Of course, the decision to accept various artifacts from Iraq

was taken at a ministerial level as a service to a brother-museum in distress.'

'Are all the Baghdad artifacts still here?' Cal asked.

'My understanding is that the Iraqi government subsequently requested for much of it to be returned and that has occurred over the years. However, I am aware of no requests for the return of the Rasouly archive during my predecessor's tenure and certainly none have been made since I took charge of the department.'

'Does that surprise you?'

'Not at all. You see, for political and cultural reasons, artifacts and writings from an early Christian monastery would not be a priority for the Iraqis. And as you can imagine, the Rasouly papyri are quite the step-children here in an Egyptian museum that concentrates on Dynastic epigraphy. That is why I was so astonished to receive two queries about these papyri in the past week when there were none before.'

Cal stopped him. 'I'm sorry. Two queries? Who else asked about them?'

'A gentleman presented himself to the director's office the day before yesterday. His name was Almasi. Walid Almasi. He said he was from the Iraqi Ministry of the Interior. He wanted to see the Rasouly papyri. However, he did not have proper identification papers and the assistant to the director asked him to return the following day after the Iraqi Embassy could be contacted. Well, the Embassy knew nothing about this man and he did not return. Very strange, no?'

Cal looked at Eve and said, 'Do you know what this man looked like?'

'I did not see him, but Mrs Elhawary told me he was a very large gentleman, perhaps fifty years old, and a bit rough in his mannerisms, which is why she was suspicious.'

Cal said nothing more about him but he knew damn well who Almasi or whatever his name was. But he didn't want to spook Nawal and distract him from helping them.

First London, now Cairo. How was the killer able to keep one step ahead of them at every turn?

Instead, Cal asked, 'Were you able to find the Rasouly papyri?'

'In truth, it was a challenge. I am quite sure that no one

has examined them since their arrival. One of my assistants spent a full day going through cabinets and boxes.'

'You have them?'

'Indeed we do. I have set up a work station in my department for you to make an examination.'

Walking through the basement, they passed through long halls of cabinets and open racks of pottery and statues, sarcophagi, storage jars of mummified animals, and dozens of human mummies. Eve paused to look into the hollow eyes of a beautifully preserved female from the Third Dynasty and had to scramble to catch up when Nawal took a turn and disappeared. She caught up with them at the door to the Papyrus Restoration Laboratory.

The large man with a floppy fedora had been loitering in the square outside the museum entrance. When he spotted Cal and Eve, he drifted inside and waited by the gift shop until he saw Nawal come to get them. Then he followed at a discreet distance. At the guard station, Barzani told the guard that he had seen a boy urinating on a statue, and when the guard ran off to investigate, he went through to the staff area and down into the basement. From a distance he saw Cal and Eve disappearing into the Papyrus Laboratory. Once he knew their destination he returned to the museum square and bought himself an ice cream.

The lab was bathed in harsh fluorescent light. There was an open plan of work stations manned almost exclusively by female conservators at drafting tables. They briefly looked up from their magnifying loupes when the visitors entered.

'You will work here, Professor,' Nawal said.

There was a file box on the table labeled *Baghdad Museum/ Omar Rasouly.*

'Will you be letting Professor Rasouly know that his papyri have been located?' Nawal asked.

'I wish we could,' Cal said. 'Unfortunately, he recently passed away.'

Nawal tutted his sympathy.

'I have a meeting I must attend,' Nawal said. 'Here are security passes that will allow you to come and go as you wish and here is my card with my contact information. Perhaps we can get a coffee when you have made some progress. I will leave you to your work.'

As soon as they were alone, Eve whispered, 'He's here!'

Cal tried not to sound alarmed, but it wasn't easy. 'I wish I hadn't brought you, Eve. Let's just get this done as fast as we can and get home. We'll take taxis. No walkabouts, no restaurants outside the hotel.'

'No pyramids,' she said sadly.

'No pyramids.'

Cal opened the file box and there it was: his father's calligraphy. The first envelope he took from the box was labeled with one of the Rabban Hurmizd grid references from his father's excavation journal – Cutting 9/ L 14. Peering inside he saw loose papyrus fragments the size of average postage stamps, some larger.

'Bingo!' he said.

A woman at a nearby desk glanced over.

'Yes?' Eve asked.

'Oh yes,' he replied, more softly, carefully tipping the fragments onto the drafting table in a small pile.

Nawal had equipped the table with the tools of his trade – tweezers, a set of magnifying loupes ranging from low to high power, a high-intensity light, dainty paint brushes, special glue for working with papyrus fragments, acid-free backing paper, and pieces of mounting glass for non-permanent fixations. Cal tweezed one of the fragments, put it under a low-magnification loupe, and adjusted the lamp.

'It's very similar to the piece we already have,' he said, 'same coloration, same striations, same kind of lettering.'

He moved over so she could have a look through the glass.

'Is it Aramaic?' she said.

'Yeah, but it's like the piece I brought with me from Harvard. They're not words I recognize.'

'Can you sound them out for me?'

Their cheeks were almost touching. He could smell her hair. He vocalized the Aramaic.

'It's Enochian,' she said. 'It says earth. Actually, of the earth.'

'Then we're in the money. How good are you at jigsaw puzzles?'

'I hate them. You?'

'I hate them too. Always found them annoying. On digs whenever we have pottery shards to assemble, I leave it to others.'

'How many pieces are there all together?' she asked.

He proceeded to do an inventory of the contents of the file box. All the samples mentioned in his father's journal were there.

'With the one piece we already have, there should be a hundred-five. They were found in three different grids reasonably close to one another but we don't know if they were scattered and represent a single torn-up papyrus or whether the ones found together are from different sheets. I think we should start with the assumption that they were from three different papyri and try to piece them together that way.'

'How should we do it?' she asked. 'Like an upside-down jigsaw puzzle or a right-side-up one?'

He grunted. 'Right-side-up I'd say. Let's work together. I'll start with shapes of pieces and the Aramaic letters, you refine by the phonetics to make sure we're looking at whole words.'

The irregular shapes and frayed edges made Cal think that the pieces had been torn by hand. One of the larger fragments gave another clue. It didn't lie flat – there was a fold through it. Cal thought that a sheet might have been folded before someone ripped it to pieces. It took ten minutes of trial and error before Cal was satisfied he'd gotten a good match of two corresponding edges.

'What do you think?' he asked

'It seems like a good fit,' she said. 'Sound it out for me.'

He pieced the phonemes together a few different ways with different intonations until she told him to stop. She started writing on a piece of scratch paper, trying a few things out.

'I think it says, let them vex.'

'Are you sure?'

'Pretty sure, yeah.'

'Okay, then. Let them vex,' he said. 'We're on the way.'

She squeezed his hand like an excited kid.

They worked for several hours but it was exceedingly slow going. The fragments were shaped similarly to one another and the handwriting was so sloppy that Cal came to believe the writer had not been a professional scribe. By the time hunger and fatigue overtook them, they had found only four contiguous pairings. They kept them pressed between two pieces of glass. Cal asked one of the conservators if there was a cafeteria in the museum and they went there on break.

After lunch they returned to the laboratory and kept plugging away, but they had so little success that Cal reached a conclusion.

'Look,' he said, 'I think we've got to abandon the idea that there were three separate sheets. It's got to be one bigger puzzle.'

'I think so too,' she said. 'You want to do the honors?'

He swore under his breath, reached for the folder, and began carefully removing fragments from the other two grid references. He laid them onto the table in their own groupings, ink-side-up. In case he was wrong in his assumption, he took multiple close-up pictures of each grouping to restore them to their original associations if need be.

A half-hour later they had their answer. One fragment from one grouping paired perfectly with one from a different group.

Cal sounded it out and asked her what it said.

She sucked in a little air and said, 'Cast down.'

'Isn't that interesting?' he said. 'Fallen angels, cast down to Hell?'

'Cal, I've got a bad feeling,' she said.

All he could manage to say was, 'Let's just keep going until they close for the day.'

When the conservators around them started packing up for the evening, they began tidying their work station. They had fourteen pairs and two triplets plated under glass to show for their efforts. The rest went back into envelopes.

At the museum exit, Cal told her to stay alert. 'He could be anywhere. Let's grab the first taxi.'

There was a taxi rank just off the museum square. They briskly walked over and hopped in the lead car. When the driver heard they were only going as far as the Four Seasons he began to argue, but Cal pushed a large-enough bill into his hand to shut him up.

As they drove off, Barzani, who had been loitering in the square, almost lost his fedora rushing to the taxi rank. He climbed into the next available cab and ordered the driver to follow Cal's car.

After a few short blocks, the lead taxi pulled into the hotel forecourt and Barzani told his driver to let him out on the street.

'Too fast, too fast!' the driver complained in his best English, pointing at the meager fare in his meter. 'I not take you if I know.'

The big man swore at him and tossed some coins onto the front seat. Then he walked to the lobby and with his hat pulled low, had a look around. Cal and Eve apparently had gone to their room, so he settled into the farthest corner of the bar, ordered a soft drink, and made a call.

'What's going on, Tariq?' Hamid asked.

'They spent the whole day in the basement, in the papyrus room.'

'They must have found it!'

'Maybe, but I don't know.'

'Where are they now?'

'Back at their hotel. I'm in the lobby.'

'Okay, listen, Tariq. This is a good development. Keep watching them but don't let them see you. Let them keep doing what they're doing. When it looks like they're ready to leave Cairo, that's when you make your move, okay? I want the papyrus. You must not fail.'

'And the stone?'

'It's somewhere in Cambridge. God willing, we'll find it.'

Up in their room, Cal was also on the phone. He got Julia D'Auria's voice mail, but she called him back a few minutes later.

'Funny ring tone,' she said. 'Where are you?'

'Cairo, Egypt.'

'You get around. What are you doing there?'

'On the trail of the papyrus.'

'Must be a lot of them there. What can I do for you?'

He told her he wanted to see if Detective Inspector Proctor from the Metropolitan Police had contacted her.

'Yeah, he did,' she said. 'He sent us a series of shots of the suspect from CCTV outside the place where Rasouly was murdered.'

'They're calling it a murder?'

'After the autopsy, yeah. It looks like his chest was compressed till he asphyxiated.'

'Is it the same man?'

'Looks like it. The thing is we haven't put a name to the face yet. Obviously, he flew into London from the States but without knowing the flight details or even the day, it's a needle in a haystack situation sorting through CCTV at the London airports.'

'I think he may be in Cairo.'

'What?' she exclaimed.

'Somebody matching his description was poking around the museum.'

'Jesus, Donovan, you've got to watch yourself.'

'Believe me, I know. We're going to get the hell out of here ASAP. But if he followed us to Cairo—'

She finished the thought for him. 'Yeah, this could help. What day did you travel?'

He told her.

'You don't think he was on the same flight?'

'We would've seen him.'

'We'll work with the British authorities. There are only one or two relevant travel days he could have used, yours and the day before. There can't be that many flights a day from London to Cairo. I'll let you know.'

'Thanks.'

'Try not to get killed, all right?'

'I've got very little interest in that outcome.'

Cal and Eve didn't venture out that night. They had room service on the balcony, watched the city lights and river traffic, and he drank half the mini-bar. Then they began in the living room and continued in the bedroom, making love until exhausted.

They dawdled in the morning; there was no point leaving until the museum opened. On the way out, Cal told Eve to take her passport in case the security guard at the restricted area wanted to check their IDs against their passes.

The conservators at the nearby desks were used to them by now and they got a few smiles as they settled in. The work progressed as before. There were no shortcuts. A couple of hours into it, Cal announced he needed a coffee badly.

The cafeteria wasn't crowded. He stirred sugar into his coffee. Eve poured hot water onto her tea bag.

Then Barzani poked his head in.

Perhaps he only wanted a coffee or a water and didn't want to go out into the hot square. But it was a sloppy bit of tradecraft.

Cal saw him right away. The squared-off, bulky body was unmistakable. Their eyes locked. Cal hadn't seen the face under the balaclava. The man was older than he imagined; he fought younger.

Barzani retreated.

Cal waited a few seconds before reacting.

'Eve, we're leaving. He's here.'

'Who? Him?' she said, looking around.

'He saw me and backed off into the gallery. We're going to leave through the courtyard.'

'And go where?'

'I don't know. We've got to lose him and figure out what to do.'

They cut through the courtyard and circled back around to the main entrance. Cal scanned the crowds by the audioguide rentals, the gift shop, and the ticket counters. He didn't see him.

Eve followed him out the door into the garden square.

'Quick, let's grab a taxi,' he said.

They were halfway to the taxi rank when Cal looked over his shoulder and saw the big man coming toward them.

'Hurry!'

The taxi rank was empty.

Barzani had a hand in his pocket around a folding knife that would open with the flick of his wrist.

He had a makeshift plan.

He'd follow them into a crowd, cut Cal's throat from behind first, then hers, and leave them to the screaming masses. Then he would backtrack to the museum, barge into the papyrus laboratory, get someone to show him what they had been working on, and take it.

Would it work?

He didn't know but George Hamid would expect him to try.

Cal knew none of this but he was scared. He reached for Eve's hand and simply said, 'Run.'

Their hand-hold lasted only until the first knot of tourists blocked their way. They went around them, Cal to the left, Eve to the right, and reunited side by side. Cal's plan was to outrun the killer back to the hotel, and once safely in their room, maybe call the police, maybe get the FBI to help with the authorities. To get there they'd have to pass through Tahrir Square, which would be packed with people and cars this time of day. The problem with the plan was that Eve was wearing loose sandals and she couldn't keep up. The sidewalks were baking hot so barefooted running wouldn't work either. The big man's long legs were getting him closer.

They had to circle around Tahrir Square to get to the Four Seasons. A quarter way around, Cal saw they weren't going to make it. He had been forced to slow down for Eve's sake and the killer was gaining on them too fast. Glancing down El Tahrir Street, Cal saw something.

Slowing the man down wasn't good enough. If they were going to get out of Egypt alive they needed to stop him cold.

'This way,' he shouted.

'The hotel's that way,' she shouted back.

'I know. Come on!'

There was a cafe with an awning a hundred meters down the street and Cal pulled her inside.

Barzani was right behind them, out of breath. He paused outside the cafe and looked like he was going to come inside, but when he saw them getting seated at a window table he backed off. He crossed the street, keeping them in sight, and leaned against a wall, panting and sweating, using his fedora as a fan.

Inside, a waiter gave them menus and a bottle of water.

Cal was drenched. Eve used a napkin to dry her face and neck. Their stalker was in plain sight, staring at them like a hungry wolf.

'Eve, here's what I want you to do.' Cal rattled off instructions and finished with, 'Can you do it?'

She nodded, took a drink of water, and asked the waiter where the toilet was.

Through the window Barzani saw Eve getting up from the table. He started to move but held off when he saw Cal staying put.

Eve ducked into the toilet, quickly washed and dried her face, then made her way to the open door at the rear of the restaurant. There was an alleyway lined with garbage cans. She went in the opposite direction from the square and at the first parallel street she made a right, heading back to El Tahrir Street, about a block from the cafe.

The police car Cal had spotted was double-parked midway between the cafe and where she was.

She slowly approached it, head down, until she was at the window. Two policemen were inside. She tapped the driver's window with her knuckle. The officer lowered it and looked at her suspiciously.

A blast of air-conditioning hit her. 'Do you speak English?' she asked. 'Can you help me?'

'What is the trouble, miss?'

Barzani was about fifty meters away on the other side of the street, staring straight into the cafe window. It didn't look like he had seen her.

She pointed. 'That large man, over there, across the street. He assaulted me.'

Both officers craned their necks. 'What did he do?'

'He was walking behind me. He put his hand up my skirt.'

The policeman stuck his head out the window a bit to look her up and down.

'Maybe you shouldn't wear these kinds of clothes in this country. Egyptian men are not used to this.'

His partner laughed.

She was dressed demurely, at least by Western standards, but Cal had told her the conversation might take that turn.

'I don't think he's Egyptian.'

'Not Egyptian. You sure?'

'Pretty sure.'

She leaned toward the officer, getting a few inches from

his face so he could hear her talking low. Even though she was on foreign soil in a culture she didn't understand, her job back home dealing with aggressive, burly contractors clamoring for her building permits prepared her for dealing with this type.

She gave him her friendliest smile. 'I know how busy you men are. You have a very important job. But I would greatly appreciate it if you could help me.'

She reached into her bag for the cash that Cal had thrust in her hand. She dangled the wad in front of his face.

'Do you think, for a thousand dollars, you could hold that man for at least two hours?'

The officer diverted his attention from her breasts to the money.

'One thousand dollars for two hours,' he said, his eyes widening.

'At least two hours.'

He took the cash and said, 'A foreign man should not do something like this to a nice lady such as yourself.'

With that, he put his car in gear, pulled a U-turn, and switched on his flashers. He stopped in front of Barzani and both policemen got out, unholstering their guns.

'You, mister, I want to talk to you.'

Cal saw what was happening, dropped some money on the table, and left the cafe.

By the time he and Eve began running toward the museum, Barzani was in handcuffs, shouting and cursing in the back of the police car.

TWENTY-THREE

Krakow, 1587

The beginning of the end was three years earlier when John Dee and Edward Kelley received the 48th Call. Dee had been entirely satisfied with the explanation that the one missing call was not for man to possess but Kelley had vehemently disagreed. He stewed with anger when Dee would not allow him to press the case to Ilemese, Nalvage, or any of the angels who appeared in the showstone.

The years in Krakow had not been fruitful for the fortunes of either man.

Nothing had come from Prague. Dee had waited for over a month for his audience with the Holy Roman Emperor. Rudolf was known to have a deep interest in spiritual, mystical, and occult matters and Dee's conversations with angels were well known. During their hour-long meeting, Dee stood or kneeled before the Emperor, lecturing him in mathematical detail on his personal forty-year quest for spiritual enlightenment and his insights into the mysteries of Creation. The monarch sat on his throne listening, his Habsburg jaw set, saying little, occasionally stroking his face in non-comprehension of Dee's arguments. Finally, in frustration, Dee lashed out as he might to a dim student saying, 'If you will not hear me, the Lord, the God that made Heaven and Earth, will throw you headlong down from your seat.' The audience concluded shortly thereafter and unsurprisingly, patronage was not granted.

Back in Poland, both Dee and Kelley increasingly turned to alchemy to solve their monetary woes. They often pressed the angels to guide them to hidden troves of treasure, but the responses were vague. Dee continued to labor at his alchemical laboratory at the university and Kelley, who had been booted from his own laboratory in the university district over failure to pay rent, persuaded some local merchants to give him money to buy glassware, scales, and burners to conduct experiments in more modest rooms, promising fat returns if he succeeded in making precious metals. When these efforts came to naught, Kelley became increasingly fixated on the belief that if only he could acquire the 49th Call, he might, from a fallen angel, receive the knowledge needed to find the philosopher's stone, the substance that would transform his meager alchemy laboratory into a gold factory. But every time he broached the topic with his employer, Dee sternly rebuffed him. For his part, Dee was so distracted by his financial predicament that he hardly had the time or inclination to use the precious angelic calls to explore the hidden springs of the universe. Most nights the showstone lay in its box, unused.

Edward Kelley had even more frustrations. As his wife Jane grew plumper and more complaining, Kelley's obsession with the other woman in the household began to dominate his waking thoughts. Jane Dee's iciness merely inflamed his passions and he resolved to find a way to have her.

Then he had an inspiration.

On a chilly early April night, he was scrying with Dee in the older man's study. Peering into the showstone, he told the magus that a black velvet curtain had parted revealing the angel Zebaoth. What followed was a sermon on their need to be diligent in obedience to their superiors and to do justice to angelic direction.

'Have we not been obedient?' Dee asked.

'The angel points his staff toward me,' Kelley said. 'He sayeth, "Therefore thou shalt have the womb thou hast barren and fruitless unto thee because thou hast transgressed that which I commanded thee."'

Dee understood the meaning perfectly well. Before Kelley took Jane Cooper to be his wife, the angels had told him not to join her in marriage. But he had defied the order. It was little surprise, then, that these years later, the couple remained childless. Dee asked what else the angel was saying.

Kelley responded, 'That we must participate one with another.'

Dee frowned deeply. He took the meaning exactly as Kelley had intended.

They should share each other's wives.

Dee angrily halted the proceedings and retired for the night. The next day he announced that his son, Arthur, would be his scryer for the time, but a fortnight later when little, if anything, appeared in the novice's showstone, he begged for Kelley's return to the table. At their first session following the brief schism, Kelley persisted in his scheme, this time describing the angel, Madimi, showing herself naked and revealing four pillars topped with four heads, 'like our two heads and our two wives' heads.' Then he announced that Madimi proclaimed that they would be resisting God and encouraging Satan if they did not have unity amongst themselves.

Dee urgently sought clarification, hoping that by unity, the angel was speaking now of a spiritual unity. But no, Kelley told him. Madimi repeated her command, this time explicitly referring to unity via matrimonial acts. And then Kelley told him that another angel called Ben had appeared and further warned that unless they obeyed the sexual injunction forthwith, they would never receive from the angels the powers to transmute substances into gold.

It was late when Dee noisily crawled into his bed. Jane awoke. She could tell by his tossing and turning that something was troubling him.

He told her about the celestial demands.

She sat bolt upright and protested, 'Surely, husband, this cannot be so. Why would the angels wish you to have carnal relations with Jane Kelley and me to have relations with Edward Kelley?'

Dee sounded deflated and powerless when he said, 'I know not the divine plan but far be it for a mere mortal such as myself to doubt the wisdom of their commandments for the angels speak on behalf of God Almighty.'

'Nevertheless, husband, I beseech you to seek further guidance and clarification.'

Dee did so two days later. This time the angel Rafael himself appeared and made it crystal clear to Kelley that unless they formed a marital pact and obeyed the directive to swap wives that they would have to prepare for God's plague to fall upon them.

The next morning, Dee and Kelley left the house and went for a walk in a nearby wood. They took a well-worn path on account of Kelley's infirmity. The younger man's walking staff sank into the wet earth with each labored step.

'I remain deeply troubled, Edward,' Dee said. 'Our marital vows are sacred and yet the angels command us to break them.'

'I too am troubled,' Kelley lied, 'but we could receive no clearer a pronouncement than the one rendered.'

'Nevertheless, I feel I cannot comply. I do not wish to have carnal relations with your wife and I am sure you do not wish to have carnal relations with mine.'

Kelley had to smile at that. 'Truer words were never spoken, Doctor Dee, but I am loath to suffer the consequences of defying an angelic order.'

'I am not saying this lightly, Edward, but I fear we must take our chances.'

Kelley lifted his staff and angrily plunged it into the forest floor, as if planting a flag.

'I cannot take such a chance with my mortal life and my immortal soul!' Kelley shouted. 'I hesitate to take such a position with a man who is my elder, my mentor, and my employer, but I must threaten dire consequences should you refuse to comply with the angels.'

Dee looked shocked. 'What consequences, sir?'

'Does the name Throckmorton mean anything to you?'

He knew full well that Dee knew of Throckmorton. And not only Dee. There were few men among the denizens of Europe's universities, salons, and cafes who did not know the juicy details of the Throckmorton plot. Four years earlier, shortly before Dee joined with Count Laski to travel to Poland, Sir Francis Throckmorton, in Paris, hatched a treacherous plot with several co-conspirators, including his brother, Thomas, Bernardino de Mendoza, Philip II of Spain's ambassador in London, and Queen Elizabeth's main rival, the Catholic Mary, Queen of Scots, her first cousin. The plan called for the assassination of Elizabeth and the simultaneous invasion of England by the Frenchman, Henry I, Duke of Guise, with an army paid for by King Philip.

Elizabeth's spymaster Walsingham intercepted key communiques between Throckmorton and Queen Mary, rolled up most of the conspirators, and expelled Mendoza. Francis Throckmorton was hung, drawn, and quartered in 1584 at the Tower of London and Mary languished under house arrest until her beheading at Fotheringhay Castle only four months earlier, in February 1587.

'I do know of the Throckmortons,' Dee said, hands on hips. 'What of it?'

'I believe you had a relationship with the gentlemen that

included a business transaction,' Kelley said. 'I believe you did cast a horoscope for them regarding suitable dates for an action of theirs.'

Dee exploded. 'How know you this?'

'I have ears, Doctor Dee, and I have eyes.'

'What of it? How does that matter bear upon our present conundrum?'

'This is how,' Kelley said, leaning heavily on his stick, sinking it even further into the ground. 'I do so fear an act of angel defiance that as God is my witness, I will make Elizabeth's Privy Council aware of your business with Throckmorton and Mendoza. Perhaps they will believe you had innocent intents. Perhaps they will believe otherwise.'

'Good Heavens, man. You would threaten me with venom and malice?'

'For the sake of my immortal soul, I have no choice.'

Under the pressure of blackmail, Dee relented, and when his decision was presented to the two Janes, the women fell into a silent despondence. To Jane Kelley, Dee was a shriveled old man. To Jane Dee, Kelley was an unctuous and morally despicable cripple. Nevertheless, this was an obedient household and when Doctor Dee told them he would draw up a matrimonial pact, they bit their lips and said nothing against the plan. A week later, no lesser entity than the archangel Michael appeared to Kelley and confirmed the new doctrine. The next day, Dee, Kelley, and the two Janes solemnly affixed their signatures to the document.

The women were given a week of preparation and on the appointed night, Jane Kelley and Jane Dee, with tears in their eyes, left their bedchambers dressed in their nightshifts and changed rooms.

Edward Kelley was lying under the blankets trying to look somber and dutiful, but in truth, he had the appearance of a cat who had cornered a vole. Jane Dee blew out the candle and slid herself under the blanket.

'Well, Jane, it has come to this,' he said. 'Our obligation unto God is to consummate our pact.'

'I am here because I am an obedient wife to my husband, sir. That is the only reason, of that you can be sure. Do what needs to be done and let me be gone.'

He felt for her nearest thigh. It was half the size of his wife's and firm. Then, rolling onto his side, he pulled up her shift and climbed on top of her. She felt his withered leg against hers and shuddered. When he rammed his way inside she gasped, not in pleasure, but in pain and distress, and that seemed to spur him on. He continued to furiously drive into her, all the while grunting like a rutting farm animal.

His sounds of pleasure intensified and in a panicked tone she cried out, 'Pull out, sir, pull out! It is a poor time of month!'

He ignored her and kept going to climax before rolling onto his back, wheezing and coughing. All she could do was to dash out of bed and stand, with the hope that being upright might prevent a calamity. She left him and waited outside her own bedchamber door until Jane Kelley emerged. When she did, flushed in the face, her hair tousled, the two women could not bear to look at one another.

The atmosphere in the household, already clouded over money issues, deteriorated further. There was little to no conversation over the supper table, except for admonishing the Dee children for this or that, and husbands and wives spoke little in private. Dee carried on with his university work, Kelley with his failed attempts at alchemy. When they passed each other in a hallway, Dee glowered at his assistant, increasingly resentful how he had been threatened over his work with the Throckmortons. The two men scryed infrequently now. When they did, Dee's questions were perfunctory, and the angels offered little in the way of profundity. From time to time, according to Kelley, the naked angel Madimi did reappear to reaffirm the necessity of honoring their command of matrimonial unity, and buttressed by these commandments, Kelley demanded sexual congress with Jane Dee once or twice a week. Kelley raised the 49th Call with Dee twice more. The first time, Dee turned around and simply walked away. The second, he exploded in rage and warned Kelley never to mention it again.

Some two months later, the Dees said their nightly prayers and crawled under the blankets. He was surprised when Jane addressed him for during these last weeks she had rarely initiated a bedchamber conversation.

'Husband,' she said with a quaver to her voice, 'I am with child. My time has passed twice.'

Despite Dee's copious intellect, he was momentarily befuddled as they had not had recent relations. 'But—' Then the realization settled in. 'My God.'

He rolled to face the closest wall and she did the same.

The next morning Dee was waiting for Kelley in the sitting room and accosted him as he was about to walk out the door.

'Master Kelley, I would have a word.'

Kelley frowned at the greeting. It had been years since Dee called him anything but Edward.

'Doctor Dee, what seems to be the matter?'

'The matter, sir, is that it is my wish, nay, my demand, that you leave this house forthwith. When I return from the university this evening I expect that you and your wife and all your belongings will be gone.'

Kelley had to steady himself on his stick. 'Pray tell, why this damnable action?'

'It is because I tire of your threats, I tire of your inclinations toward black magic, and—'

'And what else?'

Dee looked away. 'Nothing else. See to it that you vacate, or I will petition the courts for your removal.'

Kelley seethed back, 'Perhaps I will petition the courts for wages not paid.'

'Do so and I will make a demand for recompense of your lodgings and foodstuffs these past years.'

With that, Dee angrily rose from his chair and left.

The sun had set hours earlier.

Through the closed door, Kelley could hear his wife crying into her pillow. The two rooms he had managed to secure in short order from a merchant friend were meager at best. Apart from a bed with a mattress stuffed with very old straw, one table, and three unsteady chairs, there was no other furniture – not a chest, not a wardrobe. Their possessions were laid out on the rough floorboards. A baby was shrieking in a nearby apartment. The communal privy served God knows how many dwellers in the tenement. To make matters worse, there was a leather tannery on the street and the smell of tanning urine was overwhelming.

Kelley tried to put all these distractions from his mind. He did not know how much time he had before his crime was discovered. Well, partial crime perhaps, because the obsidian showstone he took from Doctor Dee's study originally belonged to him. The same, however, could not be said of Dee's spiritual table, his red silk cloth, the Sigillum Dei Aemeth, and the companion wax seals.

He began his scrying session with a general prayer then proceeded apace to the call that unlocked the gate of the fourth Aethyr. There in the shiny showstone he found Selaphiel. Immediately he began beseeching the angel to reveal the 49th Call.

'Why do you wish it?'

'I am at the end of my tether,' Kelley said. 'I must possess it and discover what powers might accrue to my person.'

'The path you seek is fraught with danger.'

'Am I not a powerful enough magician to penetrate this veil of yours and harness the powers within?'

'There has only been one more powerful magician since time began. His name was Daniel.'

'Did Daniel receive the 49th Call?'

'He did.'

'Then I too should have it.'

'The heavens shuddered when Daniel received it and they will surely shudder again this night.'

Kelley had taken writing implements from Dee's study and he used the doctor's quills, ink, and parchment to record the long chant that Selaphiel vocalized. When the angel was finished, he angrily stepped off his throne and disappeared in a ball of fire.

Kelley wasted not a second. He immediately read aloud the new call as carefully as he could to assure the correct pronunciations, and waited for something, anything to appear in the black mirror.

When the visage did appear, it sent a chill up his back. The angel he saw was perched on a dark throne, wearing the simplest of gray robes. It was his eyes that froze Kelley to the marrow, as black and cold a pair as he had ever seen.

'I am Satanail. Why have you summoned me?'

Kelley bowed to the stone, unsure how he should react and what he should say. He had been warned that the 49th Call might invoke fallen angels but this one? The Prince of the fallen? Satanail? When he found his voice, he addressed him in angel language as Telocvovim, he who has fallen. The angel seemed pleased at the appellation and showed his yellow teeth. Emboldened, Kelley asked him if he could impart unto him the secret of the philosopher's stone.

But Satanail showed little interest in the subject and said, 'My interests lie elsewhere and so should yours.'

'Where, my lord?' Kelley asked.

'Sowing the seeds of discord, that is where. There is no better way to stir men to barbarism than to wave banners of religion before their faces. Today there is a schism in your lands among Christians. You are an acolyte of the Catholic Church and yet you wear a Protestant cloak. You live and breathe the schism. Yet, the discord could be far, far greater.'

Kelley knew the dark angel spoke the truth but he asked, 'Why would you need my puny soul to aid a great lord such as yourself to sow seeds of discord, Telocvovim?'

'Because I reside in my realm and men reside in yours. I can only act on Earth through men. If it is your will then I will be the instrument of evil. Chaos and death will reign supreme.'

'Tell me, Telocvovim, how will this profit me?'

The angel's laugh was curiously high-pitched and Kelley found it deeply unsettling.

'Cunning men have always been able to profit from discord. You will know what lies ahead. You will find ways to profit.'

'Then tell me what I must do,' Kelley said, nodding to the bargain.

'Who is the Catholic king with the power to make war against the Protestant queen?'

Kelley immediately answered, 'King Philip of Spain.'

'Would you have me enter the heart of King Philip?'

'I would, my lord.'

'Then this I tell you: King Philip will gather a great armada and he will launch it against England to defeat the Protestant Queen.'

'How will it end, Telocvovim?'

'You will not have long to wait to know the outcome. All I can promise is that on account of strife a great many men will die on that day and in years to come, many, many more.' He waved a bony hand. 'Now leave me to my work.'

The stone went dark and the angel was gone.

There was a loud bang against the hallway door and then another. Jane had cried herself to sleep but he heard her wake to the noise and call out. When he opened up he saw three Polish men, one of whom he recognized as a ruffian often in Count Laski's retinue.

The man pushed his way in and said, 'Laski sent us to get what you stole from Doctor Dee. Where is it?'

Kelley backed off and glanced at the magic apparatus in the center of the room.

The ruffian instructed his men to bag it up.

'Not the black mirror,' Kelley insisted. 'That belongs to me.'

'No more it don't,' the man said, giving Kelley's face the back of his hand. Kelley's crippled leg buckled and down he went. When he was on his belly, the man kicked him in the ribs and legs.

Jane came in as the men were leaving and bent to help her husband to his feet.

'Leave me!' he hissed. 'Go to bed.'

As he lay on the floor sucking air in pain he noticed that his pointer finger was involuntarily tapping against a floorboard. He watched his own finger in fascination and soon was able to discern a pattern.

Seven taps then a pause. Then seven more taps. Another longer pause, and the pattern repeated.

Seven sevens, he thought, makes forty-nine.

The 49th Call was loose upon the world.

TWENTY-FOUR

The museum guard at the entrance to the restricted staff area seemed interested to see that Cal and Eve were pouring with sweat. But their visitor passes were valid, and their passports confirmed their identities. He let them through.

Inside the Papyrus Laboratory they tried to act as casually as possible. Cal carefully taped the edges of the glass sheets that held the matching pairs and triplets of papyrus fragments. When he was done, he slipped the glass into the Rasouly folder and did the same with the rest of the unmatched pieces. The folder went into his bag.

He asked Eve to put some supplies – glue, tape, backing paper, tweezers, and one of the magnifying loupes – into her bag.

One of the conservators at a nearby desk had been looking at them suspiciously. He made eye contact, smiled, and told her they were off to a lunch with Dr Nawal. She nodded and smiled back.

They hopped in the first taxi they could find but Eve looked at Cal strangely when he told the driver to take them to the airport.

'Our things are at the hotel!'

'There's no time. Who knows how long until the cops release him? We've got to leave now. I'll call the hotel and have them pack up our stuff and send it along. Was there anything you can't live without for a week or two?'

She shook her head. 'I'm not sure I can survive without my red blouse. Just kidding. But my plane ticket is there.'

'We've got to re-book anyway.'

She checked to make sure she still had her passport. 'Thank God we've got them,' she said waving hers.

'Or thank Cal,' he said.

* * *

There weren't many people at work at the FBI offices at lower Manhattan this early. One of them was Julia D'Auria, who was wakened by the ding of a 6 a.m. email. Her wife moaned at her when she lit the bedroom with her glowing screen. She climbed out of bed when she saw the email was from the Metropolitan Police.

The message was from Detective Inspector Proctor and read: 'Special Agent D'Auria, Based on the CCTV photos of your suspect in the murders committed in Boston and New York, and our photos of the suspect in the murder of Omar Rasouly in London, we searched CCTV files from UK Border Control at Heathrow and Gatwick Airports. To narrow down the scope of the search we concentrated on the two possible travel days you highlighted for the three hours prior to the departure of all flights to Egypt. The good news is that we believe we have a credible match from three days ago for a man who boarded a Virgin Airlines flight to Cairo. Attached are the photos of our suspect. We have gone back to staff members at the Institute of Archeology with these new photos which are clearer than the street CCTV images and they believe it is the same man seen there on the day of the Rasouly murder. Further, attached is the scan of the suspect's passport. As you can see he is an American citizen named Tariq Barzani, a resident of New York City. We are in the process of notifying the Egyptian authorities. Our records indicate that Barzani has not re-entered the UK. More later, DI, Proctor, Metropolitan Police.'

D'Auria called Richard Nesserian, her partner on the case, on his cell. He was in bed in a Boston suburb and sounded groggy.

'Hello, Dick?'

'I'm still home, Julia. I haven't had coffee yet. What the fuck?'

'We've got him. Our guy.'

'In custody?'

'No, but we know who he is.'

'And who is he?'

'Tariq Barzani. Fifty-one. American citizen, born in Iraq. Immigrated in 1994.'

'And where is he?'

'Probably Cairo, just like Cal Donovan said.'

'Then Donovan's in a world of shit.'

'I'm going to call him now,' she said.

'We should put out arrest warrants – U.S., Interpol Red Notice, the works.'

'If I send you Barzani's particulars, can you work on those? I'm going to pay a visit to his employer to see what I can find out about him.'

'Who's his employer?'

'It's a real-estate company in Manhattan called Hamid Property Holdings.'

Cal and Eve were in a long queue for Immigration Control at Cairo International Airport when his phone rang from a New York number.

'Cal, it's Julia D'Auria. Where are you?'

'At the airport. He saw us in the cafeteria at the Cairo Museum and he chased us. We got away but we're not taking any chances. We're heading back to Boston. We should land late tonight.'

'You sure he doesn't know where you are?'

'I think we're good.'

'We know who he is,' she said.

The name meant nothing to him, but he grimaced when he heard Tariq Barzani was from Iraq.

'Listen,' she said, 'we'll be casting a wide net for Barzani. I'm going to be dogging it here in New York today, but I'll fly up to Boston in the morning. Send me your flight details and text me when you land.'

The police drove Barzani to the nearest station and parked.

'Why won't you tell me what you think I did wrong?' he demanded.

'Just a misunderstanding, I am sure,' the driver said.

'What? We're just going to sit here?'

'There is no rush. We get coffee now. Want one?'

They left him sputtering and fuming in the hot car, hands handcuffed behind his back. Half an hour later, they returned with a bottle of water.

'Should I take the cuffs off?' one asked the other.

'He is a very big fellow. Better to let him drink like a baby.'

When the bottle was put to his lips Barzani told the officer where he could shove it.

'You want not to drink, okay with us.'

'What did she say to you? The American woman.'

'She says you very bad man who put hands up her.'

The other policeman laughed.

'How much to let me go?' Barzani asked.

The driver was quick to reply. 'One thousand American dollars.'

'You're out of your mind.'

'That's what she pay.'

The sweat fell from Barzani's face like rain. 'I'll give you a hundred.'

'Then you sit here for another hour.'

'Two hundred, not a dollar more.'

'Three hundred,' the officer said.

Barzani nodded. 'Three hundred if you drive me to the Four Seasons Hotel. And turn on the air-conditioning.'

Barzani ran into the lobby of the hotel and went straight to the front desk.

'A friend of mine, Calvin Donovan, called me to come to his hotel. He told me he had a problem and needed my help. Can you give me his room number?'

The clerk checked the computer.

'I am very sorry, sir, but Mr Donovan checked out.'

'When?'

'About an hour ago.'

'That's impossible.'

'He said he had an emergency and had to fly home to Boston. He has given us instructions to send his belongings to the United States via express mail.'

Barzani had his back turned on the clerk before he finished his sentence and was shouting at the doorman to get him a taxi.

'Mr Hamid will see you now.'

The executive assistant showed D'Auria into Hamid's office. The agent had to work hard to keep her cool about the amazing views stretching south to the Freedom Tower, the harbor, and the Statue of Liberty.

Hamid stood behind his large desk and showed his gleaming teeth.

'I am George Hamid. I am so pleased to welcome an agent of the FBI to my humble office.'

D'Auria introduced herself and gave him her card.

'Thank you for seeing me at short notice, Mr Hamid.'

'I am told you have a query about one of my employees. The human resources director tells me it concerns Mr Barzani.'

'I'm sorry to go straight to the top of your company,' she said, settling into a comfortable chair, 'but seeing as Tariq Barzani reports directly to you—'

'Of course, of course. What is the problem, please? Has Tariq done something wrong?'

'I'm afraid I can't discuss an active investigation. What I wanted to know is when he was last at the office?'

'Let's see. I believe it was last Friday. He is on vacation. We give three weeks of vacation per year. Employees are very happy here.'

'Do you know where he said he was going for his vacation?'

'Tariq is the head of my security detail. Billionaires need security – the world we live in. He knows a lot about me but alas I know little about his personal life.'

'I understand he was born in Iraq,' D'Auria said. 'Are you Iraqi too?'

'I am. I emigrated in 1994. Your country welcomed me with open arms and now I have a huge company. America is the greatest country in the world.'

'Yes, it is. Mr Barzani came to America the same year. Is that a coincidence?'

'Hardly. We came together with my wife and daughter. We are Christians who were terribly persecuted by Saddam. Tariq was like a son. That is why I am so distressed to hear the FBI is looking for him. Please, can you not tell me why you wish to see him?'

'I'm sorry, no. Is he married?'

'To a woman, no. To his job, yes.'

'He lives alone?'

'To the best of my knowledge, yes.'

She asked a few more questions then thanked him for his time. He got up to walk her to the door.

'Sorry,' she said, 'one last thing. Do you know a man named Calvin Donovan? He's a professor at Harvard.'

'Donovan, Donovan,' Hamid said. 'No, Agent D'Auria. I don't believe I have ever heard this name. Is he at the business school? I understand they are considering a case study on the success of my company.'

'Divinity School,' she said. 'He teaches religion.'

Hamid laughed. 'Maybe I should meet him. I often pray I will be able to raise my rents.'

Barzani scanned the departure board at the airport and got lost in the sea of destinations. He waited impatiently at a ticketing counter, and only then did he think to check for his passport. Had he left it at his hotel? He was mightily relieved to feel it in his back pocket. When his turn came he asked when the next flight was to Boston. He was told there were no direct flights but many routes via a number of European hubs on different airlines.

'I want to be on the same flight as a friend. Can you look him up if I give you the name?'

The woman replied that this was not possible.

'Okay, when is the next flight with a good connection?'

She checked her computer. 'There is a Virgin flight to London with an excellent connection to Boston leaving in ninety minutes.'

'I'm sure that's the one. He traveled through London to come here. Please give me a ticket. One way. Coach.'

She checked and told him it was sold out.

Given his streak of frugality it pained him to ask, but he inquired about business class.

'I'm afraid that is also full and there are several passengers on stand-by. There's an Air France flight via Paris that leaves in three hours, if you like.'

He needed to know for sure that Donovan was on the flight, but he would need a ticket, any ticket to get to the departure gate.

'Look, just get me to London on the next possible flight. Any airline.'

Barzani got through security and made a bee-line to the Virgin departure gate. He slowed as he got closer and removed his fedora as not to be instantly recognizable. Then, through a glass partition, he saw them, sitting together, leaning toward each other in conversation. Cal's messenger bag was at his feet. That was the target. Barzani figured the chances were high the papyrus was inside. He worked out a plan involving getting close and causing a diversion, that had, at best, a fifty-percent chance of working, but it was worth the risk. George Hamid was everything to him. He would not let him down.

He crept closer to the entrance to the departure gate and what he saw dashed his hopes. There was a secondary security screen with a security officer checking all boarding passes and passports and subjecting carry-on bags to another level of search. He walked away, grinding his back teeth hard enough to make his jaw ache.

He stood outside an Armani shop and called his boss on his cellphone number but Hamid didn't give him a chance to say anything.

'I was just about to call you, Tariq. The FBI were here. They've identified you.'

'Shit.'

'Yeah, shit for sure. Where are you?'

'At the Cairo airport. Donovan and the woman left in a hurry. They even left their bags behind in the hotel. I think they have the papyrus.'

'Can you get it?'

'It's not possible. I can't get to their gate. Their flight to London that connects to Boston was sold out. I can take another flight that will get me to Boston four or five hours after them.'

Hamid told Barzani he needed to think. After a few moments, he said, 'I'm going to have my travel people arrange a charter for you. Direct to Boston. You'll get there before them.'

'That'll cost a fortune.'

'Christ almighty, Tariq! Have some perspective. Do you know how high the stakes are and you're worrying about pennies? Look, I'll fly up to Boston tonight. I'll be at the

Mandarin Oriental. Follow Donovan from the airport to wherever he goes and call me on a disposable phone. And turn your phone off now and take out the SIM card. The FBI may try to trace you.'

'What are we going to do about them? The FBI.'

'We'll figure it out, Tariq. Don't worry. I'll always protect you. Let's concentrate on getting the papyrus and the showstone. Once we have them, everything will be good.'

Cal and Eve settled into adjoining seats in the Upper Deck cabin. Cal guzzled the champagne on offer then asked the stewardess for another. He didn't have to beg. She immediately took a liking to him and poured another, whispering that she'd keep a bottle chilled just for him.

'You seem to have an effect on women,' Eve said.

He touched her hand. 'Do I? I hadn't noticed.'

She suddenly turned sad. He noticed and asked her why.

'I'm going to miss this.'

'Miss what? Getting chased by a killer?'

'You know. It's been an adventure, like a dream. These places, the things we did. You.'

He didn't want to make fake promises. He'd be going back to Jessica and his life. She'd be going back to Arizona and her life. He had faith the FBI would catch the killer and put an end to the danger.

'Hey, it's not over yet. We've got sixteen hours till we arrive in Boston. Before we take off, I'm just going to fire off an email to Dr Nawal, apologizing for stealing his papyrus – I'll come up with some lame excuse – then we'll start working on the pieces again. Okay?'

She whisked away a tear with the back of her hand. 'Sure. I'm starting to like jigsaw puzzles.'

TWENTY-FIVE

I t was late and they were tired. Cal switched on some lights and put his bag down.

'So, this is home,' Eve said.

'Be it ever so humble.'

But it wasn't humble at all and she started admiring the books, the antiques, the serious art on the walls.

While she wandered, he checked out the keypad lock-box on the porch, where he found what he was expecting. A FedEx with the Glock. Back inside, he re-armed his security system and unpacked his new toy. He loaded it with the ammo he had bought before he left.

'Do you have any tea?' she asked.

'In the kitchen. Cabinet above the kettle. I'll have some too if you're making it. Milk and sugar, like the Brits.'

Across the street, a distance from the closest street light, Barzani sat in a rental car staring at the house. There was a security placard on the lawn that hadn't been there the last time he graced it with a visit. He yawned and placed a call to Hamid on his burner phone.

As soon as they had landed, Cal's phone was flooded with the texts Jessica had sent while they were over the Atlantic. They were all along the lines of, where are you? Call me.

He knew she was probably still awake, but he used the lateness of time as an excuse to text back:

Too late to call. Just got back

Thirty seconds later she replied.

I'm coming over

Couldn't be a worse idea, he thought.

Wiped out, Jess. Tomorrow ok?

Don't be silly. Be there in half an hr

His back was against the wall. Sometimes the only play was telling the truth.

Eve Riley is going back to Arizona in the am. She's in the guest room

The ping-ponging slammed to a halt. Cal waited for a phone-melter. It came a minute late.

You're a fucking asshole fuck you

Not poetry, but it got the job done. Getting caught sucked but he needed to get one more ball over the net, and the shot needed a lot of spin.

Not what you think. We ran into some trouble but safe now. Let's talk tomorrow over dinner. Love you.

He read it over and hit the delete key, evaporating the last two words.

When Eve came in with tea he was still looking at his screen.

'These mugs all right?' she said, sitting down and sipping.

'Yeah, fine. I'm just going to get a bottle of vodka from the freezer. Want some?'

'Tea for me.'

He returned with the bottle. He had already downed a double-shot in the kitchen.

'How're you feeling?' he asked.

'Getting a second wind even before the caffeine.'

'Want to try and finish it?'

On the longer London to Boston leg, things had really started to click. The edge-to-edge matches accelerated and now, when Cal took the work in progress from his bag, about three-quarters of the papyrus fragments were in their correct positions pressed between the glass leaves.

They set up at his dining-room table and decided to make the job semi-permanent by tacking the pieces onto backing paper with tiny spots of glue, the technique the conservators in Cairo had employed. When that was done, they started to find homes for the last twenty-eight fragments.

At a little past 3 a.m., they tacked down the last piece, filling a hole in the middle. The assembled papyrus was slightly smaller than a sheet of copier paper. They pushed their chairs back and stood to hug each other. She was punch-drunk; he was half-drunk for real. It wasn't clear who was propping up whom.

'Bed,' he croaked.

'Go ahead,' she said. 'I want to spend a few minutes with it before I come up.'

He had been dreaming of taking a long, hot shower since boarding in Cairo, but he only managed to get his clothes off before collapsing on the bed.

Eve was ready to drop too, but the 49th Call wasn't letting her go quietly. Ominous words and phrases that had come to light during its assembly were rolling around in her head and she couldn't rest until she had digested it in full.

As the pieces fell into place, she had been transcribing her own version of the call, translating Cal's Aramaic phonemes into Enochian letters and words.

She sat back down and began to read her transcribed document slowly and carefully. During its assembly even the uttering of isolated words and phrases had scared her. Putting voice to the fullness of it was terrifying and when she reached the last section, she was sobbing uncontrollably.

No af mi od faorgt Telocvovim

Now I shall enter the dwelling of him that is fallen

Aboapri Telocvovim adrpan od quasb q ting

Help me, him that is fallen, cast down and destroy the rotten

Torzv Zacar od Zamran

Arise Move and Appear

Odo cicle qaa od ozazma pla pli Iad na mad

Open the mysteries of your creation and make us partakers of your dark knowledge

She staggered from the table and went to the powder room to wash her face. The sink was black with fancy scalloped edges. The flow from the faucet exceeded the balky drain and water began to accumulate. When she turned off the faucet the pool of water was becalmed and she saw her tired reflection in it. But then another face appeared and she reached for the drain stopper.

It had been a long while since she had scryed without the trappings of Doctor Dee's table and seals, but she was a strong magician who had experienced visions long before she had learned the first things about Enochian conjuring.

She shook her head in disbelief. 'Pothnir,' she said in Enochian, 'I did not call you.'

'Perhaps it is I who have called you.'

'Why?'

'There are things you need to know.'

When the vision was over, she slowly climbed the stairs and fumbled in the dark for the knob to Cal's door. She shed her clothes, felt for the duvet, and once under it, she felt for a sleeping Cal, who was on his side facing her. She scooted her back to him so that he was spooning her, and when he awoke enough to put an arm around her, she quietly cried until sleep came.

She was up before him the next morning. When he came down there was coffee and a simple breakfast waiting. She wasn't very talkative and when he asked if she was all right, she repeatedly told him she was fine, just tired. Before he could mention the 49th Call, she asked if she could use his computer. He set her up at the desktop in his office.

'Can you show me how to scan something as an email attachment?' she asked.

He gave her a quick in-service on his printer/scanner and went upstairs to take his long-awaited shower. His phone pinged with an email from Osama Nawal, who told him he was a bit shocked that Cal had taken the papyrus from the museum without permission, but given the vague emergency Cal blamed, he said he understood. However, he insisted that it be returned to Cairo at the earliest possible date.

Eve was still working when he came back down, dressed and refreshed, so he made a call. D'Auria picked up right away.

'Welcome home,' the agent said. 'You okay?'

'Safe and sound. Did you find the guy?'

'Nothing to report, I'm afraid. We've got international and domestic warrants out for him but there's no sign of him. He's on a Customs and Border Protection watch list but there've been no hits at Logan or other airports.'

'Maybe he's still in Egypt.'

'Maybe. We'll find him. Where are you going to be?'

'In Cambridge for a while. We'll probably shoot over to the Peabody Museum later.'

'Do you have it? The 49th Call.'

'As matter of fact, we do.'

'And?'

'The jury's out. I've got no idea why someone would kill for it.'

'When you know, I want to know. By the way, did you get your pistol?'

'Yeah, I did.'

'Be careful with it.'

When Eve emerged from his office holding a couple of sheets of paper, he called her into the living room and asked her if she had managed all right.

She folded the papers and slid them into the back pocket of her jeans.

'I'm not great with technology but everything worked. All good.'

He didn't think she sounded good. She sounded flat and wasn't making eye contact.

'So, here we are,' he said.

'Here we are,' she repeated.

'You came up late. Did you spend any time with it?'

'I read through it again.'

'Verdict?'

'It's ominous. It's unsettling.'

'I think we need to understand it better, Eve. We need to know why my people are dying. I need to know why my parents died.'

She said in a monotone that she understood.

'What's wrong, Eve? You don't seem yourself.'

'I told you, I'm tired. Really tired.'

He sat beside her on the couch and she put her head on his shoulder. Her hair spilled onto his chest.

'I hate to say it,' he said, 'but I think the only way to understand what the call means and why this man wants it so badly is to use it. Let's pair it with the showstone and put it to the test. It's not something I can do. You'd have to do it.'

She didn't answer.

'I know it's a lot to ask, Eve, but I don't know how to get answers unless we go there.'

Her eyes were closed when she said, 'If you want me to do it, I'll do it. Is the showstone here?'

'I hid it at the archeology museum on the campus. We can go get it.'

'It's hard to know if I'll need the table and the seals to make it work,' she said.

'If we have to go back to Arizona, I'll fly back with you.'

He heard her sigh. 'I don't think we'll be doing that.'

'Why don't you get yourself ready?' he said. 'There's no rush. It's a nice day. We'll walk to the museum.'

They were in the living room of the presidential suite at the Mandarin Oriental Hotel. Hamid's laptop computer sat on the coffee table, the volume on maximum. Barzani had been listening to the audio feed from his hidden microphone all morning and had called Hamid to listen once he heard Cal and Eve begin their living-room conversation.

When they were done talking, Hamid looked up, as if the ceiling wasn't there and he was gazing straight into the heavens.

'Praise God,' he said. 'We have the call. We have the showstone. Get the car, Tariq. We are going to a museum this morning.'

TWENTY-SIX

London, 1609

Whitehall Palace was a gloomy and cold place to be on a late winter evening. The endless corridors were even colder than the air outside, and the secretary, making his way through corridors and courtyards, wore a heavy woolen cloak over his padded doublet and warmest leggings.

When he got to the private chambers of his lord, he threw

off his outer garment and warmed himself by the small fire. When he was sufficiently comforted he knocked politely and entered the main office.

His master was all but hidden behind stacks of books and documents tied in ribbons and piled upon his desk. Robert Cecil had to stand to see who had entered.

'Ah, it's you, Roger. What news of His Majesty?'

His secretary saw that Cecil's fire needed tending and he sprang to it while answering, 'The Dutch ambassador was exceedingly dull in his exposition and the King did all he could to prevent slipping off his throne in a stupor of boredom.'

'It was good I chose not to attend,' Cecil said, sitting back down. 'There was more important work to be done.'

Cecil was a ferret of a man, not quite five feet tall, with a face smothered by a brown beard that encroached upon his diminutive features. Even his mincing movements were like a furtive rodent, anxiously protecting its morsels of food. When he served the previous monarch, Queen Elizabeth, she mercilessly teased him about his stature, often calling him her pygmy, her dwarf. His new monarch, King James, whom Cecil served as Secretary of State, was publicly kinder to the fellow but taunted him liberally to the gentlemen with whom he drank and gambled.

Elizabeth had been dead going on six years.

Cecil's father, William, Elizabeth's first Secretary of State and Lord Privy Seal, was dead almost twenty years. His father's spymaster, Francis Walsingham, had died the same year as his father and Cecil had not replaced him. He preferred to consolidate the power inherent in operating spy networks in his own offices.

'My lord, I received word today of the death of an illustrious gentleman,' Roger said.

'Oh yes, who?'

'Doctor John Dee.'

'Goodness, I had almost forgotten about him. He must have been ungodly old.'

'Eighty-two by most accounts.'

'Quite the Methuselah,' Cecil joked.

'I wonder, my lord, if we ought not to close out his accounts.'

'When was the last time we made note of his activities?'

'I cannot recall. Not for years, I would say. Most of the entries and correspondence are from the Walsingham days.'

'Well, bring me what we have, and I shall review it before I retire.'

The secretary took considerable time locating the relevant documents in the vast security archive established by William Cecil and Francis Walsingham to keep track of the myriad enemies of the state during Elizabeth's reign. Every intercepted letter, every scribbled report from their spidery network of agents, every coded missive sent among conspirators, was there, filed and cross-referenced. When the secretary returned he carried multiple bundles of parchments, a stack so high he could hardly see his way.

'My God, man,' Cecil said. 'I could not lift such a pile.' He went to his dining table. 'Put them here. I tell you this, Roger, the King is not without enemies but Walsingham saw an assassin behind every tree.'

'Part of this trove relates to an associate of Doctor Dee's, Edward Kelley.'

'Ah yes, I remember him. All right then, I will examine the lot of it.'

John Dee's time in eastern Europe came to an end in 1589. The rift with Kelley could not be healed so he reluctantly turned to his eldest son, Arthur, to be his scryer, who employed the black mirror that Laski had returned to Doctor Dee. However, the success of this venture was marred by Arthur's general lack of ability and his absences to pursue his medical studies in Basel.

In 1588 the last of Dee's eight children was born. The boy was baptized Theodorus Trebonianus Dee. He looked nothing like Dee's other children, but father and mother would not speak of the matter. The boy was raised a Dee and Edward Kelley never once laid eyes upon him.

Dee's financial woes would not abate. His sources of Polish income dried up, one by one, Count Laski all but abandoned him, and all his entreaties to Queen Elizabeth to support his alchemical research fell on deaf ears. With the last of his funds he bundled up his family and his possessions, and made the long journey back to England.

What he found in Mortlake distressed him greatly. His rambling abode was in a sorry state. The house had been vandalized, furnishings removed, precious instruments gone, and most distressing of all, his prized library was decimated. His brother-in-law, Nicholas Fromoundes, who had lent him the 400 pounds for his journey to Poland, insisted he had no hand in the matter, but Dee was led to believe otherwise, and the two men never talked again.

Finally, the Queen took a modicum of pity upon the old magus, and although she would not release a penny from her treasury in his support, she appointed him warden of Christ's College, Manchester, a former college for the priesthood that had been repurposed as a Protestant institution by royal charter. The modest stipend attached to the position kept him afloat, but the fellows of the college did not take to the crotchety old scholar and derided him behind his back for his angel work. The arch-conjuror of Mortlake resumed his association with one of his old scryers, Bartholomew Hickman, but little of significance showed itself in Edward Kelley's black mirror that he had kept as his own.

Jane Dee died of the plague in Manchester in 1604. Dee returned to Mortlake a year later, in failing health and exhausted. He was decrepit, his house was decrepit, and he spent the remaining years of his life with his daughter, Katherine, who dedicated herself to his care, wandering the stripped and bare rooms, remembering the wonders of the universe that had been revealed to him by the angels.

Cecil removed his crystal spectacles and rubbed his tired eyes. His secretary had stood by, handing him new documents, bundling and tying ones his master had finished with.

'What a waste.'

The secretary did not fathom the meaning of the comment. 'Doctor Dee's life?' he asked.

'Not his life, Roger. That was perfectly interesting, I suppose. I mean Walsingham's efforts to cast the old fool as a traitor and conspirator. I see nothing to merit all these years of machinations and spying. All this parchment could have been put to finer use.'

'Are we done, my lord, or do you wish to look at the Kelley dossier?'

'I suppose I'll run through it quickly and be finished with the exercise.'

Kelley fared rather well following his schism with Doctor Dee. At least for a time. His alchemical work began to bear some fruit, or at least so he said, claiming he was on the precipice of being able to produce vast quantities of gold. His assertions so excited the local nobility that he was able to secure rich patronage.

Count Rožmberk of Bohemia bestowed upon him estates and generous funds to pursue his experiments, and the Emperor Rudolf, who had dismissed his master as an impudent old boor, took a keen interest in Kelley's work. When he convinced Rudolf he would shortly start producing gold, the monarch knighted him Sir Edward Kelley of Imany and New Lüben.

Six months after receiving this honor, the worm turned.

When his laboratories failed to yield any gold, Rudolf had Kelley arrested and jailed in the Křivoklát Castle on the outskirts of Prague. After a lengthy imprisonment, Kelley was once again able to persuade the Emperor's representatives that he had been able to work out why his previous experiments had failed. If only he could be allowed to return to his alchemical work with his former status restored, molten gold would flow.

Rudolf had him on a short leash and when he failed again to produce gold, he was re-imprisoned, this time in Hněvín Castle in Most. Kelley saw the future with clarity for the first time in his life. He would not be able to talk himself out of his predicament again and he would die in a cold turret. In desperation, he attempted to escape by climbing down a wall but fell and broke his good leg. The year was 1597. When his long-suffering wife, Jane, visited him in his cell, she was horrified to see bone protruding from his shin. So she obeyed his wishes and the next time she came she brought a vial of antimony powder from his laboratory.

He swallowed it in front of her and proceeded to die a most horrible, agonizing death. In his final minutes, in near delirium, he uttered the 49th Call and in a puddle of his own urine he saw Satanail sitting on his throne, showing his yellow teeth and taunting him.

Cecil handed the last of the parchments to his secretary.

'So, Doctor Dee was a fool and Edward Kelley was a charlatan.'

'Was there nothing to the angel magic?' Roger asked.

Cecil stood and rubbed at the cramp in his thigh. 'I have little knowledge of the subject and even less interest. I am off to bed and so should you.'

'What shall I do with these documents, my lord?'

'Do with them? Take them to my bedchamber and throw them onto my hearth so that I might have excellent warmth tonight. Walsingham's endeavors will finally be put to a good end.'

TWENTY-SEVEN

Constantinople, 1095

Emperor Alexios had wine and food brought to him and shared a meal with the young priest, Thaddeus.

Thaddeus had returned his showstone, table, and wax seals to Daniel's red bag. He was still shaken by his encounter with the dark lord, Satanail.

'What will happen now?' Alexios asked.

'I know not, my Emperor,' Thaddeus said. 'I am but a humble priest who sees things in the celestial world that I do not always understand.'

'Then there is nothing for us to do but wait and see,' the Emperor said. 'In months past I sent a letter to Pope Urban asking for his help against the Turks but I have received nary a reply. Everything now depends on whether Satanail did abide by his promise to enter the heart of the Pope and harden it to our purpose.'

Pope Urban II was a proud Frenchman, born Odo of Châtillon. The scion of a noble family, he took his early education at a cathedral school in Reims. Owing to his superior intellect and ambition, once he entered the priesthood, he rose through the ranks of the Church to become the Cardinal of Ostia. Eminently papabile, no one was surprised when he was elevated to the papacy in 1088.

He was refined in mannerisms and appearance, possessed of a close-trimmed beard and an expansive, tonsured dome. He was more finely attuned to political realities than his predecessor, Pope Gregory VII, and he found soon enough that he needed all of his skills to advance his reign. Rome and swathes of southern Italy were off-limits to him, as the city was occupied by the Italian Anti-pope Clement III. Moreover, the Holy Roman Emperor, Henry IV, had feuded with him over ecclesiastical appointments and the Emperor, to Urban's peril, had decided to align himself with the Anti-pope.

Perhaps the last thing Urban needed was another large conflict and thus, when he received a letter from his comrade in the east, Alexios Komnenos of Constantinople, he balked. How could he provide assistance to his battle against the Turks when he was fighting his own battles close to home?

The winds blew fierce and cold that November in the French city of Clermont, where Pope Urban had gathered with several hundred clerics and noblemen for a council to debate reforms within the hierarchy of the Church. Urban dressed in his papal regalia and made his way to the cathedral from his temporary accommodation in the abbot house he had been using during his time in the city. It was early in the morning and his intention was to spend a quiet hour alone in prayer and contemplation before the council attendees arrived.

He knelt in the empty chapel of the great church and began to pray but prayers did not come to his lips.

Suddenly he felt his face contort in a spasm of sorts, and his mind turned to the darkest thoughts he had ever had. He was a man of serenity and good cheer, fully devoted to acts of Christian charity and devotion, and now he felt only anger and hatred. His mind was filled with visions of agony and gore, and he saw, as clearly as if he were gazing directly upon it, a river running red with blood, with countless hacked and maimed bodies flowing past.

And when the Pope appeared before the assembly later in the morning, he did not present himself in the calm manner expected of him, nor did he speak on the expected subject of Church reforms.

Instead he stood before them and raged in a bellicose manner they had never heard coming from the mouth of their benign and courtly pontiff.

'A horrible tale has gone forth,' he shouted. 'The Saracen, an accursed race utterly alienated from God, has invaded the lands of the Christians and depopulates them by the sword, plunder, and fire. You should shudder, brethren, you should shudder at raising a violent hand against Christians. It is the wicked Saracen you must brandish your sword against. Go now east. Go to Jerusalem to wage war against the Turk and return the Holy Land to Christian hands. All who die by the way, whether by land or by sea, or in battle against the pagans, shall have immediate remission of sins. This I grant them through the power of God with which I am invested. O what a disgrace if such a despised and base race, which worships demons, should conquer a people which has the faith of omnipotent God and is made glorious with the name of Christ! Set out on the way with God as your guide. Tear that land from the wicked race and subject it to yourselves in this righteous crusade!'

There was a hush in the cathedral then one nobleman rose from his seat and shouted, *'Deus vult!'* God wills it, and then the entire congregation, hundreds of men, rose as one with fists pumping the air shouting, *'Deus vult! Deus vult!'* and that phrase would become the rallying call for the First Crusade to the Holy Lands.

In the months and years to come, one hundred thousand men at arms responded to Urban's call to march on Jerusalem. Most of them were poorly trained peasants, led by nobles fueled not only by piety but by the prospect of looting and riches. They killed scores of innocents on the way to and in Jerusalem, absorbing the estates of the vanquished. The Christians were initially beaten back by the better-trained Muslim armies, but through sheer force of numbers they eventually triumphed. Urban died in 1099 shortly after Jerusalem fell to the Crusaders, but before news of the Christian victory made it back to Europe. But the dark legacy of his fiery speech at Clermont lived on. Six more Crusades were fought over the following two hundred years. Two million people died in conflict and the bloody repercussions rippled through the centuries.

Thaddeus stayed in Constantinople, a guest of the Emperor, until news came from France that a liberation force was massing to defeat the Saracens. While he waited, he had little to do but ponder his life and his fate. He never used the showstone again. A wave of nausea washed over him every time he looked upon it and the papyrus, the last thing written by Daniel's hand. Now that his thirst for revenge against the hated Saracens had been sated, he reverted to the Thaddeus of old. He could hardly fathom that he had murdered his friend. His guilt overwhelmed him. When the news of the liberating army arrived to great fanfare and exult among the Christians in Constantinople, he decided it was time for him to leave. One night, without informing his host, he slung Daniel's red bag over his shoulder and began the long trek back to Al-Iraq.

As before, the journey was a lonely one and arduous, but he managed to arrive one dawn to his beloved Rabban Hurmizd Monastery. Emaciated and dragging, he presented himself at the gate where the keeper recognized him and remonstrated him for his deed.

'You return! You, who did kill our Daniel? May the Lord curse you for what you have done.'

Thaddeus dropped his head in shame and asked to be taken to the bishop. The bishop took one look at him, and guided by charity and decency, had him taken away for food, drink, and a bath before giving him a hearing.

Dressed in a clean robe and fresh sandals, Thaddeus

prostrated himself before the bishop, admitted his crime, and begged for absolution and the dispensation to return to the cloisters of the monastery.

'You have not told me why you smote young Daniel,' the bishop said.

'I was angry.'

'About what?'

'He would not give me what I wanted.'

'And what did you want?'

'The means to punish the Saracens for what they did to my family.'

'And by smiting Daniel did you get what you wanted?'

'Yes, father. The angels answered my prayers and the Pope is sending an army.'

'And you believe that happened because of your prayers.'

'Yes.'

'I see. Well, Thaddeus, it is not for me to say whether the angels or God Almighty answered your prayers. If an army is coming, I pray that innocent souls will not suffer, but that is but a hope. Innocents always suffer, do they not? It is within my power to give you absolution for your great sin. This is in keeping with the teachings of our Master, Jesus Christ. But it is also in my power to deny your request to return to your brethren here. Daniel Basidi was greatly loved and admired and I fear it would create sorrowful wounds and divisions to our household if you were to resume your vocation. No, Thaddeus, your penance for your sin is to leave here in the morrow and wander the countryside for the rest of your days, stripped of holy orders, and forever contemplating your evil deed.'

Thaddeus was given a thin mattress, a blanket, food, and beer and allowed to camp on a flat piece of ground near the scriptorium, a fair distance from the dormitory. The copyists who labored there were great friends of Daniel and they looked upon the stonecutter with contempt when they saw him upon leaving work for the day.

When dusk came, Thaddeus began to shed tears with the realization he was about to put his broodings of these past hours into action.

He found a flat stone and began digging with it. The dry, packed soil yielded slowly to his poundings and scrapings. By the time he had dug four shallow holes several paces from one another, each one large enough to hold a melon, his hands were bleeding.

In the first hole he returned to the soil the black obsidian that he himself had flaked and polished into a sacred mirror. As he was about to cover it up with dirt, he thought he saw an image in its surface of a yellow-toothed smile, but then again, it could have been his imagination. A fistful of brown soil put an end to whatever it might have been.

Then, the papyrus. He could not bear to look at the 49th Call again. Yes, he had used it willingly and many Saracens would die. To his mind, that was well and good. But in the hands of another, might not destruction be turned against faithful Christians? He folded the papyrus once then twice and began ripping it into small pieces, divided the torn fragments into three handfuls, and dropped them into three holes. The power of the Holy Trinity would defeat the evil the papyrus bore. He filled in the holes and labored until the ground was smooth and trodden over.

No one would ever again have the power to summon Satanail.

He unlatched the door to the scriptorium and looked for the jar of lamp oil he knew to be kept on a storage shelf. When he had wetted multiple sheets of parchment with the oil, he placed Daniel's red bag on an oil-soaked scribe's table and grabbed a flint and a striking stone. He cupped the flint in his palm. He loved the feel of the cool stone against his warm skin. It was one of the reasons he had become a stonecutter. With a single, expert strike, a spark caught the parchment, setting it ablaze.

He watched in fascination as melting wax from the Sigillum Dei Aemeth and other seals leaked onto the table before the bag itself was a ball of orange light and heat.

And he watched without uttering a sound as the flames crept up his robe and reached his face. His flesh was melted before the entire scriptorium collapsed around him, burying his bones for a thousand years.

TWENTY-EIGHT

J ulia D'Auria was sitting in Dick Nesserian's office at the
FBI Boston headquarters in Chelsea when he got a call. She
could only hear his side of the conversation and it consisted
of loud cursing and things like, 'You've got to be shitting me.'

'What?' she said when he hung up.

'That was Homeland Security. You know that alert we have
on Barzani?'

She leaned forward, 'Yeah?'

'Well, after the fact, a fucking half a day after the fact, they
found out he passed through customs at Logan.'

'How the hell did they miss him?'

'Because he arrived on a chartered jet and went through a
customs check at the private aviation terminal where the officer
on duty cleared him on the plane rather than the counter. He
used a tablet that hadn't been synched with the server for
several hours.'

'So, he's in Boston.'

'Looks like.'

'Fuck.'

They had been checking for a signal from Barzani's
cellphone but it had been stone-cold dead.

D'Auria searched for a number on her cell.

'What are you doing?' Nesserian asked.

'Seeing if Barzani phoned home.'

Hamid's assistant answered and told the agent that Mr
Hamid was not at the office. She claimed she had no idea
where he was.

'Is that unusual?' D'Auria asked.

She said frostily, 'Not at all. He comes and goes.'

D'Auria smiled when she asked if she could have his
cellphone number.

Then the assistant turned colder. 'I'm afraid I'm not
authorized to give that out.'

D'Auria ended the call and mumbled, 'I don't need it from you, bitch.'

The night before, she had applied to a federal judge in New York for a warrant to perform surveillance on Barzani's and Hamid's phones. The judge had ruled there was probable cause to grant the warrant to both listen to and track Barzani's phone but she limited the scope of the warrant against Hamid, ruling that his association to the murders was tenuous at best. The FBI was only granted a location-tracking warrant for Hamid's phone.

This was a good time to put Hamid's warrant into effect. They logged onto a central FBI server to activate a StingRay device in New York City but there were no hits from metropolitan-area cellphone towers.

'You don't think . . .?' Nesserian said.

'Yeah, I do think,' D'Auria replied.

They switched the search parameters to the greater Boston area and before long, the scan produced a red dot on a map of Cambridge.

Nesserian spat out, 'Divinity Avenue. Motherfucker. Didn't you say Donovan was going to the Peabody Museum?'

She was already calling Cal's phone.

It was a Saturday and the Peabody Museum was thick with tourists, coming and going. Barzani and Hamid had been lurking behind a stand of trees across the street from the entrance, from where they saw Cal and Eve walking up Divinity Avenue and entering the museum. Cal used his faculty ID to pass through the lobby quickly but Hamid and Barzani got hung up at the ticket counter.

The ticket lady said sweetly, 'It's twelve dollars each but if you're over sixty-five, sir, it's only ten dollars. And I can check your bag if you don't want to carry it.'

Hamid told her he'd keep his shoulder bag, pulled out a couple of twenties, and told her to keep the change as a donation. With a shrill thank-you ringing in his ears, Hamid watched Cal and Eve entering the small elevator.

He stared at the old-fashioned arrow above the elevator door that pointed to the stopped floors. The arrow pegged the fifth floor. They decided to take the stairs rather than wait for the elevator to return. Barzani took the bag from his boss and attacked the stairs by twos and threes but Hamid chugged along, one at a time. When he got to the fifth floor Barzani was already there, looking around the empty hall.

It was a faculty and research area with no public exhibits.

'Take this too, Tariq,' Hamid said, wheezing and sputtering at the exertion. He passed him the pistol he'd brought from New York, courtesy of flying on his own plane. 'I haven't climbed five flights since I was a slum landlord.'

They began walking down halls, looking at the plaques on office doors and the laboratories. Every door they tried was locked.

One room had a sign that said, Faculty Archives. The door was ajar.

Barzani slowly pushed it open.

The room was larger than they anticipated, much larger. There were rows and rows of file cabinets that prevented them from getting a line of sight to the voices they could hear.

They walked as quietly as they could toward the voices. When they were only one row away they heard Cal say, 'Here it is.'

Barzani came around the row of cabinets with Hamid at his heels. Cal heard the footfalls and wheeled around to see Barzani pointing a gun.

'Oh my God,' Eve said, her face going slack.

'It's going to be okay,' Cal said without a ton of conviction.

His phone rang.

'Take it out of your pocket,' Barzani said, 'and throw it to me.'

Cal tossed it over and Barzani gave it to Hamid.

It showed Julia D'Auria on the caller ID.

'She's a nuisance,' Hamid said.

Cal pointed at Barzani. 'I know who the big fuck is,' Cal said. 'He's been stuck to us like dog shit on a shoe. Who are you?'

'There's no need to know my name, Professor Donovan, but it is nice to finally meet you.'

The accent was similar to Barzani's. Cal remembered what Eve's angel, Pothnir, had told her, the night they scryed in Arizona. There was a powerful man, a magician who controlled Barzani. This was that man. 'You're from Iraq too,' Cal said.

'True, but I consider myself a patriotic American first.'

Cal looked at his fleshy, sweaty face and fancy suit. Thirty years ago he would have been in his forties. The big man would have been in his twenties.

'Why did you do it?' Cal said.

'Do what?' Hamid answered.

Cal spit venom. 'You know what you did. You murdered my father. You murdered my mother.'

'Have you ever lived through a war?' Hamid said. 'Not on TV. I mean lived through it for real. I'll bet you haven't. I did when the Americans invaded Iraq. Many people were killed. My son was killed. You accept that people die in wars and I'll tell you something. That was a just war. Saddam was a monster. Your parents died in a war too.'

Cal scoffed at him. 'What war is that?'

'The war of good versus evil, Professor. An eternal war. Your father and your mother were not – what's the term – enemy combatants. They were collateral damage. They had what I needed to fulfill my own destiny. They had the show-stone and the keys to the 49th Call. Do you know how long men like me have looked for the call? Do you know how long men like me have looked for a stone as powerful as the black mirror? Let me tell you something. I used to visit the British Museum and look through the glass case at Doctor Dee's black mirror and wonder if it was possible to steal it.' He laughed at the memory. 'You know, drop down from the ceiling like in *Mission Impossible*. This was my Mission Impossible and you, Professor, have made it possible. You did all the work and all we had to do was follow you.'

'How did you find out my mother had the showstone?'

'It was an old Iraqi man who was with your father. A deathbed confession, if you will. And now I want the stone and the papyrus.'

'What do you want them for?'

Hamid shook his head, unsmiling. 'That's another thing you don't need to know. Now give them to me.'

Cal stared at the gun in Barzani's hand. It was a large-caliber revolver with a six-shot capacity. It could do more damage than he wanted to think about.

'They're not here.'

'But they are. I know you came here to retrieve the stone.'

Cal was confused. How the hell could he know that? Unless.

'You bugged my house.'

'The sound was very clear when you were in your front room. Not so clear in others. We heard the girl give voice to the call last night but not clearly enough to understand the words. So, please, Professor, or she will be the next collateral damage, which would be a shame. I admire a fellow scryer. Tell me, Miss Riley, what Aethyr can you attain?'

Her throat was dry. 'The fourth.'

'My goodness. You are quite a powerful magician. Not as powerful as me. I can reach the second. But with the stone and the 49th Call I will explore the realm that others can only dream about.'

'The Aethyr of the fallen,' Eve said.

Hamid's plump lips twitched at that. 'Let's have no more talk. Give me the stone now or she'll die.'

Cal glanced at his bag but it was on the floor, too far away.

He simply said, 'I'll get it.'

Cal stooped at the file cabinet that had his father's papers and pulled out the padded envelope.

'Put it on the floor and slide it to me with your foot,' Hamid said.

Hamid bent to pick it up and stuck his hand inside. The washcloth that padded the stone had a smell evocative of his homeland. He sniffed at it and briefly closed his eyes. He partially unwrapped it and touched the smooth black surface with two fingers. His white teeth showed.

'Now the papyrus. It's in one of your bags, I suppose. Yours, Miss Riley?'

'I don't have it,' she said.

'Then yours, Professor.'

Cal raced through his options. If he gave him the bag they'd find his gun. If he drew it, he'd probably take a round to the chest before he could put it to work.

'I'll give it to you.'

He got his bag and pulled out the glued papyrus.

'Tariq tells me you're quite the fighting man, Professor. I don't want you near me. Hand it to her to give to me.'

Hamid took it from Eve and looked at it. 'This is Aramaic. I know you have an Enochian translation. Come on. Stop wasting time.'

Cal passed Eve the sheet with her translation and she gave it to Hamid.

A quick glance satisfied him. 'My God, such powerful words.' He looked around the archives. There were areas in the shadows and bright ones where windows overlooked the courtyard of the adjoining Museum of Comparative Zoology let in the sunshine. 'Tariq, watch them closely. I want to make a test drive and I may need them, particularly her, if I have trouble with her translation.'

'So, I'll shoot him first if they make trouble,' Barzani said.

'That would be the correct order, yes.'

Hamid took his shoulder bag and his new possessions and went in search of a perfect spot. He found it in a dark corner of the room that was bisected by a shaft of window light. There he removed his small ceremonial table and unfolded its legs, placing each one on a wooden box containing his miniature wax seals. Then he put the Sigillum Dei Aemeth onto the center of the table and covered it in red silk. The showstone had no frame or holder so he had to improvise. There were some dusty old books on a nearby shelf and he used one to prop the stone so that it caught the sun. Then he sat on the smooth floorboards cross-legged and read through the 49th Call.

From across the room Cal began to hear the rhythmic tapping of Hamid's index finger against a floorboard.

Over and over, the same pattern. Seven taps. A pause. Seven taps.

Eve heard it too and said, 'It's an Enochian code. Seven sevens. The 49th Call.'

Hamid made his preliminary prayers to God in his native

Arabic then steeled himself for what might come next. Eve's transcription was in his lap. He began to give voice to the 49th Call in Enochian, his eyes riveted to the gleaming surface of the showstone.

He read the last line of the call.

Odo cicle qaa od ozazma pla pli Iad na mad

And there he was, floating inside the black mirror, a dark presence on a dark throne.

'I am Satanail. Why have you summoned me?'

D'Auria and Nesserian were six floors below in the basement security office near the library. A guard was telling them that the only way she would know Professor Donovan's location in the building was if he had used his keycard to access a locked area.

'Well look, for fuck's sake,' Nesserian said.

She checked the online activity logs and said, 'The only area accessed in the last hour is the Faculty Archive on the fifth floor. It looks like the door's open for some reason.'

'Is there an elevator?' D'Auria asked.

'Down the hall on the left. Do you want me to come?'

'Do you have a gun?' D'Auria asked.

'I'm not armed.'

'Then stay here, sweetheart,' Nesserian said.

D'Auria and Nesserian had their service weapons drawn at the archive door. Nesserian pushed it open with his foot and they entered, listening hard for anything to guide them through the maze of cabinets and cases.

D'Auria heard something faint and pointed. They crept forward but changed course when they both heard Cal's voice.

Eve stood near him. The room was warm but she was shivering. Cal wanted to hold her but Barzani warned him not to move.

'I'm sorry,' Cal said to her.

'Please don't be.'

'It was a mistake from the start getting you caught up in all this crap.'

'I told you, it was the one adventure in my life.'

D'Auria peeked around a row of cases and saw Barzani and

his revolver. Then they heard Hamid's voice speaking an unintelligible language, coming from somewhere else.

D'Auria pointed to herself first, then the direction of Barzani. Nesserian nodded and pointed at himself, then the direction of Hamid. He crept off.

D'Auria silently counted ten seconds then stepped out and acquired her target.

'You with the gun. FBI. Drop it immediately or I will shoot to kill.'

Barzani kept his gun on Cal.

'I'm not fucking around,' D'Auria said. 'You're about to die.'

Barzani put the gun onto the floorboards.

'Kick it all the way to me and get your hands on top of your head,' she ordered.

He complied and she scooped up the revolver.

Nesserian turned the corner and pointed his weapon at Hamid.

'Hey, asshole,' he said. 'FBI. Hands up.'

Hamid kept his gaze fixed on the showstone.

In Enochian, he cried out, 'Enter *this* man, my lord. Enter *this* man's heart!'

Cal didn't think he'd ever been happier to see someone in his life.

'Agent D'Auria, you are a sight for sore eyes. I'd like you to meet Eve Riley.'

D'Auria gave her a little smile and asked Cal if he had his Glock with him.

'In my bag. It was very near but very far.'

'Use it to cover me while I cuff this baboon. My partner's circling around.'

As Cal reached into his bag there was an explosion and blood began to shoot out the side of D'Auria's head.

She fell to her knees and then onto her side.

Nesserian was standing near her with the blankest of stares. When her body convulsed he fired more rounds until she stopped moving.

Cal felt the rough grip of the Glock against his hand.

As he fired at Nesserian, Barzani was on the move, throwing

his large body onto the floor. Hamid's revolver had dropped from D'Auria's grip. It was closer to Barzani than her own weapon.

The 9mm rounds ripping into Nesserian's torso weren't bringing him down fast enough. He staggered and began wildly spraying bullets in Cal's direction, but he was missing the mark and Cal raised the sights for a head shot.

He pulled the trigger again and Nesserian fell, half on D'Auria, half off. One of his thighs landed on the revolver as Barzani reached for it.

The big man was on his belly fishing for it.

He looked up when Cal said, 'I don't think so.'

Cal was standing directly over him.

When he saw Barzani's hand emerge from under Nesserian's leg, holding the revolver, Cal grunted and put a round into the back of his bald head execution-style.

'That's for Hiram Donovan.'

He fired again.

His shoes and pant legs were blood-splattered.

'And that's for Bess Donovan.'

'Eve?' he said, turning around quickly to the sound of a moan. 'You okay?'

She was sitting on the floor, her back against a cabinet.

'One of the bullets . . .' she said.

She held her hands tightly against her abdomen. They were dripping in fast-flowing blood.

He reached for his phone and dialed 911, and as he knelt beside her he screamed into the speaker that multiple people were shot on the fifth floor of the Peabody Museum.

He added his hands to hers to put pressure on the wound, but she began to slip, her voice getting thinner.

'It's okay, Cal. It's okay.'

'It's not okay. Stay with me.'

She seemed to be struggling to see him. 'Last night,' she whispered, 'Pothnir told me this was going to happen. Didn't know how. Or when. But I'm ready. Really, it's good. At least I got to know a good man.'

As her head slumped heavily onto his shoulder, he heard quick footsteps heading toward the door. They faded as Hamid ran down the hall.

TWENTY-NINE

Jessica picked him up from FBI headquarters late that afternoon. Three different teams interviewed him, trying to make sense of the fact that one of their own had killed Julia D'Auria. Despite his credentials as a full Harvard professor, the first group of questioners thought they were dealing with a fantasist, until someone retrieved Nesserian's case notes and confirmed all the business about black mirrors and angel calls.

Cal could not identify the older Iraqi-American, but Nesserian and D'Auria's files led them to a billionaire property developer and landlord named George Hamid. Hamid's private jet had taken off from Boston less than an hour after the shootings and flown to John Wayne Airport in southern California, but from there the trail went cold. The pilots had no idea where their passenger had gone after landing and they reported that a car wasn't waiting for him on the tarmac. Hamid's New York company personnel, and even his wife, were unaware that he had gone to the west coast, and his cellphone was no longer pinging towers. The FBI field office in Los Angeles, coordinating with the satellite office in Orange County, began canvassing car services and taxi companies.

When Jessica met him in the lobby, his usual spark wasn't there. He couldn't even muster the faintest smile.

'Thanks for coming,' he said.

'You look like shit.'

'I'll bet.'

'How'd it go?' she asked.

'They thought I was a nut.'

'You are a nut. They're not charging you with anything, right? I can get a team of lawyers involved in a heartbeat.'

'There won't be any charges,' he said in a monotone.

'Come on, I'm taking you to my place.'

She didn't then, or any time later, ask him a damned thing

about his relationship with Eve Riley. As far as she was concerned, the woman was dead and so was the subject.

And Cal was Cal – take him or leave him. Right now, she was taking him.

A parade of luxury cars and limos were pulling up to the entrance of the Ritz Carlton in Laguna Niguel, discharging men in evening wear and women in ball gowns. The hotel was perched high on the cliffs overlooking the shimmering Pacific Ocean. The evening was warm and fair. Seagulls were feeding and their cries carried on a stiff breeze.

The guest room was not remotely to his standard. He had made a last-minute reservation from his plane. The hotel had been nearly sold out and there were no suites on offer. But the room had a balcony with an ocean view. He had the doors wide open so he could hear the waves and see the sea quenching the setting sun.

Hamid's only luggage was the shoulder bag filled with sacred objects.

At the museum, he had packed them in great haste. Now he unpacked slowly and carefully, treating each item with the gravitas it deserved.

There was no reason to wait another minute. For all he knew, his last grains of sand were falling from the hourglass.

He took the shade off a bedside lamp and positioned it to shine onto the black showstone sitting atop Doctor Dee's table. It would have been more perfect if he had been able to memorize the 49th Call, but he had to read from Eve Riley's transcription again.

Satanail sat on his throne and said, 'It is you.'

He replied in the angel tongue, 'Yes, my lord, it is I.'

'You summon me again.'

'It is time to ask you to help me achieve what I seek.'

'What is it you seek?'

Hamid had been holding his breath. He filled his lungs hungrily, let the air out, then said, 'I seek the destruction of the Muslim race, the race that has long persecuted me and my Christian brethren. That is what I seek.'

'I can only work through men. Which man should I enter?'

*   *   *

Gabe Lonergan was in another wing of the hotel, occupying the lavish Ritz-Carlton Suite with his wife and a handful of aides.

He emerged from the bedroom with a selection of neckties and asked his campaign manager which one he should wear.

The manager, a veteran Republican operative, one of the highest-paid in the business, said, 'Go with the red. You can't go wrong with a red tie.'

'Red it is,' Lonergan said.

He asked his wife to let him use the bathroom and knotted the tie in the mirror, fiddling with it to make it just so.

Suddenly, he felt different.

Very different.

His hands dropped to his side. He was spellbound by the look of his own eyes.

He was always supremely self-assured but there was something else coursing through him now. Something powerful and incandescent.

It was rage.

A few minutes later, he reappeared in the living room.

'You look – different, honey,' his wife said. 'You okay?'

'Never better.'

His campaign manager was getting up to leave. 'I'm just going to go down to the ballroom and make sure the speech is good to go on the teleprompter.'

Lonergan said, 'Don't bother.'

'Don't bother?' the man replied. 'You're just about to announce your run to be president of the United States in front of every cable news network in the country and you don't think I should bother making sure your speech is teed up?'

'I'm scrapping it.'

'What the fuck do you mean you're scrapping it? Gretchen, what the fuck does your husband mean?'

'I have no idea, Bob,' she said. 'He's right here. Ask him.'

'Come on, Gabe. This isn't funny.'

'I'm going with my gut tonight. I'm going to wing it. People are angry. I'm angry. It's time for authenticity. Trust me.'

Cal was on the balcony of Jessica's condo, watching in the distance as planes took off and landed at Logan. There were pleasure boats out on Boston Harbor, red and green port and starboard lights moving across the black water. It was eleven o'clock. They hadn't had dinner yet because Cal had taken a nap and stayed down for hours. Jessica wasn't much of a cook but she managed to pull together spaghetti with something.

'It's ready,' she called.

He came in. The two of them sat at her kitchen counter on bar stools. The living-room big-screen was on low but neither of them was paying much attention.

Lonergan made his entrance into the ballroom to the strains of a patriotic-sounding rock song. The room was awash in red, white, and blue. As he swept by tables, he paused to shake hands and exchange tidings with supporters.

He didn't see George Hamid, who had purchased a ticket at the door and was seated at a peripheral table. Hamid didn't seem to mind that he wasn't in the limelight. It was no longer about him.

Lonergan ignored the stairs and used his long, tennis-player legs to leap onto the stage where he waved at the crowd and smiled exuberantly. When he settled behind the podium he splayed his arms wide and rested his hands on either side.

'Will someone please take these teleprompters away,' he shouted into the microphone, 'because I don't need them!'

At that, the crowd went into overdrive.

Jessica looked at the TV and said, 'Who the hell is Gabe Lonergan?'

Cal knew the name but not a lot about him. 'Another billionaire who thinks that's a qualification to be president.'

'Should I turn it off?'

He was about to say yes but then he saw it.

'Wait a minute,' he said.

Lonergan was doing something with his right hand. He was tapping against the lectern with four fingers.

Seven taps. A pause. Seven taps.

Seven taps. A pause. Seven taps.

'Turn up the volume,' Cal said, alarmed. 'Hurry.'

Lonergan asked for quiet then began to speak. He started almost conversationally, but five minutes into his speech he was leaning into the lectern and practically shouting.

'You know, my friends, you've got to be crazy to run to be president. You've got to be crazy in love with this country. You've got to be crazy in love with freedom. You've got to be crazy in love with our core American values – and yes, I'll say it, our core Judeo-Christian values. You've got to want to protect American working men and women and protect their children. You've got to want to protect our flag, protect our right to bear arms, protect our right to worship God, and protect our right to kick the ass of anyone who would take those rights away! And here's where I'm going to be the most politically incorrect son-of-a-bitch to ever run for the presidency – tonight, as I declare my candidacy, I am declaring war on those low-lifes who want to destroy everything we've worked so hard to build since this country was founded. You know exactly who I mean. Say it with me. Radical. Islamic. Terrorists.' The crowd enthusiastically joined in and he repeated the phrase three times. 'And not only the terrorists,' he shouted, 'but all those who actively and even passively support them in the Muslim world. So tonight, I am declaring that I will be your candidate for the presidency but also *the* candidate who pledges to launch a crusade. I'm calling it a New American Crusade. We are going to take the fight to the Middle East, the Far East, to Africa, the Muslim strongholds in what used to be the great European cities, and yes, even the mosques in America if they choose to be breeding grounds of anti-American hate. And, my friends and fellow Americans, we will wipe these goddamn terrorists off the face of the Earth!'

Jessica and Cal had stopped eating during the speech.

'What the hell did we just see?' she asked when it was over.

'I think I know but I don't like it,' he said, reaching for the remote control.

'An asshole like that can't possibly win, can he?' she asked.

Cal hit the power button and the screen went black. He didn't answer her.

Lonergan was swamped by gleeful supporters as he tried to leave the ballroom. His flushed campaign manager was telling him he had to keep moving. They had a dozen interviews lined up.

Near the back door, a smiling Hamid stepped forward and caught Lonergan's attention.

'It's George Hamid, Gabe.'

'George, you made it!'

'It's an honor. I just wanted to be the first person to call you, Mr President.'

'Well, don't be putting that cart too far ahead of the horse, George. But I'll appreciate your help going forward.'

'You already received it.'

Lonergan gave him a peculiar look and bounded out of the ballroom.

Hamid was back in his hotel room, getting out of his suit. A storm front was passing overhead, and the heavy wind was blowing a fine mist of rain through the screens of his balcony doors. He was dead tired. He would sleep through the night then decide what to do next. It almost didn't matter. He had never felt so calm. He had never felt so at peace.

Three door thuds snapped him to attention.

'FBI!'

He only had time to grab the obsidian mirror and two pieces of paper.

As the door was being unlocked, he was on the balcony.

And when the first agent entered the room, Hamid was falling through the night air.

He hit the steep cliff face and careened down a hundred feet, bashing against rocks and stumps, and landing in a twisted mass of bloody flesh on the hotel access road.

As he fell, the wind caught the papyrus and Eve's Enochian transcription and sent the sheets fluttering out to sea.

The showstone slipped from Hamid's hand on his first impact and fell to the asphalt drive, shattering into a thousand sharp pieces.

THIRTY

The call had come out of the blue and it was enough to get him onto a plane.

When the flight was within an hour of landing in San Francisco, he took out the papers Eve Riley's lawyer had mailed from Tucson.

Cal had not known it at the time, but on Eve's last morning of life she had used his computer to write her lawyer a set of instructions, and had made a single change to her last will and testament. The attorney explained to Cal that although the revision hadn't been notarized, the probate court had seen fit to ratify it.

Cal Donovan was therefore duly appointed the executor of Eve Riley's estate.

The job of her executor was not particularly challenging. It turned out she was renting her house and her only significant asset was a checking account with a few thousand dollars on hand. This trip to Redding, California would fulfill Cal's only significant duty.

He waited at baggage claim for a suitcase and picked up his rental car.

The three-hour drive from the airport gave him time to think about the genealogy report that Eve had made an exhibit to her will.

The names of the men and women of each generation played through his mind. Husbands and wives, daughters and sons.

In the nineteenth century, John Riley and his wife, Mary, fled the Great Hunger in Ireland and came to America to start new lives. They first settled in New York City, then Chicago. Six generations later, Phillip and Meg Riley, residents of Denver, Colorado, had a daughter, Eve, who, in turn, had a son out of wedlock whom she put up for adoption.

But it was the European section of the family tree that Cal thought about the hardest.

Because Eve Riley's roots traced back to 1588 when a boy, Theodorus Trebonianus, was born in Poland to Jane Dee and John Dee. Yet, by all accounts, contemporary and historical, the father of the child was not the esteemed academic, but his angel-scryer, Edward Kelley.

Theodorus Dee married Eliza Church in London in 1606 and they had a daughter, Mary, who would marry William Riley of Belfast, and the Rileys, whom Cal imagined had passed their gift of scrying from generation to generation, remained in Belfast and thereabouts until the Irish diaspora.

Cal found the address on a tree-lined street. He got the suitcase out of the trunk. Inside were Eve's Enochian tools – her inscribed wooden table and wax seals, her scrying bowls and crystals, her reference books and a few copies of her own.

The woman who answered the door was Isabelle Heath. Cal had talked to her in advance and had smoothed over all the details.

On the phone she had said, 'He knows about things in general. We were always going to tell him the details of his birth-mother when it was time. I suppose it's time.'

Now she said, 'Come on in. He's in the backyard.'

'He knows I'm coming, right?'

The woman bit her lip. 'I'm sorry, I couldn't. I didn't know how to say it.'

'It's okay,' Cal said, smiling. 'I've got a little speech planned.'

Cal waited in the living room.

There were photos of the boy everywhere. Smiling pictures of a mother and father, and a boy who was now fourteen. It looked like a fine family.

Cal hoped that the kid would take to the contents of the suitcase.

He hoped that something good would come out of it.

There was so much evil in the world. Maybe a good young man with the right disposition and abilities could make a difference.

Ryan Heath came in, his long black hair wild from the wind.

Cal said, 'Hey, Ryan, my name is Cal Donovan.'

Ryan looked at him then looked at the suitcase and said, 'I kind of knew that someone was going to be coming to see me.'